LILY OF PERU

A Novel

David C. Edmonds

A PEACE CORPS WRITERS BOOK

LILY OF PERU: A NOVEL

A Peace Corps Writers Book
An Imprint of Peace Corps Worldwide

Printed in the United States of America
by Peace Corps Writers of Oakland, California.

For more information, contact peacecorpsworldwide@gmail.com.
Peace Corps Writers and the Peace Corps Writers colophon are trademarks of
PeaceCorpsWorldwide.org.

Book Cover and Map designed by Elizabeth Indianos.

Inca Pachacuti on cover based on 18th century painting by Antonia de Herrera.

David C. Edmonds web site: www.dedmonds.com

ISBN-13: 9781935925569
ISBN: 1935925563
Library of Congress Control Number: 2014959155

First Peace Corps Writers Edition, January, 2015

For Maria

The Lily of my life.

Quiero hacer contigo
lo que la primavera hace con los cerezos

I want to do with you what spring does to the cherry blossoms

Pablo Neruda, *Twenty Love Poems and a Song of Despair*

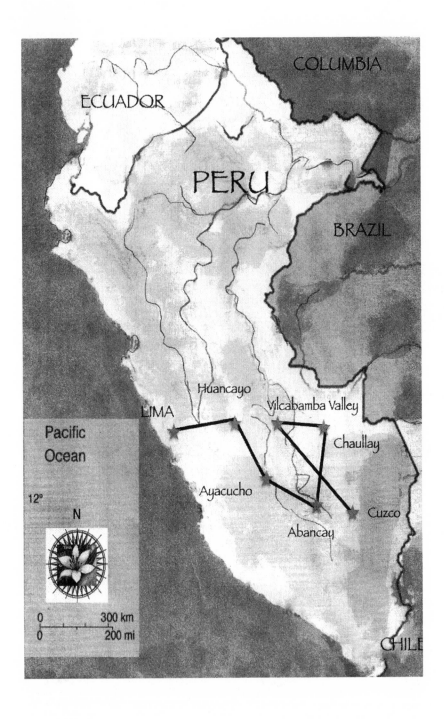

COLUMBIA

ECUADOR

PERU

BRAZIL

Huancayo

Vilcabamba Valley

LIMA

Chaullay

Pacific
Ocean

Ayacucho

12°

Cuzco

N

Abancay

0   300 km
0   200 mi

CHILE

CHAPTER ONE
Lima, Peru—the Gran Hotel Bolívar

1992

Until the general called, I'd been pacing around my suite on the fifth floor, wondering what was keeping Marisa. In the past she'd always been waiting in the room—towels on the bed, dressed in a bathrobe—as eager to catch up as I was. So when the phone rang, I expected to hear her voice, telling me she was stuck in traffic. Or the fog.

"Professor Thorsen?" said a man with a raspy voice.

"Yes, who is this?"

"My name is Reál," he said in Quechua, "General Clemente Reál, commander of army forces in Ayacucho. Would you mind if I come up to your room? It's urgent."

The uneasiness I'd felt before turned to near panic. A general? Had something terrible happened to Marisa? "What is this about, General?"

"It's about the war, Maestro. It's about secrets. It's about you."

"You must have me confused with someone else."

"No, caballero. No mistake. No confusion."

I sank onto the sofa. What the hell was he talking about? And why was he speaking Quechua? I answered in Spanish. "Listen, General, could you be a little more specific?"

"We'll discuss it when I get there. I'm downstairs. It'll take me only a few—"

The lights faded and went out. The room darkened. From somewhere came a shouted curse, and when I spoke back into the phone, I realized we'd been cut off. Or he'd hung up.

I replaced the receiver and tried to make sense of the call. An urgent matter, he had said—and in Quechua. Now why would a Peruvian general be interested in me? And how would he know I spoke the language of the Andes? Surely it had nothing to do with Marisa.

Or did it?

I took out her e-mail and read it for at least the hundredth time.

My dearest Mark:

I've left him. It's over. If you still want what we've been talking about, I'm ready. No more excuses. I can either fly to Tampa next week or you can come to our place and we can leave together, maybe spend a few days in Acapulco on the way home. You can always use the economics conference in San Marcos as your pretext.

I can hardly wait to see you again.

All my love, Marisa.

PS: Please be careful. Peru is falling apart.

Our place was this place, where we'd first made love more than ten years ago. Before my world collapsed. Before we'd gone separate ways. But now...now we were putting the world right. Let Peru fall apart. Let the Shining Path take over. All that mattered was that she'd soon be in my arms and we'd be flying home.

But why was a Peruvian general coming up to my room?

The minutes ticked by and still no word from Marisa. No general either. Nothing but fog outside the window, a noisy protest rally in the plaza, and a nasty feeling in my stomach.

I swept back the drapes and stared over Plaza San Martín, five stories below. The fog—thick here, lighter there—swallowed whole buildings, most of the demonstrators, and even the bronze horse of General San Martín. A man with a Lenin cap and red armband was pumping up the crowd with a bullhorn, shouting about the brutality of President Fujimori's *Mano Dura* policies, his voice competing with the roar of traffic and the blare of radios. The crowd cheered, placards waved, and their chant rolled over the plaza like a tidal wave.

"Strike! Strike! Strike!"

Just like the last time I was here with Marisa. I closed my eyes and pictured her in this very room: Marisa with the long dark hair and sparkling blue eyes, propped up in bed beside me, saying she'd made a terrible mistake, that she wanted to leave her husband and move back to the States. With me. Had she changed her mind? Had her husband found out?

"Strike! Strike! Strike!"

The phone rang again.

Please, dear God, let it be her.

I scooped it up and groaned when I heard the voice of my dean in Tampa, yelling in his New York accent. "What the hell's going on, Mark? Your assistant told me you'd gone to Peru. Don't you read the papers? There's a war going on."

"It's a personal matter, Dean, and you don't have to shout. I can hear you fine."

"Well, I can't hear you worth a damn. Does this have anything to do with a woman?"

"Who told you that?"

"I'm just repeating what Jenny told me. Said you went out and bought some cool new sunglasses. Ray-Ban. Also that you've been growing a mustache. Damn, Mark, a mustache?"

"Look, Dean, I'm here to attend a conference. Okay?"

"Fine by me, but why didn't you fill out a travel form? And what am I supposed to tell the president? She's been hounding me ever since your nomination to dean—wanting to know your qualifications, your administrative experience, when you can meet with her."

"Just tell her I'll be back in a few days, Monday at the latest."

"This better be good. She's not the type to be kept waiting."

The knot in my stomach twisted tighter. "Listen, Dean, I—"

"Monday," he shouted. "Nine sharp. In my office."

The line clicked as if he'd slammed down the phone. The noise in the plaza grew louder. And the receiver was still in my hand when someone knocked on the door.

Not a Marisa knock, but the pounding knock of arrogance, as if the police were outside and ready to kick in the door.

CHAPTER TWO

I opened it and looked into the face of a powerfully built man with slicked-down hair and the strong features of an Inca warrior. His hawk nose gave him a menacing appearance. If this was a general, he'd changed his uniform for a suit that might have been crafted by one of Lima's finest tailors. He thrust out a hand that was as tough as old leather.

"Elevator's out," he said in Spanish. "We took the stairs."

"We?" I peered around him into a dark hallway.

"My assistant. He's a bit slow."

A man carrying a cardboard box stepped from the darkness. He was darker and shorter than the general, with a slight build and acne-scarred face. The general introduced him as a *funcionario* with some lofty-sounding government commission. I didn't catch his name, but I noticed the cologne, the pink tie, and how he avoided my eyes.

The general marched into my suite and sat, uninvited, in a padded chair, bringing with him a smell of cigarettes. The other man took a seat on the sofa and pulled out a legal pad. His shoes were Italian looking, black and shiny, with the kind of soles to give him extra height.

"What is this about?" I asked, still standing.

The general lit a cigarette and motioned me into a chair as if this were his room. "Why don't we start by you explaining what you're doing in Peru?"

"No, General, why don't we start by you explaining what you're doing in my room?"

His face darkened, as if he wasn't accustomed to people talking back. His assistant pulled an envelope from his jacket and laid it on the coffee table. It was official looking—thick, with a red wax seal, like mortgage or divorce papers. I reached for it.

"Not yet," said the general, holding up a hand. "We'll save that for later." He popped open his briefcase, pulled out a thin folder, and opened it. "When did you check in?"

"A couple of hours ago. I just flew in from Miami."

He glanced into the bedroom. "Nice suite for one person. Are you expecting company?"

"No, General."

He consulted the folder in his hand and smiled—not a friendly smile, but the kind you'd expect from Dracula before he bites into your neck.

"According to this, you've lived in Peru on two separate occasions. *Verdad?*"

"Is that folder about me?"

"First as a Peace Corps Volunteer in Sicuani, then as a Fulbright professor in Ayacucho, which explains why you speak both Quechua and Spanish."

"Yes, but—"

"It also says you visit our country three or four times a year. Why do you come so often, Professor? Is it business"—he picked up a rose I'd brought for Marisa—"or is it personal?"

I didn't like the way he said "personal," sniffing the rose and exchanging looks with his associate as if he knew about Marisa. But how would he know? Or care? Unless that folder had information he wasn't sharing.

"Look, General, I'm a university professor. I write academic articles. Some are about Peru. I'm here to attend a conference at San Marcos University."

The assistant began scribbling on his pad as if I'd said something incriminating. The envelope on the table looked more menacing by the second. So did that folder in the general's hand. He took a puff on his cigarette, blew smoke out his nose, and fixed me in a hard gaze.

"When were you last in Ayacucho?"

"Three, maybe four years ago. Why?"

"And have you heard of the man who calls himself Chairman Gonzalo?"

"Of course. He's head of *Sendero Luminoso*—the Shining Path."

"Exactly. The most bizarre terrorists in Latin America." He pointed toward the light fixtures. "That's why we're sitting in a dark room. That's why the elevator's not working. They're always blowing up transmission lines, buildings, people. During the pope's visit, they blacked out the city, then strung dead dogs on light posts, right in the heart of Lima. They're closing in as we speak. If we don't stop them, this hotel will soon be flying the red flag of revolution."

A roar from the demonstrators interrupted him. He stepped to the window with his cigarette. I drew in a breath of frustration and joined him in time to see an armored personnel carrier rumbling past the office of AeroPeru. Police in riot gear filed out of a narrow street. Behind them came a water cannon mounted on a truck. The spectators retreated down side streets, but the protestors remained, shouting insults, shaking fists, and waving their placards.

"Stupid, deluded Indians," the general said. "Most can't even speak Spanish, but they've moved into Lima by the millions—begging, stealing, singing the praises of Communism, driving decent people into armed communities. It's disgusting.

Every day you hear about kidnappings, citizens hiring body-guards for protection. This entire city is going to the dogs."

"All they want is a better life," I shot back.

"If they want a better life, they should move back to their villages and farms. Not destroy Lima. This city used to be beautiful, a little Paris of the Americas. Now look at it."

He had a point. Even from five stories up in the fog, I could see the boarded-up buildings, the battered and broken-down automobiles, the beggars and the homeless.

"Last month we got lucky," he said. "We intercepted a mule train. It was loaded with coca paste. Here, let me show you something."

We returned to our chairs. The general pulled a newspaper out of his briefcase and handed it to me. The headline read: DRUG TRAFFICKERS ARRESTED IN JUNGLE.

"We gave them a choice," the general said, "cooperation or the firing squad." He again smiled his predatory smile, this time showing a gold crown in the midst of long yellow teeth. "They led us to the hideout of Chairman Gonzalo. In Ayacucho. We staked out the house. Then we moved in with a group of *Sinchis*, our most elite troops..."

"And?"

"And no Chairman Gonzalo. There was an escape tunnel beneath the stairwell. He'd outwitted us again. But we found something else...which brings me to you."

My heart beat faster. The rumble of armored personnel carriers rattled the windows, and the demonstrators sounded like they were about to assault the hotel. Reál reached back into his briefcase and took out a sheaf of papers. "Do you write poetry, Maestro?"

"I've dabbled in it. Why?"

"Then you must be familiar with this poem. It's called 'Lily of Peru.'"

8

I glared at him. Lily of Peru was a perfume, Marisa's perfume, but it was also the title of an erotic amateurish poem I'd composed for her years ago.

"Where did you get that?"

The lights flickered and came back on. A hum started up somewhere. Muffled cheers came from down the hall. Then this vulgar man with the raspy voice was reciting the words of my poem in fractured English, smirking as if it were a dirty limerick.

> A snowy night in Cuzco / high above the pines,
> A roaring fire to warm me / candlelight and wine,
> Marisa in my bedroom / alone with me at last,
> Whispering to me softly / of things to do tonight.

I came out of my chair—all six feet two inches of outrage—and ripped the poem from his hand. "I asked where you got this."

The gold in his teeth glittered. He snapped his fingers. His assistant dropped to a knee and began pulling out more files and folders and bundles of old letters—my letters to Marisa, my poetry, even a small book of Neruda's *Twenty Love Poems*.

"All from the bedroom of Chairman Gonzalo," said the general. "It appears that you and the most-wanted terrorist in the country are sleeping with the same woman."

CHAPTER THREE

Marisa a terrorist? My Marisa? I couldn't have been more shocked if the general had punched me in the stomach. Back when she was an exchange student at San Marcos, she'd done nothing more radical than read Mariátegui and hang around with the Trotskyites. It was the thing to do, even for American students like her. But that was years ago.

"Where is she?" I asked, certain they had her chained in a dungeon.

"You don't know?"

"I told you already. I came to participate in a conference."

He picked up a packet of old letters Marisa had tied with a red ribbon. "Too bad the Lima press isn't here. I imagine they'd have something to say about these hot little love letters." He fanned his face with an open palm. "She must be a real tiger."

I wanted to slam him against a wall, but that was probably what he wanted—a confrontation to give him an excuse to arrest me. So I excused myself, went to the bathroom, and splashed cold water on my face. No way was Marisa with the Shining Path. I couldn't imagine her stuffing dynamite into some hapless victim and setting it off. Not the woman who used to sit across from me and whisper she was wearing black bikini panties, getting me so aroused, I couldn't get up from my chair. Not Marisa. There had to be an explanation.

I toweled off, and on the way back through the bedroom, I imagined I could still see her in bed beside me, her skin warm against mine.

Where are you, Marisa?

"Hey, Professor, did you get lost?"

I tossed the towel onto the bed and went back into the sitting room. The general was now standing with his back to the window, arms crossed, glaring as if waiting for a confession. The little acne-scarred man looked sheepish, almost embarrassed, his eyes still avoiding me.

I sat back down and tried to keep my voice calm.

"Who owned the house that was raided?"

"We don't know. The name in the records was a fabrication."

"How do you know it was Gonzalo's safe house?"

"We have photos of him going in. The place was filled with weapons—hand grenades, Kalashnikovs, dynamite, Shining Path handouts, explosive devices. Also notes of people they were planning to kidnap or assassinate, including members of congress."

"That still doesn't prove she was part of it. Do you have photos of her going in and out?"

"We know from this material she was there."

"Maybe they hijacked her house."

The general rolled his eyes, and I too thought it was a flimsy explanation. "I'm a realist," he said. "When my cork sinks in the water, it's because I have a fish on the hook." He marched to the coffee table, leaned down and picked up another stack of material. "This is more recent—from your professor days in Ayacucho." He pulled out a photograph. "Is this you?"

It was clearly me, jogging through the streets of Ayacucho in sweat pants, headband, and black pullover. "Who took this picture?" I asked.

"Must have been your girlfriend. It was found in her things."

He lit another cigarette and took a long puff. "I'm going to make you an offer you can't refuse." He picked up a packet

11

of letters and shook it. "The contents of these letters are bound to leak to the tabloids. You can imagine the effect. You, a respected scholar who writes love letters and erotic poetry to the mistress of the most-wanted man in Peru. What would it do to your job as a professor? Your nomination for academic dean?"

"How do you know about my nomination?"

"We have our sources."

"Listen, General. Those letters are ancient. I wrote them a long time ago. Look at the dates."

"We're not stupid, Professor. We know you're still seeing her, that the two of you rendezvous in this hotel every few months. We also know you were seeing her in Ayacucho three years ago. And if she's half the woman you make her out to be, I'd want to keep her too."

He held up a hand to cut me off. "So here's the offer: see that cardboard box with all its evidence? I can make it disappear like this."

He snapped his fingers.

"No publicity, no public debate about your link with the Shining Path. No charges of being an accomplice. As for your girlfriend, we'll keep her out of it. I'm a general. That's as good as being pope in this country. I can arrange safe passage out of the country for both of you."

"In return for what?"

"In return for your help in capturing Gonzalo."

"I have no idea where to find Gonzalo."

"Your lady friend knows. All we want from her is an address."

In the silence that followed, I paced around the room. People like Gonzalo belonged in jail; people like Marisa didn't. But that's where she'd end up no matter what the general promised.

"Look, General, I'd love to help. Problem is I haven't seen this woman in years."

The little man made a notation in his pad. The general leaned forward and ground out his cigarette. "Where did you meet her?"

An image of a classroom at San Marcos University flashed through my mind. A journalism class to which I'd been invited to speak about the Peace Corps. Marisa sitting on the front row in short skirt and boots, long dark hair falling around her shoulders. Until then I hadn't believed in love at first sight, but oh, those eyes of hers. That olive complexion. And her nose with the slightest hint of a hook. Her Spanish was so good, I hadn't known she was American, down from Miami, and it occurred to me the general didn't know either.

"I met her at a social event," I said. "We had a fling. But that was ten, eleven years ago. I probably wouldn't recognize her if she walked into this room."

"Oh please. If I hadn't shown up, she'd have this rose in her hair and the two of you would be in that bedroom right now, humping like dogs."

My hand tightened into a fist. How dare this grinning snake talk about us in such intimate terms? "I want you leave," I said. "Now. There's the door."

He threw out his hands in frustration. "I was hoping to do this the easy way, but you leave me no choice. Have you heard of the Amado Commission?"

"The what?"

"A commission investigating terrorism in Peru. We can schedule you as first witness tomorrow morning. They'll be asking the same questions I've been asking—except you'll be under oath." He reached for his briefcase and began gathering up his things.

"I'll be at San Marcos tomorrow morning."

"I don't think so, Maestro." He picked up the mystery envelope on the table, glanced at it a moment, and thrust it into my hands.

"What is this?" I asked, running my finger over the wax seal.

The little man stood, buttoned his suit jacket, and smoothed it down. He couldn't have been more than five foot four, even with elevated soles, and when he spoke, his voice was soft, effeminate. "Is your name Markus Einar Thorsen?"

"It is."

"Then it is my duty to inform you that you are to present yourself before the Amado Commission tomorrow morning at zero-nine-hundred-hours. The location is the presidential palace at the old Plaza de Armas. You are to be sworn in as the first witness. If you need a translator, please call the number on the document, and it will be arranged. If you need transportation to the palace, please call, and it will be provided. Do you understand these instructions as I have presented them to you?"

I looked at the general, who was stuffing files back into the box. His teeth were showing. "A subpoena, Dr. Thorsen. Surely you know what that means."

He snatched up his briefcase. The little man picked up the box, and the two of them marched out the door.

CHAPTER FOUR

I flung the subpoena at the closing door. Dammit to hell.
Why hadn't I just waited for Marisa in Tampa or Acapulco
or some other city where no one had ever heard of the Shining
Path, Chairman Gonzalo, or the Amado Commission? But love
was at stake. And lust. And old wrongs to be righted. Now I'd
have to answer their questions under oath.

I grabbed the phone and within minutes was complaining
to the legal attaché at the US Embassy, a man named Holbrook
Easton. From his refined Bostonian accent, I imagined a
Harvard lawyer.

"What is your relationship with this woman?" he asked.

"I have no relationship with this woman. Haven't seen her
in years."

"Then you have nothing to fear, do you?"

"Why can't I just ignore their subpoena?"

"That wouldn't be prudent. They'd apprehend you and
haul you to the hearing in handcuffs. My advice is comply with
the subpoena. Go to the hearing and answer their questions."

I thanked him, hung up, and cursed so loud the people
in the next room probably heard. Then I emptied the general's cigarettes from the ashtrays, freshened up, pulled on my
leather jacket, and went out the door. For all I knew, Marisa
could be waiting downstairs.

Of course. What was wrong with me? She'd been warned about the general and was staying away. Probably sitting in the lobby, dressed as a tourist.

She wasn't, so I nibbled on a sandwich at the bar and looked around. A table of Brits were laughing and exchanging stories about their close encounters with violence. The French and Germans were carrying on about God knows what. But no Marisa. No Americans either. Had we grown so fat and soft and rich that we no longer had a stomach for adventure?

I waited awhile longer, hoping someone would step forward with a message. No one did. I chatted with the servers, hoping to get a signal. No signals. I lingered in the lobby, reading tourist brochures, and even asked the desk clerk if I had messages.

"No, señor, nada."

This made no sense. Marisa had to know I was in trouble. Otherwise she'd have shown up as planned. Or called. But why hadn't she sent a message? Clandestinely. Maybe she was waiting outside, sitting in a parked car. I pushed through the revolving front door and was instantly besieged by money changers, coming out of the fog.

"Dollar, dollar, dollar. I change your dollars."

I turned up my collar against the dampness and retreated down a side street, breathing in the smell of exhaust fumes and street cooking, glancing into doorways and parked cars. Nothing but fog, the money changers, beggars, and old women selling their goods from sidewalk blankets. But no Marisa. Where was she? It wasn't as if I'd be that hard to spot, not with my gringo looks.

A beat of drums rolled over the plaza. People came out of shops. Street waifs darted around me, and I too hastened my step back to the plaza.

The fog and the crowds were still there, but the shouting had given way to the prehistoric sounds of flutes, drums and Peruvian *queñas*. A troupe of musicians in native dress marched solemnly through the square, the crowd giving way as they advanced. When they reached the statue of General San Martín, the drums fell silent.

I climbed the hotel steps for a better view. The crowd waited in stony Indian dignity.

The notes of an ancient *harawi* rose to my ears, music that from Inca times had represented tragedy, and then an older man dressed in poncho and black hat stepped to the microphone and belted out a soul-wrenching tune about unrequited love, sung entirely in Quechua.

> Go away, you keep telling me / Move on, move on, you say.
> I know my bad luck, and I shall leave / But, oh, those eyes of yours,
> And long dark hair / Have stolen my heart…

The tempo quickened, higher notes sparkled, and a magnificent Andean harp joined with the *queñas*. A chorus kicked in, drums beat, but there remained an edge of desperation to the song: the last gasp of dying love. Then a flautist stepped forward and piped out a haunting coda that sent an arrow into my chest and out the other side.

Where the hell was Marisa?

CHAPTER FIVE

It was almost six the next morning, and I'd been dreaming about her all night, when I was shaken from a sleep state to wakefulness by a hellish din outside my window. Horns blared, radios played, and the street traffic sounded like a drag race between log trucks and Hells Angels.

Then I realized the telephone was ringing.

I reached over and grabbed it, hoping as always to hear Marisa's voice.

"The hell's going on, old buddy? I hear you're in deep doo-doo."

I bolted upright. There was only one person with that kind of Tex-Mex accent who called me old buddy, and he was a DEA agent named Lannie Torres, a man I'd known since my Peace Corps days.

"Lannie, what are you doing in Peru?"

"Still with the embassy. I hear you need a lawyer."

"You heard right."

"Well, I figure you'd rather an old friend than some prissy-assed Ivy Leaguer from State. How bout we meet downstairs for breakfast in, say, thirty minutes?"

❧

The dining room was packed with European-looking types, even at that early hour. The smell of bacon reminded me I hadn't eaten since the day before. A heavy-set man looked up from his newspaper and stared. Lannie hadn't arrived yet, but no sooner did I find a table than he came clomping into the room in boots, turquoise bola tie, and tan leather jacket, looking like a tourist from New Mexico. He'd aged a bit in the six or seven years since I'd last seen him, but he still had his mustache, flashing white teeth, and dark Mexican looks.

He gave me a warm *abrazo*. "Looking good, old buddy. How's Denise?"

"I guess you didn't hear. We've been divorced almost three years."

"Oops, sorry. Hope you're okay with that."

"It was a mutual decision. No fights or hard feelings."

The server took our order for the American breakfast and brought a steaming pot of coffee. After we caught up on the small talk, I asked, "Did Holbrook Easton send you?"

"Hell no. Sent myself. Damned near croaked when I saw your name on the list. 'Why, that's Markus Thorsen,' I said to Easton. 'That guy can't be in cahoots with terrorists. He's one of those mild-mannered Scandinavian types. A poet. An Eagle Scout. Doesn't cuss or smoke. Used to sing in a church choir. Why, he's the last guy you'd expect to—'"

"Wait a minute, Lannie. I was never in a choir. Not much of a poet either. And I've been known to drop a cuss word or two. So what's this list you're talking about?"

"Oh, come on. You know how it is in the embassy. An American calls in. He's in trouble. Name gets circulated to see if he's one of the bad guys: baby dealers, radical California Indians, traffickers, criminals on the run, even a few Marxists down to join the revolution." He took a sip of coffee. "That what your girlfriend is, one of those lefties who threw in with the rebels?"

"No, Lannie, she's not the type."

"Then what the hell's going on?"

I pulled Marisa's e-mail from my pocket and handed it to him. He read it and handed it back. "Well, I'll be damned. She that cute little Trotskyite you met at San Marcos?"

"Everyone at San Marcos was a Trotskyite. It's the Berkeley of Peru."

"Yeah, but she was an American, wasn't she? When's the last time you saw her?"

"Two, three months ago."

"And you didn't know she was running with the Shining Path?"

"For God's sake, Lannie. She's not with the Shining Path."

"You told Easton you were here for a conference."

"What else could I tell him? He's probably cooperating with the Peruvians."

"The hell didn't you just wait for her in Tampa? She gave you that option."

"Because Peru's a basket case. Dangerous. I wanted to be here for her, get her on that plane."

He shrugged, let out a long breath, and looked at me the way a doctor might look at a patient before telling him he had a fatal disease. "Look, Mark, I know it's tough, you having a hard-on for her and all that, but look at it from their perspective. Here's this woman with a history. A radical, a Trotskyite. Her things turn up at the digs of Chairman Gonzalo."

"Dammit, Lannie, she gave up that left-wing crap years ago. And even if she hadn't, Trotskyites aren't violent. All they do is drink wine, read Marx, and romanticize revolution."

The server returned with breakfast. Lannie ate a few bites of his hash browns. "Ever wonder why potatoes taste so good in Peru? It's because they're cooked in hog lard. Tastes good, but it's bad for your health. Like fooling around with the wrong kind of woman."

"What the hell is that supposed to mean?"

"You know damn well what it means. What's she doing in Peru anyway?"

"Relatives."

"Hell, I got relatives in Durango, but I'm not moving there."

"She's married, Lannie. Okay? But she's leaving the bastard."

"You ever meet him?"

"Of course not."

"Maybe it's Gonzalo. Ever thought of that?"

"That's so ridiculous, I'm not even going to answer it."

He pointed his fork. "I'm sorry to be the one to tell you, old buddy, but she's deeper in this hole than you're willing to admit. You might as well prepare yourself." He dug into his eggs and was reaching for his cup when he frowned and said, "Aw Christ, it's Gordo."

"Who's Gordo?"

"Fat-ass Peep agent. Sitting back there."

My indignation rose. Peep was the FBI of Peru, the Policia de Investigaciones de Peru—PIP, but pronounced "peep." I moved my chair to the side and took a furtive glance. It was the same heavy-set man I'd noticed when I entered—beer belly, slicked-back hair, and ill-fitting suit, trying to hide his face beneath a newspaper.

"Is he watching us?" I asked Lannie.

"Us, kimosabe? Hell no. He's watching you." He grabbed his briefcase off the floor. "Gotta make some calls. Why don't you finish up and meet me out front at, say, eight-hundred hours?"

"But wait, hold on. I thought you were going to help me develop a defense."

"In the car," he said, and clopped off toward the exit.

21

I shoved away my plate, no longer hungry, and called for the bill. As I was signing it, a silver-haired lady at the next table touched my shoulder.

"Excuse me," she said in a German-sounding accent, "but aren't you Professor Thorsen?"

"How did you know?"

She reached into a tote bag and pulled out a Lima newspaper. There I was on the front page, jogging through the streets of Ayacucho in sweatshirt and headband. The headline read: THE PROFESSOR, THE TERRORIST AND THE MYSTERY WOMAN.

My face heated up. People at other tables were also staring. So was Gordo. I excused myself, hurried down the corridor to the hotel gift shop, and went to the newspaper rack. There I was again, front page of all the dailies. I grabbed a copy of *La Republica*, paid cash, jogged the five floors up to my room, and sat down. By then my heart was pounding. And it didn't slow when I read an excerpt from one of my old love letters on the front page.

My dearest Marisa: How I wish I could breathe in your perfume, run my hands through your hair, look into those beautiful blue eyes. I want to kiss you the way we kissed when I read Neruda to you. I want to feel the beat of your heart next to mine. I want to...

The next few lines had been blacked out by some clever editor with a sense of humor. I flung the paper onto the coffee table, and I think if General Reál had shown up at that moment, I'd have thrown the son of a bitch out the window.

CHAPTER SIX

At eight sharp, dressed in a dark suit, I slipped out the front door into the fog. A residue of tear gas hung in the air, burning my eyes. Pedestrians held handkerchiefs over their noses. A speaker with a bullhorn was firing up demonstrators about the number of *desaparecidos*—people who'd been arrested and then disappeared—while a line of policemen in full riot gear protected the hotels and other commercial interests around the plaza.

Lannie waved from a Green Cherokee. "Over here, old buddy."

As soon as I climbed in, he rattled a newspaper at me. "Can you believe this crap? Country's going to hell—bombings, murder, kidnapping, rape—and what do they have on the front page? You." He fanned his face. "Fucking tear gas. Let's go somewhere we can talk."

He gunned the engine, made a loop around the plaza, and turned onto Jirón de la Unión for the short drive to the palace. "This must be creating a shit storm at your university."

I'd forgotten about the university, but suddenly I could picture the dean in the president's office, the president waving a copy of the *St. Pete Times,* saying she had trustees to answer to. And the alumni. And a reputation to uphold. And how could the screening committee be so stupid as to send her the name of a crypto-terrorist as their first choice for academic dean?

Lannie parked in front of a shop advertising Inca gold. Crowds of teenagers roamed up and down the street, most looking like newcomers from the Andes. Little children and old women hawked their goods from sidewalk blankets. Lannie lit a cigarette.

"We've still got a couple minutes. We can talk here." He turned to face me. "Tell me this—you and Marisa were getting it on even when you were married to Denise?"

"It wasn't like that. Denise and I had been emotionally divorced a long time."

I rolled down my window to let out his cigarette smoke, but closed it when it attracted a woman with ragged children clinging to her skirts. She tapped at the window anyway and screwed up her face in that piteous expression of beggars everywhere.

"*Señor, por favor.*"

I opened the window and handed her a few coins, but all that did was attract more beggars—kids with outstretched hands, a man on crutches, a woman pushing a child in a wheelchair.

"Christ, Mark. Don't you know better?" He turned the keys in the ignition, drove down two blocks, and parked again. "Now, keep that damn window closed."

"Fine, but put out that damn cigarette."

"What is it with you pussies in the States? You'd be smoking too if you had my job." He flicked the cigarette out the window. "Okay, back to Marisa. You say you've been meeting her for like three years. But she's married. How'd you arrange that?"

"Her husband's a businessman. Travels to Europe and the States."

"And you never asked about him? What he does?"

"Of course. She told me all about him. Bottom line is they don't get along."

"Maybe he's into trafficking. Ever thought about that?"

I had, but wasn't about to share my thoughts with a DEA agent.

He twisted around to face me. "Look, I'm gonna say something that'll piss you off, but it needs to be said." He paused at the sound of a passing truck. "This girlfriend of yours, Marisa, she's married to another man, but she's been banging you for like three years. Right?"

"I wouldn't exactly call it banging."

"Whatever, but here's the point. Women who cheat on their husbands aren't exactly the most trustworthy types. If she lies to her husband, she lies to you."

"Marisa's not like that. I've known her for over ten years. I trust her."

"Would you fucking listen to yourself? If she's so trustworthy, why the hell can't she just pick up the phone and tell you what's going on?"

I drew in a deep breath but said nothing. Lannie went on. "You know what I find weird? Back in your Peace Corps days, the two of you were, like, joined at the hip. The hell didn't you marry her?"

"It's a long story—parents, distance, hell, the stars."

"You can do better than that. What happened?"

I'd asked myself that question a hundred times. The short answer was Marisa's mom, but there was more to the story, and I was trying to form an answer when a convoy of armored personnel carriers rumbled up the street, shaking the ground and fouling the air with exhaust smoke. An officer in a jeep ordered us to take another route. Then we got tied up in traffic, and by the time we broke free, Lannie had forgotten his question and it was time to go to the palace.

"Best thing is a bad memory," he said in his Tex-Mex accent. "Don't volunteer a damn thing."

25

CHAPTER SEVEN
Palacio Pizarro

The ancient buildings around the plaza looked sinister in the mist. Soldiers in full battle gear stood around the fountain in the square or looked down from ornate wooden balconies. Sandbags, machine gun emplacements, tanks, and a long open trench lined the entire block. The palace itself, built on the site of Pizarro's home, loomed up like Dracula's castle.

"Nervous?" Lannie asked.

"What do you think?"

"Don't worry. I'll be sitting at your side. They ask a question you don't want to answer, you just turn to me for counsel. It'll be okay." He patted my knee.

A military policeman flagged us down. A search of the Cherokee followed. Then we were directed around a concrete barrier, through a gate, and into a crowded parking lot, where we parked next to a jeep.

"There's something else I'd better tell you," I said to Lannie. "You've heard of Congresswoman Peretz-Montero, haven't you—from Miami? Head of the House Committee on Foreign Affairs?"

"What about her?"

"She's Marisa's mom."

"You fucking kidding me?"

"No, Lannie."

He leaned forward and banged his head on the steering wheel. "The hell didn't you tell me?"

A side door opened in the palace. The little man who'd presented me with a subpoena stepped outside, caught our attention, and tapped his watch.

Lannie ground out his cigarette. We crunched across gravel to the little man, and within seconds were following him into a corridor that smelled old and musty.

Ceremonial guards in Napoleonic uniforms with gold plumed helmets snapped straight. The little man hurried ahead, heels clicking on the marbled floors, leaving a trail of perfumed cologne, leading us past a painting of Pizarro and his troops trampling Incas into the dust.

Presently, we heard what sounded like the noise and stir of a party. Lannie and I exchanged troubled glances. Ahead of us a ceremonial guard swung open a magnificent pair of gilded wooden doors, and when we stepped through it, I thought we'd gone to the wrong place.

"Holy shit," Lannie muttered.

A sea of faces turned to stare, the ladies in full dresses with scarves and brooches, the men in tailored dark suits. Gold glittered in the bright lights. Clouds of cigarette smoke drifted toward the ceiling. A television news crew was also there—with minicam and an attractive female reporter telling her live audience the proceedings were about to begin.

She stepped forward and thrust a microphone in my face. "What can you tell us about the identity of your love, your *novia?*"

"I don't have a *novia.*"

A ceremonial guard of five or six soldiers cleared a path to a roped-off section in front of a dais. On the wall behind it hung an enormous oil of Captain-General Pizarro. One of the guards motioned me into a chair at a small table. Lannie dragged up a chair to sit beside me.

"No, no," said our host, wagging a finger. "You can't sit there."

"But I'm his lawyer."

"Sorry, sir. The witness sits alone." He pointed to the spectator section. "You sit over there."

Hot words followed. The guards took Lannie by the arm and ushered him away, all of which was caught by the TV cameras.

"Don't worry," he hissed back.

I loosened my tie and looked around. Seats rose up behind me and on both sides, giving the place the effect of a Greek amphitheater, one of those places where great tragedies were played out. Every seat was occupied by someone with a newspaper, and every occupant looked hostile. Even Pizarro looked hostile. He stared down at me from the wall, hand on sword, armor glistening, flags flying, ready to trample me under his horse. This must have been what it was like during the Inquisition—a heretic, a screaming mob, an accuser, and a panel of judges.

If that wasn't bad enough, General Reál made his entrance, all starch and boots in uniform and aviator glasses, surrounded by aides, reporters, and TV cameras, lips curled in a sneer. The medals on his chest gave him the appearance of a much-decorated war hero.

The ceremonial guards led him through the crowd. The general stopped so close, I could hear his answers to questions from reporters.

"Yes," he said in his raspy voice, "the witness could have saved himself this embarrassment."

"Yes, she was sleeping with both men at the same time. Now what kind of woman does that?"

I was saved from further provocation by the sergeant at arms who stepped up to the dais and cried, "*Oye! Oye!* By executive order of the president of the Republic of Peru, in accordance with the protocols established by this commission, these hearings will now come to order. *De pie.*"

Everyone stood, and for the first time in years, I craved a cigarette.

Three commissioners swept in amid camera flashes and gawking, a flurry of black robes and posturing, medallions swinging from their necks. They took their chairs and looked around at the spectators and reporters. At the aides scurrying around with papers.

At me.

Introductions followed, a litany of compound names and titles that would have sounded pretentious in any language other than Spanish. Commissioner Amado, a distinguished-looking man with thinning hair, was introduced by his title, Licenciado, and then as Aurelio Amado-Saavedra Montes y Valle. His credentials were equally grandiose—Harvard degree, novelist, and the recipient of so many awards that it took the reader a couple minutes to go down the list.

Finally, Commissioner Amado glanced down at me. "Does the witness need an interpreter?"

By then my mouth couldn't have been drier if I'd been chewing cotton. Sweat from my armpits trickled down my ribs.

"No," I managed to answer.

"Very well. May I now introduce—"

Lannie came to his feet. "Mr. Commissioner?"

Every eye and camera turned to Lannie. In his southwestern outfit with the turquoise and boots, he looked as out of place as the commissioners would look at a Texas cookout.

Commissioner Amado glared over the top of his glasses. "Who are you?"

Lannie snapped to attention. "My name is Emiliano Carranza Torres y Sanchez—*Licenciado, abogado y doctorado de jurisprudencia—a sus ordenes.*" He snapped his boots together.

"I'm with the legal staff of the Embassy of the United States of America. Dr. Thorsen is my client. On his behalf I'd like to request a delay in his appearance before this honorable commission."

"On what grounds, Mr. Torres?"

"On the grounds he did not have time to adequately prepare."

"This is a hearing, Mr. Torres, not a trial."

"We'd still like a delay."

"Are you Peruvian, Mr. Torres?"

"No, Commissioner."

"Do you have a license to practice law in this country?"

"No, Commissioner."

"Then please be seated. Your request is denied."

Lannie shrugged and eased back into his chair. Commissioner Amado, sitting high and lordly in his straight-backed chair, gaveled the place to order and pushed back his glasses on his nose.

"Swear in the witness and get on with the questioning."

A clerk thrust out a copy of the Holy Bible, and it's a good thing I wasn't hooked up to a lie detector when I raised my hand and promised to tell the truth, the whole truth, and nothing but the truth, "*así Dios me salve.*"

CHAPTER EIGHT

Commissioner Amado looked down at me. "Please to state your full name, age, and place of birth."

I leaned forward and spoke into the microphone. "My name is Markus Einar Thorsen, age thirty-three. I was born in the United States of America, state of Minnesota."

"Where do you currently reside?"

"Tampa, the state of Florida."

The preliminaries went on—questions about my profession, place of employment, mode of transportation—and didn't end until an aide whispered something to Amado. Then the cameras and every eye in the place shifted to a table surrounded by a cloud of cigar smoke.

The man sitting there was smallish and stooped, with a sprinkling of ashes on his jacket. His rumpled suit looked like a recycled military uniform. He stood, bowed politely, flicked ashes from his cigar, and then strode to my table and smiled, showing tobacco-stained teeth.

"Professor Thorsen, my name is Raúl Felipe Bocanegra y Pozo, chief inspector of the international division of the Policia de Investigaciones de Peru, the agency we all know as Peep."

He marched back to his table, rummaged through his briefcase, took out a legal pad, and turned toward the dais.

"Honorable commissioners, as I sat there listening to the introductions, I found myself wishing I could apologize to this witness. Imagine the embarrassment, the delay in his rendezvous with his *novia*. But there is a problem." He pointed with his cigar toward the briefcase. "It is called evidence. The evidence will show that this witness, this learned professor, is an important link in the chain of terror that has brought so much grief to our people."

Lannie came to his feet. "Mr. Commissioner, please."

Commissioner Amado's face turned red. He pointed his gavel at Lannie. "Sit down, Mr. Torres. Don't make me have to tell you again."

Lannie dropped back into his chair. The commissioner turned back to Bocanegra. "If you have a point to make, make it, but please be aware this witness has not been charged with a crime."

The inspector ground out his cigar and digressed into a speech about the dirty little war that had already claimed thirty thousand lives. He spoke about the raid on the hideout of Chairman Gonzalo and the letters and poetry that had brought me before this commission. Finally, he turned to me.

"For the record, Dr. Thorsen, do you claim to have never met Chairman Gonzalo?"

I leaned forward and spoke into the microphone. "Never."

"What about your lady friend?"

"I wouldn't know."

"Indeed. My impression was that you came to Peru to rendezvous with her."

"I came here to attend an academic conference."

"Are you the keynote speaker?"

"No, Inspector."

"Ah, then you're presenting an important paper?"

"No, I came to attend the conference."

"Just to attend? During a war? How flattering for us." He resumed his pacing, hands behind his back. "Do you know about the hanging dogs?"

"Only what I've heard—that it's to intimidate people."

"Oh, it's more than intimidation, much, much more." He lit another cigar and blew a perfect smoke circle toward the ceiling. The room grew so quiet, I could hear the hum of the TV cameras.

"The death of a dog reaches deep into the Andean psyche. It used to be that when a man died, his dog was put to death as well. In short, the death of a person always meant the death of a dog. But over time people came to believe the opposite. In other words, the death of a dog foretells the death of someone else. The Shining Path capitalizes on this superstition. They kill dogs and hang them in conspicuous places, usually before an act of violence. It's a warning of what's to come—even graver than the cross burnings of your Ku Klux Klan."

"They're not *my* Ku Klux Klan."

Commissioner Amado lifted his gavel. "Is there a point to this dog story, Inspector?"

"The point is that Peru is a violent country. The point is that this witness should be made to understand the kind of people with whom he is associating."

Commissioner Amado pointed his gavel. "I'm giving you exactly ten more minutes. But I'm warning you, Inspector, if all you can produce is another dog story, then I plan to dismiss the witness, rescind the subpoena, and send him on his way. *Me entiende?*"

"I understand perfectly." He looked at his watch and smiled. A long period of silence followed, during which he paced the floor like a prosecuting attorney, trailing clouds of evil-smelling smoke. He stopped in front of me and seemed to reflect a moment. "Where did you learn Quechua, Professor?

33

As a Peruvian, I find it remarkable that you know the language of the Andes."

I smiled at the compliment, though I knew what he was up to—that I was guilty by association.

"I learned it when I was in the Peace Corps, in a small village called Sicuani."

"Did you ever lecture in Quechua when you were a Fulbright professor in Ayacucho?"

"I did."

"At the time of your association with Chairman Gonzalo?"

"I told you before I don't know this Chairman Gonzalo."

"Was Quechua the required language?"

"Spanish was the language of instruction. But many of the indigenous students—Runas—spoke Quechua as their first language, so we offered a few courses in it."

"Whose idea was this?"

"I think it was a philosophy professor."

"What was this professor's name?"

Lannie bolted to his feet. "Mr. Commissioner, please, I need to confer with the witness."

Commissioner Amado ripped off his glasses. "What is the basis of your request, Mr. Torres?"

"A point of clarification. The witness is answering questions based on incomplete information."

The commissioners fell into an animated discussion. Spectators whispered among themselves. Lannie caught my eye and began mouthing words I didn't understand, and I was still trying to figure it out when the gavel banged and Commissioner Amado spoke. "Mr. Torres, may I remind you again that this is not a trial. Your request is denied."

Inspector Bocanegra adjusted his wire-rimmed glasses, went into his briefcase again, and pulled out a book. "This is a yearbook from the University of Huamanga in Ayacucho. It belongs—or belonged—to you, Dr. Thorsen. It too was recovered in the raid on Chairman Gonzalo's safe house." He waved it around and handed it to me. "Do you recognize it?"

"I do."

He opened it to a page tagged with a yellow slip of paper. "Here we have photographs of the professors. Why, here's one of you." He showed it to the commissioners, then flipped to another page and jabbed his hairy finger at a photo of another professor.

"Well, look at this. Would this happen to be the philosophy professor?"

I looked at the photo and tried to place him. "That might be him. I can't be sure."

He held it up for the cameras and then handed it to me. "Would you please read the inscription?"

I took the book and examined the faded handwriting. And then I knew where the inspector was going. I even knew why Lannie was shaking his head.

Commissioner Amado pointed his gavel at me. "Please to read it for the record."

"It says, 'To my gringo friend, Marco, with warm personal regards.'"

"Is it signed?"

"He signed it as Abí."

Bocanegra took the open book and handed it to Commissioner Amado. He strode back to his briefcase, pulled out a poster, and unrolled it.

"This is a more recent photograph of the professor—the kind you see in post offices and other public buildings. Do you recognize him?"

I wanted to crawl under the table. The man in the poster was older and more coarse-looking than the picture in the yearbook. He loomed as a menacing figure with a furrowed brow and angry glare. His beefy face and bushy eyebrows stood out. His left fist—almost as big as his head—was clenched, and in the other hand, he carried a red hammer and sickle flag of the Shining Path.

"And you haven't seen him recently…or spoken with him?"

"No, Inspector. I told you I hardly knew him."

"Would you please look at the top of the poster and read aloud what it says?"

I let my eyes fall on the words at the top of the poster. WANTED FOR MURDER, TERRORISM AND CRIMES AGAINST THE STATE—ABIMAEL GUZMÁN.

"Read it aloud," Bocanegra repeated.

I read it, almost choking on the words.

"Louder, please."

I read it again.

"And what does it say at the bottom of the poster?"

"It says 'Also known as Chairman Gonzalo.'"

CHAPTER NINE

If Chairman Gonzalo had burst into the room with a fizzing stick of dynamite, he could not have stirred it up more. Journalists and reporters rushed out. Spectators with cameras came running down to snap pictures of me looking—dumbfounded—at the wanted poster of the man I'd sworn I didn't know, and the entire place turned into a madhouse.

Amado gave up his attempt to restore order and declared a ten-minute recess. He and the other commissioners left the room. Lannie hurried to my side. A detail of ceremonial guards kept reporters away. I looked at Lannie.

"How the hell was I supposed to know? That university is a big place. He was in a different building. I don't even remember him signing my yearbook."

"Maybe they forged the signing."

"So what do we do now?"

He lit a cigarette. "Only one thing to do, and that's come clean about Marisa."

"Her husband would kill her."

"Her husband already knows, for God's sake, unless he's in Alaska hunting polar bears."

Ten or fifteen minutes passed. Spectators and reporters returned to their seats. Lannie and I tried to anticipate the questions and come up with a strategy, but it was hopeless.

"De pie!"

Everyone stood. The commissioners filed in and took their places. Lannie hurried off to his seat. Inspector Bocanegra resumed his pacing across the ancient wooden floor. Blood was in the air. He stopped and pointed his cigar at me. "What is the name of your paramour?"

Before I could reply, Bocanegra picked up one of my old love letters. "According to this, her name is Maria Luisa Montero, abbreviated to Marisa. Obviously a fabrication."

"It's the only name I know."

"And yet you compose erotic poetry to her?"

He reached into his jacket pocket and took out a folded sheet of paper, and as he unfolded it, slowly, I recognized it as a yellowed copy of my 'Lily of Peru.'

Please don't read it. Please.

He read it anyway. The women in the room smiled. Lannie shook his head. Bocanegra put away the poem, then took a large red book out of his briefcase and waved it around.

"Another yearbook—this one from the University of San Marcos." He flipped through the pages. "Why, here's a picture of her. It says she's a journalism student."

I looked into Marisa's nineteen-year-old face and took in the blue eyes, the long dark hair that was combed straight down, and the smile. It was a good photo.

"Listen, Professor Thorsen. You're in enough trouble already, so I'm going to save you further embarrassment. We know she was a student at San Marcos, a Trotskyite. We know you met her on campus. We know the places you took her. We know your favorite night spot—El Parrón—where the radicals hang out. And we know she's from your country. From Miami."

My heart sank. I waited for him to announce that she was Congresswoman Montero's daughter. When he didn't, I assumed—hoped—he didn't know.

"Why are you protecting her?" Bocanegra asked quietly. He walked over to me and leaned down. Ashes fell on the table, and when he spoke, it was almost a whisper. "Where is she?"

"I honestly don't know, Inspector."

"You renewed your relationship with her three years ago, didn't you? In Ayacucho."

I said nothing. It must have been obvious to the entire world that I was defeated.

Bocanegra turned to the stenographer. "Let the record state the witness refuses to answer."

He snapped his fingers and waved. This brought out a dumpy little woman with jet black hair. She rolled out a slide projector on a cart with squeaky wheels. Another man helped her set up a screen. There was a short delay while someone went off in search of an extension cord.

When all was in readiness and the lights dimmed, I put on my glasses. Lannie looked at me and shrugged. The projector came to life with a hum. A ray of light penetrated the dimness, picking up drifting clouds of smoke.

"First slide," Bocanegra said.

A whitewashed house with a red-tiled roof appeared on the screen, with chalky mountains in the background. The hydrangeas were so lush, I imagined I could smell them. The number on the entrance gate was 143. Bocanegra's voice penetrated the darkness.

"Do you recognize the house?"

"It's where I lived in Ayacucho."

"Next slide."

The second image showed an attractive blonde with a clean athletic look standing at the gate of the same house. She was dressed in jeans and a heavy knit pullover.

"And this young lady is?"

"Denise. She was my wife."

"Aha, so you were married?"

"Separated."

"Separated? But here she is with you in the same house. What a strange separation."

"She was visiting. We had issues to settle."

"I'm sure you did, Professor. It's always difficult to explain another woman."

The audience burst into laughter. Amado banged his gavel.

"Next slide."

Suddenly I wanted to flee the building. There she was, collar turned up against the mountain air, dark glasses shading her blue eyes, wind whipping hair about her face—walking through a green gate with the number 143 in plain view. But who had taken the photo? And why?

"And who might this be?" the inspector wanted to know.

I didn't answer. Even in the darkened room, I could see the reaction of the audience: the men elbowing each other and wishing they could be so lucky, the women shaking their heads and whispering to each other. Probably saying what a prick I was.

Bocanegra saw it too. "So here we have this married man, a man with a beautiful blond wife, entertaining a female associate of Chairman Gonzalo. What did your wife say, Dr. Thorsen, this woman with whom you shared the sacred vows of matrimony?"

I wanted to yank off my tie, wrap it around Bocanegra's neck, and choke him to death. Slowly.

They showed other photographs—Marisa leaving the house, climbing into a Toyota, driving away, the license plates clearly visible.

"We ran the plates," Bocanegra said, "and came up with nothing. No name. No registration. But terrorists are like that. The trail is always murky."

The lights came on. Someone disconnected the projector and wheeled it away. I blinked back the brightness and tried to compose myself, wondering who took those photographs. Had Marisa's husband hired someone to watch her? In the silence that followed, Bocanegra stepped onto the dais with the commissioners and entered into a whispered conversation.

The minutes went by. The audience stirred. Finally, Commissioner Amado banged his gavel and looked down at me, solemnly, as if this would be painful.

"Professor Thorsen, what is obvious is you know a great deal more than you're letting on. We need to know where this woman is. You could help us. Instead you've chosen to defy us."

He hesitated as if to let the words sink in. "So what are we to do? We have two choices. First, we could remand you to Inspector Bocanegra's care for a few days of private questioning. Alternatively, we could give you another chance to stand before us and tell the truth."

I looked at Lannie. The commissioner kept talking. "On the recommendation of Inspector Bocanegra, I'm going to allow you to go back to your hotel and think about it. But tomorrow morning at oh-nine-hundred-hours, we want you back here with a full confession. Is that clear?"

I could have fainted with relief. "Yes, Commissioner."

No sooner had he banged his gavel for adjournment than microphones and questions came at me from every angle. The ceremonial guards pushed people out of the way, clearing enough of a path for us to make it out of the room and down the corridor to the exit.

"Christ," Lannie said. "I need a drink."

The damp, outside air was a refreshing change from the oppressiveness of the palace, but even there a crowd had gathered. Lannie grasped my arm like the lawyer he was and tried to lead me through the madness, saying, "Let us pass, *por favor,*" or "No comment."

We were about to make a dash for the Cherokee when an impulse seized me. Maybe it was her perfume—Lily of

Peru—though I didn't exactly smell it. Maybe I heard her call my name, though in the clamor around me, that wouldn't have been likely. Or maybe it was an indefinable current passing between us—a common destiny, a fusion of souls. Whatever the case, I glanced to my right and saw her, strolling along with the spectators.

Marisa.

The world stood still, the noise fell away, my breathing seemed to stop. Surely I was hallucinating. No one could be this brazen. But the oxblood leather jacket was unmistakably hers. And she had the same dark hair, same walk, graceful even while pushing through a mob.

She turned toward me, caught my eye, and then moved quickly away at an angle.

Lannie tugged at my arm. "Come on, old buddy. The hell outa here."

She was away from the crowd now, hurrying her pace and heading toward a line of parked taxis. A driver hopped out and held the door. She paused, turned, and looked straight at me. Heels. Dark skirt. Full lips. The distance was too great to make out the color of her eyes, but I could plainly see she was biting the corner of her lower lip, the way she always did when troubled.

"Wrong way, old buddy. We're parked over there."

Marisa climbed into the backseat and shut the door.

The engine started. The cab raced out the gate and faded into the mist.

CHAPTER TEN

I trotted back to Lannie's Cherokee, desperate to chase her down. "Hurry," I said, hopping inside and closing the door. "I saw Marisa. She just drove off in that green cab."

Lannie fired up the car and headed for the exit, but other cars were also crowding the gate, and by the time we got through, the only possibility of catching her would be if she waited.

"Can I have a cigarette?" I asked.

"The hell's this? You back to smoking?"

I lit up one of his Marlboros, took a long drag, and put it out.

We scanned side streets and parked cars, looking into the shadows. We drove around the plaza a second time, slowing at each street and alley. But all we saw were soldiers and tanks and misty fog and a steady trail of spectators leaving the palace.

"Fucking *garúa*," Lannie grumbled, using the Peruvian name for the fog. "Can't see a thing." He switched on the headlights and wiped the inside windshield with his hand. "You must have been mistaken. She got any sense at all, she'd have gone to the States by now."

"No, Lannie, it was her. I'd know her anywhere."

"You better hope you're wrong. Bocanegra wasn't being generous with you; he was being creative. He arrests you, all

43

they get is bad publicity. But cut you a little slack, and you'll run straight to her. That's how they operate. Probably got a platoon of agents on your case."

He stopped at a red light and lit a cigarette. "But I know how to outsmart the bastards. We've got planes flying every day into the jungle—gunships, crop dusters, helicopters—looking for *narcos*. Hell, we could dress you up like one of my men— helmet, coveralls, goggles—fly you over to Pucallpa and drop you with the missionaries."

"Missionaries?"

"Why not? They're always flying over to Brazil in their little one-engine planes."

He was still talking airplanes when we came upon the same convoy that had passed us earlier—jeeps with machine guns mounted on top, trucks loaded with soldiers who looked as if they belonged in high school. One of the tanks had parked sideways in the street, its cannon pointing up toward Plaza San Martín, its engine at an idling growl. Beyond it, a crowd of angry demonstrators waved placards, chanted *"Asesinos,"* and hurled an occasional orange.

Lannie slammed the Cherokee into reverse, backed down to the intersection, and took a side street, talking as he drove.

"Okay, here's the plan: I'll set up a meeting with Easton. He'll get the ambassador on it. Maybe they'll work out a solution. If not, we go with my plan."

"What about Marisa?"

"She ever bailed out of an airplane?"

"We'd have to bail out?"

"Hey, I never said it was gonna be easy."

Our route took us to La Colmena, the main street leading down to Plaza San Martín, and to a side entrance of the hotel. Lannie pulled over to the curb.

"Aw, shit, would you look at that?"

Beneath an awning stood Gordo the Peep agent—cigarette, trench coat and dark hat, looking like a gestapo agent from an old war movie. He spotted us, flicked his cigarette into the street, and nudged the man beside him, an Asian-looking type.

Lannie did a screeching U-turn, took another side street, and stopped about five blocks away. He took out a notepad, wrote on it, ripped out the paper, and handed it to me.

"Your phone's probably bugged, so we gotta talk code. Here's three possible meeting places. If I call and say, 'Number two,' that means second place on the list. Got it?"

"Got it."

"If I say nineteen-hundred hours, you subtract two hours. And one more thing—don't do something stupid like going out to meet her. You could get killed."

As soon as he drove away, I headed in the opposite direction from my hotel, stepping around blanket vendors, waving off money-changers, glancing over my shoulder. La Colmena was as cluttered and shabby as everything else in Lima, a far cry from the fashionable street I remembered. I ducked beneath a wood-covered walkway in front of a construction site. Someone had spray-painted the plywood with the words REDUCED TO RUBBLE BY A SHINING PATH BOMB.

I had hoped to get past El Parrón without wallowing in old memories, but the haunting sound of a flute brought me to a stop, and when I got a whiff of cigarette smoke that had wafted into the street, I was a twenty-two-year-old Peace Corps Volunteer again.

El Parrón had been *our* place, one of those dimly lit *boites* where bearded revolutionaries sat around debating dialectical materialism and liberation theology, and guys brought girlfriends to plot seduction. Even now I could envision Marisa in a black turtleneck, her lips moist and inviting, my copy of

Neruda's love poems on the table, a mug of hot red wine, cigarettes in the ashtray.

My eyes watered. I wiped them, drew in a deep breath, and hurried on.

Presently, I was in the elegant lobby of the Hotel Crillion near the US Embassy. The smell of freshly brewed coffee was in the air. Guests had gathered around the TV set, and the announcer was talking about hanging dogs and another bombing.

I found a pay phone and stuffed a Nuevo Sol into the coin slot.

No tone, dammit. The Lima telephone system was as antiquated as everything else in Peru.

After a few tries, I got a tone and dialed Marisa's calling service.

A woman answered. "Sorry, señor, but that service has been disconnected."

A clerk at the desk stared as if she recognized me. Would she report me to Peep?

I visualized a phone ringing in some dark inner sanctum, a little Peep guy with earphones plugging wires into an entire wall of switchboards, trying frantically to tap into this line.

I stuffed another sol into the slot and dialed another number. It clicked as if someone picked up. Then came an annoying klaxon-like sound followed by a recorded voice.

"The number you have called is no longer in service. If you need assistance…"

Damn, damn, damn. There had to be some way. She was out there somewhere, trying to get a message to me. What would she do?

Probably call me at home and leave a message on voice mail.

Of course. How stupid of me not to have thought of it before.

I stuffed in another coin and got the international operator. Behind me, a voice on the television was saying, "Do you
know this woman? Described as a North American with blue
eyes and dark hair, her height is about a hundred and sixty-
eight centimeters. Slim, very attractive. Last known residence
was Ayacucho. Anyone with information should call…"

The operator asked for my calling card number. I followed
her instructions and dialed my PIN, then my home number,
and waited to hear Marisa's message.

Instead, there was only the beep-beep of a busy signal.

How could that be? I lived alone.

Finally, I gave up and called my administrative assistant at
the university.

"Oh my God," Jenny said. "Are you all right? We've been
hearing crazy things."

"I'm fine, but listen. Are there any messages for me?"

"About two dozen."

She went over the list, but Marisa wasn't on it.

"Listen, Jenny, would you get on another line and call my
home number?"

She put me on hold and came back in a few seconds. "All I
get is a busy signal."

I thanked her, hung up before she could start asking questions, and resisted the temptation to yank the phone out by
the cord. This trip was nothing but disaster. I might as well take
Lannie up on his offer and dive out of an airplane over the
jungle. Sans parachute!

CHAPTER ELEVEN

The demonstrators were still in the plaza when I got back to
my hotel, but the protests had given way to the same gut-
wrenching tunes as the day before, the same old man, backed
up with flutes, drums, and *queñas*. The old man's voice was as
cracked and strained as my mood, but his song, rendered entirely in Quechua, almost brought me to tears.

> I waited for you on the hilltop,
> Beneath the trees / At the spring.
> And never did I see your face again…

Poor man. He looked as miserable as I felt. Probably left at the
altar by some dark-haired flower of the Andes. I marched back
into the hotel, took the elevator to my room, and heard the
ringing telephone before I opened the door.

"What is going on?" the dean yelled. "CNN called. I'm getting calls from Peru, something about you being implicated in
a drug bust. Keeping company with terrorists."

"I'll explain everything when I get back."

"It's going to take more than explaining, Markus. The president's going through the roof. There's talk about dirty letters,
and you writing erotic poetry to a married woman."

"She wasn't married at the time. We were engaged."

"Are you saying there's truth to these allegations?"

"Look, I can't talk right now. I'll be back in a couple days, and you'll understand."

"I don't have a couple days. The screening committee's meeting this afternoon." His voice took on a sympathetic tone. "I'm sorry to be the one to tell you, but they're withdrawing their recommendation for the deanship—integrity and all that crap."

It took all the willpower in my being to keep from yanking the phone out of the jack and hurling it out the window. Only a few days ago, my biggest worry had been whether or not Marisa and I should stop in Acapulco on our way home. Now it had come down to no Marisa, no deanship and no escape from madness. The dean droned on.

"I'm also disappointed in you, all these—"

I slammed down the receiver.

A loud pop sounded in the plaza, followed by screams and the wail of sirens. I rushed to the window and pulled back the drapes in time to see tear gas rising around the statue of General San Martín. Police in full riot gear waded into the crowd, swinging their truncheons.

A water cannon roared forward and sprayed the protestors with long, drenching bursts, knocking people off their feet and sending them skidding along the cobblestones. The musicians tried to retreat, but their instruments slowed them down. The old man tripped and fell. A policeman picked up his guitar and smashed it against a lamppost.

Some of the protestors tied handkerchiefs over their mouths and hurled the smoking canisters back at the police. Others counterattacked, and for a fleeting moment, I wanted to rush out, grab a flag and join the charge. But within ten or fifteen minutes, the twentieth century had beaten down the sixteenth, and there was nothing left except tear gas seeping through the windows.

The phone rang again. It was Lannie.

"Listen, old buddy. I think we found a solution. How bout we meet at, say, number one? Make it twenty-two-hundred hours. Can you lose the goons?"

I grabbed my leather jacket and hurried out the door. Fog hung over the city like a medieval plague, creating an eerie glow around streetlamps and headlights. Tires swished on the wet pavement. My eyes and throat burned from the lingering tear gas. I waved down a taxi, handed the driver a ten-dollar bill, and told him what I wanted to do.

Behind us, men in trench coats were piling into a black Mercedes.

"You that gringo they're talking about?" the driver asked.

"Is that a problem for you?"

"None, I hate the bastards too."

We raced up La Colmena, the driver complaining about all that was wrong in Peru—a fascist president, a worthless currency, taxes on poor people like him. After about eight blocks, he made a screeching right turn onto a dark side street and then slowed down long enough for me to jump out.

"*Viva Gonzalo*," he cried, and kept going.

I galloped into a doorway and pressed myself flat against the wall. The Mercedes skidded around the corner and fishtailed on the slick pavement. It too kept going, a blur of dark hats and glowing cigarettes, its single taillight disappearing into the gloom.

A few minutes later, I strolled into El Parrón.

CHAPTER TWELVE

It was just as noisy and crowded as before and still smelled of smoke, wine, and spicy food. A small band of college-looking kids was tuning up in a corner. Long-haired types chatted across their drinks, the men bearded, the women dressed in black, some with eyebrow rings and mulberry-colored hair, a few of them staring as if they recognized me.

Lannie waved from a far corner, at the very table where Marisa and I used to sit. In his jeans and boots, and a black pullover beneath a dark jacket, he looked more like an art professor than a DEA man. He motioned me into the same chair where I'd once sat with Marisa.

"Couldn't you find someplace else?" I said. "These people read the papers."

"So what? You're their hero. Don't be surprised if they ask for your autograph."

A shapely, dark-haired server took our order for pisco sours. Lannie touched her arm. "Anyone ever tell you how gorgeous you are?"

She went away, grinning. Lannie pushed his chair closer. "The ambassador had a long talk with the commissioners. They're working out a closed-door hearing. It'll be just them, Holbrook Easton and the two of us. No journalists, no spectators, no generals."

"What am I supposed to tell them?"

"That's why we're having this meeting. You tell me. I'll decide."

The pisco sours arrived. While Lannie was flirting with the server, I glanced around at posters of Che Guevara, Mariátegui, and Trotsky. Clouds of cigarette smoke drifted toward the ceiling. A bearded man at the next table was reading poetry to a woman in a black sweater. That could be us, I thought, Marisa hanging on every word I read, looking into my eyes, her feet entangled with mine.

Lannie slapped me on the arm. "She likes me."

"Who likes you?"

"Our waitress. The hell you think I'm talking about?" He took a sip of pisco and wiped foam off his mustache. "Okay, old buddy, tell me about Ayacucho. Wasn't that where the two of you linked up the second time around?"

I let my mind drift back three years to a small chapel— church bells, tuxedoes, and flowers, the women all hats and smiles. "It was at a wedding for one of my students."

"She shows up at the same wedding?"

"Not exactly. It was also the day of Inti Raymi, you know, sun festival, winter solstice, Runas on the streets in native wear, dancing, blowing horns, getting soused. The noise interfered with the wedding, but it went on, and when we went outside, I saw her across the street."

"Dressed like a Runa?"

"No, Lannie, it was like she was waiting. And the weird thing was I knew she'd be there."

"Wait, you saying the two of you have some kind of metaphysical connection—stars and planets, the moon? All that New Age bullshit."

"You wanna hear this or not?"

"Course I wanna hear it. So you go outside and there she is, but you knew in advance."

"All I know is I felt it. I pushed through the mob like a madman, calling her name, jumping on the steps for a look. But it was like an Elvis sighting—there one second, gone the next."

"Like today at the palace?"

"Something like that, but more intense. Think about it. After all those years of wondering what happened to her, not hearing a word, and suddenly she shows up in a remote place like Ayacucho."

Lannie picked up his glass and tried to ape Bogart's nasal voice. "Of all the gin joints in all the towns in all the world, she walks into mine. But we'll always have Paris."

"How many piscos have you had?"

"Sorry, just had to say it. Go ahead, I'm listening."

"Another time I saw her in a passing car. And then one snowy night, she just"—my throat tightened, but I still managed to say it—"just shows up at my front door in Ayacucho."

"The hell? What about Denise?"

"Wasn't there. We were talking divorce, so she'd gone home to visit her mom."

I took another long sip and let the scene play out in my mind: Marisa standing outside in the cold and snow, all mittens, galoshes, and ski cap, snow on her coat, shivering, looking up at me with those blue eyes, not saying a word. And me at the door, holding a book, too stunned to speak.

"You gonna tell me or not?" Lannie said.

I choked up, even with noise and stir all around and cigarette smoke in the air and a couple making out at the next table. Lannie saw what was happening and called over the server.

"*Dos más,*" he said, pointing at the glasses that were still half full.

The server grinned. Lannie grinned back. I started to pick up the narrative, but Lannie said, "Wait, hold that thought. I gotta take a leak."

He stood and weaved his way through the crowd, leaving me alone with my pisco sour and thoughts of Marisa. I wiped at my eyes and looked around. A woman at a nearby table flashed a look of recognition and pointed me out to her boyfriend. He looked over and gave me a thumbs-up. The bearded man and his girlfriend at the next table were now kissing, and they were still locked in embrace when the server arrived with our drinks and asked if I was that gringo professor who'd come to find his girlfriend. "That is so romantic," she said. "I hope you find her."

She wanted to chat, but someone called her away. Then Lannie dragged up his chair, sat down, and looked over at the kissing couple.

"Christ, they should get a room." He downed his glass of pisco. "Okay, so Marisa just shows up at your door and you pull her inside. Then what?"

"Talked for hours."

"That's it, just talked?"

"No, Lannie, we also cried a lot. It was an emotional moment."

"What did she tell you about her husband?"

"I told you already. They don't get along. He's a business-man. Travels a lot."

"You can do better than that. He's gotta be part of the problem."

"My guess is he's *all* the problem."

"So tell me."

I didn't want to tell a DEA agent what Marisa had told me in confidence—that she suspected he was into shady dealings, maybe with drugs, and she was afraid of him. And worried the authorities would go after her as well. So I said to Lannie, "This is just between the two of us. Right?"

"Right."

"The main issue is his affairs with other women."

"The hell? What I want to know about is—"

"Not only that, but he's into…swinging with other couples, you know, exchanging—"

"Dirtbag. The hell kind of man wants to watch his wife fuck another man?"

"It never came to that. She refused to participate."

A commotion erupted a few tables away, a drunk protesting his girlfriend being with another guy. A scuffle ensued. The kissers at the next table got up and left. Lannie and I waited for the bouncers to restore order, and then he said, "What I want to know about is his business dealings."

"All I know is he's into imports and exports—art supplies."

Lannie rolled his eyes. "When's the last time you spoke to her mom?"

"We're not exactly on speaking terms."

"Because?"

"Because I got Marisa pregnant."

He choked on his pisco. "Whoa! You knocked up Congresswoman Montero's daughter?"

"She wasn't a congresswoman then. I was still in the Peace Corps. We'd planned on getting married anyway, in Miami. But when her mom learned about the pregnancy, and that I was the father—a longhaired Peace Corp Volunteer—she dragged Marisa off to God knows where."

"My mom was like that too. Went ballistic when she learned my first wife wasn't Catholic."

"I thought you said it was because you met her in a strip joint."

"That too." He lifted his glass in a toast. "Here's to moms who care about their daughters."

Pain swept over me again, and I remembered the depression. The tears. The wanting to curl up and die. That helpless feeling of not knowing what to do.

Lannie reached over and touched my arm. "So what happened to the baby?"

"Miscarriage."

"Damn, Marco, that's so sad I could cry. I knocked up this gal once—a cheerleader in high school. Cutest little thing. Damn, could she screw. I thought she'd demand I marry her, but…"

"But what?"

"Blamed the quarterback. Stupid sonbitch married her."

The lights dimmed. The band came to life. A young girl with long dark hair and minidress took the microphone. "Tonight," she said in a melodic voice, "we have a very special guest, an old friend of this establishment who came to our troubled country for the love of a woman."

Chairs scraped as everyone twisted in my direction.

"This song is for you, Maestro. May you outwit the forces against you and find your love."

The crowd cheered and applauded. And then she sang about a woman whose heart was like a chameleon, always changing colors, and everyone in the restaurant sang along.

> *Ey, camaleón, mama, tu corazón,*
> *Cambia de colóres, en tu corazón…*

The noise defeated our efforts at conversation. Patrons came over to pat my back or shake my hand and wish me well. Cigarette smoke got so heavy that someone propped open the door to let in fresh air. We ate sandwiches, and were on our third pisco when a private guard with an assault rifle came inside, looked around, and hurried over to our table.

He leaned down and said one word—"Peep."

CHAPTER THIRTEEN

Lannie ground out his cigarette. "Christ, I didn't even get her phone number."

"Whose phone number?"

"The hell you think? That cute little thing that served us."

I waved to the crowd and followed Lannie out the door into the gloom. A black Mercedes was parked behind his Cherokee, with three Peep agents leaning against it. Gordo was there too—trench coat, black hat, fat face, and big mouth.

"Hey, gringo, we took turns with your little *puta*. Really hot stuff. Says your dick is like your brain. Too small. She likes real men."

"Ignore them," Lannie said. "Don't give them an excuse to arrest you."

I was at the Cherokee, ready to climb in, when I noticed the broken windshield, all spider-webbed as if it had been hit with a tire tool. Lannie said, "Shit!" and stormed back toward the agents. Angry words followed. The bouncer stepped out the door with his AK. People on the sidewalk scurried into the night. I hurried back, grabbed Lannie's arm, and more or less dragged him away from a fight he'd be certain to lose.

Behind us, the Peep men were flapping their arms like chickens.

It was going on midnight when we pulled up in front of the hotel, Lannie still cursing and grumbling. In spite of the fog and lingering tear gas and a curfew that began at one, the plaza had come to life, with blaring radios, street vendors, beggars, lovers in the shadows, and a kiosk featuring an organ grinder and his monkey.

"Straight to your room," Lannie said. "I'll call first thing in the morning."

I headed toward the entrance and was threading my way between the hotel's fleet of vintage Cadillacs when a young Runa girl in Andean garb stepped from the shadows.

"Jesus is Lord," she said in Quechua and shoved a religious flyer at me. "Read it."

I tossed the flyer into a trash bin at the entrance.

The clerk motioned me over and handed me several messages. I raced up five flights of stairs to my room and plopped on the sofa to read them. All from reporters.

Dammit, why couldn't at least one be from Marisa? Not that she'd be so careless as to leave a message that could be traced. She was the type who'd hurl a stone through my window at midnight.

Or send a note with an Indian beggar. Of course. What was I thinking.

I hurried to the elevator, caught it going down, and raced past Gordo. The flyer was still where I'd tossed it. I scooped it out and brushed off cigarette ashes.

"What is that?" Gordo said, now at my side.

I pushed around him and dashed up the stairs to my room.

A likeness of Jesus stared at me from the flyer, all thorns, blood, and halo. On the back were questions and answers about eternal hell, and on the inside was a discourse on the evils of alcoholism. But between the lines, in red ink, someone had scrawled a message: *Maestro. Son of Thunder. I know where she is. Carlos, Political Wing, Lurigancho. Bring food.*

What the hell? Lurigancho was a federal prison on the outskirts of Lima. Carlos would have to be a former student. They had all called me Maestro, and they'd all joked about the meaning of my last name—son of the god of thunder. But I couldn't remember anyone named Carlos.

I tore the flyer into little pieces and flushed it.

∾

On my third day in Peru, the hellish din outside my window woke me again. The thought of having to go back to the presidential palace made me want to plunge out the window. I was hungry, but since I couldn't bear to face the breakfast crowd, I ordered down for breakfast and a newspaper, took a quick shower, and clicked on the TV for morning news.

A grim-faced woman with a bad hairdo was reporting on the carnage of the night before—three Lima banks and a state water board blown to rubble, eight bystanders dead, ten dogs strung from light posts in a park, and two policemen shot to death. The image cut to a Shining Path poster crudely inscribed with the words, LEARN TO SUFFER. LEARN TO WEEP. LEARN TO DIE.

The phone rang. *Please, dear God, let it be Marisa.*

"It's a no-go," Lannie said in his Tex-Mex accent. "Sorry."

"What are you talking about?"

"Agreement with the commissioners. They nixed the deal."

"You mean I have to go back to the hearing?"

"Not today. They postponed it. You got the whole day to yourself. Works for me too. I'm going to get my windshield fixed. Then I'm going to file a complaint against those bastards."

I thanked him and rapped the receiver against my head. A whole day to myself in this city of fog and damp pavement. Another day to search for Marisa. To wait for her message.

There was a knock at the door.

It was room service with breakfast, along with a copy of a newspaper. The young man who brought it laid it out on the table, glanced around nervously, then motioned me into the hallway.

"Carlos needs to talk to you," he whispered.

"Who the hell is Carlos?"

"He says to tell you to think of a wedding, a priest, and church bells."

He hurried away, but his words lingered in my head—a wedding, a priest, and church bells. Why couldn't Runas just come out and say what they meant?

I finished my ham and eggs, drained my glass of papaya juice, then read about my appearance at the hearing. There were two pages of transcripts, articles, and pictures, one of which showed me looking—stone-faced—at the wanted poster of Chairman Gonzalo.

Marisa's photos were there too, along with a warning: *If you know this woman, please report her whereabouts to the local police. Do not approach. She may be armed and dangerous.*

Marisa armed and dangerous? Absurd. The only danger I'd ever seen in her was when I read Neruda to her, and there damn well better be a bed nearby.

The phone rang again.

"Bad news," said the dean in a sympathetic baritone. "You made the *Saint Pete Times* and the *Tampa Trib.* I've got both papers in front of me right now." He rattled them for emphasis. "Your photo's on the front page. This isn't good, Mark. The president's in a tizzy. Says she'll need to convene a board to review your suitability as a professor."

"Are you saying they could fire me?"

"It gets worse. Someone broke into your house. Trashed it up. Painted a hammer and sickle on the wall, also some foreign words. Indian-looking shit."

He went on, saying something about telephones being ripped out of walls, dishes smashed, mirrors busted, and all my artwork thrown into a pile and pissed on. I listened, but all I could do was sit helplessly and shake my head and wonder how it could come to this.

"Mark, are you still there?"

"You said something about foreign words."

"I can spell them out for you."

It took several minutes. The language was Quechua, and I recognized the words as a variation of an old poem by a Peruvian named José Maria Arguedas.

> *Ch'isi tutalla musqoychallaypi*...Last night in my dreams.
> *Yawar qochapi nadallachkasqani*...I saw you swimming in a lake of blood.
> *Hawan kallipis allqulla allwachkan*...Out in the street a dog was howling.
> *Kurria, wiraqocha, qhawaykamunki*...Run, foreigner, go and see.

I felt my blood go cold. "How did the police know to look in my house?"

"That's the bizarre part. That old lady who lives next door to you, with the toy poodles?"

"Mrs. Wexler?"

"That's her, poor woman—let her dogs out last night, and they didn't come back. This morning she found them on your front porch, hanging from flower hooks."

CHAPTER FOURTEEN

I wanted to smash General Reál's face. It had to be him, the bastard, making it appear as though the Shining Path had marked me as their next victim.

Worse—no telephone at my house to hear Marisa's message.

Dammit, there had to be someone I could talk to, someone who could help me get in touch with her. Then it struck me: Marisa's mom. The last time I'd spoken with her, years ago, she'd threatened me with a restraining order. It still hurt. What I'd needed back then was a hug. Someone to talk to. Instead she'd called me a loser, a stalker.

Would she even accept my call?

I changed into jeans, grabbed my leather jacket, and bounded down the stairs. There were no suspicious-looking types in the lobby, so I slipped out a side door, hurried down the street to the old Hotel Azúcar, and went into their phone booth.

A few minutes later, I had Congresswoman Peretz-Montero on the phone.

"Thank God you called," she said in her husky smoker's voice. "I've been worried sick. The embassy called. . .some guy named Holbrook Easton. Wanted to know her whereabouts, her marital status, her relationship with you. I didn't know what to tell him."

She broke down, this vindictive woman who'd destroyed our chance for happiness years ago. Between sobs she said, "Look, Mark. None of those things they're saying about her are true."

"Do you know where I can find her?"

She gave me numbers, names, and addresses, but it was information I already had.

I finally asked the question I dreaded. "What can you tell me about her husband?"

"A bad man. He abused her, lied to her. A few months ago, some men came to my office—DEA agents—asking questions about him. Now what does that tell you?"

"Did you say DEA?"

"Drug Enforcement Administration—from our embassy in Peru."

I could have kicked myself. No wonder Lannie kept hounding me about her husband. What an actor he was. "Was one of them named Lannie Torres?"

She didn't answer. I asked again, and then realized the connection had broken.

I tried again, but couldn't get a line, so I headed back toward my hotel. Damn that Lannie. What a slick liar. A noisy group of women were now marching around the statue of General San Martín in slow, ritualistic fashion—old women with sad Indian faces and placards with photos of their loved ones, one of which read, MY DAUGHTER DISAPPEARED AT THE LIMA POLICE STATION.

A sick feeling came over me. That could happen to Marisa if they caught her.

Someone touched my arm. I swung around and looked into the face of the same young girl who'd handed me the flyer the night before. She couldn't have been more than fifteen.

"Go to Carlos," she said in Quechua. "In Lurigancho. He will help you.

I pulled her into the alcove of a nearby shop. "Who is Carlos?"

"He was your student…in Ayacucho."

"How do you know this?"

"Because I'm his sister. He says it will be safe for you. All you have to do is pretend to be a newspaper reporter. They want someone to tell their story. They want—"

Where Gordo came from, I did not see. He grabbed the girl and shoved her against the plate glass window, twisting her around and trying to put cuffs on her.

The girl screamed. I tried to push between them, but Gordo held on.

"Back off, gringo. This girl is a known agitator. I'm taking her in."

"You idiot. She's only a child."

He directed his fury at me, cursing, threatening, trying to hold the squirming girl at the same time. In the process, I yanked the cuffs out of his hand and was trying to free the girl when an old man on crutches hobbled over and began yelling at both of us as if we were sex perverts.

Other passersby gathered around, shouting insults and demanding we leave the girl alone. Gordo, his breath coming in ragged gasps, took out a radiophone with his free hand and asked for backup. The girl jerked loose and raced down the street.

I trotted away as well. Behind me, Gordo was threatening the good Samaritans with his pistol. At the corner, my heart racing, I dropped the cuffs into a trash-can and flagged down a taxi.

"Where to?" the driver asked.

"Lurigancho."

CHAPTER FIFTEEN
San Juan de Lurigancho

I saw it long before we got there, a bleak compound of cement looming out of the fog, as mean and colorless as the surrounding windswept desert, looking like a fortress from an old movie about the French Foreign Legion. The closer we got, the more the air reeked.

"That place is dangerous," said the driver. "Are you sure you want to do this?"

"It's for my paper. They asked me to do a story on political prisoners."

"I hope they provide life insurance."

He let me out at the gate, said, "Good luck," and sped away, leaving me in the foul air with a sack of potatoes and onions, a few packs of cigarettes, and a copy of Mariátegui's *Seven Essays*, all of which the driver had said were necessary for entry.

Visiting hours began at two. It wasn't noon yet, so I fell in with a collection of sad-eyed women and children waiting beneath an open shed, all with bundles of food and clothing, and most dressed in colorful Andean garb—shawls, black hats and ankle-length skirts.

Back in my Peace Corps days I'd have felt at home in a crowd like this. But now, gringo that I was, I felt as out of place as a character from a Batman movie. So it didn't surprise me at all when a guard stepped from a building with his truncheon and motioned me over.

"What are you doing here?"

"I'm a journalist. I'm here to visit the prisoners in the political wing."

"Don't you people have anything better to report?"

"I'm just doing my job."

He looked me up and down and slapped his truncheon into an open palm. "This way."

We passed through a door marked Processing, and a few minutes later, I was again explaining my business to an officer of the guards.

"Do you realize how violent those prisoners are?" he said.

"That's why they're in prison, isn't it?"

"*Bueno.* Enjoy your visit."

During the next hour, they searched me, marked me on the arm with a number, confiscated my cigarettes, and shoved me into a pen near a set of iron gates with other visitors. By then the numbers had swollen into the hundreds, a herd of corralled humans with scarcely enough room to breathe, the rat-a-tat of Spanish here, the guttural sounds of the Andes there.

A woman next to me carried a newspaper-wrapped bundle of food with blood soaking through, and her mood was as foul as the air. From her I learned that President Fujimori was a crook, the opposition Apristas were no better, Peru was going to the dogs, her son was in jail for no reason other than he was a poor *Indio,* and she had a bad liver.

Presently, the officer I'd spoken to earlier appeared on a wall above us. He lifted a bullhorn to his mouth and made his announcement in both Spanish and Quechua.

"Once inside, you must proceed quickly to the block you are visiting. The inmates are supposed to remain in their quarters during visiting hours, but we are unable to enforce the rules."

He paused and looked down at me, and even from my location, I could see the grin. "We can neither guarantee your safety, nor will we go in looking for you if you do not come out."

What? I wanted to yell. I had imagined an armed guard to escort me to the political wing, a glass window separating me from the prisoners, a telephone to communicate with Carlos.

Maybe I could still get out of this awful place.

The gates swung open. *"Pasen! Pasen!"* the guards shouted.

Voices on the other side picked up the chant. *"Pasen! Pasen!"*

Others joined in. The chant rolled across the prison grounds like the bark of dogs at night. The crowd surged forward, and I was swept into the prison like just another visitor.

CHAPTER SIXTEEN

The stench from the outside had been bad; inside, the air was so foul that most of the visitors held shawls over mouths and noses. I shouldered my sack of potatoes and onions and followed the others along a well-worn path between rows of austere buildings that were odd numbered on one side and even numbered on the next.

Inmates leaned from broken windows or stared from the sides, calling out names, some making obscene gestures to the girls. Occasionally one rushed into our group to embrace a loved one.

We angled around several buildings, passed through an opening in a barbed wire fence, and walked past a mountain of reeking trash that served as a feeding station for seabirds and vultures. Inmates were now pouring out of the buildings—men with headbands, wild beards, and eye patches, looking like bands of marauding pirates.

The line of visitors dwindled at each building. I asked directions to the political wing.

"That way," said a woman in the line.

"No, it's back there," said another.

A beggar in rags held out his hands. Beyond him, a man was babbling to himself, and as we passed the so-called *maricón* block, men dressed as women stuck out their tongues and penises and made sucking sounds with their mouths.

Presently, I was alone, standing on a dirt path between two concrete buildings that might have been inspired by Kafka, vultures circling above as if waiting for me to die, a gray-white mist closing around me, trapping in the smells and my own stupidity.

Maybe there was no political wing. Maybe I was the victim of some elaborate ruse to get me inside. Any second now a steel door would spring open and release a pack of ravenous wolves.

I traipsed on and finally came to a one-legged man sitting on a concrete block.

"What are you looking for?" he asked in Quechua.

"The political wing."

He lifted his crutch and pointed to a building I'd already passed. "What is that over there?"

I thanked him, trotted over to the building he'd pointed out, and was instantly set upon by a group of ragged, unhealthy-looking men of all ages, most with dark Andean features.

By then my legs were so wobbly with fear, I could barely stand. My mouth was dry, and sweat seemed to be pouring from my armpits. It didn't help that the leader of the group, a powerfully built man with a headband and long greasy hair, took my sack of potatoes and onions, sniffed it like a dog, and then ran his free hand over my jacket.

"Nice leather. Take it off."

He put down the sack and motioned for the jacket with his hands. His friends crowded in closer, waiting for my reaction. I was grimly aware of my cowardice, but I'd been around bullies long enough to know better than to back down, so I puffed myself up with faux courage.

"You want this jacket? You're going to have to take it off me."

His eyes widened. "What is this—a gringo that speaks the tongue of the people?"

"A gringo who came for Carlos. He's expecting me. Get him. I don't have all day."

He looked around at his friends. "Where's Carlos?"

"Library," one of them answered.

They led me through a one-story building that looked like a military barracks—double-decker beds on both sides, foot-lockers and metal closets, everything tidy. The boyish good looks of Mariátegui smiled down from posters of the Peruvian Communist Party. The sight of women visitors sitting on beds with their loved ones made me feel better, and from behind a partially closed door came the unmistakable grunts and cries of a more intimate encounter.

Beyond the sleeping quarters, we came to a library where inmates sat around tables reading newspapers and books. The air reeked of cigarettes. Everyone looked up. A vulture alighted on the corrugated roof above, clanging and clattering.

I took out the book I'd brought, Mariátegui's *Seven Essays*, and handed it to a frail little man who seemed to be the librarian. He flipped through the pages, found the passage he was looking for, and read aloud. "'All things decent in Peruvian society come from the communal experiences of the Indian past, whereas all things rotten were brought by Europeans.'"

Everyone nodded angry agreement. The librarian shook a cigarette out of a pack and offered it to me. Though I hadn't smoked for years, I took it anyway, lit up, and took a long drag.

A back door swung open. In it appeared a scrawny, acne scarred man in rumpled clothes. His white tennis shoes were torn and dirty, tied loosely with broken laces, and worn without socks.

He looked confused, as if concerned he'd been called for punishment, but when he saw me, his face lit up. He mumbled the Quechua version of "Oh my God," then rushed over and hugged me as if I were his mother. "Oh, Maestro, thank you for coming. I knew you'd come."

I looked into his dark Andean face, taking in the scar, the oily, shoulder-length hair, the prominent Adam's apple, and the headband. Luís: that was his name, a former student from Ayacucho. It was his wedding that I'd attended—tails and ties and a beaming little bride in white. Lots of smiling, happy people. A far cry from the defeated faces that now surrounded me. I remembered him as an outspoken Marxist, combative and opinionated, critical of all things capitalistic, and a notorious cheater on examinations. No wonder he was in prison.

"Don't you recognize me?" he said.

"Of course. You're Luís."

"Carlos," he shot back. "I was Luís in another life." He struck a match on his trousers, lit a half-smoked cigarette and clapped his hands together for attention. "Comrades, listen up. Do you know who this gentleman is? This is Comrade Marco, the man whose letters and poetry were found at the home of President Gonzalo. He is a good friend of Chairman Gonzalo."

A flicker of recognition, then smiles, applause, and cheers. Inmates came over and patted me on the back; others shook my hand and wished me luck. And, just like that, I was among friends: Comrade Marco in Lurigancho Prison.

CHAPTER SEVENTEEN

Luís, a.k.a. Carlos, showed me around like a museum do-cent, using a rolled-up newspaper to point out the politi-cal slogans on the walls, the crafts the men were doing. He smoked one cigarette stub after the other, down to his tobac-co-darkened knuckles. From a bunk, he picked up a copy of Trotsky's *Revolution Betrayed* and waved it around.

"We are thousands—teachers and students, peasants and miners, professionals and slum dwellers—all united by injus-tice. We have to tear down the old system and build a new Peru."

The inmates near me whispered their own grievances, and even the air seemed to take on the taste of injustice. How could the United States be so stupid as to support a corrupt president like Fujimori? Why couldn't the world see the Shining Path as the freedom fighters they were?

"Look at this," Carlos said, pulling me over to a wall hung with a large photograph of Chairman Gonzalo. Around the photograph, printed on red tissue papers with gilded frames, hung dozens of Mao-like pronouncements. I leaned forward to read, but Carlos and his fellow inmates began rattling them off as if they'd come down from Mt. Sinai.

"Revolution is at hand."

"I give you a stick of dynamite. Throw it."

Carlos tugged at my sleeve and led me through a torn screen door to the outside, stopping in the shadow of the outer wall. A guard glared down from a watchtower. Carlos lowered his voice to a conspiratorial tone, his Adam's apple bobbing. "Your lady friend is in great danger."

"That's why I need to find her."

"No, Maestro, you're thinking about the danger from the government. I'm talking about her husband. He's Spaniard. A businessman. She stole money from him. Lots of money."

"How do you know this, Carlos?"

"See that Indio over there, the one with the long hair? His name is Tucno."

I followed his gaze to the man who'd threatened to take my jacket. "What about him?"

"He's an Ungacachano—an Unga. They're a jungle tribe, meaner than snakes. He worked for her husband…before he was captured. It was his job to kill her. Kill you too."

Tucno glared as if he wanted to bash in my head, so I positioned myself where I could keep an eye on him. "Listen, Carlos, where is she?"

"If you help me, I can help you. I am in desperate need. My family is poor. I have only one blanket, little food, and hardly any clothing."

I figured it would come to this, and reached into the sock where I'd hidden a hundred-dollar bill, more than a Peruvian laborer earned in a month. He took the money and stuffed it into his pocket.

"Thank you, Maestro. Thank you. I'll pray for you. Light candles for both of you."

"Where is she?"

"Ayacucho, on the plaza." He whispered the address.

"How do you know this address?"

He moved closer, unrolled the newspaper in his hand, and pointed to the photograph Bocanegra had shown at the hearing. "Who do you think took this picture?" He ground out his cigarette and lit another. "We were spying on you in Ayacucho, when you were a professor. You spoke Quechua. How many gringos speak our language? It's unheard of. We were at war with the police. Comrades being killed every day. Students disappearing. We were paranoid."

An inmate with his girlfriend came out the door. Carlos waited a moment and went on. "Kept you under surveillance for months—looked into your background, wrote reports, checked out everyone who visited you. That's why we have her pictures."

A bell tinkled. The inmates on the outside scurried back into the building like school children called to class. Carlos said, "*Coño,*" and put out his half-finished cigarette with his fingers.

I had no idea what was coming, but followed him back into the library anyway, keeping my distance from Tucno. Hats came off. Cigarettes were put out. The inmates cleared the room of tables and chairs and lined up against the walls, as solemn as mourners at a Lutheran funeral.

It grew quiet enough to hear the clatter of buzzards on the roof. Then an old man with an Indian face turned to leather by a thousand suns stepped forward. A mane of long white hair flowed down his back. His skinny arms were tattooed, and he wore a sun god medallion around his neck.

"Many years ago," he intoned in a ragged voice, "our Inca ancestors devised the perfect system. There was no unemployment. No injustice. No poverty. We built magnificent roads and cities and irrigation canals. We conquered nations and spread our language and culture. We embraced our conquered foes." He paused a moment. "But then what happened?"

"Pachacuti," everyone answered as one.

"Exactly, the Spaniards turned our world upside down. Stole our wealth, our gold, our women. They enslaved our ancestors.

Your ancestors. But the day of reckoning is upon us, the day when Pachacuti means world turned right side again." He pointed to a banner over the doorway on which were inscribed the words, TUPAC AMARU IS THE CONDOR IN THE SKY.

He smiled a toothless smile. "Let us never forget our inspiration—Inca Tupac Amaru. He struggled for freedom against the Spaniards. His cause is our cause. He is now the symbol of our movement. Of our struggle for Pachacuti."

He raised a clenched fist. "Pachacuti!"

Others picked up the cry— "Pachacuti! Pachacuti!"—and they became a fierce choir, marching, stomping their feet, singing, chanting, dancing like a war party of savages.

The room shook, windows rattled, books fell out of shelves.

"Our path is shining. Let us follow the shining path to Pachacuti."

"Pachacuti! Pachacuti!"

The old man led them into the sleeping quarters, the others snaking behind him, hands clapping, the women visitors jumping into line. I followed them out the front door and around to the back, an undulating mass of revolutionaries, flowing beneath the outer wall beneath the guards.

"The dawn is rising. The walls are crumbling. Victory is almost here."

"Pachacuti! Pachacuti!"

A whistle blared at the front gate, signaling the end of visiting hours. I waved at Carlos and hurried away as fast as my legs would carry me without running, heading for the exit with other visitors, thanking God I might live to tell about this madhouse.

Behind me, their chants sounded like a fading locomotive.

"Pachacuti-Pachacuti-Pachacuti."

CHAPTER EIGHTEEN

There were no taxis, so I took a battered bus that followed along miles of squalid slums and stucco walls covered with revolutionary slogans. Mangy dogs drank from ditches, bare-bottomed children ran around dirt sidewalks, and kids played soccer in streets strewn with garbage.

The evil smells and occasional stiff body of a dead dog added an extra touch of gloom.

The sights improved as we entered Lima, but it didn't help when I reached my hotel and found the evidence of another clash between protestors and police—placards strewn here and there, puddles of water from the water cannon, the nostril-burning residue of tear gas.

I lumbered into the lobby. What a rotten, miserable day. I was going to send my clothes down for cleaning, hit the shower, call Lannie, and have it out with him.

Or so I was thinking until a clerk behind the counter motioned me over. "Peep is looking for you," he said, wrinkling his nose as if he could smell me. "They're in your room."

I grabbed the messages out of his hand, noted they were all from reporters, trashed them, and took the elevator up to my room. The door was open, lights on, and even from the hall-way, I could see the room was a shambles, with drawers opened, clothes and personal items strewn about.

I marched inside. Gordo stood at the foot of my bed, a cigarette dangling from his mouth, going through my suitcase. "What the hell are you doing?" I said.

Someone grabbed me from the back.

"Hold him," Gordo said and came at me with a shoe from my suitcase.

Until he hit me, I never realized a shoe could be so lethal. The room flashed white. A ringing sensation went off in my head. My knees buckled.

Gordo drew back for another blow. The man behind me held on, tightening his grip, giving me leverage. I pushed backwards, raised both legs, and delivered a vicious kick to Gordo's stomach.

He screamed and doubled over. With my downward momentum, I flipped the man behind me over my head. In my rage I slammed my open suitcase into both men—once, twice—and was still pounding them when Inspector Bocanegra burst into the room.

"Basta," he cried. "Enough. What is going on?"

I struggled to the sofa, breathing hard, and grabbed the phone.

Bocanegra pointed a finger. "Put that phone down."

Gordo was still on his knees, groaning and cursing, but the other agent, the wiry little man with Asian features, yanked out a pistol and pointed it at me.

"You heard the inspector."

I put the receiver back into the cradle.

Bocanegra glared at the agent. "Get out of here, Chino. Take Gordo with you. Go."

Chino holstered his pistol and wiped blood off his lip. Gordo struggled up and staggered to the door, holding his stomach. He turned and wagged a fat finger.

"Fucking gringo. You'll pay for this."

Bocanegra slammed the door behind them and lit a cigar. I staggered into the bathroom and touched a finger to my face where the shoe had hit. It was puffy, my vision blurred. I splashed water on it and was toweling off when I noticed cigarette butts in the toilet.

Someone had also taken a piss without flushing. Bastards.

Bocanegra stuck his head in the door. "Are you okay?"

"No, I'm not okay." I touched my face. "Look what your men did."

"You're lucky I didn't let them arrest you."

"On what charge?"

"Interfering with an agent this morning. Stealing his handcuffs."

"I didn't steal anything. Besides, that girl was just a child."

"Children throw bombs in this country. They shoot policemen."

He followed me back into the sitting room and dropped down in the same chair where the general had sat a lifetime ago. "Where were you today?"

"I'm not telling you anything until I speak with the embassy."

"Very well, I can wait until the hearing tomorrow." He stood and looked around at the mess. "Get a good night's rest, Professor. From now on you're confined to this hotel."

"For what reason?"

"For your own protection." He ambled to the door and looked back. "And one more thing. Next time you go to Lurigancho, it might not be as a visitor."

I bolted the door behind him, let my heart calm a minute, and tried to call Lannie.

No answer. Damn him. Probably out with that cute little server from El Parrón.

I finally gave up, straightened the room, yanked off my smelly clothes, showered, crawled into bed, and spent another miserable night, my mind buzzing with all my problems.

And it seemed as if I'd just fallen asleep when the phone rang.

"The hell were you thinking?" Lannie raged.

I sat up and wiped my eyes. "What are you talking about?"

"Lurigancho. Are you fucking crazy?"

"How'd you know I went to Lurigancho?"

"The whole world knows. Holbrook Easton knows. The ambassador knows, and he's going batshit crazy. Turn on your TV. Have a look, then get some coffee in you and get dressed. Meet me out front at oh-nine-hundred. Shit's hitting the fan."

I swung my legs out of bed and forced myself to acknowledge the reality of another day in Peru. My body ached. I could barely see out of my left eye and didn't want to look at myself in the mirror. I called down for breakfast, then clicked on the television in time to see images of Lurigancho on the screen—bleak gray walls and scenes of chaos, with bodies covered in orange plastic sheets amid the flashing lights of ambulances.

"Christ," I mumbled.

The woman with a bad hairdo was saying something about a prison break.

I turned up the volume and listened.

"The breakout occurred around ten last night. Two guards and four inmates are dead. All the inmates were from the political wing. Two succeeded in escaping. Sources tell us they paid one of the dead guards with money provided by a visitor. A hundred-dollar bill was found on his body."

The escapees' pictures flashed on the screen, and there they were—Tucno and Carlos.

CHAPTER NINETEEN
Palacio Pizarro

When I climbed into Lannie's Cherokee for the ride down to the palace, I expected him to rage at me. Instead he patted me on the knee.

"Good job, dude. This could work in our favor."

"What are you talking about?"

"Look, they've been saying all along you know where Marisa is. Right? This proves you don't know a damn thing, that you're just another lovesick professor looking for a woman who's been lying to you. Otherwise, why would you go to a shit hole like Lurigancho?"

"What about that hundred-dollar bill? My fingerprints are all over it."

"They ganged up on you and stole your money. Who's to contradict you?"

"The inmates, Lannie. They know what happened."

"They're terrorists. Who the hell's gonna believe them?"

By the time we reached the palace, I was so convinced of his logic that I didn't confront him with the information I'd learned from Congresswoman Montero.

"Think victim," he said as we drove into the grounds. "Shed tears if you have to. Show that battered face. The inmates did it. And for God's sake, take off those fucking Ray-Bans."

The grounds and parking lot were more fortified than during our first visit, with more trenches, tanks, and soldiers, looking like a World War I battlefield in the mist.

The little acne-scarred man who had issued the subpoena escorted us inside.

Again, the place was packed, and reporters waiting with cameras and questions. Again, I ignored them. A clerk mercifully told me I would not be the first witness. A sergeant at arms led me over to a section reserved for witnesses. I sat and scanned the hall for Marisa.

She wasn't there. Or if she was, I couldn't find her.

The little man sat down next to me. I noticed how he sat there, legs pressed tightly together, reading the editorial page in a local daily. He raised the paper to his mouth as if to shield his words.

"I have a message from your friend with the blue eyes," he said in his effeminate voice.

"What message?"

"Don't look at me. This place has cameras. They can read lips."

I turned away. He went on. "She says you should leave the country today, while you can."

I pretended to be rubbing my mustache. "I need to talk to her."

"There'll be time later, when you're safe."

"No, I need to talk to her now. She's in great danger."

"Please, caballero. Do you think she doesn't know that?"

"How do I know you're not trying to trick me?"

"She said to ask you about Normán. I have no idea what that means."

I smiled. In my father's language—Norwegian—Normán means man of the north. It was a name he used for other Scandinavians whose name he didn't know. When I'd told Marisa, she used it in reference to a part of my anatomy.

"Tell her Normán is fine."

He leaned closer. "At exactly eleven thirty, something important will happen. When it does, you should go immediately to your hotel, change into travel clothes, and wait for her message."

I glanced at my watch. "What is going to happen at eleven thirty?"

"You will know when it happens."

"Who are you, anyway?"

"They call me Apu Condor."

With these words he stood and sauntered away.

More people drifted in. Orderlies began setting up folding chairs. Cigarette smoke billowed up, and for the first time since coming to Peru, I felt a glimmer of hope. *Apu* was a Quechua word for spirits that lived in the mountains, but it also referred to a person of power, a spiritual leader.

General Reál marched through the entranceway, all sharp angles and teeth, surrounded by younger men in uniform. Although he was dressed as a civilian, I thought he needed a swagger stick to go with the black tie and aviator glasses.

The commissioners filed in and took their places on the dais. Everyone stood.

A gavel banged, and the hearing was back in session. The time was 10:47 a.m.

A young army lieutenant, looking fit and handsome in his olive drab uniform, moved to the witness table. His trouser legs were tucked neatly into combat boots. His name was Bravos. The red beret on his head identified him as a Sinchi, a word that in Quechua meant warrior. It was his platoon that had intercepted the Ungacachano mule train in the jungle.

I leaned forward and listened. This was where it all began—in a dripping jungle.

"Tell us what you found," said Commissioner Amado from his seat at the dais.

"Money, Commissioner. More than a hundred thousand dollars, US. I'm told it was drug money, paid to the Shining Path for safe passage in areas they control."

"What else did you find on the mule train?"

"Coca paste, *huacos*, weapons, and ammunition."

An overweight functionary held one of the shells aloft. An army major described it as a Chinese imitation of a Soviet mortar round. He went on and on with the description, comparing and evaluating, saying how similar items could be viewed in the Military Museum.

Commissioner Amado held up a hand. "Enough. We've all been to the museum."

Everyone laughed. The proceedings went on. Lieutenant Bravos and other Sinchis hauled the captured booty before the dais. They laid out weaponry, money, bags of coca paste, and even a few pre-Columbian artifacts made of gold and silver, which they called *huacos*.

I stared at the coca paste. Could this be the connection with Marisa's husband? Did she know?

Finally, it was my turn. The time was 11:19 a.m.

Commissioner Amado looked down at me. "What happened to your face?"

Before I could answer, Inspector Bocanegra jumped up from his table. "An unfortunate incident," he said. "He and my men had a misunderstanding."

Lannie shrugged. I shrugged back. So much for his advice.

Commissioner Amado picked up a note pad and scribbled on it, and when he spoke, his voice had an edge. "Inspector Bocanegra, may I remind you again that Professor Thorsen is a guest of this commission. I expect him to be treated as such. Do you understand?"

"Yes, Commissioner."

"Very well. Get on with the questionings."

Inspector Bocanegra lit a cigar, popped open that damn briefcase again, and reached inside. By then I wouldn't have been surprised if he'd pulled out a rattlesnake. But it was a hundred-dollar bill, which he held up for all to see. "Lurigancho," he said as if it were a battle cry. "This is how much it cost for Professor Thorsen's friends to bust out."

I glanced at my watch. It was 11:26.

He marched over to my table. His tobacco-stained teeth were showing. "Professor Thorsen, would you be kind enough to tell these commissioners where you went yesterday?"

"You know where I went."

"Of course I know. The entire world knows, but we want to hear it from you."

He waited, but I was determined to make him pull every word out of me.

"Answer the question," said Commissioner Amado.

"I went to Lurigancho Prison."

"Why did you go to Lurigancho?" Bocanegra asked.

"To speak with inmates about..."

"About what?"

"About Marisa. I'd been told they had information on her whereabouts."

"Did they?"

"They knew nothing. They'd tricked me into going."

"But you paid them anyway, didn't you?"

"They mugged me. Stole my money. A hundred dollars."

"Did it occur to you that a prison filled with desperados is not the place to take money?"

"It does now."

He took another puff. "What is the name of the inmates you spoke to at Lurigancho?"

I looked at the time again. 11:31. Maybe my watch was fast. Maybe the little man had been lying. Maybe he was operating on the Peruvian concept of time.

"I asked you a question, Professor."

He was glaring at me, waiting for an answer, when an explosion shook the palace.

The lights dimmed, chandeliers tinkled. Then a second explosion left us in darkness. Glass shattered. Alarm bells clanged. People gasped and called out to one another. Words like "bomb," "earthquake," and "Shining Path" flew around the room like shrapnel. Into this madness came chants from the spectator section. "*Viva Gonzalo. Viva la revolución.*"

Cigarette lighters flared. Someone opened the emergency doors. In came light, smoke, and sharp, acrid smells. A group of soldiers dashed by the doors, followed by an army tank. Lieutenant Bravos and his Sinchis rushed out on the double-quick, the lieutenant pulling out his pistol.

I glanced at the dais and saw the commissioners fleeing into the antechamber, a flurry of robes, fear, and confusion. Spectators were now jamming the exits, screaming and carrying on as if the palace were about to explode.

Lannie grabbed my arm. "Come on, old buddy. The hell outa here."

CHAPTER TWENTY

The parking lot was equally chaotic—soldiers sprinting this way and that, automobiles burning, people yelling and cursing. From behind us came shouts to get out of the way. Horns blared, sirens wailed, and one of the army tanks rolled over a tiny Fiat, driver and all.

"Son of a bitch," Lannie cried. "You see that?"

We dashed for the Cherokee before it too was crushed, jumped in, and followed the other cars around the perimeter to the exit. Even there we had to wait amid a jam of honking motorists and cars trying to break into line. I sat there, breathing in the smells of burning tires, stunned at the violence, trying to push the image of the crushed Fiat out of my head.

"Come on, come on," Lannie muttered. "Let's get moving."

He lit a cigarette, took a long drag, and glanced into his rearview mirror. "Shit!"

I twisted around and saw the massive hulk of Gordo in the passenger seat of a black Mercedes. "Hold tight," Lannie said and shifted into reverse.

He backed into the Mercedes. Glass shattered. Then he did it again. Gordo opened his door, climbed out, and was trudging toward us when our turn came to exit.

Wheels spun. Gravel showered Gordo and the Mercedes, and then we were speeding around the plaza, Lannie laughing like a maniac.

We raced through an intersection. The Mercedes stayed close behind, blowing its horn. On the streets, people were running away from the palace.

"Okay," Lannie said, "here's what we do: I drop you at the hotel. Right? You dash in front and right out the back. Forget your suitcase. Meet me at the Hotel Azúcar in ten minutes. I've got a plane leaving at four."

"A plane to where?"

"Tingo Maria. It's on the eastern slopes."

"I'll need more than ten minutes. Marisa sent me a message. She's going to call."

"Are you fucking crazy? Opportunity knocks. She can call you in Tampa."

"Maybe she can, but I want to talk with her today, find out what's going on."

He shook his head, mumbled something about being pussy-whipped, and was still grumbling when we skidded to a halt in front of the hotel. Demonstrators stood around with their placards, staring down toward the palace. A helicopter gunship was circling the plaza.

The Mercedes with its busted headlights and grill stopped behind us.

I jumped out and trotted toward the revolving front doors, loosening my tie.

Behind me, Gordo was struggling to get his heavy body out of the Mercedes.

"One hour," Lannie yelled and sped away, tires screeching, leaving Gordo on the street.

The lobby was also in turmoil, everyone clustered around the television. The woman with the bad hairdo was reading a statement—"The Tupac Amaru Revolutionary Movement, a pro-Castro group, is claiming responsibility for the attack. For more on this story we go to…"

I raced up five flights of stairs to my room, showered off the smell of burning rubber, changed into fresh khakis, and was pulling on a shirt when someone banged on the door.

Please, dear God, not Gordo.

It was the same young man who'd brought me the message from Carlos the day before. He gestured me into the hallway. "Phone," he hissed. "Down the hall."

In my socks, with shirt hanging out, I followed him down to a vacant room. There, he picked up the phone and spoke into the mouthpiece.

"*Ya, listo,*" he said, and handed me the receiver.

"Mark," said Marisa's voice. "Can you hear me?"

I sank onto the side of the bed, breathless. She was alive. There was hope. I imagined I could see her in a dark phone booth in a public building, looking over her shoulder, collar turned up, wearing dark glasses.

"Where are you?" I asked.

"Doesn't matter. You've got to get out of there. Now. And I mean now. You've got ten minutes, maybe less. She paused to catch her breath. "Do you have somewhere to go?"

"I think so."

"Then go. Get out of the country. Go home. I'll call in a few days."

"Why don't you come with me?"

"I can't. Not now. I'll explain later. And one more thing. I love you. Don't ever forget it."

I told her I loved her too, hung up, and dialed Lannie's number. Nothing happened. Dammit to hell. Didn't anything work in this country? I glanced at my watch and dialed again.

A woman answered. "Sorry, sir, but he's with the ambassador."

"Get him anyway. Please. It's urgent. I need to talk with him."

"Sorry, sir, but I can't interrupt him."

"Listen, just tell him Mark called. I'll be at the place we talked about."

I slammed down the receiver, raced back to my room and put on my shoes. Into my pockets went wallet, passport, tickets, Swiss Army knife and toothbrush.

The young man pointed to my khakis. "You're not wearing those, are you?"

"Why not?"

"Because they're so foreign looking, so gringo."

He was right. Only Americans wore khakis—or Bermudas—in foreign countries. So with him watching, with the clock ticking, with a helicopter buzzing outside, I yanked off the khakis and pulled on charcoal slacks. Then I put my shoes back on, threaded a belt through the loops, transferred the wallet and passport and knife, and grabbed my leather jacket.

"No, no," said the young man. "Not the jacket either. They'll recognize it."

I flung the jacket on the bed and pulled on a dark windbreaker.

"Don't worry about your suitcase," said the young man. "It'll find you."

"Doesn't this place have security cameras? They'll see you helping me."

"All turned off. We're not stupid."

The phone rang. I looked at it a second, then scooped it up.

"Dipper Man?" said Marisa.

"Dipper who?"

"You know, the man with the long—"

"Okay, I remember."

"We're talking doomsday scenario, Mark. Plan C. Last resort if nothing else works. Go to the employees' entrance. Ring the bell three times. But only as a last resort. Now go."

I put down the receiver and followed the young man into the hall. He led me into a freight elevator I hadn't noticed before, and pressed the S button for *sótano* (basement). As the elevator creaked and hummed downward, he said, "It was the watch."

"What watch? What are you talking about?"

"Your wristwatch, the way you kept looking at it during the hearing. They're showing it on television, saying it's proof you knew in advance about the attack."

The elevator stopped. The door opened. In swept a steamy smell that I recognized as laundry.

"That way," he said, pointing left. "Don't worry about the doorman. He's on our team."

I handed him a twenty-dollar bill, thanked him, and hurried along a corridor beneath pipes and ductwork, passing a laundry room, a time-card rack, and a tiny glassed-in office.

A squat doorman had his radio tuned to the news, but he stood when he saw me.

"This way," he said, and led me up the stairs to a door marked *Exit to Jirón Ocoña*.

He opened it and stuck out his head, letting in cool, damp air and the chants of demonstrators. "Street's sealed off," he said. "You'll have to turn left and go to La Colmena to find a cab."

He motioned me out. "Be careful, caballero. Go with God."

I thanked him, stepped outside, and fell in with a noisy group of German tourists. No Peep agents and no soldiers that I could see, only the fog, the ever-present smell of exhaust fumes, a money-changer, and an old woman on a sidewalk blanket.

The Germans gave me puzzled looks, but I stayed with them anyway, wishing I wasn't so damn tall, and we had just stepped around a vendor's cart when I saw Gordo.

CHAPTER TWENTY-ONE

His stomach and dark hat protruded from a doorway. I danced to the side of the Germans away from him, but that attracted the money-changer, holding up a wad of paper currency.

"Dollar, dollar, dollar. I change your dollars."

I waved him off and kept going, putting one foot ahead of the other, resisting the impulse to bolt. The woman next to me leaned over and spoke to me in German, probably asking *Who the hell are you?* I shrugged and gave her that stupid look of non-comprehension, and then realized she was the same silver-haired lady who'd shown me the newspaper in the dining room.

She turned and spoke to the others in German. They nodded recognition, and by then we were at the doorway where Gordo stood.

"You," he bellowed. "Halt!"

The Germans stopped. I broke into a run. Pedestrians jumped aside. Children leaped up from their blankets and stared, and for a moment I was twenty years old again, racing for the goal line with my football. No way in hell was Gordo going to catch me. Not that overweight slob.

The intersection with Jirón Camaná was straight ahead. All I had to do was hang a left, race another block to La Colmena, and grab a taxi. Get to the Hotel Azúcar and find Lannie. Take that plane to Tingo Maria. Go home. Get the hell out of Peru. Wait for Marisa in Tampa.

And that might have happened except for Chino, who suddenly appeared to my front.

His face was bandaged from our encounter, his left arm in a sling, but he removed the sling and assumed a martial arts stance.

"*Puta madre*," he yelled, and came at me like a character in a cheap Asian movies, making slashing motions with his right hand.

Behind him came more Peep agents, young men, drawing their pistols.

I swung around and charged back through the Germans.

The silver-haired lady slapped her knees. "Run, gringo, run!"

Others picked up the chant. "Run, gringo, run!"

I galloped toward the crowd of demonstrators, darting around vendor carts and lamp posts, and was so concentrated on getting there that I didn't see Gordo until he flew into me from the side, driving me into a parked police motorcycle.

"Whore-loving *Senderista* pig!"

His truncheon missed my head and glanced off my shoulder, but it still sent an electric-like shock down my arm. This was the second time Gordo had landed the first punch; there wasn't going to be a third. I grabbed his arm, twisted it behind him, and drove him into a lamp post.

The Germans cheered. So did a few Peruvians. Then I was racing toward the plaza as if the bulls of Pamplona were on my heels, legs pumping so high, I thought they'd hit my chest.

I was almost there when a female motorcycle cop stepped out of a door in front—all helmet, boots, and riding pants—reaching for her pistol.

I flattened her.

Gunfire detonated behind me. A plate glass window shattered. A piece of brick on the wall beside me stung my cheek. The noise from the plaza was so loud that hardly anyone noticed.

The demonstrators were now surging out of the plaza and heading down Jirón de la Unión toward the palace, a sea of angry, shouting faces. I plunged into their midst and weaved my way around placards and banners, keeping my head low, moving ahead, praying.

Someone handed me a small placard marked HUELGA! I held it over my face and kept going. Two blocks down the street, exhausted and gasping, I took Jirón Cusco, raced another block and flagged down a taxi.

"Where to?" the driver asked.

"Anywhere. Just go."

The taxi was like everything else in Lima—ancient and decrepit. We sputtered along for eight or ten blocks, the transmission popping out of gear, the driver muttering, smoke pouring from beneath the dash, stinking up the cab and burning my eyes.

Finally, I paid the fare and took a second taxi to the Hotel Azúcar.

A crowd had gathered around the lobby TV. Lannie wasn't there. I hurried to the phone booth, dropped a sol into the slot, and waited for the dial tone.

Nothing.

I pressed down the holder and released it. Still nothing. I did it again and again. I cursed. And if it hadn't been for all those people in the lobby, now staring and pointing, I'd have destroyed both phone and booth. I left the receiver dangling and hurried into the fog.

Time for Plan C. Dipper Man.

CHAPTER TWENTY-TWO

Two taxi rides later, I ended up in a wooded park only four or five blocks from Marisa's place of last resort. Traffic was light, mist falling, sirens blaring in the distance, and the only person around was an old wino stretched on a bench and covered with plastic.

I turned up my collar and was about to dash away when I noticed the pay phone.

Yes, why not? Maybe I could still catch that plane.

I asked the woman who answered to put me in touch with Lannie.

"Who is calling?" she wanted to know.

"Markus Thorsen. He's expecting my call."

The phone clicked, and then Holbrook Easton was on the other end.

In my tortured mind, I imagined a dark basement with electronics and a switchboard, guys with crew cuts and shoulder holsters, turning dials, trying to get a fix on my location.

"Do you realize what you've done?" Easton raged in his refined way of speaking. "That man you assaulted was a special operations agent with Peep."

"All I did was defend myself."

"No, Professor, you were resisting arrest. You'd better hope he doesn't die."

"Why would he die?"

"Because he's in critical condition—concussion, stroke, cardiac arrest."

A stab of nausea shot up my middle. The hatred I felt for Gordo dissolved in the pitter of the mist. Holbrook Easton kept talking, but I couldn't hear because the wino was now tugging at my sleeve, begging for money. I shoved him away in time to hear Easton saying, "You can either surrender to us or get the hell out of Dodge. And I'd recommend the latter."

"Lannie said something about a plane to Tingo Maria."

"That plane has flown, Professor. You're too late. As for Mr. Torres, don't call him again."

I slammed down the receiver. How in God's name had it come to this? Less than a week ago, I was a respected university professor and a dean-to-be, all dressed in suit and tie and doing nothing more stressful than conducting seminars for graduate students. Now I was a fugitive on the run. Even beginning to think like a criminal.

"Bastards," I muttered, and trotted away.

A short while later, drenched, defeated, and on the verge of tears, I stood beneath the spreading limbs of a giant eucalyptus across the street from the Larco Herrera Museum. This was it, Plan C, the place of final resort, the home of Dipper Man and thousands of other pieces of erotic Mochica pottery. A group of chattering British tourists came out and climbed into their tourist bus. When they pulled away, I slipped through the iron gates, followed a wooded path to the employee entrance, and rang the doorbell three times.

No one answered. I rang three more times and heard a female voice on the inside, speaking English, saying "Oh my God, oh my God" as only an American could say it.

The door creaked open, and there stood a young woman who looked a bit like Marisa, even the same age, with long dark hair and brown eyes.

"Oh my God," she said again. "You've got blood on your face. Are you hurt?"

"I don't think so."

She stuck out her head, glanced around, and handed me a set of car keys. "Green Volvo in the parking lot. Get in the back seat. Lie down. Hurry. I'll bring a towel."

"Do you have a name?"

"Sonia. Now go. Hurry, before someone sees you."

Within minutes we were speeding down Paseo de la República like a race car, the radio blaring out a salsa, Sonia polluting the air with a cigarette, me lying in back with a towel.

"Where is Marisa?" I yelled above the racket.

"Please, Mark, I'm trying to concentrate."

"You're going to get us stopped for speeding."

"Get serious. They don't stop speeders in this city."

We made a series of screeching turns, drove into the trendy neighborhood of Barranco, and pulled into the drive of a multistoried brick building called Chateau Beige, an upscale apartment complex with ornate burglar bars, security lights, and bougainvillea growing up the wall.

A uniformed doorman sprang to a metal gate and pushed it open. We parked in back and hurried up the stairs into an opulent third-floor apartment.

Sonia bolted the door, slammed her car keys on a table, and then burst into tears. "This god-damn country. God-damn war. I should have stayed in the States."

CHAPTER TWENTY-THREE

Chateau Beige

She left me standing there and came back with a bathrobe and towels. "Bathroom's down the hall. You can clean up."

"Is Marisa meeting us here?"

"Are you crazy? She's a fugitive. Like you. They're searching cars. If she came here, they might follow. And all of us could end up like Bonnie and Clyde."

"Where is she?"

She held up a hand. "Please, no more questions."

"You're her cousin, aren't you? I remember her talking about you."

"Stop it, Mark. I don't exist. I'm a dream, an illusion. Now, go, get out of those wet clothes. Wipe that blood off your face."

I showered for the third time that day, cursed at the sight of my battered face, and came out to find Sonia on the sofa with two bottles of cold Cristál beer. Not until then did I notice she also dressed like Marisa—dark pants and white shirt, sleeveless and open two or three buttonholes. She also had crimson polish on her nails and a nice tan in spite of the sunless skies of Lima.

She pointed to a TV that was on in the background, the volume turned down. "They're saying you beat up a Peep agent and almost killed him."

97

I took a long guzzle of beer and told her what happened. She listened, and before long we were both grumbling about Peep agents and the US Embassy, and how the country had gone to hell with death squads, a brutal government, two groups of insurgents, citizens caught in the middle, and a media that was making me sound as bad as the terrorists.

"It's a blood feud," Sonia said, "a dirty little war with extremists on both sides."

"How do you fit into this mix?"

"I don't. I'm like most people in Peru, caught in the middle, but I might have a different take if I'd been born poor and Indian in some little village in the mountains."

We talked until dark. In spite of my probing, Sonia refused to tell me anything about herself or Marisa, and it wasn't until she pulled a little address book out of her purse—which at first I thought were cigarettes—that I realized she hadn't lit up since coming to the apartment.

"What happened to your cigarettes?"

"I don't smoke."

"You were smoking in the car."

"Only when I'm nervous. I'm better now."

She consulted her address book, picked up the phone, dialed a number, and spoke to someone about passports. She listened a moment and then looked up at me.

"What languages do you speak other than Spanish and English?"

"Quechua."

"That's no help. What else?"

"My parents are Norwegian. I can get by in that language."

"I thought you guys had blond hair and blue eyes."

"Some of us have dark hair and brown eyes."

She asked the person on the other end about a Norwegian passport. From her expression, I knew the answer was no.

"What about Danish or Swedish?" I said. "The languages are similar."

She passed along this information, waited a moment and broke into a grin. "Danish," she whispered. "You're going to be a Danish journalist." She listened a moment longer, then hung up. "But you'll have to lose that mustache. It just isn't you."

She stuffed my wet clothing into the washer, got it running, and then showed me around, pointing out rosewood furniture, a glass case filled with pre-Columbian artifacts, and a rack with wines from Argentina and Chile.

"How long have you been living here?"

"I don't live here. This isn't my place."

"Whose place is it?"

"It's best you don't know. Also, in case you're wondering, I don't work at the museum either."

"So what were you doing there?"

"Visiting a friend."

She led me into a bedroom and pointed out a painting in which a barely pubescent girl with dark Runa features lounged on a sofa wearing nothing but combat boots, black beret, and a red scarf embossed with a hammer and sickle, looking like the Shining Path version of Goya's Nude Maja. An AK-47 rested across her stomach. A hand grenade topped a basket of fruit, and all around were the results of her work—demolished backdrop, smoke, and dead soldiers.

"Her name's Carla," Sonia said. "Part of a series called *The Girls of Pachacuti.*"

I stepped closer and took in what looked like four or five loads of semen on her chin, breasts, abdomen, and thighs. "Is that what I think it is?"

"It's a metaphor."

"For what?"

"The indigenous people fucked by the ruling elite."

"Who's the artist?"

"Francisco de la Vega."

The name sounded familiar, and I was trying to place it when she said, "You'd think he'd care about poor girls like Carla. But no, he gives them a few soles to model for him and then he forces them to service his friends. They say he gets his goodies by watching."

The lights dimmed and went out, plunging us into darkness. The hum of the washing machine stopped. Sonia said, "Peru" as if it were a disease instead of a country and went looking for a flashlight. I sat on the bed beneath the painting, and in that moment of darkness remembered what Lannie said about Marisa's husband back at El Parrón:

The hell kind of man wants to watch his wife fuck another man?

Sonia appeared in the doorway with a candle in her hand, face all aglow, the candle emitting the smell of coconuts. "Damn complex," she grumbled. "They're supposed to have a generator, but it's like everything else in this country—broken."

She lit other candles and lamps, told me to make myself at home, and then pulled on her jacket and headed for the door. "If anyone knocks, don't answer."

"Where are you going?"

"Would you please stop with the interrogation? And don't go out either. Or answer the phone. And whatever you do, don't make any calls, especially to your friends at the embassy. They can track you down in minutes."

She opened the door. "Oh, and one more thing. I'll order out for Chinese. The doorman delivers. He'll ring and then leave it at the door. He's very discreet."

She closed the door, hurried down the stairs, and drove away in her Volvo, leaving me watching from the window and still wondering whose place this was, why the doorman had to be discreet, and who the hell was Sonia?

I took a lamp and began snooping like a Peep detective.

CHAPTER TWENTY-FOUR

The books on the shelves were mainly by well-known Latin American novelists: Isabel Allende, Gabriel Garcia Marquez, Mario Vargas Llosa. There were also music cassettes. Tangos, flamenco, jazz. But no family photographs, letters, bills or receipts. Nothing of interest in the kitchen drawers and pantry either. Or in the closets. Not a hint of who owned the place.

Maybe it was a safe house, a hideout for Chairman Gonzalo and fellow travelers.

But shouldn't it have guns and grenades? And revolutionary pamphlets?

The only sign of occupancy was Sonia's suitcase in the master bedroom. But it was locked. No name tags either. I glanced into her bathroom and saw a makeup kit, hairbrushes, and toothpaste. In the closet were designer jeans, a red poncho, an alpaca sweater, and blouses.

Then I stepped to the nightstand and pulled open the top drawer.

Trojans, a small bottle of K-Y, and a pink dildo.

Christ, was this place a love pad for Sonia and a lover, and I'd interfered?

No wonder she was so snappy. No wonder the doorman was discreet.

The lights suddenly came on. No warning. And for an instant, I thought I'd been caught by Sonia in her bedroom, sneaking around like a sex pervert. I closed the drawer, hurried out, picked up Gabriel Garcia Marquez's *Love in the Time of Cholera* and began reading.

Not long thereafter, the food arrived—beef chow mein.

I ate in silence and watched the evening news about the palace bombing. President Fujimori had ordered more troops into the city and imposed a nighttime curfew from 10 p.m. to 5 a.m. The media had also acquired the Germans' film, and I saw myself bounding over an old woman on the sidewalk, struggling with Gordo, slamming his head into the light post, then flattening the policewoman. They ran it again and again, in slow motion, and asked for tips on my whereabouts. They even flashed a number to call on the screen.

Why, I wondered, in a time of crisis for the country, did the media give a damn about me?

The chow mein didn't agree with me either, and in bed that night, beneath a ceiling fan, I dreamed of poison mushrooms in my chow mein, and Chino the Peep agent serving it up for me. And Marisa and Sonia posing for a painting, all combat boots, red scarves, and black berets, spread-eagled on the sofa while Francisco de la Vega and his friends took turns with them.

Worse, Marisa seemed to be enjoying it.

My brain turned feverish. The swish-swish of the ceiling fan became the sounds of what they were doing. Hurt and anger overwhelmed me. I went for the AK-47 and was shooting the place to pieces when Sonia shook me awake, and I realized it was daylight.

"Are you all right?" she said.

I sat up, my heart pounding, and rubbed sleep from my eyes. Sonia was now dressed in something silky and scanty and black that looked like a new purchase from Victoria's Secret.

She sat on the bed and rubbed my neck. "Poor Mark, you've had a rough time. I'll fix breakfast."

I showered again, but it took a long time for that nasty feeling to leave, and it didn't help when I looked in the mirror and saw the imprint of a shoe heel on my face. The only good thing about the morning was breakfast with Sonia, who was in a better mood than the day before.

And still dressed in that little teddy with white-lace trim.

In spite of Sonia, my despair deepened when I sat down in front of the TV and saw Inspector Bocanegra with his cigar, saying his men would track me to the ends of the earth. Chino was there too, speaking in singsong Spanish, bragging he'd personally see that I answered for my crimes. Next came the policewoman with her arm in a sling. And her chief saying how brave she was for trying to stop a dangerous fugitive like me.

Dangerous, mind you. Me, a college professor. Of economics.

A final image showed Gordo lying in an oxygen tent in the hospital, next to a sad-faced little woman. "Don't feel sorry for him," Sonia said. "He'd have killed you in a heartbeat."

Sonia went out again that afternoon, and while she was gone, I shamelessly took another peek into her nightstand drawer. Everything still there. Surely she hadn't left it by mistake. And surely she must know I'd be snooping. Was it there to tease me? Like that teddy?

I needed something to take my mind off my troubles—and Sonia for that matter—so I found a legal pad in a kitchen drawer, sat at the table, and began scribbling. In verse.

> All I wanted was a night together / an explanation,
> And a flight home for the two of us.

Yes. Why not write about all that had happened to me? Get it on paper while it was still fresh. Write it for the lawyers

103

and judges and the embassy and my university. And Marisa too.

I started with the general. Then the hearings and my trip to Lurigancho. And I was getting beaten up by Gordo when Sonia returned with newspapers and sandwiches, along with medication for my cuts, a pair of lounging slacks, a sweat-shirt, and a little box of chocolates.

Then she took a shower and pranced around the apartment wearing only a towel, all sweetness and smiles. God, was she that clueless about guys?

Or was I that clueless about women?

James Bond would have yanked away the towel and dragged her into his cave. But I wasn't Bond, and I wasn't about to fall into that trap. Hell no. Years ago, in my senior year at the University of Minnesota, I'd had a fling with a young cutie named Ingrid, and in a moment of weakness, had also bedded her dorm mate. Several times. And thought I could get away with having them both. Until Ingrid found out—and things turned ugly.

But I'd learned a valuable lesson. Women kiss and tell.

∾

A jangling telephone woke me on the next day. I stumbled out of bed, still half-asleep, and found Sonia in the living room in her black teddy, talking to someone in English.

"Sounds like a plan," she said into the mouthpiece. Then she hung up and looked at me. "We're leaving Thursday, taking the train to Huancayo."

My heart gave a little kick at the thought of leaving the security of this place and going into the unknown. "Will Marisa meet us in Huancayo?" I asked.

"We'll know when we get there, won't we?"

She bleached my dark hair blond and took photos for the stolen passport. We rehearsed our plan. She also brought me clothes a Dane might wear—blazer, overcoat, and gray slacks—and even Danish books and newspapers. And a small suitcase. But she continued to walk around in stages of dress that tortured me. And on our last night together, with our bags packed, she put a tango on the player, uncorked a bottle of Cabernet, dropped onto the sofa beside me in her little spaghetti strap nightie—the lavender one that barely reached her thighs—and began lathering an aromatic lotion on her arms and legs.

"I'm going to miss you," she whispered.

"I'll miss you too, Sonia. You've been a wonderful—"

She leaned over and kissed me.

Not a lingering romantic kiss. But not innocent either. Just enough to take away my breath. Then she sat there, the tango playing, her lips moist and inviting, looking into my eyes as if waiting for me to respond.

The tango ended. A look of sadness crossed her face. Her eyes watered. She stood, turned off the player, went to her room, said good-night, and closed the door, leaving me alone on the sofa, still thinking about that luscious body with the soft, inviting lips.

And the nightstand drawer.

What would I have done if she'd kissed me again?

Or invited me into her room?

The next day, on a dreary Thursday morning, we took separate taxis to Lima's Desamparados train station, checked our bags, and fell in line with other passengers for the 7:20 to Huancayo.

CHAPTER TWENTY-FIVE
Ferrocarril Central Andino

Until Sonia lit a cigarette and began glancing around like a nervous bank robber, I'd been optimistic about our chances, thinking how good it felt to be outdoors again, to feel the cool damp air on my neck, to see all these European tourists who didn't seem the least concerned, to hear the chatter of different languages, even to smell exhaust fumes.

But now, looking at the wide-eyed expression on Sonia's face, I knew she was as scared as I was, which made me wonder why she'd dressed in a red poncho with a little knit cap. I wanted us to remain as unobtrusive as a lamppost in daylight, as gray as the overcast sky. Yet there she stood in that red poncho as if saying, *Hey, everyone, look at me.*

I shook a Gauloises out of the pack she'd provided, lit up like everyone else in line, stepped closer to her, and repeated the lines we'd rehearsed, pretending to make conversation with a stranger. "Please to excuse," I said in the best Danish-accented English I could muster, "but do you happen to speak ah English?"

"I can manage," she said, faking an accent.

"Is it always this ah foggy in Lima?"

"Only this time of year. Where are you from?"

I was about to say Denmark when a black Mercedes drove up and screeched to a stop.

Out popped three men in dark hats and trench coats.

Sonia's face went so white I thought she'd faint, and I probably looked just as terrified.

The Peep men hurried past, went to the front of the line, and began working backward.

Sonia took a deep breath and lit another cigarette. A Brit in front of us, all red-cheeked and dressed in a safari jacket, turned to me.

"Nothing to worry about," he said. "They do this at each station."

Easy for him to say. He was probably just another thrill-seeking tourist. But I was doomed. Nothing was going to save me now. Not the cigarette. Not my Danish passport, not my blue eye contacts or faux blond hair or Danish blazer with the brass buttons. Not even the raincoat I wore over my shoulders European fashion, empty sleeves dangling.

In spite of my terror, I pretended to be flirting with Sonia, though it was a clumsy, halfhearted effort whose artificiality would have been obvious to anyone paying attention.

"Where are you ah going?" I asked like a robot, forcing a smile.

"Why, I'm going to Huancayo. What about you?"

"The same place. Now, isn't that a coincidence?"

Never mind we were about to board the Huancayo train.

They were almost on us now. I felt it in my heartbeat and in the sweat trickling down my ribs. I heard it in the strain of Sonia's voice, and saw it in the eyes of other passengers. The only hope now was to run, to dash up the track, to jump into the river, and start swimming.

Then I felt a stir of air as they passed.

Sonia closed her eyes and drew in a deep breath. A whistle blew. The line closed up. I felt blood returning to my face. We climbed aboard a car marked Tren de Sierra and took our seats. No searches, no policemen and no Peep agents, nothing but a car full of tourists. What was wrong with these people? Didn't they know that half the countryside of Peru was controlled by the Shining Path? Or that the government was just as brutal as the terrorists?

Did they care?

The train lurched and pulled out of the station, following the cocoa-colored Rimac upstream. Through the window I noticed a woman near the riverbank with a long pole in her hand, watching the water as if she expected to see a relative floating down.

The train gathered speed, clattering along the tracks and taking us away from the tortured city of Lima, passing alongside little shantytowns of woven straw-and-bamboo huts. Across the aisle, the Brit was explaining the fog to his wife, saying it was a coastal phenomenon caused by warm winds interacting with the cool water of the ocean.

It grew brighter. The blurred edges of distant objects became clearer, more sharply defined, and suddenly the train burst through the cloud of perpetual mist into the open sunlight. Passengers clapped and cheered. I slipped on my Ray-Bans for a look. The Rimac was cleaner now, and all around was bare open desert.

I turned to Sonia. "Now that we're out of Lima, can you tell me our plans, where we're going, when we'll link up with Marisa?"

She gave me a shut-up look, then took an Isabél Allende novel from her tote bag and began reading. I took out my Danish newspaper, *Kobenhaven Dagbladet,* and tried to read, but found myself listening to the Brit, who was telling his wife that our first stop would be Chosica.

"It's a resort town, love. It's where Lima's rich go to escape the gloom."

He was telling her there wouldn't be enough time for shopping when we pulled into the station. A swarm of locals gathered around the train—pigtailed matrons swinging baskets of bananas; barefooted children holding up oranges and chewing gum; beggars with sun-parched faces, all tatters and grime, tapping on the window. Some of the passengers gathered their belongings and headed for the door. Sonia stood and stretched.

"Be right back," she said, and sauntered down the aisle.

Other people came aboard: lighter-skinned people in our car, darker-skinned locals with their bags and boxes and chickens to the "Indian cars" in the rear. The sign outside read 860 meters above sea level. Out the window I could see Victorian mansions shaded by palm and eucalyptus trees, elegant hotels with balconies, and shops advertising Inca jewelry.

The train jerked and began to move. I half stood and looked around. Where was Sonia?

Then I saw her, coming down the aisle—red poncho, dark hair, knit cap, and dark pants.

I picked up my Danish paper and buried my face in it.

The Brit leaned over and touched my arm. "What's that paper you're reading?"

I told him it was Danish. He said Tivoli Gardens was on his bucket list, and he was yapping about all the other places he and his wife had visited when Sonia brushed past me and settled into the window seat, bringing with her a faint whiff of Lily of Peru.

Lily of Peru? Why was she wearing Marisa's perfume?

The train entered a tunnel, plunging us into darkness. The clickety-clack grew louder. Sonia leaned against my shoulder and reached for my hand, and somewhere in the darkness of that tunnel, even before we emerged into the light, I realized the woman beside me was not Sonia.

CHAPTER TWENTY-SIX

I tried to speak, to say hello or make some other comment, but all I could do was stare. Marisa's blue eyes were now brown. Her nose, unlike Sonia's, had just the slightest hint of an arch. Her tan was deeper, and she was an inch or two taller than Sonia, but from her overall dress and appearance, no one but me would have noticed the switch.

The whistle blew. We entered another tunnel. Marisa came into my arms and sobbed against my chest. I also choked up. Two months of absence and a basket of mysteries does that to a person, and when we came out two or three minutes later, straightening up and wiping at our eyes, the Germans behind us were laughing and chattering as if nothing had changed, the Brit in the safari jacket was lecturing his wife about the eucalyptus trees alongside the tracks, and outside the window the entire world seemed like a brighter place.

"Thank you for believing in me," Marisa whispered.

"I never for a moment doubted you. Your husband's the problem, isn't he?"

She put a finger to my lips and traced it up the side of my face, below the bruise that was purpling beneath the makeup. "Tonight," she whispered.

The train climbed higher, maneuvering zigzags, bridges and switchbacks, passing through places where Inca warriors with slings and leather shields had met Pizarro's cannon and horses. Marisa and I sat together like strangers on a train... except when we entered a tunnel.

And there were lots of tunnels, each more passionate than the last.

After the third or fourth or fifth tunnel, when I was arranging the newspaper over my lap to hide the embarrassing bulge, Marisa leaned a little closer.

"Guess what I brought?"

She reached inside her tote bag and pulled out a copy of Neruda's *Twenty Love Poems.* "Here, why don't you read this to me?"

She flipped it open to a dog-eared page. "This line."

At a glance I saw the verse I'd first read to her years ago in El Parrón—*I want to do with you what spring does to the cherry blossoms*—after which we'd checked into the Gran Hotel Bolívar and made love all night. "You want me to read this to you here?"

She moistened her lips. "No one's paying any attention."

"If I read this, are you going to behave yourself?"

"Do you want me to behave?"

My breath caught. One of the things I loved about Marisa was that poetry always had that effect on her. Flowers wouldn't do it. Neither would wine, music, or expensive gifts. But get her talking poetry, and there'd better be a bedroom nearby. Or a dark tunnel.

"I'm waiting," she whispered, and reached beneath the newspaper on my lap.

Sometimes we seemed airborne over valleys and roads far below. Each turn brought fresh views of streams running through groves of eucalyptus, Inca terraces that covered entire mountains, and shepherds looking after flocks of llama and alpaca.

The Brit was telling his wife about Henry Meiggs, the American engineer who'd built the track with Chinese labor, when I felt the onset of *soroche*. It began as dizziness and a slight headache, followed by nausea and a general malaise.

I knew the feeling well, knew I was going to get it anytime I went above ten thousand feet; we were already at thirteen thousand and climbing.

"It's bothering me too," Marisa whispered.

Conversation around us ceased. I began to perspire in spite of the cold. The Brits looked ghastly: all limp and pale, and even Marisa was sitting back with her eyes closed. At Ticlio Station, 15,611 feet above sea level, a little man in a white smock hurried down the aisle with an oxygen tank and a broad grin, giving passengers a pull from the nozzle.

A few minutes later, at Galera Tunnel, we passed a sign that read "Highest Passenger Station in the World." Marisa touched my arm. "You'll soon feel better. It's all downhill from here."

∽

It was going on five when we rolled into Jauja, an ancient town where Pizarro had once established his capital. Conversation picked up. People began to stir. I was still headachy, dizzy and nauseated from the elevation, but managed to struggle out of my seat and head to the doorway. Marisa joined me, and we were breathing in the icy mountain air when I noticed a green army bus—followed by the slap of running feet.

Marisa grasped my arm. "Sinchis."

We hurried to our seats and had barely settled in when an officer with a clipboard clambered aboard. Around me, I saw faces of fear and nervous twitching. I glanced behind us like a trapped rabbit, looking for a vacant seat, thinking it best for us to be separate, but soldiers were already filing in the rear door, bronzed men with assault rifles, pants tucked into combat boots, some of them wearing black ski masks, which made them look even more menacing.

Dammit, why hadn't I thought of separate seats before? It had to be oxygen deprivation.

A passenger in a seat in front opened a window as if he wanted to jump out, but a Sinchi beside the train lifted his rifle. Outside, a patrol was dragging a young man alongside the train, probably from the Indian car. Blood dripped from his nose and chin. He was crying, and behind him, wringing her hands and pleading, trotted a dumpy little woman in a short, tight skirt.

Marisa put on a pair of glasses. "Get out a book and start reading."

I did as she told me. The words on the page were a blur, my head throbbed, and when I glanced up again, the officer with the clipboard was coming down the aisle, peering into faces. Behind him came more soldiers with ski masks. The officer looked familiar, but I didn't place him until he was two rows ahead, body-searching the man who'd opened the window.

Lieutenant Bravos from the hearing.

Marisa let out an exasperated sigh. I muffled a curse. Bravos would unravel our little deception as surely as he'd found that cluster of mortar shells with the bananas.

Then he was standing over me.

He looked from me to Marisa as if he'd seen our pictures on a wanted poster. Then he turned and spoke in Quechua to the Sinchis behind him.

"What do you think?"

"They're about the right age," said one with stripes on his sleeve, his voice muffled.

My heart beat faster. My mouth felt dry. Bravos spoke to Marisa, now in Spanish. "*Con perdón, señorita,* are you traveling with this gentleman?"

"I'm traveling alone. I don't know this gentleman."

Bravos touched my shoulder. "*Y usted, caballero.* What is your business in the country?"

"I don't think he knows Spanish," Marisa said.

Bravos switched into fractured English and repeated his question. I answered in my Danish accent. "I'm a newspaper journalist—from ah Denmark."

"A reporter who doesn't speak Spanish?"

"I have a translator. He's ah meeting me in Huancayo."

"Please to stand."

I turned my legs into the aisle and stood, hoping my legs would support me.

"Right height," Bravos said to the other soldiers, and they all nodded.

The Sinchi with the stripes and ski mask stepped closer. They conferred in Quechua, saying the blond hair didn't look natural, that it made no sense to send a journalist to Peru who didn't speak Spanish, that the woman fit the description.

Bravos turned back to me. "Passport, please."

I dug it from my jacket, trying to keep from shaking. Bravos took the passport and compared the photograph with my face. Then he turned to the Sinchi behind him and again spoke in Quechua. "Those two ladies up front—second row. Where are they from?"

"Denmark," answered the one with the stripes.

"Get them. Let's see if this gentleman is who he says he is."

CHAPTER TWENTY-SEVEN

My headache grew worse. The Norwegian I spoke was *gammel Norsk*—old Norwegian—difficult to understand even in modern cities like Oslo. The real Danes would know immediately I was a phony and probably cheer when Bravos dragged me off the train.

Presently, the Sinchis came back down the aisle with a pair who looked like mother and daughter, all thick glasses and rosy cheeks, one of whom was old enough to remember the Nazi occupation of her country. Their eyes and the way they clutched their purses told me they were as terrified as I was. And as woozy from the elevation. The older one adjusted her hearing aid and protested to her daughter. Loudly.

"JEG IKKE OPFATTE HVAD DE ONSKER."

Which I was pretty sure meant, "I don't understand what they want."

"Please, Mother, not so loud. It'll be okay."

Bravos touched his beret and spoke to them in English. "Please to pardon, but this, eh, gentlemen claims to be Danish. Would you be so kind as to…how you say, *verificar?*"

I stepped around him and thrust out my hand to the ladies, praying they'd understand.

"*God aftermiddag,*" I said. "*De forteller meg at du er Dansk.*" They say you're Danish.

"*Ja, ja,*" answered the younger one. "We are Danish." She offered her hand. "I'm Anne Lise, and this is my mother, Mette. We're from Skagen."

"Hans," I replied, "Hans Prebin Hoelvik. How nice to meet fellow Danes."

Their smiles turned to skeptical looks, but before they could ask, I told them in *gammel Norsk* that I was a journalist with the *Kobenhavn Dagbladet* and had taken a few days off to visit Huancayo, and what a coincidence it was to meet other Danes in Peru.

The older one, Mette, pushed closer and cupped a hand over her ear. "HVOR DU SAGDE DU FRA?" Where did you say you're from?

Bravos touched my arm. "What did she say?"

"She said what a nice surprise to meet another Dane in Peru."

Anne Lise's mouth opened as if to contradict me, but I quickly said, "Please, Anne Lise, I need your help. If I don't convince these soldiers I'm Danish, they're going to arrest me."

She slapped her forehead. "*Åh min Gud.* You're that American professor, aren't you?"

My heart beat faster. In Danish, the word for American professor was almost the same as in English—*Amerikansk professor.* I half expected Bravos to yank out the cuffs and clamp them on my wrists. When he didn't, I turned back to Anne Lise.

"I don't know what you heard, but those things they're saying about me aren't true."

Mette tugged on Anne Lise's sleeves. "*HVAD SAGDE HAN?*" What did he say?

Bravos had heard enough. He slapped my passport into my hand and turned his attention to the Brits. Mette headed back up the aisle, shaking her head, but Anne Lise lingered.

"You should work on that Danish accent, Professor."

∾

It was dark when our train rolled into Huancayo and came to a stop with a loud screech. Not until then did Marisa tell me the bad news that her network—whatever that was—had arranged for us to stay in different hotels.

"I don't like it either," she whispered, "but it's best that way."

"How long are we going to be here?"

"They'll let us know."

"Who is *they*?"

"You really don't want to know."

Through the window, I saw the usual buzz of baggage handlers, taxi drivers, beggars, and pigtailed matrons in bowler hats and bright clothing. Sinchis were there too—red berets, officers in dark glasses, enlisted men hiding their faces beneath ski masks, a jeep with a machine gun mounted on top. Over the intercom came warnings in French, German, Spanish and English that Huancayo was almost eleven thousand feet above sea level.

"You may experience dizziness and shortness of breath. If you become ill, you should immediately seek medical attention."

I managed to step down on the platform without stumbling. The air was as cold and damp as my feelings about staying in separate hotels. Baggage handlers and beggars came at us from all sides, and down by the Indian car, Sinchis were pulling passengers aside for questioning.

We waited for our bags. The Europeans, who seemed to be in a tour group, left in a waiting bus. Marisa hired a porter and followed her luggage to a line of waiting taxis. I turned up my collar against the cold, grabbed my little suitcase, and found my own taxi.

∞

A jangling telephone brought me back into the world of the living. It was almost ten p.m. The last thing I remembered was falling into a squeaky bed in a hotel that was as run-down,

117

broken, and depressing as everything else in Peru. I rolled over and grabbed the receiver.

"I'm lonely," Marisa's voice said. "Wanna come over?"

"How do I get past the desk?"

"You don't. They monitor all comings and goings, but I've got it figured out."

"Tell me."

"Not on the phone. Someone could be listening."

She was probably right, but the likelihood of them understanding English in this cheap hotel was almost nil. "So what's the plan?" I asked.

"Meet me in the dining room. We'll take it from there."

I downed an Alka-Seltzer with bottled water, cleaned up, put on my blazer with the brass buttons, pulled on an overcoat, and crossed the street to her hotel, passing around armored personnel carriers, tanks, jeeps, and knots of soldiers warming themselves around fire barrels. I didn't like the idea of showing my fugitive face in public, but it had been four long months since Marisa and I had spent the night together. Four months was too long.

Another minute was too long.

CHAPTER TWENTY-EIGHT
Hotel Turismo Huancayo

The soldiers guarding the entrance waved me inside as if I was just another tourist. No one stopped me in the lobby either. No one glanced up from a newspaper, and no one looked like a Peep agent, only a few European-looking types chatting over drinks. So I hurried through the lobby like any other guest and marched straight into the dining room.

Marisa, dressed in black, nodded from a table near the fireplace. I nodded back, then stepped to the bar, ordered a pisco sour and took in the surroundings. Unlike my hotel, which had all the charm of a home for derelicts, this one could have been a ski lodge, with beams in the overhead, the pleasant smells of food and a wood fire, guests sitting around in colorful sweaters, servers in tuxedoes, musicians in native attire on the stage—and the faint glow of a stairway sign behind Marisa's table. Perfect. All we had to do was wait for the right moment and get to that door.

I settled with the server, then took my pisco sour and ambled over to Marisa's table, passing the Brit and his wife and tables of Germans and French.

A candle flickered on her table. In the dim light, I thought she'd never looked so desirable. She had tied up her long hair, exposing a pair of dangling sun-god earrings that sparkled in the light. The slope of her neck was like ivory.

"May I to join you?" I said in my faux Danish accent, loud enough for the Brits to hear.

"Please," she said, and motioned me into a chair.

I took off my overcoat and dropped into a chair. "That the stairway?" I whispered.

She grinned. "No guards either. This is just like the old days, when you'd sneak me into your room. Back then we didn't care if we got caught."

"How long should we sit here?"

"Long enough to eat."

"We're going to eat here—in public?"

"Why not? Besides, I've already ordered."

"For both of us?"

"Both of us, Mark, and stop glancing around. You look like a fugitive."

"I am a fugitive."

"I'm scared too, but we've got to stay calm. Act like a married couple."

"Married couples don't talk to each other."

"Sure they do. Look at that Brit. Hasn't stopped yapping since Lima."

I wanted to ask a hundred questions—like why her things had turned up at Chairman Gonzalo's hideout—and had the words in my mouth when the food arrived and then the power failed, plunging the room into darkness. Groans and a smattering of applause followed.

Someone said, "Peru" as if that explained it, which it did.

A procession of servants came around with lamps and candles. The ambience grew softer, conversation took on a hushed tone, and the band struck up a traditional Andean number, heavy on the flutes and drums. So we ate. Music played. Couples danced. Cigarette smoke billowed up from tables around us, and we were on tiramisu when Marisa rubbed my leg beneath the table.

"Remember that night in Cuzco? The snow, the ice cubes?"

I sighed, and for a moment we were back in the old Inca capital of Cuzco. Just the two of us, a snowy night in the mountains, a roaring fire, a bucket of ice cubes.

God, those ice cubes.

She lowered her voice. "You wrote a poem about it, didn't you?"

Before I could answer, she moistened her lips, grinned that wicked little grin that was always a prelude to an interesting evening, and began whispering the lines.

> Fire and ice in Cuzco, both did serve us well.
> A thousand inquisitions, yet, I shall never tell.
> For pleasures are my secret, and nights in heaven too,
> With music, wine and lamplight, and Lily of Peru...

The noise around us faded away. Marisa sat there looking into my eyes as if I were the only man in the world, her breasts rising and falling. Candlelight glinted in her hair.

"Know what?" she said, rattling the ice in her water glass. "I think it's time to go upstairs."

She said she'd already settled with the server. I left a ten-dollar tip anyway, and we were coming to our feet when the band struck up "El Condor Pasa." Flutes, *queñas* and drums came to life. Tables emptied as couples headed to the dance floor.

"That's our song," Marisa said. "We can't leave without dancing."

She took my hand and pulled me across the room, passing gracefully around Frenchmen, Germans, and Englishmen, drawing admiring looks from the men and envious stares from the women. When we reached the dance floor and she came into my arms, I tried to hold her at arm's length. But Marisa, who loved to tease me about how easily I got aroused, pulled close.

"Know what I'm going to do when we get to the room?" she whispered.

"I don't want to hear it."

"I'm going to order a bucket of ice cubes."

"If you don't behave yourself, I'm never going to make it to the room."

"We could do it on the elevator."

"Elevators don't work during a power failure."

"God, I am so wet."

"Do you want to dance, or do you want to go to the room?"

The violinist hit a sour note.

Marisa stiffened. I spun around. And there in the dining-room doorway, in a little pool of lamplight, stood Lieutenant Bravos with three or four Sinchis.

In an instant, without thinking, I danced her toward the table we'd just vacated and grabbed our things. The Brits glanced from us to the soldiers as if they knew what we were up to. So did the Frenchmen. I guided Marisa to the door behind our table anyway and pulled on the handle.

It was locked.

CHAPTER TWENTY-NINE

I cursed. I rattled the handle. But nothing gave. By then we'd attracted even more attention. Even the Danes were staring. Our server hurried over to us.

"Sir," he said, "you'll have to use the lobby to get upstairs."

I pulled out my wallet. "Look, young man, we're not exactly, you know, married. At least not to each other, and if we go through the lobby, they won't let us...."

"No need to explain," he said, and pulled a key ring from his pocket. It was huge, with a dozen or more keys that all looked alike. He stuck one into the lock and jiggled it.

"Oops, not this one."

He tried another, and yet another, but none seemed to work.

Marisa and I moved deeper into the shadows. Far across the room, beyond the dancers, Bravos and the Sinchis were pointing toward the back. Then they headed our way.

"Oh God," Marisa said. "They'll see us."

"Aha," said the server, and the door swung open.

Marisa plunged into the darkness beyond. I followed, but not before handing the server a twenty-dollar bill. I took Marisa's hand and tried to pull her up the stairs.

"Wait, I want to see what they're up to."

"No, Marisa, come on."

She jerked loosed and peeked back into the dining room. "They're just here to eat."

She closed the door and fell against it, giggling like a child who'd just pulled off a prank. I giggled too. Laughter turned to kisses, the wonderful, moist fusions of passion that come with moments of danger. And then we were against the wall, fondling like teenagers. Right there at the bottom of the stairs. In the darkness. With only a door between us and a tableful of Sinchis.

"We could do it here," she whispered between kisses.

"Are you crazy? We could get caught."

She reached for my zipper.

"No, Marisa. We shouldn't—"

"Hush."

Voices came from the landing above. Someone was coming down with a flashlight, speaking German. We pulled apart and flattened ourselves against the rear wall.

Down they came, mere shadows in the darkness, the arc of their light flashing on the door. They pushed it open—no problem from this side—and entered the dining room, letting in the sounds of music and merriment, and the smells of cigarettes and food, and giving us a quick glimpse of Lieutenant Bravos at the table with his Sinchis, laughing and drinking.

The door closed. By then Marisa had come to her senses, and I led her up the stairs in the darkness, feeling the blood returning to my head.

We stopped on the second-floor landing to catch our breath in the thin air.

We kissed and fondled again in the third-floor corridor. In total darkness.

And by the time we reached her room, I'd forgotten all about Bravos and the soldiers.

Her room had a wonderful, sensual scent of Lily of Peru. A candle burned low on the nightstand. From the street below came the wail of a flute and the beat of primal drums. I kicked off my shoes and watched her take off her earrings. She did it slowly, the way a stripper might remove an article of clothing, tilting her head, smiling, wrinkling her nose.

Her watch came off next, then the sandals.

"Be right back," she whispered, and padded into the bathroom. While she was gone, I took out the contacts that had turned my brown eyes blue, and was stripping off my shirt when she came back out, her hair down, contacts gone, her eyes now blue.

She wore a towel and nothing else. "Do you want me?"

"Desperately."

She came into my arms and kissed me with the same intensity she'd shown on the stairs, and on that first night in Lima when I'd read Neruda to her, and when we'd linked up the last time in the Gran Hotel Bolívar. The towel fell to the floor. She mumbled something about how much she'd missed me, and then we were on the bed.

"Touch me," she pleaded. "Tell me what you're going to do."

I told her, again and again, in the graphic words she liked, and I did all the other things that drove her wild and that I'd fantasized about for months. The bed creaked. It shook. Who cared that people in the next room could probably hear? Or in the next village?

This was what life was about.

In time, mindless pawing gave way to tenderness and an occasional spasm. I began to notice things I hadn't noticed before, like sticky wetness, the outside sounds of people and traffic, and another Andean tearjerker from the musicians on the street below, rendered in Quechua.

*Iglisia punkuchallapi...*In the doorway of the church,
*Suyakuykiman karqa...*I stood waiting.
*Munaspa mana munaspa...*Even if you didn't love me,
*Casaraykiman karqa...*I would have married you.

We listened. I translated the words for her and told her I'd been collecting lyrics of Peruvian folk music for inclusion in my book of poems—if it ever got published. She propped herself on an elbow, her lips and face pale in the candlelight, her hair a stringy mess.

"Mark?"

"What?"

"Can we do it again?"

By the time we finished the second round—or maybe it was the third—the musicians outside the window had long since quit their posts, and I figured it was time to get some answers about why her things had turned up at the hideout for Chairman Gonzalo.

So I propped up in bed, leaned against the headboard, and asked her.

"Mark, please, it's late. Can we talk about this tomorrow?"

"It was your husband, wasn't it?"

"Ex-husband, now come on. I'm sleepy."

"What's his relationship with the terrorists?"

Loud voices came from outside the room, angry voices, like a domestic quarrel. I eased out of bed, wrapped a sheet around me, padded to the door, and opened it a crack. Down the hall, a woman was saying, "You have no right to come in my room. No right whatsoever."

I peeked out in time to see flashlights and a pair of boots disappearing into a doorway—combat boots. "Sinchis!" I said. "They're searching the rooms."

Marisa bounded up and began gathering my things. "Hurry. You've got to go."

I yanked on my trousers and shoes and pulled on my jacket. Into my pockets went socks, shirt, and shorts. At the door I pulled on my topcoat, fluffed my hair, and put on my glasses.

"Contacts, Mark. Put on your contacts. Your eyes are supposed to be blue."

Somehow I got them in, got back to the door, and pushed it open a crack. Other doors were open now, people with candles and lamps peering out, the looks of fright and amazement.

Seeing no soldiers, I stepped into the corridor and dashed into the darkness: no socks, no underwear, no shirt, and no answers from Marisa.

CHAPTER THIRTY

The rumble of a passing truck brought me out of a troubled sleep. The reddish glow of dawn filtered through the curtains. When I remembered where I was and the circumstances of the night before, I rolled out of bed and was yanking on my trousers when I heard movement in the hallway. Then a tap at the door.

"Mark, are you there?"

She was dressed in jeans, sweater, and a fur-collared jacket. Her hair was damp and straight, as if she'd just washed it, and in her hand were steaming mugs of coffee.

"Bribed the desk clerk," she said. "Also ordered breakfast."

She handed me a mug and trailed a fresh soapy smell into the room.

"What happened last night?"

"Checked my passport, asked a few questions, and left. Big fright, but no big deal."

She reached into her jeans and pulled out my necktie. "Next time you sneak out of a woman's room, Don Juan, be sure to take the evidence with you."

I took a cold shower in a cold bathroom without lights and was trying to shave in cold water when room service knocked on the door with breakfast. We ate at a table next to a window that looked out over the soldiers in the plaza—young conscripts with blankets over their shoulders, caps pulled low over their ears, warming themselves around barrels of fire, stomping their feet against the cold. Marisa downed the last of her papaya juice and looked at her watch.

"Better get dressed. We don't have much time."

"Where are we going?"

"Ayacucho. We're taking a truck. The ruts are too deep for cars."

I groaned at the thought of another high-elevation trip. The road to Ayacucho rarely dropped below thirteen thousand feet. Worse, it was at the center of the war between the Shining Path and government forces, a city under martial law, the place where General Reál was quartered.

"Don't look so worried," Marisa said. "They'd never expect us to go there."

"Where are your things—your suitcase?"

"Already taken care of."

I finished dressing and was about to head downstairs to settle the bill when Marisa handed me the newspaper that had come with breakfast. The headline jumped out at me:

DETECTIVE DIES IN HOSPITAL. SEARCH INTENSIFIES FOR FUGITIVE.

Gordo dead? I turned away and stepped to the rear window. The early sunlight cast a warming glow on snow-capped peaks, but the chill inside me was as cold as a Norwegian winter.

"I've never killed anyone before," I mumbled.

"You didn't kill him, Mark. He attacked you. It was self-defense."

She was right, of course, but tell that to Peep. Tell that to Gordo's cocky little sidekick. Or to Bocanegra. If they got the chance, they'd gun me down like a rabid dog.

"We'd better go," she said. "Those truckers don't wait."

We took a taxi to a warehouse on the outskirts of town. Not until we hopped out did Marisa tell me that she'd be going in one truck and I'd be following in another.

"It's better that way. The papers said we'd be traveling together."

"What about checkpoints?"

"You're still a Danish journalist. Remember?" She leaned into me and rubbed my back. "Forget Gordo. If he'd had his way, you'd be rotting in a dungeon."

She handed me an apartment key, instructed me on where to go in Ayacucho, and was telling me it would be okay when a battered ten-wheeler Mercedes with a canvas-covered bed roared up. Marisa climbed in, and off she went amid a grinding of gears and popping of exhaust.

My truck didn't show up until forty minutes later.

"Ayacucho," the driver announced as if he were a bus driver. "Hop in."

CHAPTER THIRTY-ONE
Highway of the Sun

We climbed all morning, the road winding and twisting like a corkscrew, up and still up. Rain turned to sleet, then to snow and back to sleet and rain. The driver, a burly man with a heavy mustache, never accepted that I didn't speak Spanish and rattled on.

"Don't know about you," he said, grinning at me sideways, "but I think Chairman Gonzalo could run the country better than that crooked little Jap in Lima. What do you think?"

I looked at him and shrugged.

Many hours later—dusty, nauseated, shivering in spite of the heater, and suffering from a pounding oxygen-deprivation headache—I glanced out at the lights of Ayacucho, sparkling in the night air like a thousand campfires.

We passed muster at the army checkpoint, drove past a mud wall on which someone had spray-painted the words VIVA LA LUCHA ARMADA—Long Live the Armed Rebellion—dodged around large stones that littered the road, and reached the old Plaza de Armas just as the clock on the cathedral was chiming two in the morning.

Back in my Fulbright days, the plaza had been the kind of place where poets read sonnets beneath the colonnades, and old women and girls sold flowers in the shade.

Now it was a giant army camp, with tanks, soldiers, trenches, sandbags, and tents, and for a moment the scene and its smells reminded me of a Goya—bright blazes beneath the trees, the faces and arms of soldiers all aglow, the wheel of a jeep illuminated, or the glint of fire on stacked rifles, then the gloom of night shutting down about it.

"It's an occupied city," the driver said gloomily. "People disappear all the time."

He turned left at the corner and screeched to a stop in front of the buildings facing the plaza, at a doorway flanked by white colonnades. "Be careful," he said, laying a leathery hand on my arm. "Last week they shot twelve dissidents right here in the plaza."

In case I didn't get the message, he curled his hand into a make-believe pistol and fired three rounds into my chest. "Boom, boom, boom. Dead."

I settled with him in dollars, thanked him in English, hopped down with my bag, and looked for the green doorway next to a flower shop Marisa had told me about.

It was the same address Carlos had given me back at Lurigancho.

A burst of gunfire sent me dashing into the shadows. Across the street a group of masked soldiers were howling with laughter.

"Hey, *compañero,* come on over for a drink. We won't shoot you."

I fumbled with the key, got the door open, hurried in, and bolted it behind me. Even there, in a dark hallway that smelled of floor wax and kerosene, with the door bolted, I didn't feel safe. This city was like a dystopian nightmare. Nothing but chaos, perfect for a Hollywood movie.

The only light came from cracks around apartment doors. There was no elevator, so I dragged myself up a gloomy flight of stairs. With a suitcase that felt like it contained Gordo's body.

Why did her place have to be in Ayacucho, 9,000 feet above sea level?

Why did it have to be the fifth floor? Why not the second floor? Or the first?

I put one weary foot in front of the other and climbed another flight. And yet another.

Above me, a Chopin sonata was playing softly, as if the inmates had not yet taken over.

At last I was on the fifth floor. Marisa had said top of the stairs, left side. I waited a moment to catch my breath, not wanting her to see me wheezing and gasping like an old man.

The door swung open.

Light and music filled the hall. And there, in a faded burgundy robe, a damp towel around her head, looking and smelling as if she'd just come from the shower, stood Marisa

CHAPTER THIRTY-TWO
Ayacucho

When I rolled over the next morning and found her next to me, breathing softly in her sleep, I allowed myself a moment of joy. Hardly a day had passed in the last ten years that I didn't wake up and wish for this moment. Now she was in bed beside me, warm and soft and nude and cuddly. No way was I going to leave this country without her.

I kissed her on the shoulder and breathed in the lingering scent of her perfume. She didn't wake, so I slipped out of the warmth of the bed, pulled on a robe, and fumbled around until I got coffee brewing and a kerosene heater going.

Last night I'd been too exhausted to look around the apartment, but now, with the smell of coffee in the air, with Marisa asleep in the bedroom, with me safe and rested, I saw similarities to the place I'd shared with Sonia. The same kind of rosewood furniture. The same kind of etched gourds and pre-Columbian artifacts. The same kind of books in the shelves.

And the same kind of paintings by Francisco de la Vega.

The one I like best—a reclining semi-nude called *Carmen*—hung over the living-room sofa. It surpassed all the others for color and mastery of detail. No semen or dead soldiers, only a beautiful Runa girl with tears in her eyes, clutching a bouquet of wilting roses.

Marisa stirred in the bedroom. "Mark?"

She was propped against a pillow when I came in with coffee, her face pallid, eyes swollen, dark circles beneath, her hair a tangled mess. Yet she was more seductive than *Carmen* in de la Vega's painting, and I felt that surge of arousal that had always been part of our bond.

She took a sip of coffee, set it on the nightstand, and held out her arms.

When we finally collapsed in an exhausted heap, the coffee was cold, the cathedral clock was chiming noon, and we could hear the clang of shopkeepers closing for the midday break. I sat up and pointed to another de la Vega on the wall facing the bed. In it, fat army officers sat around a table in a restaurant while ragged children stared from an open window.

"How does he get away with it?" I asked. "Peru isn't exactly a country of free expression."

"Maybe because he's a cultural icon for the oppressed— like Rivera for the Mexicans."

"Is that why you like him?"

"I don't like him. This isn't my apartment."

"Whose is it?"

She twisted around to face me. "Look, Mark, I know I should explain. But I can't. Not now."

"Why not? I can keep a secret as well as anyone else."

"Not if they take you to Dracula's House."

"What the hell is Dracula's House?"

"It's where they'd take us if we're captured. The neighbors say you can hear screams at night. We'd give up our secrets in no time. And it's not just us; other lives are at stake."

She eased out of bed and headed for the bathroom. I brewed more coffee, stirred up an omelet with onions and peppers from the refrigerator, made toast with cheese, found an Andean music station on the radio, and was waiting at the table when she came out in her robe.

"There's something I should tell you," I said.

"What?"

"It's about the inmates in Lurigancho."

As we ate, I told her all the details about my visit, how scared I was, and how I'd met a former student named Luís, a.k.a. Carlos. "But there was this other inmate—Tucno. All scars and greasy hair. Wore this headband like an Apache. They said he worked for your ex-husband."

She pushed away her plate. "What about him?"

"He escaped, busted out the same day I was there. Do you know him?"

"What about him?"

"They say he's a hired killer, and that you're on his hit list."

"Who is *they*? Who told you that?"

"Carlos. The inmate I went to visit. He says you stole your husband's money."

"That's absurd. I didn't steal his money. All I did was…" She stood, marched to the balcony door, looked out, and came back to the dining table. "Look, I wish I could explain everything to you. But I can't. Not until we're safely out of the country. Trust me. Please."

"There's something else I'd better tell you."

"There's more?"

"Carlos knows about this place, this address. He says he followed you here…three or four years ago. He's the one who took those photos they showed at the hearing. He also escaped. But the worst part is he's from here, Ayacucho. He has family here."

Her face turned red. She said, "Bastard" like she meant it, and again bounded up to peek out the balcony doors.

"Settle down," I said. "He's not going to report us."

"Don't you understand anything, Mark? There's a reward for us. He'll get one of his family members to turn us in. And even if he doesn't, they could capture him. Take him to

Dracula's House. They'll have him talking in no time. He'll offer us up in exchange for his life."

She came back to the table, emotions showing on her face. "I need to make some phone calls. Figure we've got a day, two at the most, before they kick in the door."

CHAPTER THIRTY-THREE

Marisa made a phone call, went out, came back, and said her contacts were putting together a plan to get us out tomorrow. No details other than the next stop was Cuzco, and the people in her shadowy world were as unhappy as she was that our "safe house" had been compromised.

We slept poorly that night, listening for the sounds of boots on the stairway. Sirens blared. Trucks roared. Now and then the shouts of soldiers sent me to the window. And once, when we were awakened by gunfire, Marisa burst into tears.

"There's no end to it," she said, sobbing. "No matter how well you plan, something's bound to go wrong."

At daybreak she rolled out of bed and grabbed her robe off the floor. She made a phone call, gave me one of her "don't ask" looks, and headed for the bathroom. The noise of running water came on, and while she was showering, I made coffee, toast, and boiled eggs.

She came out in a bathrobe. "Do you know where the cemetery is?"

"I know exactly where it is."

"It'll be our rendezvous—just in case."

"In case of what?"

"Plan C. Worst-case scenario. You know the drill."

She ate a boiled egg, drank some coffee, then marched to the living room, and pulled a wad of money from a desk drawer. "Two thousand dollars, all in hundred-dollar bills. If I'm not back by dark, take this and go out the back window. There's a rope in that drawer over there."

"Rope for what?"

"It's five stories, Mark. No fire escape. I don't think you want to jump."

"But why are you going out? I thought they were picking us up in front."

"That's the plan, but I have to go out first."

She put away the money, blow-dried her hair, dressed in jeans, and red poncho, put in her brown contacts. Then she took a black beret off a hook and ticked off a long list of instructions: Bolt the door. Get the rope out. Stay dressed and ready.

"It'll be at least an hour. If the phone rings, pick it up but don't say a word. It could be me."

I pulled her into my arms. "Promise me you'll be okay."

"I promise, Mark."

She managed a smile, a light kiss, and then she was gone, but her final words, "I promise," floated in the air like the chorus of one of those tragic Andean tunes.

I followed her progress from the balcony doors, watching her cross the street and buy flowers from an old woman near a covered arcade. She glanced back as if she knew I'd be watching, and followed a radiating walkway toward the center of the plaza, passing around soldiers, a balloon vendor, and a tank. At the monument to General Antonio Sucre, she raised her flowers in a final salute, and when she disappeared behind the monument, I'd never felt so helpless.

I should be the one getting us out of this mess, not her.

I took a quick shower, dressed, packed my shoulder bag, and did what I'd done at the other apartment—snoop—beginning in the cabinets beneath the bookshelves.

They were filled with paperback novels, stacks of leftist-oriented magazines and pamphlets on healing, magic, and Andean folk medicine. But no personal items to identify the owner.

Nothing of interest in the kitchen cabinets either. But in the desk, in the same drawer as the money, I found a loaded Glock. Damn, why couldn't it be a simple revolver? A semiautomatic was as alien to me as a ray gun. I examined it carefully, removing the clip and pushing back the slide to eject a cartridge, then I reloaded it and left it on the desk.

It got more interesting when I rummaged through a collection of movie videos and found porno cassettes of gay guys. There were also books and magazines touting a gay lifestyle, and condoms and lubricants in the nightstand, and literature on safe sex.

Safe sex? Whoever owned this place was probably an enemy of the state, a man who could be captured or gunned down like a dog, and yet he practiced...safe sex.

Finally, I looked in the bedroom closet. There, next to Marisa's clothing, hung a collection of tailored suits and shirts of the finest quality. From the size, I determined the owner was slight and no taller than about five foot three. There were silk ties too and racks of shoes with the kind of elevated heels that only a person of short stature would wear.

And that was when it struck me. These clothes and this apartment—and probably the apartment in Lima—almost certainly belonged to the little gay man back in Lima.

A man who called himself Apu Condor.

CHAPTER THIRTY-FOUR

The next couple of hours passed in paralyzing slowness. I made a cheese sandwich I couldn't eat. I started a book I couldn't continue. I even watched a Mexican soap opera on television, but the program was interrupted by a report of a gun battle in one of the outlying barrios.

"Peru," I sighed, and was rummaging around for another book when someone knocked on the door. I froze. In my panicked mind, I imagined a SWAT team of Sinchis.

There were more knocks, each more forceful than the last, each like a kick in the stomach.

Dammit to hell. I needed to get out of here.

I crept to the kitchen, took the rope, and was debating whether or not to go out the window when the phone rang. Now what? If I picked it up, the person or persons at the door would hear the interruption in the ring.

But what if it was Marisa? What if she was trying to warn me?

It rang and rang—shrill, grating, like an alarm bell.

I picked up the receiver as carefully as if it were a bottle of nitroglycerin.

"Hello," said a man's voice. "Is anyone there?"

I hung up. Who the hell was that?

There were footfalls on the stairway, going down. I hurried to the balcony door and peeked out in time to a man crossing the street and looking around like a fugitive.

It was Carlos/Luís. Damn him anyway. What did he want? More money?

The phone rang again. Again I picked it up.

"I know you're there," said the man. "Speak to me."

I hung up.

The calls continued, the rings growing more shrill, the caller more insistent. Finally, I stopped answering and started pacing. In my imagination I saw a man with a dark hat in a phone booth, a man wearing a black overcoat, a man who looked like Chino.

Was this a test to see if I was here? Well, he'd learned that already, so why keep calling?

Ring-ring. Ring-ring.

I sank onto the sofa and closed my eyes. The clock on the cathedral chimed three times. Shops were beginning to open, and the clang and rattle of metal security doors echoed up and down the streets. But that infernal phone wouldn't stop ringing.

I grabbed the receiver off the cradle.

"Professor Thorsen," the voice said. "I know you're there. Speak to me."

I stared at the mouthpiece. This wasn't part of the scenario I'd gone over with Marisa.

"Listen," said the voice. "I have a message from your lady friend. There's been a terrible accident. She's at the hospital. She's asking for you."

My heart jumped. "Which hospital?"

"Our Lady of Mercy. It's across the plaza. You can see it from your window."

I stumbled to the balcony doors and swept back the curtains. In the distance were the chalky white hills of Ayacucho, and there too was the white cross of Our Lady of Mercy, brilliant in the afternoon sunlight.

"She was wounded in that shootout in Santa Victoria," the voice said.

I hung up, grabbed the money, the pistol, and was wondering if I should go out the front door or the back window when my sanity returned.

Why hadn't the caller told me about Marisa the first time he called?

Why hadn't Marisa herself called?

And why hadn't Marisa told him to use our secret code, Normán?

No, Marisa wouldn't have given him my name. This was a ploy, an attempt to verify that I was in the apartment, to lure me outside so they could shoot me dead.

And I'd fallen for it.

Stupid, stupid, stupid.

CHAPTER THIRTY-FIVE

Plan C came to mind, and I was in the kitchen, gathering my things, when from somewhere in the plaza came the rat-a-tat of a jackhammer. It was too loud for me to think, too grating, but as I stood there with the rope in my hand, I discovered a rhythm to the noise, an ebb and flow.

And in it came a message: *A trap. A trap. You must warn Marisa. Trap, trap, trap.*

Of course. What was I thinking? I had to warn her. But how?

Fire shots into the air.

Call the fire department.

Set a fire.

A fire. Yes, why not? Not a big one, nothing that would burn down the building. All I needed was smoke. Marisa would see it and know something was wrong.

I raced into the kitchen, pulled the metal trash can from beneath the counter and stuffed it with dish towels, magazines, the videos, newspapers, and damp towels. Then I doused the contents with kerosene from the heater, and lugged this entire smelly mess to the balcony doors, thinking to light it up and shove it onto the balcony.

The jackhammer fell silent, as if the hard hats had glanced up to tell me to slow down, to think it over, that I was moving too fast. Once I set that fire, I'd have to make a quick exit. Best to lower my things out the window first.

So I stuffed a few more things into my shoulder bag, took the pistol and money, and was at the window, ready to lower the bag to the courtyard, when a movement caught my attention.

Sinchis. The bastards were already in the courtyard. Red berets and all.

Terror swallowed me. Now what? Couldn't go down the stairs. Couldn't go out the back window. Couldn't hide in a neighboring flat either. They'd search every apartment.

The jackhammer started again, but instead of giving me new possibilities, it sounded like a wrecking crew, dismantling my world, destroying my dreams of a life with Marisa. I could just as well have been *Carmen* in the painting, crying, holding a bouquet of wilting flowers.

The phone rang again.

"It's over," said the raspy voice of General Reál. "There's no escape. You're surrounded."

I slumped onto the sofa. "What do you want, General?"

"A talk, Professor, nothing but a friendly chat."

He paused and barked out orders to his men. "Would someone get out there and stop that infernal racket?" When he came back, the jackhammer was still blasting, and he was still shouting. "Remember that deal I offered in Lima? It's still open. All I want is an address. All you have to do is come out with your girlfriend, hands in the air."

It took a moment to absorb the meaning. He thought Marisa was in the apartment.

I slammed down the receiver.

My mouth was dry. I was sweating. Gravity seemed to be tugging at my throat. In desperation I looked at the ceiling, at the dangling chandelier, at the swirls and spirals that some craftsman had put in the finish. At the flaking paint and water stains.

Water stains? Were we on the top floor? If so, there'd almost certainly be an attic.

And if I could get into the attic, I could get onto the roof.

I dashed to the closet, looking for access. Nothing. I looked in the bathroom. Nothing. Nothing in the kitchen either. Well, by God, I'd just have to make an opening.

An engine roared to life, followed by shouts and rough military commands.

I hurried to the balcony doors for a look. A tank was moving past the cathedral, clanking and screeching on its treads, its cannon moving side to side and up and down. Behind it came Sinchis on the double-quick, assault rifles at the ready, officers trotting alongside.

Lieutenant Bravos was there too, shooing away civilians, pointing this way and that.

He waved at someone, and that was when a single bullet crashed through the balcony door, exploding the pane and showering the room with glass.

Down I went, certain I'd been hit, that I was going to draw my last breath right there on the living-room floor next to a trash can. But when I didn't die or feel pain or see blood, I looked around and found nothing but broken glass on my clothes and a neat hole in the trash can.

"Bastards!" I shouted as loud as I could. "You missed."

More bullets tore into the room, shattering the doors, the television, the pre-Columbian relics and gourds on the bookshelves. The soldiers in back joined in the fray, shooting out the kitchen window and blasting holes in the ceiling.

Chunks of plaster fell to the floor. Dust filled the place. Pieces of glass and other debris whizzed about and bounced off the walls, and the worst of it was that they blew *Carmen* off the wall and onto the floor, splintering a corner of the frame.

Sick bastards. *Carmen* was a masterpiece.

In this moment of illogical thinking, I crawled to the painting and slid it across broken glass into the bedroom. I could picture it hanging in the Prado a hundred years from now, next to a Goya, a docent pointing to the bullet holes, saying some poor bastard gringo had been shot to death trying to save *Carmen.*

The shooting stopped. I raced to the bathroom and sprang onto the sink counter.

Portions of plaster had already been shot away, bullet holes everywhere.

I stuck my hand into a hole and pulled down plaster and rat droppings. Insulation too, and the accumulated dust of three hundred years. Once the hole was big enough, I scrambled back to the kitchen and snatched up my bag and rope.

In my fury, I tripped over the kerosene heater and went sprawling amid glass and debris.

The sight of blood on my hands infuriated me even more.

Bastards. They'd be coming any second now. I had to slow them down.

I shoved the sofa against the door. No, that wouldn't stop them. I unscrewed the lid on the heater, doused kerosene on the sofa, put the trash can atop it as well, and set it ablaze.

Now they could add arson to my list of crimes.

A tear gas canister crashed through the French doors and skidded across the floor.

There were footfalls on the stairway, soldiers coming up.

In sudden protest I fired three or four rounds into the door, then grabbed my things, raced through choking fumes back into the bathroom, and climbed into the attic.

CHAPTER THIRTY-SIX

Dust swirled around me, thick as a Lima fog, penetrated here and there by shafts of light from the busted roof tiles. But I was so giddy to be out of that hellhole that I bounded from joist to joist like a cat burglar, climbing over pipes and cables, ducking beneath support beams, comforting myself with the thought that Marisa was alive and well.

Until I came to a brick wall.

A door connected to the other side, but it was one of those heavy colonial things with protrusions and strap-iron hinges—and it was locked. I pounded on it. I kicked. When I realized I wasn't going to get through it, I took a quick inventory of my choices. I could either kick a hole in the ceiling and drop into the flat below, or take my chances on the roof.

The roof, I decided, and crept along a joist until I reached the overhead tiles. I pushed a few of them up and stuck out my head. No Sinchis. Nothing but sky and roof and chimneys.

I tossed my bag and rope onto the roof and crawled out into fresh air and daylight.

A muffled boom shook the building, probably the soldiers blowing the apartment door. I could almost visualize the splintered door, the smoke in the apartment, a SWAT team rushing in with assault rifles and tear gas masks. They'd be in the bathroom in about twenty seconds, and in the attic a few seconds after that. I grabbed my things and took off at a sprint.

Tiles crumpled under my feet. Birds flew off chimneys, shrieking in protest. My lungs felt like fire in the thin mountain air, and although I couldn't see over the peak into the plaza in front, I could hear the shouts, the blaring horns, the tear gas canisters popping like firecrackers.

At last, gasping for air and sweating in spite of the cold, I reached the gable at the far end of the building. The street below was crawling with people and vehicles, probably on their way to see what the fuss was about. No escape there.

I tied the rope to a vent pipe, crept to the ledge, and had a quick look into the rear courtyard. No soldiers. Only jacaranda trees, four or five tables with chairs, and a bubbling fountain. Better yet, the building had balconies. I tossed the free end of the rope over the ledge, drew in a deep breath, and down I went, down and down until I reached the second-floor balcony.

There, I paused for another look, and was about to descend into the courtyard when two women with brooms came out and began sweeping.

Dammit. Now what? The Sinchis were probably already on the roof.

A sliding-glass door on the balcony was partially open. Why not? I thought and burst inside, ready to confront whoever was there with the Glock.

"*Hola,*" I called out. "Anybody home?"

No answer. I closed the sliding door behind me, locked it, and glanced around—unmade bed, suitcases, camera equipment, clothes on the floor. Of course, this was the Hotel Andino, a favorite for foreigners. Denise and I had stayed here years ago, when we were house hunting.

I checked the bathroom. No one there either, but the image I saw in the mirror was covered in dust. I couldn't hit the street looking like I'd crawled out of a flour bin, so I stuck my head under the faucet, toweled off, and made a quick survey of the clothes on the bed.

Yes, a floppy rain hat. I put it on. There too was a rust-colored poncho, the kind Clint Eastwood wore in his spaghetti westerns. I pulled it over my head and stepped into the hallway. No one in sight. No one on the stairway either, or in the lobby. Only a television set noisily broadcasting the drama in the plaza. I pulled my hat a little lower, went out the revolving front door, and stepped into the madness I'd created.

Every branch of every tree was filled with kids. A few daring souls had perched on top of cars. There were old folks on crutches, women in native garb with babes strapped to their backs. Students with backpacks. Foreigners with cameras. Students chanting, "*Viva Gonzalo.*"

The balconies were as crowded as the street. People stared from rooftops and windows.

A fire truck screeched around the corner and packed us even tighter. Behind it came a water cannon and an army truck with soldiers in full riot gear.

At last I managed to get myself off the sidewalk and onto the street, all the better to diminish my height. But no one gave me a glance. I was just another gawker.

"Look," shouted a man beside me.

I followed his gaze to the apartment I'd vacated, from which swirled clouds of black smoke. Firemen in yellow gear were wrestling the burning sofa onto the balcony. They heaved it over the side, and when it hit the street and disintegrated in a cloud of smoke and sparks, the crowd erupted in cheers. The man next to me captured the scene on film, and when I finally broke free and hurried away from the scene, looking for a taxi, I couldn't help but puff myself up a bit.

General Reál was going to be mighty pissed.

CHAPTER THIRTY-SEVEN
Recoleta Cemetery

Marisa, just as she'd promised, was waiting in front of the cemetery, sitting on a stone bench and looking as if she'd just buried her best friend. In her hands was a large bouquet of mixed flowers. She'd been crying and at first didn't recognize me in my poncho and floppy hat.

"Oh my God, oh my God," she said, and flew into my arms. "I thought they'd trapped you."

"It's okay," I said, holding her, wiping away her tears.

I explained what happened. She pulled me through an enormous pair of iron gates and led me into the cemetery, down a tiled walkway flanked with hibiscus and sweet-smelling gardenias. Here and there we came upon other sad-faced visitors, some laying wreaths, others quietly praying over the tomb of a loved one.

Marisa laid her flowers on a tomb for someone named Edith Lagos and then turned to face me. "That apartment was safe," she said, wiping her face. "We've been using it for years. It must have been that jailbird friend of yours from Lurigancho."

She stopped in front of a granite tomb adorned with life-sized angels and saints. Tears welled up in her eyes. She tried to speak, but words wouldn't come out.

"It's okay," I said again. "We're together now. That's all that matters."

"No, Mark. That's what I'm trying to say. We can't stay together."

"But why? We've got money. We can find a place."

A procession of mourners came down the path: old men and women, white-robed children with flowers, a sad-eyed priest and a band with blaring horns, flutes, and muted drums. Marisa led me to a concrete bench beneath the spreading branches of a Royal Poinciana and sat me down. When the procession ended, she placed a hand over mine.

"You're going to hate me."

"For what?"

She stood, ambled around, wiped her face and came back, bringing with her the sweetness of gardenias. "I have to go back to my husband."

It took a moment for the gravity to sink in, and when it did, she might as well have driven a stake through my heart. All I could manage was one word.

"Why?"

She burst into sobs and came into my arms and blurted out something about being sorry, and it couldn't be helped, and she didn't want to hurt me, and it was equally painful for her.

I finally found my voice. "Are you saying it's over between us?"

"It'll never be over between us."

"Then why are you doing this? What's going on? What is it you're not telling me?"

"Please, Mark, we've been through this. You could be captured, taken to Dracula's House. Or I could be captured and tortured. It's best we don't share secrets, not yet, not until we're out of the country." She pressed my hand a little tighter. "Please, I've arranged transportation for you. Just go home. I'll be in touch...and explain. You'll understand."

"When will that be?"

"I don't know."

"Just tell me this. Is it for love you're going back to him?"

"You're the only one I love. Don't you know that by now?"

The darkness in the shadows deepened. Marisa's sobs grew louder, and I held her, not wanting to let go, and didn't until a horn honked on a side street—three times.

"Your ride," she said, and stood.

"Where are they taking me?"

"Cuzco. You'll be safe there."

Time was short. Little sentences contained a lifetime, and the answers to Marisa's secrets lay somewhere down the road. We resumed our slow walk along the path of the dead, clinging to each other as if this were our last dance together.

"Remember what I told you about planning," Marisa said. "No matter where you are, what you're doing, always have an escape route."

She pulled me off the path and lowered her voice. "Abancay," she whispered. "It's the largest town between here and Cuzco. I've got a friend there. It's for Plan C."

She told me how to find the place and made me repeat the directions back to her.

At last we came to a stone wall and a side exit, beyond which waited a white Ford van that for me could have been a funeral hearse. A man wearing a ball cap sat behind the wheel, ready to drive away my lifeless body. The sliding side door was open. Beside it stood a dark-skinned young woman in tight jeans and earth tone sweater.

"That's Ana," Marisa said. "You'll be going with her."

Ana nodded and spoke to me in a thick Quechua accent. "Come on. We have to go."

Marisa reached into a pocket and pulled out a little cloth doll, the kind that came from ancient Inca tombs. "A guardian witch," she said. "It'll keep you safe."

Again she came into my arms, and we held each other with a desperation born of the knowledge we might never see each other again. Then she pulled away.

"Always have a Plan C," she said, and ran down the street.

"*Que triste*," said Ana. "You two must really be in love."

CHAPTER THIRTY-EIGHT

I climbed into the second row of seats and sat there like a zombie. How could this happen? How could Marisa dump me and go back to her dirtbag husband? After all these years of lovemaking and assurances that I was the only one she loved? After I'd lost my job for her, and my reputation, and killed a man and become a fugitive on the run?

The driver gunned the engine and swerved around, making a U-turn that took us up on the tiled sidewalk. At the corner I thought he'd turn left toward Cuzco. Instead, he turned back toward the university.

"Where are we going?" I asked through a haze of tears.

"Another pickup."

Our route took us down the same cobble street where I'd once lived with Denise, the same street where I used to jog when I was a visiting Fulbright professor. As we bounced along its uneven surface, passing beneath tall eucalyptus trees, I felt small and weak. It grew worse when we passed the house with its hydrangeas and bittersweet memories and the number 143. I had failed in my marriage, failed in my career, and now I'd failed with Marisa. I should be angry. Should be cursing and pounding my fists. But it hurt too bad.

God, did it hurt.

When I looked up, we were driving past the university with its red-tile roofs and another bucket of memories. Before I could seize on one, we rounded a corner and pulled up at El Baccará, a restaurant where I'd once lunched with Professor Abimael Guzmán.

Ana lit a cigarette, hopped out, and followed three or four students though open double doors. More students came and went. The smell of spicy food permeated the air. From the inside came the tune of a dreadful *harawi*, and through the open doors, I saw a group of college-looking girls in jeans, sweaters, and ponchos, swaying to the music.

Like Marisa used to do.

Out came Ana with another young woman and an older man. The driver sprang out as if they were important, ran around the van, and slid open the side door. As they climbed into the seat behind me, the man patted me on the shoulder.

"Well, hello, my gringo friend."

I twisted around and looked into his dark face, taking in the white hair, the hawk-shaped nose and wire-rimmed glasses. "Do I know you?"

He coughed, cleared his throat and spoke again, this time in the effeminate voice I'd first heard in my hotel room back in Lima. "They call me Apu Condor."

I stared in disbelief. Was this the same little gay guy who'd issued me the subpoena? The one who'd sat beside me at the hearing? He waved his hand in a circular motion and widened his eyes as if he were a spiritualist gazing into a crystal ball.

"Except for power, everything is an illusion. Maybe I'm the *maricón* you thought I was. Maybe I am the assistant to General Reál. Or maybe I truly am...the Condor in the sky."

Or maybe you're a lunatic, I thought. But before I could say anything, he laid a hand on my shoulder. "What happened to you at the apartment? How did you escape?"

I told him the same story I'd told Marisa, and he came to the same conclusion.

"We have a *suplón* among us," he said, his face distorted by rage. "A mole, a traitor. How else could General Reál have known about that apartment?"

He glared as if to say I was the mole. It grew so quiet, I could hear the rattle of dishes in the restaurant. Then he leaned forward and got so close, I could smell coffee on his breath.

"Tell me, gringo. Do you believe in our cause?"

"All I know is I'm caught up in it."

"That is not the question. Do you understand the motives for our rebellion?"

"I understand your grievances."

"Then you are sympathetic to our cause. No?"

"Your fight is not my fight."

"Listen, gringo. Peru is not Switzerland. Either you are with us, or you are against us."

"Exactly," said the woman beside him. "There is no room in this van for neutrality."

Ana piled on, lecturing me on the evils of Peruvian society—the exploited masses, the bourgeois institutions, the brutality of the Fujimori government. Outrage burst from her mouth in agitated spurts of cigarette smoke. Centuries of oppression floated through the van like ghosts, crying for revenge, and she didn't let up until Condor nodded out the window.

"Look, there he comes."

A young man in a hooded parka came hurrying down the sidewalk, glancing about as if he expected to be captured or shot any second. I noticed the greasy hair and bobbing Adam's apple, but it wasn't until he slid into the seat beside me that I knew for sure.

Luís, a.k.a. Carlos, the escapee from Lurigancho.

CHAPTER THIRTY-NINE
Highway of the Sun

C ondor gave the word to go, and we were soon bouncing along a potholed road that was once the Inca highway, passing army trucks and buses, leaving the sagging tiled roofs of Ayacucho far below. In time the pavement ended, plunging us into the hell of another rutted dirt road.

I leaned back and tried to force myself to accept reality. Back at the apartment with Marisa, I'd been an innocent, a victim of an unjust system. But here in this van full of psychopaths on this cursed road in the Andes, I was just another scared terrorist.

I turned to Luís, who was now sitting beside me. "Should I call you Carlos or Luís?"

"In Lurigancho I was Carlos. Now I am Luís."

"Why the name change?"

"Because we do not use our real names."

"But isn't Luís your real name?"

"No, Maestro. Luís is a Spanish name. My real name is a beautiful Quechua name that I will tell you soon, after the walls of injustice come tumbling down."

Don't hold your breath, I wanted to say, but instead leaned back and watched village after village roll by the closed windows: a blur of mud walls, Runas in native attire, and an occasional church. Once, when we passed a cemetery, I pulled out the little rag witch and stared into its wide eyes. The image of Marisa giving it to me made it all the more precious.

Luís reached down and touched it. "They say the spirits of the dead live inside those things."

"Who told you that?"

"It's common knowledge. Ask anyone. You can also feel the spirits."

All I felt in mine was the mystery of Marisa, so I put it away and spoke to Luís about happier times at the university when he'd been my student. But when I mentioned the wedding I'd attended and asked about his wife, his expression changed to hatred.

"She wants a divorce," he said, spitting out the words. "Imagine that. Here I am, an innocent victim of Fujimori's purge, and what does she do—takes up with a policeman!"

Ana swiveled around. "I hope you killed them."

"Haven't had the chance. Not yet." He went on, telling us he'd already killed three policemen and a Sinchi, and killing another meant nothing to him. There was madness in his face. His dark eyes shone with a yearning for revenge. He was going to get even with that bitch, and get even with the policeman, and the men who'd sent him to prison.

"I'll get them, Maestro, you'll see. They're going to pay."

When Luís finished his story, Ana told hers. Spanish gave way to Quechua, and in a voice shaking with emotion, she said she'd been living in a little village when Shining Path rebels came through and demanded food.

"We shared our food with them. What else could we do? A few days later, the soldiers came and accused my father of providing comfort to the enemy. They shot him. Then they violated my sister, and me, and all the other women. Even my mother. Then they killed all our animals and burned our village to the ground."

In the silence that followed, I could hear mud hitting the underside of the van.

The driver told a similar story. So did the woman in the seat behind me. The air became so contaminated with hatred that a new round began, each uglier than the last. They directed their stories at me as if I didn't believe them, saying I could read about the atrocities in the papers, and in independent studies such as Americas Watch. And they couldn't understand why foreign governments labeled *them* as the terrorists instead of the government in Lima.

My stomach churned. No wonder these people were so angry and sick in the head. And the same could happen to me. Only two weeks in Peru, and I'd already killed a man and could wind up in Lurigancho with all the other lunatics. In another year I could be Luís with the mad eyes and bobbing Adam's apple, raging about how I was going to get even with Marisa.

At dark we stopped to eat in one of those little mud-and-brick villages where pigs roam the streets and old men hobble along babbling to themselves. My comrades devoured the kind of stew my fellow Peace Corps Volunteers used to call UFO's— unidentified floating organs. I had no appetite and ate nothing, and then we were on the road again, twisting and laboring upward, our headlights revealing the loneliest road I'd ever traveled.

Condor tapped me on the shoulder. "What about you, gringo? What is your story?"

"I don't have a story."

"Of course you do. Otherwise, why would Peep and the army be after you?"

"Exactly," said the woman sitting beside him. "You're on the run like the rest of us."

"Look, I killed a Peep agent, but my story is nothing compared to yours."

"Aha," the driver said. "How could you not have a serious story if you killed a Peep agent?"

"It was self-defense. Besides, I didn't exactly kill him. He died of a stroke."

This brought such a howl of laughter that I felt my face growing warm. When it died down, Condor patted me on the back and said it was another victory for the people.

Luís rationalized the killing as if it were a golden rule: "Those to whom evil is intended should do evil first."

Ana reached for her bottle of Inca Kola and twisted around to face me. "To you, gringo, I drink a toast. May you kill more of the bastards before they kill you."

This was not the kind of toast I could drink to, and I was still squirming in my seat when we rounded a hill and came upon a series of flashing lights. Then, like the menacing monster of a nightmare, an army checkpoint rose out of the darkness.

CHAPTER FORTY

O ut came pistols and AKs. I took out my Glock and chambered a cartridge the way I'd seen it done in movies.
Condor told us not to fire until he gave the word, and in that
panic-stricken moment, I imagined my dean in Tampa, sitting
in his office with his mug of coffee, looking at a picture of my
bullet-riddled body on the front page of the *St. Pete Times,* saying, "Poor Mark, who would ever believe he was so fucked up?"

A helmeted guard with a flashlight waved us into a graveled
lot. Other soldiers stood back in the shadows.

"Turn off the engine," commanded the guard. He took
a clipboard from a wooden box, noted our tag number and
stepped to the driver's window. "Destination?"

"Cuzco," answered the driver. "My wife has cancer. I'm taking her to a specialist."

"Cuzco has many specialists."

"Our specialist is the best."

He shone his light into the van and let it play over all six of
us. "How many in the van?"

"Two. Just me and my wife."

He made a notation, then handed the clipboard through
the window. "Sign, please."

The driver signed, placed a wad of money beneath the clip, and handed it back.

The guard said, "Have a nice trip," and then we were back on the road.

I drew in a sharp breath. "What was that about?"

Condor laughed. "Welcome to the world of code talk, gringo. If he cooperates, he earns half his monthly income. Don't cooperate and he dies. It's as simple as that."

We stopped for the night in the ruins of an old Inca *tampu*— a relay station for the empire's runners—now only three walls and a pile of broken stones. The air was cold and dry. The Milky Way stretched to the horizon. The Southern Cross had never been brighter, and as I sat there in the rubble with my fellow travelers, shivering, my breath misting in the thin air, wishing I'd worn heavier clothing, I again wondered how hope had so quickly turned to despair.

Why hadn't I just stayed in Florida?

The driver pulled sleeping bags from the van and passed them around. Condor built a fire. Everyone gathered around, faces all aglow, cigarettes burning, and for a moment I thought they'd start relating their awful stories again. Instead, Condor gave a little lecture on Inca relay stations, saying they were like the Pony Express, except with human runners. He told us that Inca warriors had fought Pizarro on this very spot, and the place was haunted.

"They come to you in your dreams," he said, lowering his voice to a whisper.

It grew quiet. The flames crackled. Condor went on, saying the Incas had possessed special powers that enabled them to build mystic places like fortress Sacsahuaman and Machu Picchu, and that all Inca ruins were possessed with magic.

"He's right," hissed the young woman whose name I didn't know. "There's this ruins near my hometown. At night you can see strange lights...and hear screams."

By then Ana's eyes were so wide I could see the whites. "I don't want to stay here," she said, her voice breaking. "Let's go someplace else to spend the night."

"No, no, it's okay," Condor said. "They won't bother you if you toss a stone against the wall."

Ana found a piece of broken rubble and flung it against the wall. It struck with a loud thunk. The others did the same, each trying to outdo the other in the force of the throw. I also threw a stone, as much out of frustration as to keep spirits out of my dreams. When it was Condor's turn, he picked up a stone about the size of an apple, threw it...and it disappeared.

"How did you do that?" asked Ana.

"My Inca friend over there. He caught it."

Everyone twisted around as if an Inca warrior actually stood there. Condor tossed another rock that disappeared, and yet another. His stories of Inca magic resumed—lights in the sky, special powers, old gods he could summon—and by the time I crawled into my smelly sleeping bag and zipped up, he was talking about extraterrestrials.

Wind whistled through the ruins. I heard voices, footsteps, the wail of a flute, a woman crying. And then Gordo the Peep agent shook me awake.

The same Gordo I'd killed.

His face had turned green with decay. In his hands were the cuffs I'd taken from him.

"It's over," he snarled. "Now you'll have to come with me."

"But I threw a stone against the wall. It was supposed to protect me."

"I caught the stone." He held it up for me to see.

"Where are you taking me?"

"Abancay. Wasn't that your Plan C? They're waiting for you."

"Who is waiting?"

"Francisco de la Vega. He's going to paint you while you watch your little slut fucking all his friends. Then he'll slit your throat and paint that too."

He reached down to put the cuffs on my hands, and in the kind of logic that made sense only in dreams, the cuffs turned into a green parrot, and the parrot spoke.

"Come on, gringo. Time to go."

I bounded up, my heart racing. It was daybreak. I was still in my sleeping bag, and the driver was standing over me.

"Come on, gringo. Time to go."

We drank coffee that Condor prepared, munched on bread and cheese, said nothing about our dreams, and were soon bouncing and twisting along the road again.

Dust seeped into the van from the rear, mixing with cigarette smoke. My stomach hurt. The dream lingered in my head like the rancid aftertaste of a bad meal. And then I saw a road sign for Abancay, only thirty-four kilometers ahead, Marisa's Plan C.

Before the dream I'd pictured a safe house in a little town no one had ever heard of, a house with a garden and flowers. A place to rest and wait out the storm. Now I imagined an art studio with easels, canvas and paint, and an evil little bearded man with a smock.

Condor leaned over the seat. "Slow down," he said to the driver. "It's just ahead."

The driver slowed. We passed a cluster of large boulders and turned left onto a narrow trail, and just like that, Abancay with its mysteries dissolved in the dust behind us.

"I thought we were going to Cuzco," I said.

"Cuzco is like Rome," Condor answered. "Eternal. It'll wait for us."

The trail took us down through the clouds. It grew warmer. Plants turned greener. A ditch that had started as runoff swelled into a stream and then a river.

"Almost there," said Condor.

An uneasy feeling came over me. What on earth was down here, on a dirt trail in the middle of a forest, many miles off the main road? The girls took out makeup kits and began applying lipstick and brushing their hair as if they were going on a date. We wound around a creeper-covered rise of boulders, headed into a dense tree line, and stopped.

Barking dogs rushed out. Heads popped up. A dark-skinned man with binoculars scrambled down from the boulders and motioned us into a parking spot, waving his arms and yelling like an angry traffic cop.

"Be careful of that one," Condor said. "He just busted out of Lurigancho."

"Oh shit," Luís muttered beside me. "It's Tucno."

CHAPTER FORTY-ONE
Camp Pachacuti

A mob of teenage-looking kids emerged from the brush, the guys in jeans and earth-tone ponchos, the girls sauntering along arm in arm, some carrying assault rifles. Introductions followed, and then I became the object of attention, a tall, light-skinned gringo in a sea of dark children of the Andes.

Even a dog came over and sniffed me.

Tucno kicked the dog and got so close, I could smell him. He was dirtier and more fierce looking than I remembered, with bad teeth, scars on his face, a headband around his long greasy hair, and an enormous knife stuffed into a cartridge belt.

"Why is this gringo here?"

"He's with me," Condor said.

Tucno spat on the ground and stalked away.

Matches flared, cigarettes burned. More vans and pickups arrived, with more volunteers and more dogs. Back in Lima, I had pictured the terrorists as shaven-head evildoers who looked like Tucno. But here I saw only skinny kids in dirty jeans and ball caps, sipping Inca Kolas with a straw, munching chocolate bars, smoking cigarettes, and checking out newcomers as if they were hanging out in a mall. A few of the girls were pretty, and I wondered if any of them had ever posed for Francisco de la Vega. Or if Carmen and Carla were in the crowd.

Tucno blew a whistle and formed them into orderly lines of ten. Slump-shouldered teenagers were told to stand straight. Pimple-faced girls were pushed from this line to that one. A beefy man who looked a lot like Chairman Gonzalo stepped forward and made a welcoming speech.

I stared at him. Could it be the leader himself?

"They call me the Engineer," he said in Spanish, his voice cutting through the air. "Welcome to Camp Pachacuti. How many of you have read Mao?"

A few hands shot up.

"Here is what Mao teaches you—you must not swagger, you must not identify yourself as a guerrilla. You must meld into the population as fish swim with other fish in the sea. Under no circumstances are you to get drunk or consume drugs or brag. Do you understand?"

"*Sí*," they answered as one.

"You are never to use your real name. You do not ask questions of others. It's best for all if you know nothing, see nothing, hear nothing. Do you understand?"

"*Sí*, Comrade Engineer."

"Louder. I want the mountains to shake with your ardor. I want our enemies to tremble."

The shouting and lectures went on. Team leaders were introduced, after which Tucno, Condor, and the Engineer marched each line to a training station.

Then someone touched me on the shoulder. "Comrade Marco?"

I turned and looked into the face of a thirty-something woman in boots and green army fatigues. In the brim of her cap was a pink wild flower. She was dark and thin, with a gold-capped tooth and a nose like an eagle, pretty in a Runa sort of way.

"I'm Faviola," she said, and thrust an AK-47 into my hands.

"What is this for?"

"To kill Sinchis."

"Are we expecting Sinchis?"

"They don't announce their plans in advance."

In a girlish voice, she explained how to pop in the magazine and slide back the lever to chamber a round. From her demeanor, enunciation, and grammar, she was clearly a cut above the common order—like Condor—and I was wondering what motivated a woman like her to join this bunch when she hung an Inca Kola bottle on a bush limb and told me to shoot it.

"Go ahead," she said. "You need to practice. Just in case. I'll take notes."

I took aim, pulled the trigger, and destroyed the bottle and the bush.

"No, no, gringo. Easy on the trigger. Press it slowly, gently, like you'd touch a woman if you were making love. One short burst will do." She hung another bottle on a bush.

"Do I have to do this? I don't need a weapons expert to show me how to shoot."

She took off her cap and brushed back her frizzy hair. "I'm not a weapons expert. I'm a journalist, the PR rep for our movement."

"Why does the Shining Path need a PR rep?"

"Haven't you seen the Lima-controlled TV? The papers? They depict us as savages—Communists in the mountains, terrorists in the pueblos. Someone has to tell the truth."

It probably wasn't the moment to tell her the rebels were in fact Communists in the mountains and terrorists in the pueblos. So I listened to her rant and pretended to sympathize, after which I asked if her name was really Faviola.

"You heard Engineer. We're not supposed to talk about ourselves."

"But that's not fair. You know all about me."

"How could I not know about you? Your face is all over the newspapers. And on TV."

169

"Were you a school teacher? A university professor?"

"Stop it, gringo. I'm a ghost. I don't exist."

I shrugged. She managed a smile, brushed back a lock of hair the way women do, and then showed me around the camp as if we were in a James Bond movie. Here an instructor was teaching hand-to-hand combat. There a woman was talking about explosives, and yet another was lecturing on what it meant to be poor and dark-skinned.

"We look around and see the great ruins of our ancestors," she said. "We read Garcilaso and Mariátegui and learn that our system was infinitely superior to what the Europeans brought. And yet the cretins in Lima look upon us as *Indios,* lower than rabid dogs."

Faviola raised a clenched fist and shouted, "*Pachacuti!*"

"*Pachacuti,*" they all answered back.

A neighboring team took up the chant. It spread to the next team and the next, and by the time we got back to the hill where Condor was waiting, the ground itself seemed to be shaking.

Condor placed an arm around my back. "What do you think, Comrade Marco?"

"I think they're devoted to the cause."

"What about you? How do you feel?"

"I understand why these young people are disillusioned by the system."

Faviola yanked a notepad from her pocket and began jotting down my words as if I'd said something profound, mumbling as she wrote, "Comrade Marco is clearly sympathetic to our cause. His observation is that—"

"No, no," I said. "Hold on. That's not what I meant. I'm in enough trouble."

She looked up. "What exactly would you like me to write?"

"I don't want you to write anything about me. I was never here."

She slapped her pad shut and stalked away, and as she disappeared into the foliage, Condor wagged a finger. "Anger not a journalist with a pen and notepad."

The teams rotated, the hours passed, and when I could stand it no longer, I sank to the ground against a tree. A sad-eyed little mutt cuddled up beside me and rolled over, showing her lactating teats and a few fleas. I rubbed her stomach.

"Where are your puppies?" I said. "You're as sad as I am."

She looked at me with those big eyes as if to say they were all gone, and that was when I heard the voice of Tucno, talking to Engineer. Though I couldn't hear all their words, I heard enough to know they were discussing an attack on an army outpost.

"What about the *gringu?*" Tucno asked, using the Quechua word for gringo.

"Why not make him part of the plan? We could use him for propaganda. I'll get Faviola to take a picture of him—posing in black beret."

I sat straight up. No way in hell was I going to become the Patty Hearst of the Shining Path. Better to swim the river and trek to the safe house in Abancay. Yes, why not? I could do it now, while they were dreaming their delusional dreams.

I shouldered my AK and pushed through the undergrowth toward the river, passing beneath willows and eucalyptus, the sad-eyed mutt trotting behind. Birds fluttered out of the bush. The roar of the river became so loud, I could no longer hear gunshots or commands of the instructors.

The AK grew heavier. My anger increased with every stumble, every mosquito bite, and tangle of creepers. How dare these lunatics make me part of their plan? Me, a university professor whose only desire was to take Marisa home and live a peaceful life.

Well, by God, it was time to take charge of my own destiny. To hell with Tucno and Condor and the Engineer.

I slid down a mossy embankment, fought my way through another tangle of foliage—and groaned at the sight of the river.

What had started as a trickle in the mountains now crashed down like Niagara Falls, a raging torrent of mineral-green water that no white-water enthusiast would attempt.

I was stuck. There'd be no escape, at least not by the river.

CHAPTER FORTY-TWO

I sank onto a wet boulder and tried to compose myself. Back in Florida, this place would be a tourist attraction for northerners, with uniformed guides pointing out the dangling moss, the little blue flowers that grew out of tree bark, the spiked bromeliads, and the mist thrown up by churning water. But here it was nothing but a cursed river next to a cursed forest that was home to terrorists and a large green parrot that fluttered down to a tree limb beside me.

A parrot? What the hell was a parrot doing here?

It just sat there, fearless, like a family pet, as if I'd summoned it with my rage, and it didn't move, even when Faviola pushed through the brush with a camera dangling from her neck, looking this way and that.

"Gringo," she yelled above the roar of the river.

"Gringo," squawked the parrot, and flew away.

I jumped up. Did that damn parrot just speak? A parrot in the wild?

Faviola motioned me away from the noise, so I hitched up my AK and followed her back up the incline, through a tangle of forest and creepers until we were at a place we could speak. Not until then did I notice she'd prettied herself up with a touch of lipstick, hoop earrings, a crimson ribbon around her neck, and even nail polish. She'd also put on a dash of perfume, something that smelled like honeysuckle.

"I'm supposed to take your picture," she said in an uncertain voice.

"I don't want my picture taken."

"It's not what you want; it's what *they* want. You'll also need a beret and military shirt."

"For what?"

"To enhance your image. Give you that Che Guevara mysticism."

"You've got to be kidding."

"I'm not happy about it either, but we've got to follow orders."

"Are they also going to call me Che Marco?"

She rolled her eyes. "Please, comrade, I'm only doing my job."

"You're from Ayacucho. Right? I've heard that accent before. I bet you went to school at the same university where I used to teach. Am I right?"

She turned and hurried away, and I returned to camp in time to see Tucno marching back and forth in front of his warriors like a marine sergeant, kicking up dust with his feet.

By then they all wore new fatigue caps and army shirts. Some wore handkerchiefs over mouths and noses like bandits in an old Western, and the skinnier ones looked like kids prancing around in their daddies' clothing.

Tucno said Sinchis could attack at any moment. In that event we were to split into three groups, which he designated as red, black, and blue. His assistants brought out baskets of bandannas corresponding to the three colors and passed them around. Flags were staked. The groups separated by colors. Tucno said we were to practice by charging the ridge behind him.

He leveled a thick finger at me. "You, *gringu*, over there. Group Red."

Someone handed me a bandanna, which I grudgingly tied on and fell in with Group Red. A few minutes later, with Condor looking on, with Faviola watching from the side with her note pad and camera, Tucno consulted his watch, then raised a flag and dropped it.

"Attack! Go! Go! Go!"

Whistles blew. Everyone bolted, and as I dashed up the hill with my fellow terrorists, stumbling, tripping, cursing, stirring up a suffocating cloud of dust, I understood why armies were made up of young people instead of thirty-three-year-old professors.

We did it again and again. Up that damn hill until I thought I'd collapse. Take cover. Lock and load. Aim. Then it was back down, wipe off the dust, take a swig of water, and attack again. What was Marisa thinking when she sent me away with these lunatics? Surely she didn't know.

Or maybe she did, and that was the frightening part.

The sun sank at last, bringing out first stars and unfamiliar sounds, and when we finally broke for dinner, I could have cried in gratitude. Coolers and corn *chicha* appeared. Fires were made. Meats and peppers and onions went onto skewers, and the whole camp took on the pleasant smells of cooking and burning oak. I still wasn't hungry, not after what happened with Marisa, but I forced myself to eat a boiled egg, some goat cheese, and a shish kabob.

All around was talk of victory. Public sentiment was shifting in their favor. The government was on the verge of collapse. The Shining Path would soon be marching down La Colmena like Castro had marched into Havana, their hammer and sickle banners flying.

"We'll rename the palace," shouted an adolescent voice, "call it Palacio Gonzalo."

"No," said someone else. "It should be Palacio Libre."

The discussion went on and on. Logic evaporated in the smoke, and pretty soon it sounded like that campfire scene from *Blazing Saddles*. Puppy Sad Eyes came up beside me, drooling. I gave her a few scraps, then leaned back and tried to picture Marisa sitting with us beneath the trees, gnawing on a chicken bone, drinking *chicha* from a fruit jar, cradling an AK-47 and talking about how to arm a bomb. But the image didn't fit. Marisa was roses and candlelight, wine and French lace, the rustle of silk on a warm summer night.

Stabbing a knife into my heart.

A whistle blew, followed by the order to extinguish fires. Everyone groaned and protested, but this brought out Tucno.

"What is wrong with you people? Don't you realize Sinchis have spotter airplanes? How would you like napalm for dessert?"

Fires were put out. Temperature plummeted. I hiked to the van for my hat and poncho, and returned in time to hear a flautist playing the shepherd's tune for piping in the flock, an epic tune that went back to Inca times. The final notes lingered like the smell of burning wood, and when I settled back in my place, I saw these young rebels as no different from soldiers anywhere else—frightened, exhausted, uncertain, and lonely, thinking of home and loved ones.

Sad Eyes, her stomach now swollen, curled up beside me. Then Faviola sat down and touched my arm, bringing with her the sweetness of honeysuckle. In the dim light of a rising quarter moon, I could see her fatigue cap pushed back on her head, her wild hair sticking out.

She handed me a beret. "We're still looking for a shirt big enough for you."

"What's wrong with my poncho and hat?"

"Not very military looking. You'll also need an ammunition belt."

"Can't you just tell them I'm a commissar, in the civilian wing of the party?"

I wasn't sure what a commissar was, but it sounded important. Faviola must have thought so too, because she went silent, and then I felt like a jerk for giving her such a hard time.

"Look," I said, "I know you're only doing your job, but I'm in enough trouble already."

"I still have to take your picture."

"Don't I have a choice in the matter?"

"You can always take it up with Tucno. Aren't you and Chairman Gonzalo good friends?"

"Who told you that?"

"It's common knowledge. Everyone's talking about it."

There was awe in her voice. It grew quiet enough to hear the cooing of the night birds. I couldn't so much see the stares as feel them, and I was fumbling for an answer when Luís ambled out of the shadows, thumping his chest.

"I'm the one who introduced them."

The lie glittered like a fake Rolex, but it didn't matter. No longer was I the *gringo*; I was Comrade Marco, a close disciple of the messiah. And I might have embellished the lie except that a whistle blew, followed by the dreaded voice of Tucno.

"Fall in!"

Groaning, stiff from the cold, I took my rifle and fell in like the soldier I was, a good head taller than the shivering kids around me. Tucno's voice cut through the darkness.

"Listen up, Comrades. Have you sworn your allegiance to the cause?"

"*Sí, Camarada Tucno.*"

"What is the punishment for desertion?"

"Death, Comrade Tucno."

That wasn't what I wanted to hear, but since I'd not taken an oath, I assumed it didn't apply to me. Or did it? What if I'd managed to cross that river and they'd caught me?

A match flared beside me—a young woman cupping a hand around her mouth to light a cigarette. Tucno lunged through the lines like an attack dog.

"Are you stupid? Don't you know a burning cigarette can be seen from a kilometer away?"

He slapped the cigarette from her mouth and kept yelling until the poor girl was in tears. I wanted to smash in his ugly face, but that didn't seem practical in a camp he commanded, so I turned up my collar and tuned out his foulness.

My stomach churned. I was cold, so I broke ranks, hurried to the van for a blanket, leaned the AK against the fender, and opened the door.

The interior lights came on.

Oh shit. Who would have thought in this rattletrap of a van that the lights would work?

I closed the door and tried to slip away, but it was too late. There stood Tucno as if he'd swung down from a tree, his breath blowing white. He shoved me against the van.

"Didn't you hear me, *gringu?* Do you have a hearing problem?"

His face seemed satanic in the darkness, and he had the smell of a man who hadn't bathed or brushed his teeth for a long time. He jabbed a finger in my chest.

"You might have friends in high places, but I'm the one running this camp. Understand?"

"Yes, Comrade Tucno."

"If you need anything, you ask me, even if it's only to take a piss. Is that clear, *gringu?*" Again he jabbed that damn finger into my chest. "I asked you a question."

I shoved him backward. "Get your fucking hands off me."

I couldn't see his expression in the darkness, only his shadowy bulk, and I don't know what would have happened if it hadn't been for the alert sounded by the lookout on the hill.

"Headlights! They're coming fast."

CHAPTER FORTY-THREE

Whistles blew. Tucno darted away. Men and women came crashing out of the woods with their weapons. I stumbled up the hill with my assault rifle and dove into my pre-assigned position.

"Lock and load," Tucno cried.

From all around came the clack and slide of metal against metal.

"Do not fire unless I give the order! Understand?"

"*Sí, Camarada Tucno.*"

Three pairs of headlights came speeding down the mountain, twisting this way and that, sometimes disappearing behind foliage. Dogs barked. Commands rang out to hold fire. I touched the little witch in my pocket and again asked myself how it could come to this. Why would a respected university professor, wannabe poet, and dean designate be lying in a foxhole with a bunch of teenage terrorists in Peru? Holding a rag witch for protection.

And the answer was simple—Marisa.

Faviola crawled up beside me, bringing with her a pleasant, feminine smell.

"I've never shot anyone," she said, her voice breaking. "Never been in a battle."

I put an arm around her. "It's okay, Faviola. We're safe on this ridge. If they attack, we can always escape into the forest behind us. Just stay with me."

"But what if they send airplanes? You heard Tucno. They could napalm us."

I pulled her a little tighter, as much to comfort myself as her. "Listen, Faviola, you shouldn't be out here, not with your talents. You should be back at the university."

"What about you? Why are you here?"

"Circumstances, not by choice."

They were upon us now—SUVs and vans rather than army trucks. Faviola relaxed. The vehicles bumped around the hill and stopped. Lights went out. A horn tooted three times.

Tucno's thick voice cut through the silence. "Stand at ease."

The orders were repeated from Group Red to Blue to Black, and soon we were climbing out of our hiding places and peering into the darkness, Faviola at my side like a child.

Tucno ordered us to wait in our positions, then he, Condor, and Engineer trekked down the hill. I heard voices from the vehicles, the squawk of a CB, and then it was Tucno again.

"*Gringu.* Get down here on the double-quick. Someone wants to see you."

I half ran, half stumbled down the hill in the darkness, wondering who wanted to see me, hoping it was Marisa, but knowing it wasn't. Faviola trotted behind like the journalist she was, as if she could smell a story. As we neared the SUVs, someone grabbed my arm. It was too dark to make out the face, but I recognized Condor's voice.

"Hold on, gringo. They just want to see you."

"Who wants to see me?"

"Haven't you learned anything by now? You ask no questions, see nothing, hear nothing."

He guided me to the side of the lead vehicle, near a back window on the driver's side. In the pale moonlight, it looked like a Cherokee, the same as Lannie's, except black. The engine was running, its exhaust polluting the air. I squinted, trying to see inside, but it was too dark.

Then a light flashed on beside me—Tucno with a flashlight. He who didn't want light.

"Turn sideways," he ordered in his nasty way of speaking.

I obeyed, blinking back the glare.

"Face the window."

"Which window?"

He grabbed my arm and pushed me to within inches of the rear window, and I stood there like a blindfolded slave at an auction, waiting for someone to buy me.

"Smile," Tucno ordered.

"You smile," I shot back, knowing he wouldn't dare rough me up in front of whoever was in that Cherokee. The scene was so bizarre that it reminded me of an old horror movie I'd once seen in which an automobile had taken on a life of its own—an evil black automobile without a driver, the low throaty growl of an engine, a faceless entity sizing up its victim for the kill.

Tucno switched off his light. Condor ordered me to step back. He engaged someone inside the SUV in conversation. The engine roared. The Cherokee made a U-turn and drove away. The other vehicles followed, their exhausts a cloud of white confusion in the air.

"Get your things," Condor said. "You're leaving. Better grab a sleeping bag too."

CHAPTER FORTY-FOUR

I knew better than to ask, so I rushed to our van a second time, lit it up in spite of Tucno, grabbed my things, and hurried back to Condor. Word of my departure had spread, and it seemed as if half the camp wanted to see me off. There were handshakes, slaps on the back, and well wishes. Until then, I hadn't realized I was so popular.

Faviola kissed me on both my unshaven cheeks. "We'll miss you," she said.

I squeezed her arm and was trying to think of an appropriate response when Tucno appeared beside me. "Let me tell you something," he growled, getting in my face again with his stinky breath. "You saw nothing at this place. You were never here. Understand?"

"*Si, Camarada Tucno.*"

"If I ever read about it in the papers, or in a book, or see it on television, then mark my word, I'll come after you with this knife." He slapped his hand against the scabbard.

I opened my mouth to say he'd better bring an army, but thought better of it. Luís took my shoulder bag. Condor told me to follow. I hitched up my AK, and as we tromped out of camp, passing beneath overhanging limbs, Sad Eyes at my feet, I thanked the river for being too dangerous to cross. I thanked whoever was in that black Cherokee. I thanked the little rag witch in my pocket. And I thanked God that Tucno hadn't pulled out that damn knife.

At first the trail followed the river, but in time it angled away. A cold, penetrating wind blew down from the mountain. The trail grew steeper. We trudged along for at least a half hour, maybe more, and my legs were growing weary when Condor said, "I can smell it."

I smelled it too, a rich mixture of barnyard droppings, hog wallow, and fireplace smoke.

Presently, we came to the kind of one-room, dirt-floor, adobe-and-stone shack that served as home to Runas. The only hint of occupancy was a faint glow around the shuttered windows. Behind it, in the pale light of a bottom-heavy quarter moon, stood a clump of trees where I guessed they'd hidden the vehicles. Out came a guard draped in so many blankets, he could have been an ox. Condor spoke to him in Quechua, then laid a hand on my arm and lowered his voice.

"Remember what I told you yesterday in the van?"

"You told me many things."

"Yes, but one thing I want you to remember—except for power, everything is an illusion."

Some illusion, I thought, standing beneath the stars on this godless trail with an assault rifle over my shoulder and my breath misting in the night air and a houseful of terrorists behind me.

But before I could comment, Condor laughed, slapped me on the shoulder, and faded into the night. Luís handed over my shoulder bag, gave me a limp handshake, and trotted after him, leaving me alone with the ox and my illusion.

"Leave your guns outside," said the ox in a rough voice, speaking in Quechua.

I handed him my AK and the Glock, but he frisked me anyway, pulled out my Swiss Army knife, and flashed a small pen light on it.

"We're not the airlines," he said, and handed it back.

I pocketed the knife and followed him up to the shack, our footfalls crunching on gravel. The front door was closed, but rays of light pierced the cracks. From the inside came laughter, the smell of food, and the buzz of conversation. Ox slumped into a chair beneath a little overhang and adjusted his blankets around him.

"They're eating," he grumbled. "You'll have to wait."

That was fine with me. My stomach was in turmoil. I was nauseated. I unrolled my sleeping bag and draped it over my shoulders. Animals snorted down by the barn. A meteor streaked the sky. The squawk of a nocturnal bird seemed to signal trouble, and the smell of greasy food was doing to my stomach what Condor's words had done to my head. I tried to will away the rising nausea, but those boiled eggs wanted to come up, so I bolted into the darkness.

It all came out, a purge of bad food and bad scenes that left me clutching my stomach and cursing my luck. Damn Marisa anyway. What was she thinking?

I stayed on my knees until I felt better, then struggled up, cleaned myself at the hand pump, and crunched back to the cabin in time to see four or five guards passing around binoculars.

"We'd better report this to Paco," said one of them.

"Report what?" I asked.

"A light. Didn't you see it?"

I didn't, but climbed atop a boulder for a look. There were no lights or airplanes that I could see, only an ice-capped mountain, the quarter moon, the Southern Cross, and a mass of steadily burning stars receding into space.

The front door opened. Out came a woman pulling a poncho over her head, bringing with her the smells of a wood fire and perfume. She was different from the other women I'd seen: older, whiter, and better dressed. She glanced at me and hurried into the darkness. Two men also came out and fell into a discussion with the guards about the light.

"Send him in," said a gruff voice from the inside.

I stepped into the hut and closed the door. Lamps hung from the rafters. A sinfully warm fire blazed in the fireplace, and the walls were decorated with the same kind of Jesus and Mary prints I'd seen in other peasant shacks, all swirling clouds, halos and celestial light. On a rough wooden table were wine bottles, plates, used napkins, and a pile of rib bones.

The man who sat there was dressed in rumpled army fatigues, grinning at me. Could it really be Him, the most-wanted man in Peru, or was it Engineer? In the dim light, I couldn't be certain. In the three or four years since I'd seen him at the university, he'd put on a few pounds. A week ago I'd have been shocked to see him; now I was beyond shock.

He came to his feet and thrust out a thick hand. "My God," he said in a familiar booming voice. "What have they done to you? You look like hell."

I took his hand and shook it. "Good to see you too, Professor."

CHAPTER FORTY-FIVE

Chairman Gonzalo—if it was really him—motioned me into a chair and poured me a glass of red wine. "There's a rumor going around that I'm dead. Do I look dead to you?"

I looked into his beefy face, taking in the bushy eyebrows, the hair that was streaked with gray and combed straight back, the furrowed brow that was just as prominent as the day I'd met him three or four years ago. "You look better than I do."

"My dog looks better than you, Marco, but that's not the point. Point is these rumors have a way of sapping life out of a movement. It's part of the government's misinformation campaign. That's why I'm here—to show my face. Prove I'm alive. There'll be photographs. I'd like to include you in them as well, get you standing next to me with an AK."

I suppressed a groan. "Is that necessary? I'm in enough trouble already."

He burst into laughter. "Trouble? You killed a Peep agent. You made General Reál look like a bumbling fool. If they catch you, they'll shoot you anyway." He leaned forward in his chair. "Besides, it isn't every day I get a chance to be photographed with Romeo."

"What is that supposed to mean?"

He reached beneath the table, picked up an Ayacucho newspaper, pointed to a headline that read: ROMEO ESCAPES

AGAIN, and handed it to me. The front page, in typical Latin overkill, was devoted to the commotion I'd created in Ayacucho. It even had a photograph of General Reál standing amid the crowd on the sidewalk with hands on hips, his face a picture of rage, staring at the smoking sofa as if wishing it were my charred corpse.

"Not there," he said. "It's in the inside." He took the paper and shook it open. "They published excerpts of your poetry—even had it critiqued by an art professor, one of those butter-flies from the university. It's a good review. Here, I'll read it to you."

He put on a pair of thick eyeglasses and read it aloud.

"'Lily of Peru' is a love dance, a song, a cry in the darkness, the despair of love catching the scent of death. It even evokes the same passions as Shakespeare's *Romeo and Juliet*: Romeo fleeing the city of Verona because he killed for love. Romeo visiting the apothecary for his vial of poison, except in the pro-fessor's case, he visits the altar of revolutionaries. Venom by any other name is still just as deadly."

He put down the paper and pointed to the shuttered win-dow like an actor doing Shakespeare in the Park. "'What light through yonder window breaks? / It is the east, and Juliet is the sun.'"

His eyes blazed. "My God, Professor. Shakespeare? Romeo? And they call me the Fourth Sword of Marxism. But you, Marco, you're...Romeo."

No, I thought, I was a loser, the guy Juliet had dumped.

He stood, threw another log on the fire, and kicked it a couple times to get it going. "One thing I learned long ago," he said, warming his hands at the fire, "you can take the measure of a man by his dreams. You want Juliet; I want Peru."

He turned around, picked up his goblet, and clinked it against mine. "To Juliet and Peru."

"To Juliet and Peru," I answered, almost choking on the words.

He dragged up a chair and sat beside me. "Tomorrow, after the photo session, I'll be going one way; you'll be going the other. I'm sending you with Paco. He'll help you escape."

"Why are you helping me?"

"Isn't it obvious? You're Romeo. Your mystique is getting bigger every day. The press is romanticizing you. Even people who don't like us are pulling for you. Secretly, of course. But if you come to a bad ending, it'll reflect poorly on us. On the other hand, if we get you out of the country, alive, it'll be a great victory. We, the Shining Path, will have done something noble. We saved Romeo. And you, my gringo friend, will be a hero."

I stared at this man whose face was on wanted posters all over Peru. Didn't he understand how I'd be crucified in the States, labeled a commie, a pinko, a traitor, a criminal?

"Hey, don't look so depressed," he said. "You can always get a job at Berkeley."

He laughed. We drank and chatted about mutual acquaintances and slapped each other on the back like a couple of old buddies, and when we'd grown mellow with the effects of wine, I said, "Listen, comrade, there's a question I have to ask."

"Ask it, Marco."

I stood and walked to the fireplace. "It's about, well, Marisa. They're saying her things were found at your place. How did that happen?"

"Didn't she tell you?"

"We haven't had enough time together to—"

There was a knock at the door. Gonzalo—if it really was him—stood, went outside to speak with someone, then came back and grabbed his shoulder bag.

"Business. I have to run." He shook my hand and went out the door.

I sat there, not knowing what to do next, and was thinking of going outside when Engineer marched in, he who could pass for Comrade Gonzalo. The only difference was the clothing.

"Are you two related?" I asked.

He poured himself a glass of wine and took a long drink. "It helps to have a body double, doesn't it? Lots of famous men had a stand-in. Stalin. Churchill, all those Arab tyrants. Besides, for all you know, I could be the real Chairman Gonzalo."

I stared into his beefy face. "Maybe neither of you are Chairman Gonzalo. Maybe you're both imposters. Or maybe the two of you are the same person, like Clark Kent and Superman."

He roared with laughter. I laughed too, and was reaching for my glass when Engineer held up a hand. "Listen, what's that?"

From the front came what sounded like a scuffle, then a thud as if a body had fallen against the door. A dog barked. Then someone ran around the cabin, someone in a hell of a hurry.

Engineer grabbed an AK and was chambering a round when the front door burst open and in rushed two of the men I'd seen earlier.

"Sinchis," one of them cried. "They got Flaco."

Lights were doused. Paco splashed a bucket of water on the fire. It spit and steamed.

Engineer eased open the rear shutters. "Raúl. Are you out there? Héctor. Answer me."

No one answered. There were no sounds, not even from the animals down by the barn.

Engineer stormed around the room, muttering and cursing. "Dammit, Paco, didn't you tell me this place was safe? You said we had a secure exit. What is going on?"

"I don't know, Engineer. We had five men out back. Someone must have betrayed us."

I felt them staring at me.

"It wasn't me," I said like a child. "I don't even know where we are."

Engineer peeked out the window. I crept up beside him but saw only the darkness, the stars, and the outline of a forest that loomed up in back.

"How far are those woods, Paco?"

"Thirty, maybe forty meters."

"You go first," Engineer said. "We'll cover you. When you get there, you cover us."

Paco scooped up an AK and stepped to the rear door. Engineer and the other man waited, one at the window and another at the door. I had nothing to do, so I pulled out my little rag witch and clasped it like a security blanket.

"Ready?" Engineer hissed.

"Ready."

"Go!"

CHAPTER FORTY-SIX

Paco flung open the door, but he might as well have flipped on a light switch.

"*Joda!*" he cried, and dove back into the room. "We're fucked."

We closed the doors and shutters in a fury. Engineer raged and cursed and again blamed Paco, saying if he got out of this alive there was going to be hell to pay. Paco yelled right back, saying it wasn't his fault, and their shouting didn't end until the other man pushed between them.

"Stop it, you two. Isn't there some way we can signal Tucno?"

"Grenades," Engineer said. "Let's make some noise."

The three of them skittered around me, then came the clack of grenades being fixed to rifles. I needed something other than a rag witch to take my mind off the danger and was glad when Engineer ordered me to throw open the shutters on his command. Neutrality was no longer an option, yet I realized, even in that moment of pounding heart panic, that anything I did to help would make me an accomplice. At least in a US courtroom.

Not that I'd live to see the inside of a US courtroom.

"Ready," Engineer said.

A rumble came from the outside, like the sound of wheels on gravel, punctuated occasionally by the high-pitched grinding of bad bearings. All four of us peeked out.

"Trucks," Paco cried. "They're coasting. That's why we didn't hear them. It's all downhill."

Engines roared to life. Transmissions whined, gears crunched, and soon they were maneuvering around our little cabin and bumping along the rocks.

One screeched to a halt directly in front. A canvas flap opened.

Out bounded Sinchis in full battle gear, all AKs, boots, berets and ski masks.

"Now!" Engineer shouted.

I flung open the shutters. Percussion caps popped around me. Grenades whooshed out the window. Explosions rocked the cabin and lit the night. Then came a louder explosion, as if an ammunition truck had blown up, shaking the ground and slamming the hut with debris.

I threw myself on the floor, wishing I could burrow into the earth, but my fellow warriors, like heroes in a bad action movie, kept loading and firing. Smoke and acrid smells filled the room. My eyes stung. Something outside was burning, throwing off light and shadows.

Then, as if the door to hell wasn't open wide enough, the Sinchis began shooting back.

Shutters blew off the hinges. The front door shattered and fell apart. Tracers buried themselves in the wall. Splinters and other debris buzzed around like swarms of angry bees.

How long this lasted, I have no idea, but at some point it slacked and went away like a passing tornado, leaving me in shadowy darkness. I lifted my head and looked around, thinking I was the lone survivor until Engineer's voice rang out from near the fireplace.

"Paco, are you alive?"

There was movement around me, barely visible in the firelight that came through the shattered door. We brushed ourselves off, assured one another we were okay, gave thanks for the thickness of the stone walls, and sat there breathing in the nasty smells of battle.

"Let's give them another blast," said the man whose name I didn't know.

"No," answered Engineer. "Don't provoke them. Tucno should be here any minute."

We waited, hovering together like victims of a shipwreck, hoping for help that might never come. I expected a grenade to finish us off, or the blaze of a flamethrower, but heard only the cries of wounded Sinchis, the crackle and pop of a burning truck, and the drone of an engine.

"*Joda,*" Paco said, "is that what I think it is?"

An airplane roared low overhead, rattling what remained of the door and shutters. Then came another, followed by an enormous blast in the woods.

The ground shook. A massive fireball lit the night. The air was sucked right out of my lungs, and for one horrifying moment I thought the walls would crash in on us.

"*Hijo de la gran puta,*" Engineer said, "They're dropping napalm."

Until that moment I had thought there was hope for us, that Tucno and Group Red would come storming out of the night. But not even Tucno would expose himself to napalm.

Sinchis called out to each other by name, asking if they were okay. Trucks began moving away. Then came a voice on a bullhorn.

"*Atención, atención!* You are surrounded! You cannot escape! Throw out your arms. You have two minutes. If you do not surrender, we will bomb you with napalm."

He repeated the warning in Quechua, and this time I recognized the voice.

Lieutenant Bravos.

What was it with that man? There was no escaping him. He was like a nasty little jack-in-the-box, always popping up when you least expected him.

Paco, now on his belly, crawled over to Engineer. "They're going to napalm us," he cried, strain showing in his voice. "The bastards are going to napalm us."

"No, Paco, they're bluffing. They want us alive."

"*Atención, atención!* You have one minute!"

Seconds ticked away. I leaned against the wall and clutched my little witch. This wasn't my war. I wasn't driven by some ideological imperative to kill or fight for change. All I wanted was Marisa and a flight back to the States. And yet, somewhere out there, Lieutenant Bravos was waiting with a maniacal grin on his face. He didn't care about Engineer or Paco. No, it was me he wanted—Romeo. He was one of those Latin sorts who favored Cervantes over Shakespeare. He hated the story of Romeo and Juliet. He hated me. And he could hardly wait to give the order to drop the bomb and turn me into carbon.

"*Atención, atención,* you have thirty seconds to live! Thirty seconds!"

I could hear the airplanes, the pilots making their turn and coming in for the kill, their engines screaming, homing in on the burning truck. Paco let out a whimper. Engineer slid over to me.

"What about you, comrade? You're in this too. What do you say?"

There was no time to waste. "If we surrender, we'll at least have a chance."

"I'm with the gringo," said the other man.

"*Atención, atención!* You have ten seconds...n*ueve...ocho... siete...seis*—"

Engineer flung his AK-47 out the window.

"Wave off the planes. We're coming out."

CHAPTER FORTY-SEVEN

We stepped out the door, four defeated men, hands over our heads, Engineer leading the way. Ox lay on the porch in a pool of blood. The air that before had been so clean now reeked of burning tires, diesel, and charred flesh. Fires flickered. Things sizzled and popped.

I looked into the darkness for Lieutenant Bravos, but the only soldiers I saw were either dead or wounded, some in the burning trucks and others strewn on the ground like debris after a hurricane, clothes still smoldering.

Lights flashed on to our left, beams throwing dizzying arcs over the ground, shadowy figures behind them. They came closer; the shadows behind them took on the shape of humans, and there came Lieutenant Bravos in a fur hat and Russian-looking greatcoat.

He stepped up to Engineer. "Look what we have here," he said, shining a light over the three of us. "Follow the gringo, and you'll catch the big one."

Trucks roared out of the darkness, maneuvering back and forth until they had us in the cross glare of headlights. Sparks rose into the sky. Soldiers ran here and there, all silhouettes and the tramp of boots. Someone shouted for a stretcher. Other soldiers tended the wounded, and as we stood there, a patrol marched out of the darkness with three more prisoners, among them the woman I'd seen leaving the cabin earlier.

"Isabél," Paco muttered beside me.

Isabél and the two men with her, standing in the glare, looked as defeated as we did. Bravos lined us up facing the lights and searched us, taking my fake passport and money. Then a Sinchi sergeant stepped forward and counted us.

"Seven," he said. "That makes seven prisoners and four enemy dead."

"How many casualties on our side?"

"Eight dead and ten wounded."

"Then we'll have to even the score, won't we?"

I had a pretty good idea what that meant and looked around for a place to run. But there were too many Sinchis, too much open ground, and not enough darkness. What would Marisa say when she heard I'd been shot just to even a score?

Another soldier, apparently the official photographer, stepped forward with a camera and began snapping close-ups. He marched up to me.

"Smile, gringo."

Beside me, Paco said, "Tell him to fuck himself."

The photographer laughed, took out a pad, and made a notation as if it were a profound comment, repeating the words, "Tell him to fuck himself."

Afterward, he lined us up by height for a group photo—me in the center and Engineer at my side. Someone said we looked like the losing players of a soccer game.

Bravos ordered the photographer to get him in the picture, and he stood there holding a rifle on us like a big-game hunter with his trophies.

"What a great photo for the Lima papers," he said, "Romeo, Chairman Gonzalo, and me."

Soldiers exchanged glances. Apparently they hadn't been told who we were, and the revelation that they'd captured a man they thought was Gonzalo sent a little shock through their ranks. Some shuffled back into the shadows as if they wanted no part of this. Others pushed in closer, and my guess was that except for the call of the conscript officer, these children of the Andes could just as well have been fighting under a Shining Path banner.

Bravos ordered his soldiers to step back. Then he strode along our line, peering into faces, his eyes squinting, breath pluming. The insignia on his fur hat glistened in the lights. He stopped in front of Isabél, brushed back the hair in her face, and spoke to her in Quechua.

"*Ima sutiiki?*"

She gave him a puzzled look.

He asked her again, this time in Spanish. "What is your name?"

"Isabél," she answered in a small voice.

"Your eyes are blue, Isabél. Are you the gringo's woman?"

"No, señor, tonight is the first time I've seen him."

Bravos grabbed her arm and dragged her over to me. "Is this your little slut?"

"No, Lieutenant, I don't know her."

He punched me in the stomach.

The blow sent me to my knees. It hurt. God, did it hurt. Then he kicked me with his boot. And as I lay there, gasping for breath, he dragged Isabél down the line and stopped in front of one of the other prisoners, a young man who was probably a bodyguard.

Bravos pointed at Isabél. "Isn't this her? Isn't she the gringo's little blue-eyed whore?"

"No, *Teniente*, they don't even know each other."

"You're lying, you Indian prick." He took this poor kid by his hair, pushed him to a spot where a dead Sinchi had lain only moments before, and turned to the sergeant.

"Shoot him!"

I struggled to my feet. "No, he's telling the truth."

Isabél also tried to reason with Bravos, but the order had been given, and nothing short of an order from God was going to change it.

The sergeant appointed five executioners.

"*Preparen!*"

The condemned man dropped to his knees, crossed himself, and began praying. Behind him, soldiers scurried out of the line of fire. The sergeant raised an arm.

"*Apunten!*"

The executioners took aim. This was a bluff, I told myself. It had to be a bluff.

"*Fuego!*"

A fiery blast sent the poor fellow sprawling backward.

My knees went weak. The whole world seemed to swim away. Isabél began to sob, loudly. Then Bravos was marching in front of us again, his face a picture of grim determination.

"That makes it five. Who wants to be next?" He stopped in front of Paco. "You."

Paco bolted, weaving his way in and out of the startled conscripts, and for a moment I thought he'd make it, that his defiance would set him free. But two or three Sinchis tackled him at the rear of the truck and wrestled him to the ground.

He bit, he cursed, he kicked. "I'll see you in hell," he shouted at Bravos. "Fuck you and your General Reál. Fuck President Fujimori, and fuck all of you for supporting the fascists in Lima."

Bravos marched over to him with his pistol and pumped two shots into his chest.

"Six," he said as calmly as if he'd shot a snake. "Who's next?"

In the quietness that followed, I could hear the whistle of the wind. The truck crackled as it burned. The moon still hung low in the sky. And then a universal truth came to me. The death of a fellow human meant nothing in the greater scheme of things. The sun would come up tomorrow. The trees would still be green. The earth and the sky didn't care. Only humans cared.

Bravos took another slow walk along our diminishing line, his footfalls crunching on the loose gravel. He stopped in front of Isabél and pulled her up. She seemed to wither under his stare, but then he patted her on the shoulder.

"Not to worry, *amorcita*. We've got other plans for you."

He stopped in front of Engineer, whom he thought was Gonzalo. "Not you either. You're going to Lima for the trial of the century. Then we'll shoot you."

He turned to me. "You, Romeo, say your prayers."

My breath seemed to go right out of me. My legs buckled, and I'd have collapsed right there if the soldiers hadn't grabbed me. They led me to the spot where the first man lay dead. The photographer came over and adjusted the setting of his camera. There was a flash of white, and when my vision came back, I saw Bravos talking to the executioners.

The sergeant motioned his men into position.

"*Preparen.*"

I closed my eyes.

"*Apunten!*"

Ridiculously, an image of Marisa flashed into my head, Marisa reading about my death in a newspaper, a headline that read: ROMEO IS NUMBER SEVEN.

"*Fuego!*"

A volley of shots rattled out, lighting the ground with their flashes, and I fell backward onto the body of the man who'd gone before me.

CHAPTER FORTY-EIGHT

I thought I'd died a merciful death: no searing jolts, no thrashing about, and no blood gushing from my mouth. But why wasn't I floating in the air looking down at my body? Where were my dead parents? Where was Jesus? Why could I still hear the wind and the laughter of the soldiers?

I rolled over and shaded my eyes against the glare of headlights. Bravos was still there, his breath pluming in the night air. He was laughing. The bastard was laughing! What could possibly be funny about a fake execution?

He crunched over and wagged a finger in my face. "Don't think you're getting off easy. You're going to Dracula's House. You'll wish we'd shot you."

I wanted to curse him, but no words came from my mouth. I tried to stand, but made it only to my knees. I was sobbing and shaking, and I still thought they'd shoot me. Bravos had stripped me of the last of my dignity and all I could do was cry. If somehow I got out of this and got away, I was going to track him down and kill him with my bare hands. Slowly.

He stalked away. "Get them into the trucks."

The sergeant yanked me to my feet and pushed me to the rear of the nearest truck. He threw back the canvas flap and ordered me inside. I managed to get a foot on the bumper and was trying to pull myself up when a loud pop sounded in the woods. A light streaked up, arcing above the trees toward the stars, higher and still higher until it burst into a flare.

"Who fired that flare?" the sergeant shouted. "Who was it?"

Another flare went off, then another. Night turned into day, and before anyone could react, Tucno's guerrillas burst upon us like a party of Apache warriors.

Tracers blazed into the night. Bullets kicked up dirt. One slammed into the sergeant and drove him against the truck. Something smacked against my leg.

I dashed for the woods, running past the hand pump, past another truck, praying, hoping, thanking God for Tucno, and was almost at a ravine when the earth exploded in front of me, lifting me into the air and slamming me to the ground.

How long I lay there, senseless, I don't know. I was vaguely aware of people running this way and that, fire belching from weapons. My trousers were smoldering. My left leg hurt. So did my back, but all I could hear was a shrill ring, like a siren stuck at high pitch.

And then that damn parrot appeared. "Come on, gringo, you've got to move."

I crawled, pulling myself along the ground. There lay a body, all crumpled and broken. Little pieces of fiery debris fell like raindrops. The parrot flapped around me, still squawking and demanding that I hurry. Then it morphed into a woman. Her mouth was moving, as if she were also saying "Come on, gringo," but I couldn't hear a word.

Someone else came running over and pulled me up, and the three of us made it into the ravine, a shadowy place that was blessedly cool. Others were there too, looking like they'd been attacked by vicious dogs. The woman lifted a canteen to my lips, and as I sat there, my memory and the sounds of battle came back.

"Gringo," Isabél said. "Are you all right?"

"I think so. What about you?"

"It was awful. We made it, though."

Engineer, who'd been following the fighting from the edge of the embankment, came over and laid a hand on my shoulder.

"Can you walk?"

"I think so."

"Tucno's got it under control. Let's get out of here."

The pain in my leg couldn't have been worse if I'd been run over by a truck. A portion of my pants leg had burned away, but still I managed to hobble along. Trees and underbrush burned around us. The place stank of petroleum and death. The charred remains of dead hogs lay about like smoking logs, and I wondered if Sad Eyes had also been incinerated.

At length, we collapsed beside a small stream. Flares still popped and floated in the overhead, giving the illusion of a troubled daylight. The faces of my fellow terrorists went from white to blue and back to white. The water was like ice and probably polluted. But I was so thirsty that I dunked in my head and drank. I also soaked my burned leg in the water, and as we sat there catching our breath, the sounds of battle turned into single gunshots.

Isabél sat up. "Listen, Tucno's finishing the wounded."

The shots continued, one and then another. Lives were ending, yet there was nothing to mark their passing: no shooting stars, no salutes, and no laments on the killers around me.

Engineer came to his feet. "Come on. They might call in another air strike."

We struggled up, found the river by its sound, and followed it into camp. No one challenged us. No one noticed. If we'd been Sinchis, we could have shot the place to pieces.

People were shouting orders and running this way and that with flashlights. Vehicles had lined up bumper-to-bumper, doors open, engines running. The girls who'd been left in camp were throwing in coolers, sleeping bags, weapons, and other gear. Wounded lay about on blankets, and even as we watched, a man trotted into camp with a girl on his back.

"Who is in charge?" Engineer called out, hands cupped around his mouth.

A flashlight came toward us, behind which I recognized Faviola.

"*Madre de Diós*," she cried. "We thought you were dead." She yelled for a medical team.

Out of the darkness trotted three young women, one of whom had a white patch on her arm. I thought they were coming to look after me. Instead they passed right by and began fussing over Engineer as if he were a reincarnation of Inca Tupac Amaru.

I limped to the van, found a blanket, and was looking for a place to collapse when Faviola appeared beside me and took my arm.

"Oh, my poor gringo," she said. "Look at you."

She eased me onto the blanket, took off my poncho and sweater, and announced that shrapnel had lodged against my ribs. There was also a jagged hole in my lower leg, exposing the shinbone, and a burn around my ankle.

Worse, the left side of my face felt as if I'd been splashed with scalding water.

She put ointment on my wounds, bandaged me, and was helping me into a sweatshirt when Tucno came straggling in with news that they'd killed all the Sinchis.

"At least thirty," he announced between swigs of corn *chicha*. "Destroyed all their trucks."

Engineer sat up from his blanket. "What about the lieutenant?"

"What lieutenant?"

"The Sinchi in charge. I want you to find his body, cut off his head, and send it to General Reál in a box. Understand?"

"*Sí*, Comrade Engineer. I'll take care of it."

The last flare fizzled and died. The shooting ended, and the only sign of battle was the distant glare of a huge fire. Tucno blew his whistle for assembly and was ordering them to pick up and evacuate when Condor limped out of the darkness.

"Not so fast," he yelled. "Hold on."

Beams of flashlights played over him. His left arm was bandaged. There was blood on his shirt. He was supporting himself on a crude wooden staff.

"Hasn't it occurred to you people that there's a *suplón* among us?" he said, his voice strained. "The soldiers didn't find us by accident."

Flashlights turned in my direction.

"Not the gringo," Condor growled.

He limped to the rear of a dust-covered van and rapped his stick against the side. The back door swung open. Out jumped a husky young man. He reached back inside and dragged out a prisoner, and even before I saw the bobbing Adam's apple, I knew the traitor was Luís.

CHAPTER FORTY-NINE

Invectives flew around him like bullets from a machine gun. Ana, the girl who'd been riding in the front seat of the van, spat on him. Then Condor held up a small black object.

"Look what he was carrying—an electronic homing device. The Sinchis gave it to him at Dracula's House. Right, Comrade Luís?"

Luís let out a little whine and broke down in long racking sobs. "They tortured me," he cried. "Threatened to kill my children. My mother. What else could I do?"

"You could have died like a man," Tucno said. "Like a loyal comrade."

He dragged Luís away from the van and unsheathed his knife. Luís fell to his knees, pleading. Tucno circled him like a dog after a snake, shifting the knife from one hand to the other.

Then he looked up at me. "You do it, gringo. He betrayed you too."

Tucno slapped the knife into my hand. The crowd surged around and pushed me forward. Even the girls egged me on. "Kill him" became a chant, a cry for blood punctuated with a rhythmic clapping of hands. "*Matalo!...Matalo!... Matalo!*"

I looked into Luís's pleading eyes. The chants around me grew louder. Luís deserved to die, but I wasn't an executioner. This wasn't my war. Hell no.

I flung the knife to the ground.

Ana scooped it up. "I'll do it."

I stumbled to the van and slumped against the tire, and when I heard the cheers, I knew it was over, that poor, stupid Luís had died the death of a traitor. I gagged again, but all that came up was pain and the gut-wrenching realization that I was stuck with this mob of young killers.

Faviola brought me a cup of warm coca tea and sat beside me.

"You were right," she said. "This life's not for me. I want to get away. Maybe go to Miami."

She snuggled against me as if I were her only friend. Tears glinted in her eyes. I put an arm around her, and we shared a moment of intimacy, right there in that horrid camp while they were stringing Luís to a tree by his feet.

Someone had scrawled a large sign that read, *SUPLÓN,* and they pinned it to his chest, absurdly upside down. Then Tucno blew the whistle for assembly.

They fell in, everyone except the wounded, people like me. Engineer stepped to the front, his face illuminated by flashlights, his voice cutting through the night.

"Listen up, fellow soldiers. I want all of you to take the hand of the comrade next to you."

Faviola's hand closed over mine, warm and soft. Engineer went on. "Tonight we destroyed the enemy. It was a great victory. There will be other battles, other victories."

He paused as if to let his words sink in. "Do you know why we are fighting?"

"*Pachacuti, Pachacuti, Pachacuti,*" they chanted as one.

"Go now to your homes and villages. Say nothing of tonight. A loose tongue can doom your comrades." He snapped to attention and raised his hand in a clenched-fist salute. "To you, comrades, I salute you. You are my brothers and sisters. Victory will soon be ours. Peru will soon be ours. Now, go. Dismissed!"

There was a great rush of feet across the grounds. Doors slammed, engines revved, vans took off with a spinning of wheels. Faviola took my arm.

"Come on, comrade. We're going to Cuzco."

Ana and the driver piled into the front. Into the back went a man I didn't know, along with the young woman who'd traveled with us before. Then someone pounded on the side.

"Wait, wait. Take Tika. She's in bad shape."

They picked up this unconscious girl whose name meant flower in Quechua and loaded her into the backseat with the other two passengers. I struggled into the middle row and sat next to Faviola. All the vehicles in front turned in the direction of the main road, but we turned left.

"Why are we going this way?" Faviola asked the driver.

"Tucno says the gringo is the only one who can identify the lieutenant."

"Are you serious? The gringo can barely walk."

"Tell that to Tucno."

Within minutes we were back at the scene of my nightmare, breathing in the smells of burning tires, napalm, and death. Trucks were still burning, sending up spirals of smoke and sparks. The barn was also in flames. The driver maneuvered around bodies and stopped at the site of my fake execution. I climbed out slowly, wincing from pain, searching the sky for signs of an airplane or helicopter, ashamed of my cowardice and the way I'd broken down.

Tucno and a detail of five or six others were already there, gathering weapons and turning bodies face up. He stalked over to me and slapped a flashlight into my hand.

"Go find that lieutenant," he yelled above the roar of the burning barn.

Faviola took my arm and we stumbled around the debris, looking into the faces of dead Sinchis, shading our eyes from the glare of the burning barn. Less than an hour ago, these people had been monsters. Now I saw them as the teenagers they were—and would forever be.

There lay the sergeant, the photographer and three of the executioners. Others lay in heaps along the trail, but there was no sign of the lieutenant, nothing, *nada*, not even his bullhorn.

Dammit to hell. Bravos was like an indestructible vampire. Drive a stake through his heart, and he still jumps up to get you. I rolled the photographer over, hoping to find his camera. It wasn't there, but I found the note pad on which he'd scribbled *Tell him to fuck himself.*

The old dread swept over me again. Bravos could be out there in the darkness, sighting me through the lens of his telescopic rifle, waiting for me to stand still.

Tucno ordered Faviola to take photos, and while this was going on, I limped to the little shack where I'd sat with Gonzalo, hoping to at least retrieve my shoulder bag.

Doors and shutters were gone, shot to splinters. Table and chairs overturned, bottles on the floor, everything a mess. But no shoulder bag. And then I bumped into Puppy Sad Eyes, hanging from a rafter. Some sick bastard had killed her and strung her up like Luís.

I choked back tears. Other than Faviola, that little mutt had been my only friend.

A whistle blew. "Time to go!" Tucno yelled. "Let's move it!"

Faviola helped me back to the van, and as we pulled away, I broke down in tears. Our little battle would probably never make it into the history books, never even have a name, but for those who struggled and died there, it could just as well have been Gettysburg.

CHAPTER FIFTY

Every pothole jarred my insides. Every twist or turn was like a knife in the ribs. The fever came back. I fell in and out of a troubled sleep. I saw Gordo in my dreams, and Lieutenant Bravos, and even that damn parrot, dressed in a Sinchi uniform. And suddenly it all made sense. The parrot was the *suplón*, not Luís, and it was following us, flying overhead. I warned everyone in the van that they were waiting down the road to ambush us, parrot and all.

"He's hallucinating," Faviola said. "It's the loss of blood."

"Maybe it's the elevation," said a voice behind me. "gringos aren't used to it."

"How is Tika?" the driver asked.

"She's not going to make it."

"The gringo doesn't sound like he's going to make it either."

"He'll make it," Faviola said. "I know this doctor in Cuzco."

There was talk about airplanes and napalm again, and roadblocks, and to be on the sharp lookout for lights.

"Parrots too," someone said, and they all burst into laughter.

Once or twice we may have stopped and turned out our lights. Or I may have dreamed it. All I know is I fell asleep again and saw Marisa in bed with an artist, and when I woke, my head was pounding. My ears hurt. I was freezing. Faviola threw a smelly blanket over me and gave me a coca leaf to chew on. In front Ana was talking to the driver.

"What about the Apurimac checkpoint? They'll search the van and find the gringo."

"Stop worrying. I've got it all figured out. We'll dump him at Saywite."

"What is that?"

"A *huaca*—one of those secluded shrines with baths and bamboo groves."

Faviola leaned forward. "Are you crazy? The gringo and Chairman Gonzalo are friends."

"He'll be dead by the time we get there anyway. If not, we'll help him along."

"Suppose it was you?" Faviola said. "Would you want us to help you along?"

"He's almost dead anyhow. Besides, we can't leave him for the Sinchis. He can identify us."

"How can he identify us? He doesn't know our real names."

The discussion heated up. Ana said there had to be a better way. Faviola argued for dropping me off in the next village. The woman in the backseat disagreed, saying I could be a spy.

"Enough," said the driver, and slammed his hand on the dashboard. "I'm not going to risk my life for a dying gringo. It's best to just finish him off and dump his body."

He pulled to the side of the road and stopped.

My survival instinct kicked in. I fumbled in my pocket for my pistol. Gone. All I had was the rag witch, the photographer's note pad, and a Swiss Army knife. How ironic that I'd survived Gordo, General Reál, a battle, and a firing squad only to be done in by "friends."

"Why are we stopping?" Faviola asked.

"That light up there. See it? It could be a Sinchi helicopter."

We waited. I heard the drone of the engine. Or maybe it was my heartbeat. Then it was gone.

"What's that smell?" the driver asked. "Did someone step in shit?"

"It's Tika," said the voice behind me. "They got her in the stomach."

"Is she alive?"

"Barely."

Windows were partially rolled down and we resumed our journey, the heater blowing, icy wind whistling through the windows, Ana and the driver still wanting to dump my body beside the road. Why couldn't they all be like Faviola—warm and caring—the way I remembered Peruvians from my Peace Corps days? Now it seemed as if everyone I met was either chasing me or wanted the earth to open up and swallow me.

"That checkpoint still worries me," Ana says. "Isn't that place supposed to be cursed?"

"It's not cursed," Faviola said. "It's a historical site."

"For what?"

"The setting for a book. Thornton Wilder's *Bridge of San Luis Rey*."

She was explaining the plot like a schoolteacher—an Inca suspension bridge collapsed, plunging five travelers to their deaths—and they were all listening when far below us, sparkling in the thin air like a thousand jewels, appeared the lights of a city.

"Look," Ana said. "That must be Abancay."

My heart jumped. Abancay, Marisa's place of Plan C.

"We need to tank up," said the driver.

"It's not even five," Ana said. "You think they'll be open?"

"Open or not, we've got to stop."

Down we went, twisting and turning through clouds, everyone wide-awake and grumbling for a bathroom or coffee.

Finally, we crossed a long bridge and bounced along the city potholes.

There were no signs of life. No automobiles either and precious few lights, but for me it was Jerusalem, Mecca, Salvation. As we rolled into the station, I tried to ape the breathing of a man in deep sleep. The driver opened his door and looked back at Faviola.

"How is the gringo?"

"Comatose. You were right. He's not going to make it."

"How about Tika?"

"Dead," said the guy behind me. "She's not breathing. Eyes are open."

Ana bounded out and made the sign of the cross. "I don't want to ride in a van with a corpse."

"She's not going to bite," said the driver. "We'll dump her with the gringo."

"Tika was my friend," said the woman in back. "Let's bury her."

"We don't have a shovel."

"What about the river? We can dump her there."

"That's disrespectful. Drop the gringo in the river but not Tika."

Everyone climbed out. The men took a noisy leak next to the van, sighing relief, then zipped up, marched to the building, and began banging on the station door.

Faviola reached back into the van and shook me. "Marco, are you awake?"

"I'm awake."

The driver yelled at her to come on, saying they'd opened the place.

"Coming," she said.

I heard voices and slamming doors, and then Faviola was tugging at me.

"They're inside," she said, her voice frantic. "Come on You've got to get away."

I struggled out the door and onto my feet. "They'll know you helped me."

"They'll think you crawled out and died. Besides, they'll be happy to be rid of you." She adjusted the blanket over my shoulders and helped me to the corner of the building.

"That way," she said, pointing uphill. "Find yourself a doctor and stay alive."

"You stay alive too."

I squeezed her arm and lumbered into the darkness, following a cobbled street uphill, trying to remember Marisa's instructions. There were no streetlights, headlights, or lights burning through windows, nothing but stars above and darkness below. Every step jarred my injury. My eyesight was blurry, my strength failing. Every breath of cold air burned my lungs.

Was I on the right street?

Was I even in Abancay?

Marisa had said to follow the street uphill three blocks from the station. But why couldn't it be one block? Why did it have to be uphill?

A dog came snarling out of the darkness, barking clouds of steam. Christ, was there no end to my bad luck? Where were the guerrillas when I needed them? Here was the perfect candidate for a light post. The dog followed, growling and baring its teeth, and didn't give up until I was another block up the street and out of its territory.

At last I came to the end of the third block, turned left, and felt my way to a gate.

Could this be it, a green stucco house, a sign that read DENTAL SURGEON? It was too dark to know, but I pressed the doorbell button anyway. Again and again.

Please, dear God, let this be the place.

A light came on. The front door opened. An old woman stuck out her head.

"Get away from here, *Indio,* or I'll call the police."

"It's Mark," I answered hoarsely. "Marisa sent me."

The door slammed. More lights came on. Through the burglar bars, I saw the movement of two people. The door opened again, and out ran a younger woman in a housecoat.

"Mark. Is that you?"

The language was English. The gate opened with a loud creak. The woman grabbed my arm and looked into my face. "Oh my God, oh my God, what have they done to you?"

Sonia, beautiful, blessed Sonia.

CHAPTER FIFTY-ONE

Abancay

In my feverish dreams, I relived all the horrors—the firing squad, Luís hanging upside down, Puppy Sad Eyes dangling from a rafter, lifeless bodies, and burning trucks. Then I was back in the Ayacucho cemetery with Marisa, crying, begging her not to leave me.

"I'm not going to leave you," she said and climbed in bed beside me, all warm and cuddly and smelling of Lily of Peru, which made perfect sense in my dream.

We talked, we cried. Marisa said our separation was only temporary, and she was saying how sorry she was for hurting me when that damn parrot fluttered down from a tree and alighted on a tombstone next to the bed.

"Wake up, gringo. Time for assembly!"

I opened my eyes. The pillow that had been Marisa was now just a pillow, all crumpled and lifeless. Sunlight streamed through a window. My left arm was attached to an IV. There were bandages around my chest and leg and on my face.

Was I in a hospital? Everything ached. I needed to pee. I lifted my head and was looking around when the door opened and in came Sonia, she of the Marisa looks and shapely body, now dressed in a medical smock.

She sat beside me. "How do you feel?"

"Not so good," I answered in a weak voice. "Is this a hospital?"

"No, Mark, this is my house. Don't you remember?" She picked up a metal bucket and rattled it. "This is what came out of you. You're lucky it didn't go past the ribs."

I lifted my head again, thinking to tell her I didn't feel very lucky, but before I could form the words, she said, "Marisa knows you got away."

"How would she know?"

"She'd have to be living on Mars not to know. It's on TV and in all the papers."

"Is it also on TV that she dumped me?"

I choked up. It hurt to think about it. God, did it hurt.

Sonia began rubbing my neck the way she'd done back in Lima. "Oh, Mark, poor Mark. You're as messed up as she is. We've got to get you well."

"I need the bathroom."

She removed the IV and helped me sit up. Not until then did I realize I was naked.

"Where are my clothes?"

"If you mean those filthy rags, forget them. They went onto the burn pile."

"You burned my rag witch?"

"No, Mark, your little witch is safe."

She showed me a basket that contained the photographer's note pad, my pocketknife, some loose change, and the little rag witch. Then she wrapped a sheet around me, led me down a hall to the bathroom and handed me a toothbrush, towels, soap, and a bathrobe.

"Take your time. I'll fix something to eat. Try to keep water off your bandages."

There was no blood in my urine, which was a good sign, but my bandaged face and body looked like I'd just escaped from the operating room after a bad accident. I cleaned up as best I could, and when I came out, stiff and limping, dressed in a bathrobe, I almost ran into Sonia coming up the stairs with a food tray.

"This way," she said, and led me into a small sitting room.

A bay window overlooked a rear courtyard and distant mountains. The sofa, cushions, and throw blankets exuded the same kind of flowery perfume I remembered from the apartment in Lima. It even had a TV. There were also paintings of indigenous scenes on the walls, but nothing that looked like a de la Vega.

"This your retreat?" I asked. "Your place to unwind?"

She motioned me onto the sofa and laid out a bowl of soup on a coffee table. "First you take this," she said, and handed me a pill. "It's an antibiotic."

"You didn't answer my question."

"Yes, Mark, my office is downstairs. I'm a dentist. I live alone. I work all day, and when I'm finished, I come upstairs, clean up, and come here to relax."

"Who was that other woman I saw last night?"

"Aunt Sofía. She was visiting when you showed up. Take your pill."

I downed it with a glass of papaya juice and started on the soup, but didn't have an appetite. Bad memories and a love affair gone bad do that to a person.

"Tell me what happened," Sonia said, sitting in a wicker chair and nursing a mug of coffee.

I told her, leaving out the part about the fake execution. She listened and told me I'd done nothing wrong, that I was an innocent victim caught up in a dirty little war.

"Too bad you can't tell your story to the newspapers," she said. "Their version is different."

She picked up the tray, went downstairs and came back with an armload of newspapers. One of the headlines read: ROMEO AND CHAIRMAN GONZALO IN BLOODY ESCAPE. Below it were photos of strewn corpses, Luís dangling from a tree, and what I hoped wouldn't be there—the images captured by that army photographer. Bravos was there too, face blacked out, holding his Kalashnikov on us as if he were the sheriff rounding up outlaws.

The caption identified Engineer as Chairman Gonzalo, which he wasn't.

General Reál was quoted as saying my presence at the scene was proof of my guilt. Ditto for Inspector Bocanegra. Even Holbrook Easton chimed in. "Rest assured that we at the US Embassy are cooperating with the authorities to bring Professor Thorsen to justice…"

"Oh, my God," Sonia said. "Didn't you say you were riding in a Ford van?"

She handed me the paper she was reading, and when I saw the headline—FIVE TERRORISTS KILLED AT CHECKPOINT APURIMAC—my wounds began to throb. The picture showed a bullet-riddled white Ford van with five bodies propped against it.

Ana and the driver.

The man and woman who had sat behind me.

And Faviola.

CHAPTER FIFTY-TWO

Nausea swept over me. Faviola dead? Faviola with the frizzy black hair and flower in her cap. Faviola, who wanted to escape the madness and move to Miami.

Even more bizarre was the location of the shooting—the setting for Wilder's *Bridge of San Luís Rey*. I could still remember Faviola discussing it in the van. The collapse of a bridge. Five travelers dead. A Franciscan monk asking, "Why those five and not me?"

Now I asked the same question. *Why those five and not me?*

Why Faviola and not me?

I prayed for her soul that night. I dreamed about her. I told her how sorry I was for being so difficult. I cried, something I rarely did before I came to Peru. Now it seemed as if tears were always below the surface, a little lake of sadness, waiting to bubble up and spill over.

A cold drizzling rain didn't help the next morning. Neither did the pain in my left leg. Or my jittery nerves. A passing car became a truckload of soldiers. A distant buzz became an airplane loaded with napalm. The ring of a doorbell meant Bravos at the gate.

And I still didn't know Marisa's secrets or why she'd left me.

Not until the fourth day, after lots of painkillers, salves, water soaks, and antibiotics, did I stop jumping at sounds and wallowing in misery. Sonia went shopping and came back with shoes and clothing that more or less fit. We had a candlelight dinner to celebrate my improving health. A tango played in the background, and on the table were fresh flowers and a pitcher of sangria. I had shaved my stubble and dressed in my new jeans and a dark pullover. Sonia was dressed in black, with dangling earrings and pearl necklace, looking almost like Marisa in the dim light.

"Are you ever going to tell me about yourself?" I asked.

"What do you want to know?"

"Everything."

"Marisa would kill me."

"Marisa's not here."

She dialed down the tango and began talking. Sonia's mom and Marisa's mom were sisters and had both come to Miami from Cuba after Castro took over the island. Marisa's dad was a Spaniard. Sonia's was Peruvian. She and Marisa had lived in the same Miami neighborhood, attended the same Catholic schools, and had both graduated from the University of Miami.

"Marisa got herself a scholarship to study in Peru," she said in her soft voice. "That's when she met you. I wasn't as lucky. I got involved with this beer-swilling, pickup-driving, womanizing redneck named Duke. But oh, what a sweet talker he was."

She stood, put our plates in the sink, came back, and sat down. "It still hurts."

"Look, it's okay if you don't want to talk about it."

"No, it'll make me feel better." She drained her glass and poured another. "Fishing was his thing—fishing and Gator football. I could live with that, but it was the womanizing I couldn't take. He chased every skirt that came along. Lied to them too. Told them he was single. I even caught him with a girl in our bed. That was it. Packed my bags and left."

She took another sip of sangria.

"That's it—end of story?"

"Ha, if only. He stalked me, promised he'd be faithful, said he couldn't live without me. So what did I do? Moved back in, stupid me. And what did he do? Started cheating again. Then he became abusive, getting drunk, hitting me. So I left him again."

The story got uglier by the minute—beatings and threats, a restraining order.

"So where is he now?"

"They say I killed him with a shotgun."

I put down my glass. "You what?"

"Why else would I be in Peru? The alternative was fifteen to twenty in Starke Prison. It's been two years. Funny thing is, I left because of domestic violence and ended up in a bloody civil war. You're not the only one who came to Peru and walked into a buzz saw."

CHAPTER FIFTY-THREE

During the day, while Sonia and her assistant tended patients downstairs, I exercised to the tune of her dental drills, trying to regain my strength. I read newspapers, I watched television. And I composed poetry. Not just poetry, but the story of what happened to me in verse—coming to Peru with high expectations, only to have everything dissolve in heartbreak.

Funny how when I was with Marisa, sated with lovemaking, I couldn't compose a damn thing. But throw in danger and adversity and getting dumped, and a woman like Sonia in the house, and I was Darío in Paris, Neruda in Capri, Comrade Marco with a hard-on.

Some mornings I'd wake up telling myself I was going to crawl out of the cesspool into which I'd fallen, only to read in the papers that I'd sunk deeper. All my financial accounts had been closed, records seized, credit cards canceled. The bank was talking foreclosure. The FBI was involved. My world was collapsing, and all I could do was write poetry.

Then one rainy afternoon, Sonia danced into the sitting room and waved a newspaper in my face. "You've got to see this," she said, all grins and cheer.

I took the paper and read about a conference in Lima, the Society for Radical Artists. The theme was leftist poetry and protest music, but it had turned into a discussion of "Lily of Peru." Art professors had critiqued every word and verse as if it were a lost and found work of Lord Byron, pointing out metaphors and symbolism I'd never intended. Most of the comments were negative, biting into my soul with words like "lovesick puppy," and one imaginative professor even para-phrased Shakespearean verses as if they'd been composed by Marisa.

> Give me my gringo, and when he shall die,
> Take him out and cut him up in little stars,
> And he will make the face of heaven so fine,
> That all the world will be in love with night.

I laughed. Sonia laughed. I hobbled around the room, and then an idea crashed down like an Andean avalanche. Why not send my verses to the newspapers? Tease the bastards. Wasn't that what Dillinger did? And Bonnie and Clyde? After all, I was Romeo. Talk about platform.

I told Sonia my idea and asked how I could send it to Lima without a local postmark.

"Write it up, and I'll take care of it."

I sat down, grabbed a pencil, and scribbled a few lines.

> Give me a column, and I shall write,
> Of love turned to ashes, and being on the run.
> From generals with subpoenas, and Peep agents with guns.

Sonia leaned over my shoulder to read. "It's not exactly Shakespeare."

"You don't like it?"

She wrapped her arms about my neck, and then her lips were on mine—soft and moist and warm. "How could I not like anything composed by Romeo?"

She smiled again and sauntered out of the room, leaving me with a brain turned to mush.

ॐ

As the days rolled by, I wrote my story the way it happened, beginning in Lima and progressing to the camp in the wilderness, leaving out names of those who helped me, but using the real names of Gordo, Reál, Bravos, Bocanegra, and even Holbrook Easton. Sonia critiqued every word and verse like an art professor, and even joked that I'd soon become so famous they'd want to keep me in Peru as a national treasure. She also fell back into the habit of coming out of the shower with only a towel wrapped around that beautiful body, running around in a thigh-length T-shirt, sans bra, and rubbing aromatic lotion on her arms and legs in the sitting room where I was working. Making it difficult for me to concentrate.

Oh, those long legs and damp hair, and that Marisa-like face with the soft, inviting lips.

And then one night when I was preparing for bed, and the clock striking midnight, she came into my room and kissed me again on the lips.

"Sweet dreams," she whispered, and again destroyed my sleep for the night.

Any other guy would have followed her right down to her room. But I was still so hung up on Marisa, so heartbroken, that I couldn't bring myself to do more than fantasize. Never mind that Marisa probably had her legs wrapped around her husband at that very moment.

Telling him all the things she used to tell me.

Begging for more.

Bitch!

I had to get over it, I told myself, had to put Marisa behind me. So the next morning, while Sonia was downstairs, I crept into her bedroom, and looked into her nightstand drawer.

And there it was—the pink dildo.

The image of her with that dildo, writhing in pleasure, tortured me all day. And it was still on my mind that evening when she left the door open while showering, and later invited me down to the kitchen for a dinner of spaghetti and meatballs.

At first I thought it was going to be just another evening— eat, talk about poetry, and discuss our problems. But when she lit scented candles, closed the curtains, opened a bottle of Merlot, and put on a Louis Prima, I knew this was going to be different.

"I love Louis Prima," she said, and moistened her lips as if inviting me to moisten them for her. She sat down across the table and put a meatball in her mouth as if to say carnivores made better lovers. Then she licked the sauce off her finger, slowly.

"Duke wasn't all bad," she said, looking at me with those big brown eyes. "He was one of those daring types who wanted to do it everywhere. In elevators, parking lots, stairways. One time we even did it in the bed of his pickup."

I had a vivid image of her in the bed of a pickup, long legs wrapped around Duke.

"Been with only two guys since, both losers. It's been a while. Thought I could handle it, but it's not easy. Maybe if I was sixty-one, or eighty-one, but I'm thirty-one."

She shoved away her plate. "How do you handle it?"

"Not easy for me either. Last night I almost…"

"Almost what?"

"Came down to your room."

"Why didn't you?"

I shrugged. She sighed, and we sat there looking into each other's eyes. Pheromones and dopamine swirled around like static electricity, crackling and popping in tune to "Just a Gigolo." And then we were in each other's arms.

Our lips met. We moved to the sofa, fondling and kissing like the starved lovers we were, and it wasn't until her tank top was off and she was tugging at my belt that the phone rang.

She pushed me away and sprang up. "I have to get that."

She picked up the receiver and said hello, and I knew from her expression that no one was on the other end. "Dammit," she muttered. "This happens all the time."

"Who do you think it was?"

"I don't know, but no one calls at this time, not unless it's bad news."

"Maybe they'll call back."

"Maybe they can't. Telephones in this country suck. Let's give it a few minutes."

The magic was gone, the moment destroyed, so she put her tank top back on and we nibbled at our spaghetti, staring at the phone. It didn't ring, but the mystery remained. Finally, we put away the dishes, climbed the stairs, and said good-night.

No kiss.

Again I couldn't sleep. From the tossing I heard in the next room, I guessed she couldn't either. Was she worried about that phone call, or was she as frustrated as I was? All over the world, couples were making love without *being* in love, and here I was, separated from the bed of a beautiful woman because of my love for a woman who dumped me.

How stupid was that?

I tumbled out of bed, lit a candle, padded down the hall, and was about to tap on her door when it opened, and there she stood in candlelight, dressed only in lavender-colored panties.

"What took so long?" she whispered.

CHAPTER FIFTY-FOUR
The Road to Saywite

The next day was a Friday. Sonia was in her panties, blow-drying her hair, smiling through the open door, and I was sitting at a table with pen and paper, thinking I wouldn't dare put into verse what happened between us, much less that she was a screamer. Or that she was insatiable and liked to talk dirty. Or that the sheets had become so wet, we had to change them. Or that I couldn't keep up with her, and I was exhausted from not sleeping.

And wondering how long this would continue. And whether or not she'd tell Marisa.

Or if Marisa gave a damn.

And that's when the doorbell rang.

Not once, but three or four times, as if Bravos was at the gate with his Sinchis.

Sonia flew out of her bedroom. The two of us hurried to the window. An older woman stood at the gate, all bundled up against the morning chill, looking this way and that as if vampires were on the loose.

"This can't be good," Sonia said.

She pulled on a robe and dashed out. I watched from the window and didn't like what I saw—the woman gesturing, Sonia glancing up at me, looking as frightened as that day at the railway station. The woman hurried away. Sonia burst back into the house.

"We've got to go. Gather your things. I'll explain in the car."

She made a phone call, said something about Plan C, listened a minute, and said, "Oh my God. Today?" She drew in a flustered breath, said, "Okay," and within minutes we were in her battered Land Rover, heading east toward Cuzco on the old Inca highway.

Sonia sat in the driver's seat, all sunglasses, poncho and ball cap, smoking a cigarette; I was hunkered down in the back, partially covered with a blanket.

"Are you going to tell me?" I asked.

"I'm trying to concentrate. Just keep down. Relax."

Relax? How could I relax when we were on the same road where they'd gunned down Faviola? The soldiers could still be out here, waiting. And in a day or two, our photos would appear in the papers, propped against the bullet-riddled Land Rover.

At last Sonia stopped and let me crawl in front. She shook out another cigarette. "Here's what happened: When your friends in the van stopped for gas, they woke half the neighborhood. This old witch who lives next to the station looked out and saw you stumbling up the street. Reported it to Peep, said it was a tall man, maybe a gringo. Now they're going house to house."

She offered me a cigarette. I took one and lit up, figuring it was no more dangerous to my lungs than a Sinchi bullet.

"Who was that lady?" I asked her.

"Tia Sofía. My aunt. She tried to call last night to warn us."

"Where are we going?"

"You'll know when we get there."

We took off again, climbing higher and twisting along the crooked road. Here and there we passed herds of llama with their shepherds, trucks and buses with wobbly wheels, and Runa women with straw hats, shawls, and baskets, walking in single file along the road.

"What about that checkpoint at the Apurimac?" I asked her.

"We turn before we get there."

"Are you angry?"

"I'm fine."

She was on another cigarette, still looking pouty, when we left the main highway and drove into the Saywite shrine, an Inca archaeological site of carved stones, ancient terracing, walls, steps, baths, water channels, and fountains.

"Pit stop," Sonia said, and hopped out.

It was as neglected and run-down as everything else in Peru, overgrown with bamboo, thorny brush, and creepers. Was Tika's body here? I wondered. What if Faviola hadn't helped me? My rotting corpse would be here as well, hidden in a bamboo thicket.

We used their facilities, bought some sweets from a woman selling her goods from a basket, and climbed back into the Land Rover. Sonia's face still had that look of disappointment, as if she'd expected more from our lovemaking.

"Where's the warmth?" I asked her. "The smile?"

She shot me a "don't ask" look, fired up the engine, and we were back on the road, following a winding Inca trail to the north, descending alongside a mineral-colored stream that grew from small to large, just like the stream that led to the training camp.

"Tell me about Lannie Torres," she yelled above the roar and rumble.

"Why do you want to know about him?"

"Because I might be going to Lima. I can pass along a message."

I figured that morning phone call had something to do with Lima, and told her about Lannie. She asked questions, and by the time we finished with Lannie, the temperature had warmed, my ears were popping, and the flora had changed to ferns, banana plants, and broad-leaf trees smothered with creepers. The road also became straighter, the gorges fewer, and soon we were speeding along a tree-lined road where a person could run around without falling into a bottomless chasm.

"Only a few more kilometers," she said. "You're in for a big surprise."

"What surprise?"

"It wouldn't be a surprise if I told you."

The road narrowed. We took a side lane that bumped and twisted beneath flowering poinciana and acacia trees, stirring up a trail of dust. Then I saw it, a large house in the Spanish-Moorish tradition, framed against a backdrop of green trees, as hidden as Marisa's secrets.

"Dos Pasos," Sonia announced. "My family's ancestral home. It used to be a sugar plantation, but that was before land reform. Now it's only a hundred-hectare cattle ranch. No phones, but it's got a generator for power. I own a quarter of it."

"Who owns the rest?"

"An uncle. You've met him."

"I don't remember meeting an uncle."

"Sure you do. They call him Apu Condor."

CHAPTER FIFTY-FIVE
Dos Pasos

A pair of German shepherds rushed out from the shade, snarling and baring their teeth. A young servant girl drove them away with a stick, shouting at them in Quechua and shaming them for their manners. Geese, ducks, and chickens ran loose in the yard. Dirty-nosed children hurried over from a nearby servant's house, chanting and holding hands.

Sonia pulled out a plastic bag and began passing out chocolates.

"I take care of their dental problems," she said, still looking moody.

The girl led us into the house and into a sitting room that had the pleasant smell of a wood-burning fireplace. I went to the bathroom, splashed water on my face, rinsed my mouth to get out the taste of cigarettes, and looked in the mirror. God, did I look awful—hair scraggly, face splotched with shrapnel wounds, clothes baggy. No wonder Sonia was so cold.

When I came out, I noticed another large painting by Francisco de la Vega, this one of the marching mothers in Plaza San Martín, their dead loved ones swirling in the clouds above them, lighting the scene with their radiance.

"It's Condor's favorite painting," Sonia said.

"Tell me about Condor. One minute he's the assistant for General Reál. Then he's a palace official. Then he's an insurgent leader. And he doesn't look anything like you or Marisa."

She poured herself a glass of lemonade and sat on a piano stool in front of an ancient Wurlitzer. "It happened almost fifty years ago. The soldiers came. There was a rape. It's an old story in this country—a raid, a rape, a child. Back then it was a terrible disgrace, a white family with a dark-faced Indian child. Still, they sent him to good schools. He studied medicine and magic and Andean healing. I love him. Just wish he wasn't involved in so much intrigue."

She popped up. "Come on. There's more to see."

The rest of the house was just as imposing as the sitting room—crystal chandeliers, rosewood floors, exposed wooden beams, and more of de la Vega's *Girls of Pachacuti*, all with tiny breasts and shy smiles. The back porch overlooked the remnants of an old Inca trail and beyond it, barely visible in the trees, raged a white-water rapids.

"Where does that trail go?" I asked.

"All Inca roads lead to Cuzco. But if you go that way—north—you'll end up in the jungle. It's not a place you'd want to go. The servants say an old devil lives there."

A horn sounded, causing my heart to jump. Dogs barked. Geese honked.

Sonia grabbed my arm, concern in her face. "About last night," she said.

"What about it?"

"It never happened. It was only a pleasant dream. Okay?"

The dogs and geese had calmed by the time we went out the front door. A blue pickup was parked behind the Land Rover, and at its tailgate stood a young girl in jeans, striped knit pullover, and tennis shoes, pulling out luggage. She rushed over and hugged Sonia.

And then my heart almost stopped. Marisa was there too, looking as troubled to see me as I was to see her. Was this an accidental crossing of paths? Would there be another painful parting?

She glided over and looked into my face, at the scars that were still healing. "Oh, Mark," she said. "Look what they've done to you. Are you all right?"

My voice failed. I turned to the girl. She couldn't have been more than ten or eleven, and her eyes were light brown, the same as mine.

Marisa frowned and bit her lower lip as if this was going to be painful. "This is Cristina," she said, and pulled the girl to her. "She's the unfinished business I couldn't tell you about."

I stuttered something about how pretty she was and how the two of them looked alike.

"I've always thought she looked like you."

I glanced from her to Cristina and then at Sonia for an explanation, but they all avoided my eyes and looked like they'd rather be somewhere else. The servants, who didn't understand English, scooped up the bags. Marisa and Sonia followed them into the house, and then I was alone with a daughter I didn't know I had.

I smiled at her, not knowing what to say or do. "Did you know about this?"

Her eyes filled with tears. She opened her mouth as if to answer, and then she too ran toward the house, creating a storm of honks from the geese.

CHAPTER FIFTY-SIX

How long I stood there, trying to absorb the shock, I don't know. Why the hell hadn't Marisa told me? Condor was a surprise. But this—this was like a ten on the Richter scale. Well, by God, it was time to get some answers.

I stormed into the house and found Marisa in an upstairs bedroom, unpacking her suitcase beneath another de la Vega painting. Sonia and Cristina were with her, but when they saw me, they headed for the door.

Sonia poked my arm on the way out. "Go easy on her. It wasn't her fault."

I closed the door and drew in a deep breath. Marisa avoided my eyes.

"I can't talk about it right now."

She pushed aside the suitcase, sat on the bed and burst into tears.

I plunked down beside her. "Why, Marisa? Just tell me."

"Not now, please. Just give me some time." Her sobs grew louder.

When Marisa got like this, I might as well go outside and shout at the moon. So I kicked aside a shoe and stomped out of the room. Then I almost ran into Cristina, heading down with the stairs with a bag. The drooping corners of her mouth told me she wasn't happy either.

"Here," I said, "let me help you with that."

"I can manage," she said in a little-girl voice.

I followed her out the front door and watched her climb into the Land Rover. Marisa came flying out behind me and rushed over to say good-bye. Sonia, standing on the driver's side, sauntered over to me.

"Not a word," she said, and pecked me on the cheek. Then she climbed back into her SUV with Cristina, said "Bye," and drove away, gears crunching, gravel flying, leaving me alone with a flock of noisy geese and a ton of questions for Marisa.

"Where are they going?" I asked her.

"Cuzco airport. They're flying to Lima. Then Miami."

She turned and headed toward the house, tears streaming down her cheeks.

Dammit to hell, what was it with women? Why couldn't they confront the issue—like a man? Denise had been the same way. Go to her room, close the door and cry.

My injured leg was aching, so I limped to the room that had been assigned to me, only to find a servant putting on fresh sheets. Servants were in the sitting room too, one pushing a vacuum, another arranging flowers in a vase. With nowhere to go and no one to talk to, I hobbled out the back door and made friends with the dogs.

They were male. They understood.

We followed the Inca trail alongside the river, passing beneath eucalyptus and poinciana trees, heading down toward the jungle. Any other time I'd have enjoyed the sight of orchids and bromeliads in the trees, and the river that boiled green in the sunlight, and impatiens that grew wild along the sloping bank, but all I could think about was this sudden turn of events. Marisa coming back into my life. With a daughter. Our daughter. My child.

Poor thing. This must have been hard for her as well.

The dogs sniffed around in the underbrush. Parakeets flitted from tree to tree, all blue and green and chirping, and here and there the trail stair-cased into wooded ravines and up the other side. At the top of one of those ravines stood another Inca ruin. The roof had long since collapsed, but the massive walls, covered with lichen and creepers, were as solid as the day the Incas had cut the stones and fit them together like a puzzle.

Did Cristina play here? Was it still haunted by the old gods?

As if in answer, the wind picked up, thunder rumbled, and a flock of birds fluttered out of a tree. I stepped inside the ruins, ducking beneath the low entrance. The dogs followed. The air was cool and musty, with a faint smell of crushed mint. In the center rose a fountain, covered with ivy, and beyond it, against a wall, lay a raised earthen-and-stone bed.

I swept off the debris and stretched out my leg like an injured Inca warrior. Five hundred years ago, some other poor bastard had laid on this very spot, thinking about his girlfriend. Maybe he'd also knocked up a honcho's daughter. But had she gone off and married another man? Had she kept him ignorant for ten years?

I was still lying there, searching for answers, when another of those fuzzy-headed green parrots alighted on the broken wall, looking remarkably like the one I'd seen back at the training camp. Thunder rumbled again. The dogs, so tranquil before, jumped to their feet, barked, and dashed away. Then Marisa appeared in the doorway with a stone and flung it against the wall.

"For the old gods," she said. "Just in case."

CHAPTER FIFTY-SEVEN

She had changed into khaki shorts and a white T-shirt. Her hair was pulled back in a ponytail. At first she just stood there, biting her lower lip, seeming to search for words. Then she wiped her tears on her sleeve and looked at me through those big sad eyes.

"It wasn't supposed to happen this way."

"Well, it happened, so you might as well tell me."

"Look, I was nineteen years old—nineteen and pregnant, stuck with my parents in Miami. And you were here, in that little Runa village. No telephones, no e-mails, no way to get in touch. I didn't know what to do. I was alone. Desperate."

I motioned her onto the Inca bed beside her. "What did your dad say?"

"The problem was my mom. She was running for city commissioner. In Miami. With a pregnant daughter. It was a tight race. A few votes would make a difference. She wanted to send me away and give the child up for adoption. I told her that you and I were getting married anyway, as soon as you were out of the Peace Corps. Then Sonia's dad—Mom's brother-in-law—came up with a solution. This place. *Dos Pasos.*"

"You came here?"

"It was the perfect solution. I could return to Peru, find you, and we'd be married. But you'd already left. The embassy

238

tried to help me find you, but the closest we got was an uncle in Minnesota. He said you were in Norway, visiting relatives, and he didn't have a clue how to get in touch. My mom said you were probably avoiding me."

"And you believed her?"

"I didn't know what to believe. I was confused. It wasn't until later I learned you'd gone to Miami, looking for me. As for my mom...well, she told you I was in Spain."

I stood and paced around the ruins, kicking creepers out of the way. letting my mind play back over the years. Wars had been fought because of poor communications, and I'd lost ten years with Marisa and our daughter for lack of a telephone.

"Why didn't you tell me three years ago?"

"How could I, Mark? I was married. Suppose you'd made an issue out of it? Suppose things didn't work out between us? So I kept putting it off and putting it off."

"And now you're sending Cristina to Miami?"

"I had to. Soldiers could show up without warning. Or the guerillas. And both sides do terrible things to young girls. That's why I had to leave you in Ayacucho."

"Why didn't you just explain that in Ayacucho?"

"Because my husband—make that ex-husband—was holding her hostage. He wanted me back. Said I'd never see her again if I ran off with you. I had to make a painful choice—you or Cristina. If I'd told you, I don't know what you'd have done."

"Did Sonia know about this?"

"I made her promise not to tell you."

"Did Sonia know we might get back together?"

"How could she know? I didn't know. All I could think about was Cristina."

"You said he was holding her hostage. How'd you get her away?"

"Short version is he does drugs."

"You didn't..."

"No, but I'd like to kill him. By now he'll think I'm in Miami."

The storm was closer now, the wind gusting, blowing more debris into the ruins and bringing in damp, earthy smells. I told her again about wandering heartbroken around Europe, visiting relatives in Norway, and then going back to graduate school, and she told me she'd stayed heartbroken until Cristina was born and didn't get married until she'd given up on me.

"It was a mistake. People do things at nineteen they'd never do at thirty."

Tears fell like rain, suspicions dissipated in the mist, and then she came into my arms.

"Tell me you love me, Mark. Tell me it's okay."

Our lips met, we fondled, and we were yanking off clothes when my conservative Minnesota upbringing kicked in, reminding me I'd been with Sonia only a few hours before, and it didn't seem right. Not now. Not yet. But we were already out of our clothes. Marisa wanted my love, I wanted hers, and thunder was crashing around us, the wind howling, rain falling sideways.

CHAPTER FIFTY-EIGHT

In time the thunder diminished, the rain slacked, frogs came to life, and we discovered that getting back into drenched clothing wasn't nearly as easy as getting out. Marisa's hair was a stringy mess, and her eyes were red from crying, but I thought she'd never looked so beautiful.

"We'd better get back before they send out a search party," she said, buttoning her shorts.

"You still haven't told me why your things showed up at Gonzalo's hideout."

"I thought you'd figured it out."

"Your ex?"

"Of course."

"He's an associate of Comrade Gonzalo?"

"It's more complicated than that."

"Tell me."

"Not until we're out of this country."

I knew the explanation—that we could still be captured and taken to Dracula's House and be tortured, and they'd find out about Cristina and possibly go after her as well—so I didn't badger her, and we hiked back in the mist, showered in an outside bathhouse, draped towels around our bodies, and sneaked back into the house without being seen.

Marisa took my arm. "Come on, I have something to show you."

I followed her down the hall to my room. On the bed was my old suitcase that I'd abandoned in Lima, and laid out beside it were all my clothes and shoes. I picked up my leather jacket and breathed in its richness.

"How in God's name did you manage this?"

"God had nothing to do with it. You'd be surprised what money can buy in this country."

༺

The generator kicked off around nine that evening. By then, we'd eaten and lit candles and I'd told Marisa about my experiences of the past couple of weeks—everything except what happened with Sonia—and she was apologizing for sending me off with a bunch of lunatics, saying she had no idea, when a motorcycle drove up in front.

Marisa dashed to the front door. I followed her out in time to see a uniformed man from the Saywite Telephone Exchange handing her a sealed envelope.

She gave him a tip, rushed back inside, read the message in lamplight, said, "Thank goodness," and handed it to me. It was a one-liner from Sonia.

In Lima. All is well. C aboard American and on her way to Miami.

༺

The next morning I tumbled out of bed and pushed open the balcony doors. Fresh air and the smells of sweet growing things swept in. There were no soldiers or wail of sirens, only the crow of roosters and flow of the river. Still, I figured we had a week, two at the most, before Lieutenant Bravos showed up with his trucks and airplanes and a platoon of Sinchis.

Marisa stirred. "Why are you up so early? It's not even seven."

"I'm ready to go exploring, maybe take a dip in the river."

"That river's runoff from the mountains. It's like ice."

"Okay, forget the river. Let's talk escape."

"After breakfast. We're safe for now."

"That's what we thought in Ayacucho. Shouldn't we at least have a plan?"

"I'm working on it with Sonia. She'll be back tomorrow."

"But what if we have to leave today? What if the unexpected happens?"

She rolled out of bed and yanked on her robe. I thought she was going to hit me. Instead, she motioned me onto the balcony. "See that Inca trail?" she said, pointing downriver. "That's our Plan C. We can follow it into the jungle."

"Good, let's eat breakfast and go have a look."

"Are you crazy? That place is creepy, full of snakes and wild animals."

"Better snakes and wild animals than Lieutenant Bravos."

CHAPTER FIFTY-NINE
The Jungle

We followed the same trail I'd taken the day before, passing the Inca ruins we'd christened with our lovemaking. The dogs ran ahead. Marisa and I stopped now and then to admire orchids and bromeliads, or rainbows where the river threw up a mist against the rocks. Here and there we passed through copses of eucalyptus and blue-flowering jacaranda, and I had just bent down to inspect a flower when a small airplane buzzed overhead.

I grabbed Marisa and pulled her beneath the trees.

It flew on. My heartbeat returned to normal, and then I had a flash of genius.

"We could rent a plane. Get them to fly us to Brazil."

"Oh really? And how are you going to explain why your picture's on their bulletin board? Twenty-five-thousand-dollar reward. They'd fly you straight to Lima."

"That's all—twenty-five-thousand? How much for you?"

"Thirty-thousand the last time I looked, but they want me alive."

We trod on, traversing an open field where horses and cattle grazed, and at last came to a stone fence. The jungle beyond it rose like a mountain of green, pulsing with noise and life. The trail with its paved Inca stones led into it, disappearing like a track entering a dark tunnel.

"Far enough," Marisa said.

"Oh come on, don't be such a scaredy-cat." I pulled her down to a wooded gully that defined the perimeter. Butterflies floated around us like tiny, rainbow-colored bubbles, rising and falling.

"See," I said. "No snakes or forest devils."

We jumped a tiny stream, followed the uneven Inca steps up to the other side, and found ourselves in a place that only the makers of a Tarzan movie would love.

Trees as broad as houses loomed up like monsters, all bell-bottomed and covered with creepers, tentacles, and ferns. Water dripped like rain. Fog blanketed the ground, and things moved in the overhead, screeching and croaking.

"We should go back," Marisa said, clinging to my arm.

"But look at this trail. Someone's been using it."

We crept on. Mosquitoes and biting flies swarmed around us. Things chirped and croaked, and we had gone no more than about fifty paces when we came to a cluster of feathers and sticks, dangling from overhead by a red cord.

"A warning sign," Marisa said, tugging at my arm. "We should go back."

"A warning for what?"

"Look, all I know is what happened last year. Some German hikers came here. They said they were going to follow the trail up to the Vilcabamba Valley. We warned them, but…"

"But what?"

"Never came out. Their families came looking for them, but they were never found."

We turned back, our progress faster than before, and were almost at the ravine when something crashed, like a limb falling from a tree. The jungle fell silent, as if every bird, frog, and monkey had looked up to see what had happened.

Then a gunshot shattered the stillness.

We plunged into the gully, landing about halfway down, sliding through ferns and dampness. Marisa bounded up and was clawing her way up the other side when I grabbed her arm.

"No, it's open field up there. They'll see us."

I pushed her along the gully to the right, crashing through ferns and palmettos, jumping over fallen trees and sloshing through water, hoping my leg wouldn't give out.

"There," I said, and pointed to a patch of giant philodendron. I poked around for snakes with my walking stick, and then we crawled underneath and pulled the foliage around us.

Marisa pressed tight against me, and for a moment I was back on that hilltop with Faviola, the vans rolling down the hill, the smell of perfume and fear.

"Didn't I tell you?" she said, almost in tears. "Why are you so damn stubborn?"

Frogs and crickets and overhead creatures started their infernal racket. Mosquitoes found us, and then a man appeared on the trail, a coppery-colored Indian with a straw hat, AK-47, and bandolier of ammunition. Around his neck were strings of monkey teeth. A machete hung from a strap around his shoulder, and even through the foliage, I could see tribal markings on his face.

"Machiguenga," I whispered to Marisa. "They're friendly."

"No. He's Unga—an Ungacachano. They're bad news."

We sank lower. The Unga drank from the stream, glanced around, and seemed to notice the skid marks we'd made on the embankment. He sniffed the air. Then he unslung his AK and began creeping toward us like an animal stalking his prey.

Marisa let out a little whimper. I took out my Swiss Army knife and opened it to the long blade as if that would protect us against an AK. Why the hell hadn't I listened to Marisa?

He came closer, looking left and right and into the trees. What if he smelled us? What if he opened fire? Maybe I should pounce on him with my knife. Maybe we should surrender.

From somewhere came a shout. The Unga turned around, grunted something, and retraced his steps to the Inca trail. I breathed again.

"Is he gone?" Marisa whispered,

"Not yet. He's smoking a cigarette."

Another Unga appeared beside him, leading a mule. They conversed in their Indian language. Then came more mules and men, the mules strapped together and loaded with bundles, the men armed with machetes and assault rifles. Now and then I caught a whiff of cigarette smoke, kerosene and the pungent odor of sweaty mules.

"They're traffickers," Marisa hissed.

"Did you know about this?"

"All I know is if we don't bother them, they don't bother us."

Mules and men drank from the stream. The men swatted at flies and smoked cigarettes. And then I realized I'd seen this scene before. General Reál had shown it to me in a newspaper back in Lima, a headline that read: DRUG TRAFFICKERS ARRESTED IN THE JUNGLE. And here they were again: another mule train and another load of coca paste—déjà vu in the jungle.

"Look," I whispered. "They're leaving."

Up the embankment they struggled—five mules and five men, the mules snorting and shitting, the men with their AKs and machetes, as nasty and fierce looking as Tucno. They clopped away, and when the noise died, I raised my head and breathed in the fading smells of cigarette smoke and mule manure.

"Let's give them a few more minutes, just to be sure."

We waited, swatting at mosquitoes and bloodsucking flies. Marisa explained they sometimes stopped at the house and stole chickens and geese, and frightened the servants, and the only one who could control them was Apu Condor.

At last we eased out of our hiding place and climbed up the embankment, emerging into a dazzling sunlight. Our clothes were drenched and filthy, our faces mud-streaked, and we were covered with insect bites and scratches, but the air had never seemed so fresh and cool, the butterflies so colorful—or sunlight so welcome.

Marisa clapped her hands for the dogs. "Tupac! Huascár!"

There was movement in a thicket of trees near the fence. The dogs bounded out.

And behind them came the Ungas.

CHAPTER SIXTY

They circled us like a pack of wolves, barking commands in a language I didn't understand, poking and prodding with their AKs, bringing with them the stench of unwashed bodies. The tallest barely reached my chin, and the entire group had fewer teeth than a child. The leader, an older man with facial markings that looked like cat whiskers, began shouting in my face, polluting the air with his putrid breath.

"I don't understand a word," I told him in Spanish.

"Quechua," Marisa said, "try Quechua."

I didn't have to. He narrowed his eyes and asked if I understood *Runasimi,* which was the Quechua word for tongue-of-the-people.

"*Arí,*" I answered. Yes.

He yelled something to his fellow Ungas, and then asked, "How is it that we, the people of the forest, have come together at this place with a white foreigner, a *wiracocha?*"

I pointed upriver and said, "*Jatun wasi,*" meaning the big house. "We are guests. We came out for a walk. We heard a gunshot. It frightened us. We hid."

He translated for the others. They conferred among themselves in their guttural language, pointing and glancing, swishing machetes through the air, showering each other with spittle.

The old man turned back to me. "They say you are one of those *wiracochas* who poison the coca crops and destroy our livelihood."

"*Manan*—no. We have nothing to do with those people. We are alone, only a man and a woman." I held up two intertwined fingers in the Quechua gesture for lovers. "We are like this."

Again he translated, but this set off another tirade of yelling. They spat. They shook machetes at one other and at us. The old man turned back to me. "My people say they know the family in that house, but they do not know you. They say they know the master in that house, but that man is not you. They say you are a liar and a spy for the *wiracochas*."

One of the Ungas looked into Marisa's eyes and uttered a word that probably meant "blue." He then made a lengthy speech that was translated as, "I know this woman. I have seen those eyes. This man is not her man. He was sent here by the *wiracochas* to destroy us."

Marisa pushed me aside and pointed a finger at the Ungas as if she were a witch casting a spell. "*Apu Kuntur*," she said in a voice that was barely a whisper.

The word itself seemed to carry magic, as if the wind had spoken. The butterflies floated away. Even the insects and the frogs seemed to listen. She said it again, a word that in Quechua meant condor, as in a man called Apu Condor.

"*Apu Kuntur* will not be pleased," she said, speaking in the halting Quechua I'd heard her use with the servants. "If you harm us, you will answer to him."

The old man stared. "Where is *Apu Kuntur*?"

"In the City of the Corner of Corpses—Ayacucho. Through me, he sends the following message: 'May the light of the sun shine on your path. May your children prosper. May the Sinchis—the men of the shiny buttons—die a slow and painful death.'"

A toothless smile crossed the old man's face. He yelled for the mules. Out of the trees they came, led by a boy with teeth in his mouth instead of around his neck. The old man opened the gate in the stone fence, and then these people of the forest who only moments before had been ready to hack us to death clopped away with their mules.

Marisa watched them go, fire in her eyes. "Bastards. Now they'll report what they saw—a Quechua-speaking gringo with a blue-eyed woman. Then somebody's going to show them a wanted poster with your picture on it. And they'll come back for our heads."

"Where are they going to report it?"

"The airstrip. That's what the airplane was about. They take their paste to the airport."

"Why didn't you tell me this before?"

"Because you'd have started with your questions, asking if I had anything to do with it. The answer is no. I don't. Neither does Sonia."

"But Condor does?"

"He charges them a safe passage fee, a toll. It's how the Shining Path finances their operations. General Reál does the same. That's why he wants to capture Chairman Gonzalo—not because Gonzalo's a terrorist, but because he's the competition."

Lannie had told me the same thing back in Lima, but back in Lima, I hadn't shed any blood. Hadn't seen dead men either, or Ungacachanos with machetes.

"That airstrip is only about ten miles away," Marisa said. "They usually spend the night, then load their mules with kerosene and come back this way. They could come as early as tonight."

We trod on, following the Inca trail back toward the house, discussing our options. The house was too big to defend. It had too many doors and balconies, and even if we held them off, they could burn us out.

"What about Condor?" I asked. "Can't he stop them?"

"Condor can't stop anyone. He's in the hospital."

"He was fine when I last saw him."

"He took a bullet in that battle. It's serious."

We passed the Inca ruins, came to a wooded ravine, had a long look to make sure Ungas weren't waiting with their machetes, and hurried through it, the dogs tagging behind.

"Maybe we should get in touch with Lannie Torres," I said. "He'll help me."

"Are you crazy? He's DEA. He'd send in the black helicopters...and the troops. They'll shoot the place up, level the jungle, poison the crops."

"Why should you care? Look at all the lives they're destroying."

She stopped and glared. "I don't give a damn about the Ungas. It's the farmers I care about. They're all over this valley, small family farmers. It's their only livelihood." She picked up a stone and flung it into the river. "Do you know how many people died in the US last year from cocaine? Five thousand. Compare that with cigarette deaths—almost half a million. Why don't they poison tobacco crops in North Carolina?"

"Look, point is—Lannie can get us out of the country."

"Like he got you out? No, Mark. I don't trust anyone at the embassy. Forget it."

We were still arguing when we reached the house, and would have kept arguing except for all the dead geese and chickens in the yard, along with entrails, blood, and feathers. Vultures were already descending on the place, alighting on the roof and in the trees.

The servants rushed out, their faces a picture of distress, all of them talking at once. They said the Ungas demanded food. The servants gave them leftovers, but they wanted more.

"They went on a killing spree," said the woman who did most of the talking, screwing up her face in disgust. "Wrung the chickens' necks. Drank their blood. Ate them raw."

Marisa turned to me, her eyes wide. "We should get out of here, now."

"What about the servants?"

"It's us they'll be after, not the servants."

"But where can we go?"

"The Saywite shrine. We can spend the night there...in the truck. Sonia should be passing early tomorrow. We can flag her down."

I didn't tell her that Tika's body was probably at Saywite. Didn't really care so long as we could hide there. So we made sandwiches and coffee, gathered our things, and went outside to load the pickup. Vultures were there too, even on the truck, dozens of them, flopping around and fighting over the carcasses, and still more coming.

I took the keys from Marisa and told her to wait on the porch. Then I pushed my way through the vultures, climbed into the truck, and turned the ignition key.

Nothing happened. Not even a click, and when I looked under the hood, I saw that every wire had been ripped out, the hoses slashed, the battery missing, radiator fluid dripping.

CHAPTER SIXTY-ONE

"Bastards," I muttered, and slammed the hood shut. I tromped back through the buzzards to the porch. "It's hopeless," I said. "Is there someplace else we can hide?"

She paced around, made a few unkind comments about Ungas, and shooed away vultures that were lighting on the railing. "There's another Inca ruins about five or six miles up the road. We can hide out there, but it's creepy. They say it's haunted."

"It's either that or Ungas. Do you have any guns here?"

"Condor has an entire arsenal."

She asked one of the male servants to bring around the tractor and trailer, then went inside with the women. A few minutes later they came back with AK-47s, extra clips of ammunition, a bandolier, gun vests, and pistols. Marisa had changed into military fatigues and boots and had a pistol strapped around her waist, and would have looked right at home in Camp Pachacuti.

"Let's do it," she said. "Ever driven a tractor?"

It was an ancient Allis Chalmers with a torn seat, bent fenders, and broken muffler. Marisa climbed into the trailer with our luggage and weaponry. I strapped on a Glock, climbed into the driver's seat, and fired it up. Then, like pioneers fleeing an

Indian uprising in a covered wagon, we sputtered off toward the ruins, following a trail of Unga hoof-prints and mule droppings.

Cliffs and dense vegetation soared up on both sides. Vultures followed in the overhead as if they knew something we didn't. Here and there a deer or some other animal darted across the road. The wheels wobbled and pulled to the right. The sun sank lower. Shadows grew longer, and when we finally reached the ruins, I could have cried with joy.

It was about fifty yards off the road, an enormous building covered with vines and ferns. The roof had long since collapsed. Rubble lay all around, but the thick cut stone walls remained intact, perfect for defense.

"Where are the ghosts?" I asked.

"Too early. They only come out at night."

She explained that Pizarro's conquistadores, on their way to Cuzco, had attacked the place and slaughtered everyone—men, women, and children—and their spirits were said to be waiting for the day of Pachacuti. She picked up a broken stone, said, "Just in case," and tossed it against the wall. I did the same. We chose a place that had a view of the trail, then unloaded our gear, cleared away spider webs and creepers, spread our blankets and sleeping bags, put our weapons within easy reach, and watched darkness spread over the valley.

Fireflies flickered like little stars. Orion burned cold and blue, and in the air was the smell of a distant wood fire. Marisa leaned into me and told me more about the valley and the farmers and how Condor ruled over the place like an Inca lord. She spoke lovingly of him, telling me he'd studied drama in Lima, been a stage actor and magician, and could make things disappear and reappear. "The Ungas are terrified of him."

"If they're so scared of him, why'd they kill his chickens and geese?"

"They don't know it's his place. No one does. I'm guessing the reason they were so nasty is because of you. The only foreigners they've ever seen are Lannie Torres types, come to destroy their operations. So when they learned you were staying there, they—"

She stiffened and grabbed my arm. "What's that?"

"What?"

"Back there. In the ruins. It's moving."

Her grip on my arm tightened.

I peered into the darkness, listening to the crickets and frogs and the coo of night birds. From somewhere came movement, the snap of a twig, and then all was quiet.

"Just an animal," I said.

"I'm scared."

"It'll be okay. It's only—"

Something screamed. Loud. Like a woman being murdered.

I bounded up with my AK and clicked off the safety.

"What is it?" whispered Marisa.

"Maybe a bird."

"Birds don't sound like that. Maybe you should shoot."

"It'll give our position away."

"It already knows our position."

We waited. Things croaked and hooted. Patches of fog drifted around us—cool, damp, and alive. As a child I'd read James Fennimore Cooper's Pathfinder Series and fancied myself a frontiersman with a musket and coonskin cap, protecting my family against savages, all romance and glory. But there was no glory now. Only the darkness and the kind of fear that sends shivers up the spine and causes hair to stand on end.

"It's moving," Marisa said, "coming toward us."

There was a deep, throaty growl, like a wild animal.

Then it shrieked again, louder, closer.

Marisa almost knocked me over trying to climb out the window. I followed her out with my AK, the shriek still in my ears. We dashed to the tractor. Marisa hopped into the trailer. I dropped down in a shooter's stance, finger on the trigger.

Nothing happened. No one or nothing came, but every piece of rubble took on the shape of that old forest devil, ready to spring on us and sink its fangs into our necks.

"Maybe we should just stay here," I said. "In the trailer."

"Fine by me, but it's cold. We need our sleeping bags and blankets. Our food and coffee."

"You expect me to go back in that place?"

"One of us has to do it."

∾

The first rays of light found me still sitting in that smelly trailer with my AK, blanket around my shoulders, scratching at insect bites, sipping coffee from a thermos, and thinking this was no way to live. Marisa stirred and asked what time it was. I looked at my watch and was about to tell her when the distant blare of a car horn shattered the morning, followed by a burst of gunfire.

Marisa bounded up. "Oh my God. That could be Sonia."

I raced the short distance from the tractor to the road. No sooner did I get there than Sonia's Land Rover came tearing down the road, trailing a cloud of dust.

She skidded to a stop beside me, her face a picture of terror.

"Ungas," she cried, "They shot at me, the bastards. Busted a back window."

"Are you all right?"

"I think so, but they're coming this way."

Marisa trotted toward us with her AK. Sonia looked at me. "You didn't tell her, did you?"

"Hell no, and you better not tell her either."

"Tell me what?" Marisa said.

"Ungas," I said, pointing up the road. "They're coming."

The three of us fell into a spirited discussion of what to do. Couldn't go back to the house because they'd corner us there. Couldn't drive through them because they'd open fire.

Couldn't hide because they'd already seen us.

By then we could hear them, yipping and shouting like the savages they were. "We'll have to confront them," I said, and began giving orders like Tucno.

CHAPTER SIXTY-TWO

They clopped into our midst—seven mules and seven men—bringing with them the familiar smells of leather, unwashed bodies, mules and kerosene. Vultures circled above them like a black cloud of doom. Sonia had pulled her Land Rover to the side, and now stood behind it with an AK and grenades. Marisa waited behind a tree, also armed and dangerous.

And I stood next to a tree like a badass character in a Schwarzenegger movie, all done up with dangling grenades, bandolier, and Kalashnikov at the ready.

"Stop right there!" I commanded in Quechua, my finger on the trigger.

They stopped, but stayed on the side of the mules away from us, their rifle barrels vertical. It grew so quiet, I could hear the hoot of an owl.

A head popped up from behind a mule.

"Who are you?" came a reedy voice.

"Apu Wiracocha, the man you met yesterday."

"What do you want?"

"Only to talk. Stand down with your weapons. And don't get any ideas. My men are all around. Both sides of the road."

"Which men?"

"Men of the Shining Path. My men. My friends."

They began yapping among themselves, probably arguing.

"Enough," I yelled. "Who is in charge? Get out here so we can talk."

The toothless old man who'd confronted me the day before stepped from behind his mule, all monkey teeth and faux cat whiskers, a cigarette in his mouth.

"Over here," I said, "and put down that damn machete."

He dropped the machete to his side by a strap, and stepped up to me.

I slapped the cigarette out of his mouth. "Which one of you lowlife snakes shot at Apu Kuntur's car?" I jabbed a finger in his chest. "Answer me, old man. Who shot at that car?"

He turned and supposedly translated my words. Or maybe he told them to shoot. Whatever the case, no one answered and no one shot, so I kept yelling, using every foul word I knew in the Quechua language, getting so worked up, I felt my face growing hot.

"You and your men also killed chickens and geese in that big house. The people who live there are my friends. And friends of the Shining Path. Do you understand what I'm saying?"

"Yes, wiracocha."

"It's Apu wiracocha. Now turn around and tell your men what I said."

He swung about and spoke to them in his language.

"And tell them this: Apu Kuntur sends word by this woman"—I gestured at Sonia—"that if any of you vulture-face bastards ever again touch one of those chickens or geese, or any of my friends' property, or trouble the servants, he will send the old forest devil after you. Or maybe he'll send me, and I'll destroy you and your piece-of-shit operations in the jungle. Kill your dogs and all your mules. Take your women. Your children too."

Behind me, Marisa said, "Don't overdo it, Mark."

I wanted to overdo it. I was sick of being kicked around by the likes of General Reál and Bravos and Gordo and Tucno and these scrawny little creatures of the jungle who'd put such a scare into us the day before and caused us to spend a sleepless night in a creepy ruins.

"What did you tell them about us at the air strip?" I asked him.

"I said nothing about you, Apu wiracocha."

"You lie. You told them everything. They sent a messenger to say you were coming for us."

By then he looked like he was about to cry. "It was their idea," he said.

"How much money did they offer?"

"No money. Only free kerosene."

Not until then did I notice that each mule was loaded with two drums. "How much kerosene?"

"Kerosene for a year."

"Did they want us dead or alive?"

"They did not say."

"So you were coming to kill us, weren't you—for kerosene?"

He backed away and glanced at his men. Sonia, still standing behind her Land Rover, said, "Don't push him, Mark. If he thinks you're going to kill him, he'll go down fighting."

I turned back to the old man. "Today I will not kill you. But if you ever again come after me—or these women, or my friends in that big house, or the geese and chickens, I will send death and destruction to you and your people. Do you understand?"

"*Arí,*" said the old man, his face a picture of dread.

"Say it again. Say, yes, Apu wiracocha. I understand."

"Yes, Apu wiracocha, I understand."

Just to show what a mean bastard I was, I took one of the grenades off my jacket and waved it in his face. "Go, get out of my sight before I change my mind and blow you and your fucking mules to pieces. I never want to see you or your ugly face again."

The old man took the reins of his mule, yelled a command to his men, and they clopped away, urging their mules forward. But I was so worked up that they'd come with murderous intentions that I pulled the pin from the grenade and flung it across the road anyway.

It exploded with a roar, throwing up smoke and dust and singing debris, and sending the Ungas into a panicked trot.

I flung another grenade. Then, just for the hell of it, I fired a burst of gunfire into the air, venting my anger on the clouds and the vultures and the sky.

Afterward, with smoke and smells still in the air, and the Ungas nowhere in sight, Marisa stepped in front of me, all wide eyed with shock.

"Have you gone mad? Is that the way you deal with students in your economics class?"

"Only if they're not paying attention."

Sonia trotted to her Land Rover, pulled out a Polaroid, and took my picture. By then I was so pumped up at becoming the kicker instead of the kickee that I think if a Kinkos had been nearby I'd have made copies for all the newspapers in Peru, all the TV stations, and even for my dean in Tampa, and written across each one—*Make my day.*

CHAPTER SIXTY-THREE

We gathered our things and loaded them into the Land Rover. Marisa climbed in front with Sonia. I piled into the back. We took off with a spinning of wheels, and a few minutes later, with the vehicle twisting and groaning up the mountain, with my ears popping and the valley falling away behind us, the *soroche* visited me again, this time with nausea and a pounding headache.

Sonia, who was used to the elevation, told us how frightened she was at being shot at by the Ungas. Marisa told her about our scare in the ruins. Sonia said she'd rather face Ungas than spend a night in a haunted ruins, and then they were speculating about the scream.

"A screech owl," I mumbled from the back.

"Not a screech owl. It was something sinister."

My headache got worse when we reached Saywite and turned west. In the past, I'd always been traveling east, away from Lieutenant Bravos and General Reál. But now, looking out at the same boulders and road signs and political slogans, at the same bleakness of twelve thousand feet, I felt like that character in Greek mythology who was doomed forever to roll a heavy rock uphill, only to have it roll down again.

We were passing through another of those nameless little mud-and-stone villages that hadn't changed since Pizarro's time when Sonia said, "I almost forgot. The Lima papers printed your verses. I brought copies. Wanna read them?"

I didn't feel like reading. Didn't feel like doing anything except crawling into bed. But Marisa, who didn't seem to be suffering, pulled out the papers.

"Look," she said. "They put your verses on the front page." She began reading aloud.

> Send me your Sinchis, and Peep agents too.
> But never will I abandon her / My Lily of Peru.

"That's so sweet," Sonia said. "I wish someone would write poetry like that for me."

Marisa skipped to the editorial page, still reading aloud. Sleet began to fall, pelting the windshield and drumming on the roof of the Land Rover. Marisa raised her voice to compete with the roar. I closed my eyes and tried to listen, and somewhere amid the noise of windshield wipers, engine, rain, heater, and swish of tires, I heard the words, "basket of self-serving nonsense wrapped in a ribbon of I-did-it-all-for-love."

"Oh my God," Marisa said. "They put you in a cartoon."

She held it up for me, and through the haze of my misery, I saw a caricature of myself in the puffy attire of Shakespearean times—pointy-toed boots, striped pantaloons, and a feathered beret, running my sword through the heart of Gordo, saying, "Juliet, Juliet, how sweet smells the blood of thine enemies."

"Can you stop?" I asked Sonia. "I think I'm going to be sick."

In time we entered Abancay, which was covered in fine snow, and turned left at the station where I'd last seen Faviola. Up the hill we drove in low gear, following the same street that had been so agonizing for me. But instead of going to Sonia's house, we drove past it and ended up on the next block, in the drive of an imposing two-story Mediterranean.

"A friend's house," she said, "a doctor. He and his wife are in the States."

"What about that house search?" I asked Sonia.

"Finished. They found nothing."

Sonia unlocked the door and showed us around. I didn't care about the walnut floors or beamed ceilings or the entertainment center. All I wanted was a nap, and might have gone straight to the bedroom until Marisa pulled Sonia into the kitchen and closed the door.

Dear God, no. Was Marisa going to question her about what happened?

Their voices rose and fell. Something clattered. I crept to the door and tried to listen, but they were now speaking in hushed tones, and all I heard was Sonia saying, "Tell him."

Tell me what?

They came out, neither of them looking happy. Sonia nodded and left. Marisa got a fire going in the fireplace, brewed coca tea, and turned on the television. She adjusted the rabbit ears and finally got a fuzzy image of the woman with the bad hairdo, reporting on the latest carnage—an assassination in Lima, a car bomb in Callao, a street lined with hanging dogs.

The scene cut to Inspector Bocanegra at a podium, holding up a newspaper with a headline that read: ROMEO CLAIMS INNOCENCE IN VERSE. "Pure fiction," he said. "Professor Thorsen is just another left-leaning academic who sees romance in rebellion."

I watched until the reception went bad, at which time Marisa turned it off, poured more tea, and sat on the sofa next to me.

"We need to talk."

CHAPTER SIXTY-FOUR

Nothing good ever followed those words, so I braced myself, waiting for the interrogation about Sonia, certain that Sonia had confessed. She squirmed as if this wasn't going to be easy, then stood, strolled to the window, turned back, and bit her lower lip.

"Back in Ayacucho you told me this guy had been contracted to kill me."

I breathed easier. "His name is Tucno."

"Right, but his job wasn't to kill me; it was to drag me back to my ex."

A log settled in the fireplace. Marisa took another sip of tea. "Here's what happened. I was managing my husband's money. Putting it into joint accounts in Miami."

"Drug money?"

"Not at first. He had a profitable business. Legitimate. But a couple years back, the profits started to multiply. By huge amounts. That's when I found out he'd gotten into that toll business with the narcos. Not only that. He was skimming from the Shining Path."

I sat up, suddenly forgetting my headache. "You've got to be kidding."

"No, Mark. I'm not kidding. You don't steal from the Shining Path. Can you imagine what they'd do to him? To us? Maybe even Cristina. That's when I knew I had to get away."

"Why don't you just give the money back?"

"Can't. At least not yet. Did Sonia tell you about her legal troubles in Florida?"

"She told me."

"Did she also tell you she jumped bail? Or that it cost a half million? Not that I'm complaining. It was for a good cause. I put up the money and then encouraged her to run. Otherwise she'd be rotting in prison."

"So all the money's gone?"

"There's more, lots more, but I'm not returning it until I'm safely out of the country. It's my insurance. It's another reason he hasn't sent Tucno around to kill me."

"Where's it now?"

"The States. In different accounts. Different passwords. I'm the only one who can access it. I also wrote down all the dirt on him. Names, dates, statements, all his activities. Sealed it in a thick envelope and gave it to my mom for safekeeping. He knows that. I told him a copy would go to the Peruvian Embassy in the event of my death

ᖆ

Four or five days went by. Marisa fussed over my wounds like a loving wife. Sonia came around every evening with food, newspapers, and a ton of memories. Sometimes she lifted an eyebrow and grinned as if to say she hadn't forgotten either, but my heart still jumped when she and Marisa headed to the kitchen for a private talk.

What were they talking about?

I also tried to continue my story in verse, but it was hopeless. Nothing came out the way I wanted. No rhythm, no lyricism or passion, nothing but pedestrian blah. It troubled Marisa more than me, and then one morning at breakfast, she finally put words to it.

"Maybe it's because you got the girl and now we're like an old married couple."

"Maybe it's because I'm so preoccupied with escape."

"You didn't have any trouble composing for Sonia."

She marched into the kitchen and came back with newspapers. "I finally got around to reading these," she said, a glint of fire in her eyes. "You called her Little Gypsy Girl. Good stuff. But then I came to this."

I took the paper and began reading, and knew immediately I was in trouble.

> She tended my wounds when I was hurting / and listened to my tales of woe.
> She brought me food when I was hungry / and filled my days with hope.
> And yet she bewitched me with her beauty / and cast a sticky web...

"What kind of sticky web?" Marisa asked.

"I was hurting, Marisa. Sonia helped me. Stuck her neck out for me. Twice."

"You slept with her, didn't you?"

"No, Marisa, but even if I had, who the hell are you to complain? You dumped me. Remember? Sent me away with lunatics. Went back to your husband."

"I didn't sleep with him if that's what you're implying."

"How could I know that? You didn't exactly call to let me know."

A car drove into the driveway. Marisa hurried to the door for a look.

"It's Sonia, and you're not going to believe who's with her."

CHAPTER SIXTY-FIVE

Lannie Torres marched into the house like he owned it, all boots, sunglasses, leather jacket, and turquoise bolo, a grin as big as Texas.

"Hey, old buddy. The hell's going on?" He embraced me and slapped me on the back. Then he planted a big kiss on Marisa's cheeks, Latin-style. "Finally we get to meet," he said.

Marisa glared at Sonia as if she'd brought leprosy into the house. Sonia, who had that ashen-faced, just-got-laid look, motioned Marisa into the kitchen. Lannie plopped onto the sofa.

"The hell didn't you call me back in Lima? I was waiting."

"I called you three…four times. Didn't Easton tell you?"

"All he said was you popped Gordo."

"I didn't pop him. I defended myself. Then I called you. Easton said to stop calling."

"That prick. I had a plane waiting. We could have got you out, avoided all this crap."

"How'd you find me?"

"Easy. Just followed the bodies."

"That's not funny."

"It wasn't meant to be."

I told Lannie my version of events, which he'd already heard from Sonia. He lit a cigarette and began carping about the embassy, saying they were in bed with the Peruvian army, and the army was in bed with the drug runners, and nobody at the embassy gave a damn so long as they could send Washington a list of figures on how many hectares of coca crops destroyed, how many processing labs burned, how many drug runners killed. Then he ranted about Ivy Leaguers, saying the ambassador was a Princeton man and Easton went to Harvard, and they didn't give a damn about his views because his law degree was from New Mexico.

I held up a hand to cut him off. "Can we talk escape?"

"The hell reason you think I came?" He popped open his briefcase, pulled out a map, spread it on the table, and smoothed out wrinkles. "Okay, we're here—Abancay. Here's Rio Antabamba, outside town. See this trail on the east side? Follow it downstream to here. You'll find a tiny airstrip. That's where we pick you up."

"Who is we?"

"You can bet it won't be British Air. And don't ask when. Could be tomorrow, could be next week. I'll call with a coded message." He went over the codes with me and then said, "As to destination, don't know that either, but it'll be either Barcelona or Paris."

"They're flying us to Europe?"

"It's code, Mark. Barcelona's a shitty little landing strip in Brazil. Get there and your troubles are over, at least in Peru. But don't count on it. Paris is more likely." He took out another map, spread it over the first, and stabbed his finger at the terminus of the Cuzco-to-Machu Picchu rail line. "Here it is—Chaullay. Looks like the wild west."

"We're taking a train?"

"No, Mark, didn't I just explain? There's an airstrip outside Chaullay." He ground out his cigarette and lit another. "An associate will pick you up—El Gato—Cat Man."

"Cat man?"

"You'll understand when you meet him. He'll drive you to here, end of the road. Then it'll be a two-day trek through mountains. Ever ridden a mule?"

"You gotta be kidding."

"No, I'm not kidding. There's no Greyhound service. It's treacherous. Narrow trails. Anyhow, there's this gringo pilot, a missionary type from Pucallpa. Flies in and out regularly. Brings gospel and medicine to the natives. He'll fly you over to Brazil. But there's a catch. Only comes once a week. Miss him, and you'll have to wait another week. Either that or trek into the jungle to another airstrip. But that's worst case scenario. I wouldn't advise it."

"Why?"

He leaned forward and lowered his voice. "Ungas. Mean little bastards."

Marisa and Sonia came in with coffee, Marisa still with that concerned look. Sonia plopped next to Lannie and stirred cream into his cup, looking at him like a love-struck teenager. Lannie lowered his voice and kept talking about Ungas.

"Few months back they murdered a missionary. Mutilated his body. Buried him upside down. Then some journalists went to investigate. Murdered them too. One of these days, I'm going to blow their sorry asses out of the jungle."

Marisa looked up. "Who are you going to blow out of the jungle?"

"Just talk. I was telling Mark how we're going to fly you out of here." He turned back to me. "When that plane lands, a man will stick out his head and ask where you're going. Your answer is Cairo. Don't say Cairo, and they'll leave you on the airstrip." He took a sip of coffee. "Oh, and one more thing—Sinchis might be getting off the plane. Ignore them."

"How can we ignore Sinchis? They'll recognize us."

"Not if all they see is an old geezer with his daughter."

He stood and went out to the Land Rover. Sonia followed, and while they were gone, Marisa turned her wrath on me.

"He's DEA, for God's sakes. Why'd you bring him in on this?"

"I had nothing to do with it."

"That's not what Sonia says. You told her he was the only one who could help. So she looked him up in Lima. Now she's got a thing for him. Condor would croak."

I was still explaining when they returned with backpacks, a camera, and a bag containing what Lannie called a disguise kit. "We'll need a passport photo, so might as well get you geezered up right now. You can't go to the States as Markus Thorsen."

They named me John Keats, after the poet. Marisa and Sonia did my hair, and when it was over, my hair was as white as the outside snow. Lannie stuffed cotton between my cheeks and gums for the photograph, and even Marisa laughed. We went over codes and instructions again, after which Sonia jotted down a phone number and handed it to me.

"When you're ready to leave, call this number. Tia Sofía will drive you to the airstrip."

"Why can't you drive us?"

She leaned into Lannie. "Because I'm going with him to Lima."

CHAPTER SIXTY-SIX
The Antabamba Runway

The phone call came three days after Lannie's visit, a coded message to stand by. We dressed, gathered our things and waited. Darkness fell, and still no phone call. At ten we headed to bed, but neither of us slept well, kept awake by too much caffeine and the worry of heading into the unknown. I kept glancing out the window. No lights anywhere, but the moon was full, throwing a silvery image over the town, like a black-and-white photograph.

When I finally fell asleep, I dreamed of Ungas with machetes and monkey teeth beads. Marisa mumbled in her sleep and seemed to be carrying on a conversation with someone named Pancho. At six o'clock, when the first rays of light illuminated the room, I sat up and was thinking about making coffee when the phone rang.

"Oh, I'm sorry," said a woman's voice. "I must have dialed a wrong number. I was calling seven-one-eight… Wait, let me check. Yes, seven-one-eight. Oh, never mind."

She hung up.

"That's it," I said. "Seven means morning. The last two digits are eighteen. Cut it in half, and it gives you nine. The plane lands at nine."

We ate a hasty breakfast, called the number Sonia had given me, and pulled on our caps and insulated jackets. A few minutes later, Tia Sofía rolled into the drive in a pickup truck.

The ride was short, and then we were standing in the snow at the edge of an airstrip with our bags, shivering, stomping our feet to keep warm, waiting for an airplane to take us to a warmer place. An army transport truck rolled up and stopped—all sinister looking with its big wheels and canvas covering. Marisa huddled against me.

"Relax," I said. "Lannie told us this would happen."

"I still don't trust Lannie."

The two soldiers inside the cab crawled out with their cigarettes and nodded at us. My mouth with the cotton in it went dry. Marisa didn't look so brave either.

She pointed toward the trees on which icicles were forming. "The river's over there...about a hundred yards. If they come after us, that's our Plan C."

"We'll freeze to death in that river."

"Do you have a better plan?"

The soldiers climbed back into the truck. At eight fifty we felt a vibration that grew from hum to roar. Then we saw it, a two-engine prop that looked like a relic from another era. It touched down and bounced along the runway, an airplane as black as the bruise on my leg.

Please, dear God, please don't let this be a trap.

It spun around, roaring, throwing up snowy debris, looking like a scene from an old war movie. The door opened. A ladder came down. Out jumped a dozen Sinchis in red berets and full battle gear. An officer lined them up and marched them to the waiting truck.

Then a muscular black man in fatigues and combat boots appeared in the airplane doorway, holding an assault rifle. "Your name Keats?"

"Yes, sir."

"Destination?"

"Cairo."

"Will Paris do?"

"Paris is fine."

He motioned us aboard. We threw in our gear and climbed in. A second man sprang to the door and secured it. No one else was in the cabin, only empty seats, but there lingered the smells of leather, gun oil, and Sinchis.

The man with the M-16 handed me a manila envelope and pointed to the seats.

"Anywhere you want. Cabin's not pressurized, but see that oxygen tube? Keep it under your nose. Otherwise you might pass out and die."

"Lovely," Marisa said.

We strapped in, the engine roared, and then we were airborne.

CHAPTER SIXTY-SEVEN
Chaullay

The plane shook. It lurched. It was colder than a Norwegian winter, noisy and violent, and the worst of it was an occasional free fall that left my stomach in my heart. Outside the window the magnificence of the Inca Empire spread to the horizon: terraced mountains, aqueducts, roads, and ruins. Marisa huddled against me, holding her oxygen tube beneath her nose, shivering.

"What's in the envelope?" she yelled.

I fumbled with it, got it open, and pulled out a passport. The name on it was John Keats of Silver Spring, Maryland. There was also an envelope containing two thousand dollars in hundred-dollar bills. Marisa yanked the passport out of my hand and looked at the photo.

"Oh my God, I've been sleeping with Santa Clause."

In time it grew warmer. Misty granite mountains rose up on either side, green and wildly beautiful. Then the land flattened out, with jungle as far as the eye could see, broken only by a serpentine river. An open patch of land appeared below us. The landing gear went down. Cables whined. And then we were bouncing along a dirt runway.

Our host jumped up and headed to the door. "Once this door opens, you've got ten seconds."

The plane stopped. The door opened. Down went a ladder, and we hopped out into a world of sweltering heat and blazing sunlight. The plane spun around and roared away, throwing up a suffocating cloud of red dust and leaving us alone with the trees, the runway, a vulture that looked down from a dead limb, and a single windsock hanging limp from a pole.

Marisa took off her cap and jacket. "Where's Cat Man?"

The minutes ticked by. No one came. There was nothing but a runway and circling buzzards, and I was beginning to feel like that character played by Cary Grant in *North by Northwest,* when a dirty Land Rover came racing across the strip, bringing another cloud of red dust.

The driver hopped out and opened the tailgate. He was a skinny little fellow with pale eyes, goatee, ponytail, and tattooed arms. "El Gato," he said.

The sight of his bony fingers and long, dirty nails kept me from offering my hand. We threw our things into the back and were climbing in when Marisa said, "Oh my God. What is that?"

A jungle cat, all spots, teeth, and yellow eyes, sat in the front passenger seat, snarling at us. El Gato reached in and stroked its head.

"Now, now, *dulce,* just settle down."

We slid cautiously into the back. The interior smelled of cigarettes, old socks, and what was probably cat piss. El Gato made a U-turn on the runway and took us down a trail that came out on a dirt road. He didn't say where we were going and I didn't ask him, not with that damned jaguar glaring over the top of the seat, tongue hanging out.

At length we entered Chaullay and followed its muddy streets to the square. It had the same smoky smells and squalid appearance I remembered from five years earlier, the same unpainted wooden buildings, mules swishing their tails, and groups of armed men sitting in the shade.

"Paris," Marisa muttered. "Where's the Eiffel Tower?"

We stopped in front of a hotel that looked as if it had been built for a Western movie, complete with a hitching rail, watering trough, skinny wooden columns, and a pair of swinging doors. A Machiguenga Indian in native dress and long dark hair stared at us. So did a man holding the reins of a sore-infested mule. El Gato popped out, took a leash from the back, and led his cat away, disappearing into the hotel.

"What a creep," Marisa said. "I hope he's not going with us."

A little boy and girl driving a family of squealing pigs ran over and began begging. I handed them a few coins and rolled up the windows, but they remained, pressing dirty noses against the window. The pigs squealed. The inside air became so stifling and stinky that I rolled the window back down and was about to pay the kids to leave when Marisa sat straight up.

"Is that Sonia? What's she doing here?"

She was standing at the swinging doors, dressed as if she'd just come from a Banana Republic outlet. She looked angry. The beggars saw her and rushed over. Then Lannie burst through the doors with their bags, and he too looked fighting mad.

He put down the bags and grabbed Sonia's arm.

"Leave me alone," she said, and marched to Land Rover. She yanked open the front door and hopped into the seat where the cat had been, bringing with her that familiar lotion smell. Then she slammed the door and twisted around.

"Lannie says I can't go with you."

"But you weren't supposed to be here," I said. "Neither of you. What's going on?"

"Ask Lannie. He's the man." She fanned her face. "What's that disgusting smell?"

Lannie opened the tailgate, flung in luggage, and climbed into the driver's seat.

Sonia turned away from him. I sat forward.

"What are you doing here, Lannie?"

"Business. I need to get into that part of the country to see what's growing. Sonia wants to go with us, but I'm not letting her. It's too dangerous."

"Hear that?" Sonia railed. "*El hombre manda*—the man rules. All you Latinos are just alike."

"Dammit, Sonia. I've already lost four men in those mountains. It's dangerous."

"Marisa's going. Why isn't it dangerous for her?"

"Marisa has no choice, but you're going to the train station."

"Says who?"

"Says me." He lit a cigarette, started the engine, and sped away, almost running over an old man leading a donkey. Sonia said she wasn't getting on the train. Lannie said he couldn't mix with the natives if Sonia came along. Sonia asked how he could blend with the natives with that Mexican accent. And they were still arguing when we reached the train station.

Lannie hopped out and stormed around to unload her bags.

Sonia locked the door. "I'm not getting out."

There followed one of those childlike, yes-you-are, no-I'm-not debates that drew beggars, old men wanting to help with the luggage, and a group of soldiers.

Marisa leaned forward and touched her arm. "Please, Sonia. We don't need a scene."

"Fuck," Sonia said. She sprang out, slammed the door, and marched to the station platform. The argument continued at the ticket window, but it was clear Sonia was weakening.

She broke into tears, then came back and wished us a safe journey.

"I love you guys. Be sure to call and let me know when you get home."

Lannie pulled her aside. They kissed. The soldiers applauded. Marisa began wiping at her eyes. "That's so sweet. Aren't they going to make a great couple?"

CHAPTER SIXTY-EIGHT
Vilcabamba Valley

The road into the mountains followed alongside the Rio Vilcabamba. It was potholed and boulder-strewn and passed through tunnels cut out of rocks, over makeshift bridges and beneath overhanging limbs with vines and orchids. Lonely thatch-roofed huts perched on hillsides, surrounded by banana and papaya plants. Chattering parrots blazed scarlet against green foliage, sweeping down to the river in flocks.

"What was that business about losing four men in these parts?" I asked Lannie.

"Later. I need to concentrate on my driving."

He had a point. The road was little more than an uphill trail, with washouts, hairpin turns, and occasional patches of fog. It grew cooler. Places with Inca-sounding names like Cuquipata, Lucma, and the ruins of Vitcos went past the window, some shrouded in swirling mist. We even passed a checkpoint, but it was one of those thatch-roofed places manned by locals whose only interest was the hundred-dollar bill Lannie placed beneath the clipboard.

On we went, moaning along in four-wheel drive.

It was almost dark, with rain blowing sideways, when we came to a cluster of thatch-roofed huts on a high bluff. Every wall and fence was covered with graffiti and political slogans, things like, "Viva Gonzalo," or "Tupac Amaru Lives."

Lannie stopped in front of a tin-roofed hut on which hung an Inca Kola sign.

"Grocery store," he said, "but it doubles as an inn. We spend the night here."

At daybreak we found Lannie outside with two pack mules, two guides on the wrong side of sixty, a machete man, a dozen or so ragged children, several dogs of low pedigree, and an assortment of domesticated animals. Lannie had changed out of his khakis and was now dressed in poncho, battered hat, and faded trousers, looking like one of the guides.

Marisa looked over this sorry gathering. "Why can't we get saddle horses?" she asked Lannie.

"Terrain's too treacherous. We'll have to walk." He shoved back his hat and grinned. "It's only a day and a half to the airstrip. If we push it, we'll make it by tomorrow noon."

He waved an arm and we set off amid the confusion of barking dogs, snorting mules, and the thin wail of a Runa flute. The children and dogs ran behind, waving as we single-filed out of the village and headed west toward the mountains.

After about an hour, the children and dogs dropped out, but on we went, up and still up, suffering and complaining, following narrow trails that hugged mountainsides, looking below at jungles and swirling clouds, getting sunburned.

Noon came and went. Mountains rose up on either side, lush to the north, snowcapped to the south, cutting saw-toothed patterns against the sky. The hours passed. Then it was downhill, zigzagging, sometimes following the sinking sun, and it was low in the western sky when we came to the angriest stream I'd encountered since my adventure with the guerrillas.

It raged down from the left and cascaded a hundred feet or more into the Pampaconas on our right, throwing up mist, rainbows, and such a crash, we had to shout to be heard.

The bridge—if it could be dignified by that name—consisted of three eucalyptus logs strapped together over a span of about thirty feet, and the spaces between them were filled with limbs, rocks and soil. The mules refused to cross, but the guides, who'd done this many times, unloaded them, covered their eyes with blankets, and led them over, one by one.

"It'll soon be dark," I said to Lannie. "Why don't we find a place to camp?"

"Not until we take down this bridge."

"Why?"

"Precaution. DEA agents aren't very popular in these parts."

"Who knows you're DEA?"

"Cat Man knows. I don't want him sneaking up on us."

"What is it you're not telling me, Lannie?"

"Let's get this bridge down."

The guides objected, saying they'd have to rebuild the bridge to get home, but when Lannie pulled out a wad of Peruvian bills, the logs were soon floating down the Pampaconas, swirling in the current. Again we loaded the mules, trekked up a little rise, and came to the crumbling remains of an Inca lookout tower, a stone structure that loomed above the countryside.

The head guide, an old man named Policarpo, pushed back his felt hat. "The Incas called it a *tukuy rikuq*," he said, "to see all. In Spanish it's called a *mirador*—a lookout."

"And that's why we're camping here," Lannie said.

The muleteers lit a fire and began setting up tents as if they'd done nothing more stressful than spending a day in the office. Marisa and I meandered over to the tower, and in spite of my aching muscles, I trampled down the growth at its base and climbed the narrow steps that curved around the perimeter, holding vines for support. Marisa yelled to be careful. The guides shook their heads as if they expected the thing to collapse.

At the top, inside a depression large enough for four or five people, with wind blowing in my face, I pushed creepers aside and had a long look. Five hundred years ago, some poor Inca sentry had probably stood on this very spot and eyed the approaching Spaniards, and I could only imagine his terror at seeing horses and cannon and flags and dogs and bearded men in armor.

"See anything?" Lannie yelled.

"Nothing but mountains, jungle, and a river."

I eased back down and found Marisa resting amid the roots of a spreading eucalyptus, rubbing her feet. Lannie was there too, assembling a telescopic rifle. It was as black and sinister looking as a weapon from a futuristic movie.

"M-24 Sniper," he said. "With this baby, I can shoot off a witch's tit at six-hundred meters."

"Okay, Lannie. What's going on?"

"Look, I've lost some good men up here. I want to know who did it."

"And you're using us as bait?"

"Hey, I never said this was going to be easy." He reached into his pack and pulled out a battery, a coil of wire, and a green canister marked Flare. "Trip wire. I'm going to set it around our perimeter. Step on this thing and it'll light up like the Fourth of July."

He laid a hand on my shoulder. "I understand your concern, old buddy. You're a professor. Guys like you reason with your brain. Guys like me, we blow shit up."

CHAPTER SIXTY-NINE

At the fading of the last light, just as the green hills were melding into evening, we bundled up in blankets and attacked a pot of rice and beans. Machete Man threw more wood on the fire, creating a shower of sparks that danced with the stars. Policarpo took a mandolin from his gear and knocked out a few notes to "El Condor Pasa," plucking with his fingers. He twisted the pegs and tilted his head to get the right sound, executing one tremolo after the other, and when he spoke, his voice as cracked and harsh as his leathery face.

"It is a sad tune."

Marisa pulled her blanket around her a little tighter. "I'd still like to hear it."

"You will cry."

"I'm already crying from blisters on my feet."

The old man positioned his instrument as lovingly as if he were holding a grandchild. The fingers of his left hand crawled up and down the strings like a spider. The chords quavered. The music cried. It cascaded at an exhilarating pace, and just when it seemed as if he should be playing in Carnegie Hall, he laid his hand across the bridge and muted the strings.

"Inca Tupac Amaru was a god to our people. That is why the Spaniards cut off his head and hung it from a pole. But the head turned into a condor and soared into the sky. And now all we have is the song and the rebellion against the ruling class."

Everyone fell silent, for "El Condor Pasa" was one of the great songs of human heartbreak:

> *Yaw kuntur llaqtay urqupi tiyaq...*Oh majestic condor of the Andes *maymantam qawamuwachkanki...*take me home, to the Andes,
> *Apallaway llaqtanchikman, wasinchikman...*I want to live in my beloved land...

The other old guide, a man called Saturnino, stepped to the fire with a bamboo flute and piped out a melody as grim as death. The glow of the fire shimmered on their faces, and on the leaves of the eucalyptus. Marisa took my hand. Lannie sat mesmerized, and together we listened to these two old men with a flute and mandolin sing about the condor in the sky.

∾

We were up at first light, groaning from blisters and sore muscles. The weather was clear, with the promise of a brilliant sunrise. Smoke billowed up from the campfire. Mules snorted and pawed, and the aroma of coffee scented the dry, winter air. Lannie climbed the tower with his telescopic rifle. I pulled on my poncho and hat and walked to the fire with Marisa, stretching my arms to work out the stiffness.

"Anything?" I yelled up at Lannie.

"Too dark to see."

I poured coffee and handed Marisa a cup.

"No thanks," she said, and pushed it away.

"What's wrong? I thought you liked coffee."

"Not today. The smell makes me want to throw up."

"We got company," Lannie yelled from the tower. "Pack up."

Marisa dashed back to the tent. I told the guides to get ready and then scurried up the tower. Lannie was looking over the protective wall through the telescope of his rifle, his poncho over his head, burlap over his rifle.

"Stay down," he barked. "They're over there—near the downed bridge. See them?"

He handed me his binoculars. I raised them to my eyes and focused on a spiraling column of campfire smoke. There, at the edge of shadows and the first rays of sunlight, stood tents, mules, and men. The early-morning light glinted off the shiny buttons of their uniforms—Sinchis.

Bravos.

Panic seized me, and for an instant I relived the glaring headlights, the short bursts of gunfire, blood, death, and Bravos. And there he was again—come to finish the job.

"Keep your eye on that large tent," Lannie said.

As I watched, I counted five mules, five guides, and twelve Sinchis, including Bravos, who was looking in our direction through binoculars.

"Can he see us?"

"Sun's in his face, but don't make any sudden moves." He chambered a round in his M-24. "There," he hissed, "coming out of the tent. See him?"

I swung my binoculars back to the tent. The flap was now open. A man was coming out, a man leading a spotted jungle cat by its leash: El Gato.

"You son of a bitch," Lannie grumbled. "I suspected it was you all along."

"Please don't tell me you're going to shoot him."

"The hell you think we should do? Those Sinchis are younger than us. In better shape. They can out-trek us, outrun us, outgun us. They get across that creek, we're screwed."

"But it's only four hours to the airstrip."

"Christ, Mark, don't you understand anything? The likelihood of that pilot being there at the exact hour we arrive is nil. We may have to wait a day or two."

"What about that bridge we destroyed? Won't that stop them?"

"Two hours at most. Then they'll be on us. You don't have the stomach for it, don't watch."

Marisa appeared at the edge and climbed in beside us, her hair and poncho whipping in the breeze. Lannie twisted around. "The hell? You trying to get us shot?"

I pulled Marisa down and focused my binoculars on Cat Man. He was conversing with Bravos, pointing upstream, when the buzz of a chainsaw came to my ears.

Beside me, Lannie muttered, "Good-bye, you sick motherfucker."

The shot went off like a firecracker.

Cat Man threw up his arms and slumped to the ground.

Bravos dove for cover.

"Shit," Lannie said, and shot a mule. He fired again and again, dropping one mule after the other, working the bolt with his right hand, muttering "Yes" after each shot.

When he finished with the mules, he popped in a second clip and shot the cat.

The entire episode probably took less than fifteen seconds.

Lannie slung his rifle. "The hell out of here. Move it."

CHAPTER SEVENTY

If there'd been time, I'd have been on my knees, puking up my guts. But there wasn't time, so we grabbed our things and set off in a fury, bullets snapping over our heads, the guides lashing their mules, Machete Man running ahead, Lannie shouting, "Go, go, go."

We forded a small stream and sloshed across a swampy plain, tripping and cursing, and each time we ventured into the open, I imagined the back of my head in the cross hairs of a telescopic rifle. How long we kept up the pace, I do not know, but at last we rounded a bend and plopped down next to small stream, trying to catch our breaths.

I turned to Marisa. "Are you all right?"

"No, Mark, I'm not all right. I still don't understand what happened back there."

Lannie clomped over, still holding his rifle, breathing hard, his poncho covered in plant debris, face all sweaty. "Look, Marisa. Cat Man worked for me. Okay? He was on my payroll. For that, I expect loyalty. He's already cost me four men. If I hadn't taken him out, he'd have murdered all of us. As for the mules, I shot them to slow the Sinchis."

"What about the cat?" Marisa asked. "Was that necessary?"

"If I told you, it'd make you sick."

"I'm already sick."

"Look, Cat Man has this animal farm back in the jungle—snakes, cats, monkeys. Stinks so bad, you can hardly breathe. Couple months back I was there, interrogating this kid no more than fifteen. He accused Cat Man of being the go-between for General Reál and the narcos. Said he could prove it, but before he could finish his story, Cat Man whips out a pistol and shoots him between the eyes." He took a deep breath. "Want to hear what he did with the body?"

"No, I don't want to hear what he did with the body."

"Fine, but let's just say that's why I shot the cat."

"How are you going to explain all this to the embassy?" I asked him.

"Explain what? I wasn't here. Neither were you."

"Bravos knows you were here."

"Bravos is a crook, a narco, General's Reál's butcher man. He exposes me, I'll expose him. Besides, with any luck at all, I'll get him before we're outa the jungle. As for those other Sinchis, they're kids. Illiterate conscripts. They don't know anything."

We trudged on, uphill and downhill, sloshing through swamps, crossing lunar-like boulder fields, stopping now and then to shake pebbles out of our boots or splash water on our faces or share a piece of cheese. In time we reached an almost vertical escarpment, one of those places with washouts and zigzags and a narrow trail with Inca steps that hugged the face.

"Oh God," Marisa said, looking up. "Can't we go around it?"

"There is no other way," answered Policarpo.

Machete Man led the way, throwing debris off the trail and slashing at overhanging vegetation with his machete. The mules clopped along in single file. Lannie, Marisa, and I followed in the rear, sweating and cursing, laboring to keep up.

We were near the top when I heard it—a steady drone, like the engine of a lawn mower. It grew louder. Lannie looked up.

"The hell?"

A small aircraft dipped over the crest as if it had been cata-pulted from a ramp.

"Spotters," Lannie shouted. "Take cover."

The guides pulled their mules against the face of the cliff. Marisa dashed over to a small waterfall, but slipped in the spray. She grabbed her ankle and cried out in pain. I helped her into the cover of a projecting boulder and was unlacing her boot when the plane made a long turn and came back. From its color—camouflage green and khaki—it had to be military.

"Son of a bitch," Lannie grumbled, "that's one of the planes we gave them."

It flew straight toward us, engine screaming, bringing with it a flashback of that nightmarish battle in the mountains. When it seemed as if it would crash into us, it rose over the crest, showing its belly and stirring up a storm of dust.

Lannie took an AK-47 off one of the mules and handed it to me.

"Know how to use this thing?"

I clicked off the safety and chambered a round. "I'm not helpless."

"Maybe they just want pictures. Don't shoot unless I do."

We waited. Nothing happened. We thought it had gone and were about to resume our trek when it appeared in the sky to our left, a speck that grew larger with every second. It came close and still closer, banking left and then right.

The passenger door was open. A man was leaning out.

With an assault rifle.

He opened fire, his bullets lacing the trail and slamming into the cliff. Lannie shot back. Marisa yelled at me to stay down, but I did what I'd wanted to do since that night in the mountains—pull the trigger. Kill the sons of bitches who were trying to kill me.

My first blast went wide, tracers arcing into the sky.

Lannie was more accurate, his shots raking the plane. Pieces fell off. The man at the door jumped back inside. The plane veered and sputtered away, trailing smoke or oil or both. I kept shooting until the clip played out, hoping to see it explode in a fireball.

Then Marisa grabbed my arm. "They got Venus."

"Who the hell is Venus?"

She pointed to the three guides. They were on their knees and huddled around a mule. It lay on its side in a pool of blood, next to the little waterfall, struggling to get up. Saturnino was rubbing her head, speaking to her in Quechua.

"Oh, my poor baby."

He looked at us through teary eyes. "She's suffering. We can't leave her like this."

Lannie touched the old man's shoulder. "Get the bags off."

I slid back down to Marisa and was helping her to her feet when the gunshot went off. Saturnino let out a wail. Marisa burst into tears.

"Nothing goes right for us," she said. "Nothing. Those Sinchis are probably in helicopters right now. They'll get to the airstrip before we do."

"Not if we hurry."

"How can we hurry? I can barely walk. I think I twisted an ankle."

I helped her to her feet. "We've still got one mule."

"What about our gear?"

"Fuck the gear. We'll take what we can and leave the rest."

CHAPTER SEVENTY-ONE

On we trudged, arriving about two hours later in a tiny no-name village that was little more than thirty or forty thatch-roofed huts and a muddy street shaded by mango and papaya trees. Pigs wallowed in the mud. Dogs barked. Bare-bottomed children and their parents eyed us from doorways, and the entire place reeked of pigs, wood smoke, and open-fire cooking.

Lannie yelled to a man on his porch. "Which way to the airstrip?"

The man shrugged as if he didn't understand Spanish, and I could only imagine how we looked to him—three dirty guides loaded with gear, another who might be a guide, a blue-eyed Madonna atop a mule, and a tall *wiracocha*.

I approached the man, told him in Quechua that we were explorers, and asked about the airstrip. He pointed down the street, beyond the pigs and dogs. "There, *wiracocha*. Close."

"Are there any brass buttons in the village?"

"No, *wiracocha*. Soldiers are not welcome here."

We lumbered on, our excitement rising, and found the airstrip at the far side of the village, recognizable only by a grass runway and a fluttering windsock. But it was as abandoned as a high school football field in midsummer. No missionaries and no airplanes.

By now the entire village and their animals had turned out to stare, the kids pointing and laughing as if we were clowns from a circus, the dogs sniffing. An old priest pushed his way through the crowd and spoke to us in Spanish.

"Are you looking for the missionaries?"

"Yes, Father, we were supposed to meet them here today."

"They don't come until day after tomorrow."

Everyone groaned. Lannie pulled out his map and consulted it. The villagers pushed in so close, the priest had to shoo them away. Lannie turned to the priest. "According to this map, the missionaries have a permanent station about a day's trek to the west. Is that true?"

"*Sí, Señor,* but to get there you must pass through Unga territory."

I muttered a curse. Somehow I knew it would come to this. Lannie and Marisa looked equally perturbed. "Dammit to hell," Lannie said in English. "I figure we've got an hour before the helicopters arrive. No way in hell I'm waiting in this shitty little village."

"He's right," Marisa said. "We'd better get going."

I agreed. Lannie said something about a rock and a hard place, and I was helping Marisa back on the mule when the guides began grumbling and shaking their heads.

"No," Policarpo said. "We promised to come only this far and no farther."

Lannie reached for his wallet. "How about I give you each an extra hundred dollars?"

"What good is money if the brass buttons shoot us?"

I pulled Policarpo aside, out of earshot of the villagers. "Tell them we forced you."

"How can I say you forced us when everyone here is a witness?"

Marisa spoke up. "I'll make it an extra two hundred for each of you."

Policarpo consulted with the other two guides in private and then came back. "First you must to buy us another good mule. You must also to force us to go."

"Not a problem," Lannie said and turned to the priest. "Where can we buy a mule?"

The priest pointed west. "About five minutes that way."

Policarpo, who should have been an actor, began feigning protest. Lannie poked him with the AK and cursed him in Spanish. I cursed him in Quechua, saying we'd shoot them right here in this village. Lannie fired a blast into the air. The villagers scurried and we soon were back on the trail with an extra mule and each of the guides richer by three hundred dollars.

The next few hours were as agonizing as the morning trek, made worse by a downpour and another of those sinister-looking forests with giant trees and evil smells. Finally, we came to a large ravine, beyond which spread a field of boulders and a small hill.

"Unga country," Policarpo whispered. "From now on we must to be silent as death."

"Maybe we should wait until dark before crossing that field," Lannie said.

"No, *wiracocha*. That field is near their village. It is most dangerous at night. They post guards. They shoot. No questions. But once we cross it, we will to be safe."

He consulted with the other two guides and then said, "It is best for us to cross first. We are poor. They expect nothing from us. With you it is different. You can watch. If we are not stopped, then we wait on the other side. If you are delayed, we will go on to Vista Alegre."

I had a pretty good idea what delayed meant, and didn't like it. Neither did Lannie or Marisa, but the other option was to go back and face the Sinchis. So we kept one mule, two AKs and Marisa's backpack, handed over our backpacks and the sniper rifle to the guides, and watched them cross the open field and meld into the foliage.

Lannie stood and brushed off his trousers. "They made it. Let's go."

"Hold on," Marisa said. "We need a Plan C."

Lannie patted the AK-47 he'd tied on the mule. "This is my Plan C."

"Maybe it is, but suppose we get separated?" She took Lannie's map and opened it. "See this river? It's the Tunquimayo. Follow it south to the Inca lookout tower. It's a good place to hide."

"How do you know about that place?" I asked.

"Don't ask."

We settled her on the mule and set off across the field, Lannie holding the reins, looking like one of the guides in his straw hat, sun-parched face, and rumpled poncho.

After three or four minutes, we zigzagged into another ravine, struggled up the other side, and found a side trail that led south. It was marked by one of those hanging bundles of sticks and feathers, giving me the same distressed feeling I remembered from the jungle at Dos Pasos.

"Their village must be that way," Marisa whispered, fear in her voice.

We kept going, hardly daring to breathe, Lannie in front and me behind. The clop of the mule sounded like the beat of a drum. Monkeys crashed around in the overhead. Parrots squawked, and every other heartbeat something rustled in the underbrush.

We were almost across the field, ready to enter the forest, when a horrifying shriek rent the air. Then, as if the doorway to hell had opened, Ungas burst from the shadows, with feathers, painted faces, monkey teeth necklaces, machetes, and assault rifles.

The same miserable bunch that had accosted us at Dos Pasos.

CHAPTER SEVENTY-TWO
Ungacachano Territory

We surrendered our weapons and stood helplessly as they circled us like wolves, yipping and howling, sniffing us as if trying to decide which one to pee on. From their smells and the way they were stumbling, it was obvious they'd been drinking something more potent than papaya juice. The old man with cat whiskers held up a hand to stop them. Then he sniffed Lannie, apparently dismissed him as a guide, and turned his attention to me.

"You are the *wiracocha* from Dos Pasos. And now you are here. Where are your grenades, *wiracocha*? Where are your men? Why have you come to the land of the people of the forest?"

"My men and women are fighting the brass buttons back in that little village," I said, trying to sound bolder than I felt. "They will soon be here. They sent us ahead—to Vista Alegre."

He translated my words for the others. Again they went into their routine of yelling at one another, swishing machetes through the air, and spitting on the ground.

The old man got right in my face, fouling the air with the smell of alcohol and rotten breath.

"My people say you are a spy for the *wiracocha* agents."

"Your people are wrong. I am a leader with the people who allow you safe passage at Dos Pasos. We let you pass without harm. We expect the same from you."

"You threatened to kill me at Dos Pasos."

"You do not look dead to me."

"When are your people passing through?"

"Maybe tonight."

"Then you must wait for them here. With us. In our village."

"No," Marisa said. "Apu Condor is waiting in Vista Alegre. He will not be pleased."

"Apu Condor is king of his forest. I am king of mine."

He took the reins of the mule on which Marisa was sitting and led us back along the trail, turning south at the fork that led to their village.

Lannie fell in beside me. "This wasn't accidental," he said. "They were waiting."

Marisa, still riding the mule, gave him a sharp kick. "Shut up, Lannie. You're supposed to be a guide. Our guides don't speak English."

"Get real, Marisa. These idiots don't know the difference between Spanish and English."

We forded a murky stream and emerged in sight of a wretched little mud-and-thatch village at the upper end of a sloping pasture. Grazing cattle and mules glanced up. The snowy Cordillera Vilcabamba served as a backdrop, blood-colored in the sun that had sunk beneath the horizon.

"Behold," said the old man, pointing to his village as proudly as if it were Athens or Rome, "I give you the home of the people of the forest."

"Piece of shit," Lannie muttered.

We marched on, following an animal path that took us around three screened buildings, a radio antenna tower, and a stack of metal drums.

"Kerosene," Lannie hissed. "You can smell it from here. It's a processing plant."

One of the Ungas dashed toward the village and began shouting like a warrior at a victory celebration. Out from the huts poured women, children, old folks, and barking dogs. A red flag appeared above them, then another. A tiny woman in black pranced around and made a speech in a high-pitched voice, her words echoing down the hollow. Flags waved. They cheered. Then, with one continuous roar, they rushed down like Barbarians attacking the Romans.

They danced around us—chanting, laughing, showering us with spittle. Some of the kids hurled animal dung. The old woman who'd made the speech, an ugly little witch with long fingernails and coca-blackened teeth, danced up to the mule with a switch of brambles and began lashing Marisa's legs, shrieking in a hideous voice.

The old man laughed. "She says she is going to poke out your eyes and eat your heart."

Marisa kicked the woman in the chest.

The chanting stopped. So did the dancing and conversation. Everyone stared at Marisa, openmouthed, as if wondering how she could be so brazen.

Marisa climbed off her mule and got right in the witch's face. "I have heard of you," she said in halting Quechua. "They say you are a witch because no man will come near you."

The old man translated. Everyone howled with laughter.

The woman flew into Marisa again with her brambles, arms flailing.

Marisa smacked her in the face. "Do you not know who I am, old witch? I am the wife of *Supaypa*, the old forest devil. He comes to me on the wind."

It grew so quiet that even the dogs stopped yapping.

"What shall I tell him tonight when he comes to my bed—that you attacked me? Attacked my friends? Tonight I will send him into all your huts to ask you. And you. And you."

Marisa pointed with her fingers. The old man translated. Everyone backed away, the children hiding behind their mothers.

Marisa climbed back atop her mule like a princess. The old man took the reins and led us away, taking us down a muddy winding street that passed between their shabby little mud-and-stick huts. The villagers stayed well behind, quieter now.

Lannie elbowed me. "These fuckers must be into female worship."

At the end of the street, we came to a large circular building framed against the jungle. One of the young men rushed to the door, slid back a latch, and pulled it open. A nasty smell escaped, as if Cat Man had been housed there with his animals. The old man helped Marisa off the mule and was guiding her in when she said, "My backpack, please. Give it to me."

He gave her the pack, but not before confiscating the chocolate bars and a can of sausages.

"I hope you choke on it," Marisa said.

He laughed as if she'd complimented him, then followed us into the darkness. There were no windows, no furniture, and no mats, only an earthen floor, a pile of dirty blankets, a nasty smell, and a center pole that held up a thatched roof.

The old man lit a lantern, set it on the ground, went out the door, and latched it behind him.

I peeked through the cracks and saw him leading away our mule. Four or five Ungas lingered with their assault weapons, barely visible in the fading light. A few women were there too, staring as if waiting for the building to burst into flames.

Lannie came up beside me. "Hate to mention this, but according to my map, this is the same village where the missionary and those journalists were murdered."

CHAPTER SEVENTY-THREE

We took the lantern and examined the circular wall, prodding for weak spots. It was mud, thick and impenetrable. But on it, scrawled crudely, were the names of previous prisoners. Marisa took a note pad from her pack and began writing them down, moving along the wall.

"For their families," she said, "in case we get out."

It grew cold. We huddled beneath our dirty blankets and spoke like condemned prisoners. Lannie talked about Sonia and said his biggest regret was not getting to know her better. Marisa said she wished she'd had the courage to leave her husband years ago. I mentioned how things that once seemed important, like getting a deanship at my university, now meant nothing. And that kind of talk went on until it grew quiet outside and Marisa came to her feet.

"Enough of this depressing talk. Let's bust out of here."

I peeked through the cracks. No lights, no guards, and no movement, only the stars and flicker of fireflies. But the night had come alive with the chirp of crickets, the grump of frogs, the hoots and shrieks of other things, and something that sounded like a snore.

"You believe that shit?" Lannie said. "They're sleeping it off."

He scooped up the lantern and strode to the center pole. It disappeared into the darkness above us. "That thatch ceiling is nothing," he said. "We can bust right through it."

"I'll do it," I said."

"No," Lannie shot back. "I'm skinnier than you. Besides, I know how to take out the guards."

He doused the lantern and began his climb, mumbling and cursing, Marisa and I holding the pole to keep it from shaking. It was too dark to see, but we knew by the falling thatch when he reached the peak.

"Nothing here," he hissed from the blackness above. "I'm going sideways."

We followed his lateral progress along one of the joist poles by sound. In my mind I could see him putting one hand in front of the other, feet dangling.

"At the wall," he said.

More thatch fell. I saw stars and fireflies. The hole grew larger. Fresh air swept in.

"Going out," he hissed. "Wait by the door."

The hole darkened as he crawled into it. The stars appeared again. There was a thump as he dropped to the ground outside. We crept to the door and waited.

And waited.

"Maybe they captured him," Marisa whispered.

"No, we'd have heard the fuss. He's looking for weapons."

The drone of an engine came to my ears. Dogs barked. People called out to one another. There were voices at the front door.

"What's that?" I said to Marisa.

"Sounds like an airplane."

The drone grew louder, more pronounced, and then I recognized the thump-thump of rotor blades, a helicopter. "Bravos," I said, hearing the strain in my voice.

"How could it be Bravos?" Marisa said. "Ungas and Sinchis are enemies."

"Maybe they came to shoot the place up."

"Maybe they did. You should get going. Get up that pole."

"You go first."

"No, Mark. I can barely walk. My ankle's sprained. It may be broken."

The helicopter swept over us, shaking the thatch and illuminating the room with its landing lights. Dogs barked. Men shouted. Through the door cracks, I saw Ungas rushing out of their huts, a sea of flashlights, guns, and swaying lanterns.

"Wait at the door," I said. "I'll get you out."

I sprang to the pole and began climbing. It was more difficult than I imagined, and took more time than I wanted. Precious minutes. But at last I was at the hole Lannie had made.

"Hurry," Marisa said. "They're almost here. I see them."

I stuck out my head for a look. Men with rifles and fatigue jackets were surging up the street, lanterns glowing like the eyes of animals, flashlights making dizzying arcs, just like that awful night in the mountains. But why weren't the Ungas putting up a fight?

"Go on," Marisa cried. "You can still make it. Forget about me."

"No, Marisa. I'm not leaving without you."

I dropped back to the earthen floor, Marisa still protesting, saying I should have gone.

They were at the door now, men speaking Quechua. Marisa shrank against me. At a sharp command, the latch slid back. The door opened. The beam of flashlight lit the room.

A man wearing the ragtag clothing of a Shining Path guerilla marched in.

Tucno.

He shoved past me and grabbed Marisa's arm. "Don Francisco is waiting."

"Tell Don Francisco I'd rather rot in hell."

"Who is Don Francisco?" I demanded to know.

Tucno spun on me. "Stay out of this, gringo."

A second man came in with a lantern—a good-looking fellow about fifty, slightly built, European features, gray hair pulled back in a ponytail, revealing an earring. Except for his belt, which was silver coated, he was dressed in black, looking as if he'd just come from an art exhibit. And when he spoke to Marisa, it was in the sharp Castilian of Spain.

"They're waiting for us in Cuzco, *dulce*. Time to go."

"You go," she said. "I'd rather stay with him."

He turned around and fixed me in his gaze. "Ah, so this is Romeo."

He took a step toward me, clicked his heels and bowed like a bullfighter for his introduction at the Corrida de Toros in Madrid. "In case my lovely wife hasn't told you, I am Francisco de la Vega. Perhaps you've seen my paintings at Dos Pasos."

I looked at Marisa.

"My ex," she said.

CHAPTER SEVENTY-FOUR

I should have made the connection a long time ago, when his paintings kept showing up. Not that it would have made a difference. I'd still be on the run. The road would still have led into the jungle. And I'd still be a prisoner in this miserable little mud-and-thatch hut in the jungle.

Don Francisco turned back to Marisa. "Come on, *dulce*. The helicopter's waiting."

"I'm not going anywhere unless you release him."

"Listen to yourself, woman. Do you think you have bargaining power?"

"Please, Pancho. You know what these savages will do. He hasn't done anything wrong."

"Hasn't done anything wrong? How about being an accomplice in the theft of my money? How about fucking my wife?" He slapped her. "*Puta*. Where is my money?"

I grabbed his arm and swung him around and would have bashed in his pretty face if Tucno hadn't pulled his knife.

"Back off, gringo. This is between a man and his woman."

The argument went on. Arms waved. The lantern threw grotesque shadows on the wall. Other men came into the room with their AKs—young men I recognized from the training camp. They looked from me to Marisa as if confused. Don

Francisco ordered them to take Marisa to the helicopter. They glanced at me as if to say, "Sorry," and took Marisa's arm.

She fought. She screamed, she cursed, but her efforts were as fruitless as my trip to Peru, and they were soon hauling her into the night, feet first.

"Get out," she yelled back in English. "Go to Plan C."

Then I was alone with Tucno.

He waved his knife and took a step toward me, his eyes boring into mine, his ugly face even more satanic in the flicker of the lantern. I retreated to the opposite side of the center pole and grabbed a blanket off the floor. Tucno shifted the knife from one hand to the other.

"I saw your story in the papers, gringu. Didn't I warn you not to write about us?"

"You're not my master, Tucno. I don't take orders from you."

He feigned an attack from one side of the pole and then the other. I danced left and then right, trying to keep the pole between us. Not that it would save me. His friends were outside. Even if I took away his knife and slit his throat, his comrades would finish me off.

But no way was I going to make it easy. Hell no.

I slapped at the knife with the blanket.

I flung Marisa's pack.

"You're a coward, Tucno. Without that knife you're nothing but an old woman."

He lashed at me again.

"Come on, Tucno. Put away the knife and fight me like a man."

From the outside came a shout. "Tucno, we've got to go."

"What about the gringu?"

"We promised him to the villagers. They'll have him for breakfast."

Tucno spat on the ground, backed away, and went out the door.

It slammed behind him.

The bolt slid into place.

Then I was alone in that nasty hut, holding the pole for support, my body shaking, my breath coming in ragged gasps, hardly able to believe I was alive.

I stumbled to the door and peeked through the cracks. Lights were moving away. The bastards were leaving, taking Marisa with them. In my tortured mind, I imagined myself busting out, overpowering a guard, taking his AK-47, and killing Francisco de la Vega. Then Tucno.

Yes, why not?

Within seconds I was high above the floor, swinging along joist poles like a monkey, making my way over to the hole Lannie had created. Only a minute before I was a dead man, my throat slit by Tucno, my blood spilling onto the earthen floor. Now I was Batman, Superman, Double-Oh-Seven and Spider-Man. I had enough adrenaline to scale the Matterhorn.

Hell, I might even be able to shoot up that helicopter.

The door swung open. A light played over me.

"The hell you doing up there?"

Lannie stood at the door with a flashlight, looking like a commando on a mission—rifles slung over his shoulder, pistols around his waist, and a long bamboo pole in his hand.

He hurried inside. "Get your ass down and help me hide these bodies."

I didn't ask, didn't want to know, didn't want to debate the relative value of human lives. It was self-defense. Easy call. So I dropped to the floor, landing on Marisa's blanket, and hurried into the fresh air. Two dead Ungas lay near the door. I dragged them inside and turned around to see Lannie fashioning a torch from a blanket and the bamboo pole.

"What's that for?"

"Diversion." He doused the blanket with oil from the lantern, set it ablaze, and propped the pole against the ceiling thatch. Then he headed for the door.

"Come on. The hell outa here."

I grabbed an AK and Marisa's pack and plunged into the darkness, bolting the door behind me. The village looked abandoned, everyone gone to see the helicopter, and the only signs of life were a million fireflies mating with the stars.

"This way," Lannie said. "Behind the huts."

We crossed and re-crossed a shallow stream. Frogs croaked. Insects chirred, and for all I knew, it could have been a home for alligators, venomous snakes and creatures from the Black Lagoon. But all I cared about was getting away from that horrible hut and finding Marisa.

Finally, we emerged from the jungle into an open pasture. Below us, amid a sea of lights and swaying lanterns, stood the helicopter.

"Probably taking on a load of paste," Lannie said. "Either that or unloading kerosene."

We crept on, skirting the tree line toward the paste factory, Lannie glancing back to see if the hut was burning, me staring down at the helicopter, wondering if Marisa was inside.

A mule snorted. We darted into the brush and waited, not knowing what to expect.

The moon came out from behind a cloud, illuminating a stone corral that housed their animals. There were no guards that I could see.

"Let's get our mule," I whispered to Lannie.

"Forget the mule. It'll slow us down."

We opened the gate anyway and shooed them out, the logic being that Ungas chasing mules would have less time to chase us. A few more steps, and I smelled kerosene.

Then I saw it—the paste factory. A lantern burned in the radio hut. A battery-powered radio was tuned to Radio Andino in Cuzco, a voice saying something about the Festival of Inti Raymi that was only days away.

"This is too good," Lannie said. "Let's torch it."

"Are you crazy? It'll have guards."

"Then we'll have to take them out, won't we?"

CHAPTER SEVENTY-FIVE

The Paste Factory

There were three open-air buildings, each protected from rodents and insects with heavy-gauge wire screen. We crept into the closest one. No guards and no workers, only a pile of chicken bones on the table, a couple of hammocks slung from one wall to the other, posters of nude women from porno magazines, and Andean music on the radio.

"Unguarded," Lannie said. "These people are really stupid."

He went back to the door and glanced out. "Look at them, running around that chopper like kids at a merry-go-round. Let's overturn some drums. Get the kerosene flowing."

We popped the lids on a few drums and began rolling them along the ground in front of the buildings, pushing them inside, the liquid gurgling, stinking up the place.

I found a five-gallon container and splashed around kerosene like a mad arsonist, dousing tables, tools, supplies, and machinery. At the radio shack, I splashed the transceiver, the backup batteries, the generator, and everything around it, and was about to douse a metal filing cabinet when Lannie stopped me.

"Hold on. Let's see what's inside."

"It's padlocked."

"So what? Don't you professors know anything?"

He wrapped a blanket around his pistol and fired a single shot into the lock. The sound was no louder than the drop of a book on the floor. Even the sound of the opening drawers was louder.

"Holy crap," he said. "Would you look at this?"

He held up a packet of hundred-dollar bills, neatly bound with rubber bands. "Can you believe this shit? Must be two or three million dollars."

"Let's burn it."

"Hell no. Empty that pack and give it to me."

I dumped the contents of Marisa's backpack onto the floor. Even in the poor light, I recognized her alpaca sweater, her black panties with the frilly borders, and her makeup kit with its small bottle of Lily of Peru. The sight of it increased the pain inside me.

"Get out there and stand watch," Lannie said.

I hurried out with my AK, glad to get away from the smell of kerosene. A mule sauntered by. The helicopter was still on the open field no more than two hundred yards away, rotors turning, people and lights moving around it. Was Marisa inside it, crying? Thinking I was dead?

"Marisa," I whispered to the night. "I'm here. I escaped. I love you."

I said it over and over, silently, right there at the edge of the jungle with a mule looking on, with the stench of kerosene in my nostrils, pouring my soul into that indefinable little current that passed between us, trying to suck up the energy around me.

Can you hear me, Marisa?

The wind was my answer, and the snort of the mule, and the rise and fall of Unga chatter, and another tearjerker from Radio Andino, live from Cuzco.

*Munankichu willanayta…*Do you want me to tell you, *Maymantachus kanichayta?…*Where I'm from?

*Haqay urqu qhepanmanta...*I'm from behind that hill,
*Clavelinas chawpinmanta...*Amid the carnations,
*Azucenas chawpinmanta...*Among the lilies.

Lilies, as in Lily of Peru.

The helicopter lifted in a dazzling display of light and noise. I said a silent prayer for Marisa and turned around in time to see Lannie hurrying out of the building with her pack.

"Look," he said, pointing toward flames that were rising above the village.

The sight of the burning hut thrilled me. What a joy. What sweet revenge.

The Ungas saw it too. They cried out to one another, and then they were running toward the village like stampeding buffalos, lanterns swaying, dogs barking.

When the last light vanished into the village, Lannie marched back into the paste factory, picked up a towel from Marisa's things, soaked it in kerosene, and lit it with his lighter.

His face took on a ghostly look in the glare; madness shone in his black Mexican eyes.

"Hell's the point in living if you can't have fun?"

He flung the burning towel onto a pile of cardboard boxes. The flames spread across the floor and up the walls, crackling and smoking. We did the same in the next building, and the next.

Then we were crashing down the trail to the tune of exploding kerosene drums, Lannie laughing like a madman. "Two million fucking dollars, Mark. Now I know how D.W. Cooper felt when he bailed out of that airplane."

CHAPTER SEVENTY-SIX
Vista Alegre

The cawing of a bird woke me the next morning. I rolled over and found myself in a ruins overlooking a squalid little village that might have been Vista Alegre. My clothes were damp from the streams we'd forded. My hands still reeked of kerosene, and I itched from insect bites. But the worst of it was that empty feeling of failure, as if someone had ripped out my heart.

Lannie stepped out of the bushes, zipping up. "The hell's wrong?"

"The hell you think?"

He tromped over and put a hand on my shoulder. "You'll get her back. She'll bust loose. Probably get to the States before you." He picked up his rifle and pointed down toward the village. "See that building with the barn? It's an inn. They've got running water. We can clean up. Get some breakfast. The guides should also be there."

We hid the pack with the money and stumbled down the hill like a couple of derelicts, looking over our shoulders for Ungas, Lannie still trying to cheer me up.

A dog rushed out to sniff us. There was the usual stir of crowing roosters, laughing children and blaring radios. The smell of coffee and bacon reminded me I hadn't eaten a full meal for days. Lannie put a hand on my arm.

"We better check it out." He pointed to a grove of trees. "Wait over there with the AKs."

"What if Ungas show up?"

"Christ, Mark. Shoot the fuckers."

He pulled down his hat and lumbered on, passing around a wagon that was loaded with melons, looking like a local in his tattered poncho. At the door he turned back and waved, leaving me alone with my memories, a pistol, and two loaded assault rifles.

Vultures circled overhead. An old man came out, hopped onto the melon wagon, and drove away. I heard music and voices, the chirr of insects and songbirds. Then Policarpo staggered out the back and down toward the stables, carrying Lannie's sniper rifle and my old backpack.

Before I could digest the meaning, Lannie trotted out with his old backpack, munching on a banana. "Found our guides," he said, and handed me a banana. "All three shacked up with local beauties. Same room. Everybody buck-ass naked, rum bottles all over the floor."

"Policarpo's over there," I said, "hitching up the mule."

"Yeah, but look at him. Poor bastard can barely stand. And that's not the worst part." He put a hand on my arm as if to comfort me. "They say the village is crawling with Sinchis. So is the trail to the missionary post. We'll have to hide out another day or two."

"Where?"

"The ruins. Policarpo's going to haul our gear. Send us food."

I didn't know whether to curse or cry. Sinchis to our front, Ungas to our rear, another haunted ruins to sleep in, Marisa gone, and I was developing a caffeine deprivation headache.

"What about Marisa's Plan C? The lookout tower. We could go there."

"Marisa's Plan C is a two-day trek in the wrong direction."

Policarpo came clopping toward us, stumbling and stagger-ing. He smelled worse than his mule, and his sullen expression told me he wished we'd never come into his life.

"That way," he grumbled, and led us back up the same trail we'd just come down, following alongside slopes covered with impatiens gone wild, brilliantly pink and white in the morning sun. When we reached the ruins, he pushed back his hat and mopped his face. "They say it is haunted by the old gods. They send rain. Thunder. Lighting. It is dangerous."

A rumble of thunder shook the ground. "See," he said.

I took my backpack off the mule, flung a stone against the wall as if that would protect us from lightning, and was look-ing for a place to set up a shelter when a young woman came sauntering up the trail and over to Policarpo.

"Well, I'll be damned," Lannie said. "That's the old geezer's squeeze."

She wasn't bad looking, and had the soft features of most Machiguenga women—high cheekbones, black eyes, and raven-colored hair. But her skirt was too short, makeup too heavy and her perfume strong enough to drive away mosquitoes.

Policarpo motioned us over. "She brought food," he said, and the two of them began laying it out on a cloth—hardboiled eggs, ham, boiled yucca and potatoes, a loaf of fresh bread, and a thermos of coffee.

He and the girl stayed off to the side while we ate, con-versing quietly in their Indian tongue, and when we finished, Policarpo took his mule by the reins and said he'd wait for us in the inn.

"Not to worry," he said to me in Quechua. "The girl will bring you food and information." He pushed back his battered hat. "May the spirits keep you safe from the brass buttons."

I paid the girl for the food, gave her a generous tip, and watched her meander back down the trail with Policarpo and his mule. As soon as they rounded a bend, Lannie retrieved

Marisa's pack. "We should bury this money." He tossed me a small packet of hundred-dollar bills. "Ten thousand dollars. Keep it. I'll take another packet. We might need it for travel expenses."

"How much money is in that pack?"

"More than two million. With this kind of money you can hire Allen fucking Dershowitz."

It rained most of the day, forcing us to huddle in our little shelter beneath a canvas tarp. A helicopter flew over us twice. Lannie said he didn't like the idea of putting our trust in the hands of three drunken guides and a Machiguenga girl who made a living by sleeping with guests. I didn't either, and we were debating what to do when the girl came tearing up the trail.

"*Wiracocha! Wiracocha!*"

We grabbed our weapons and hurried out to meet her.

"The brass buttons," she said in halting Quechua, her voice frantic, her hair and clothing drenched. "They come to the inn. Take Policarpo."

She made a drinking gesture with her hand. "He is much with the liquid spirits."

When I translated for Lannie, he rolled his eyes and slapped his forehead.

"That stupid old geezer. They'll have him talking in no time."

I thanked the girl and gave her a hundred dollars from the drug money, which was probably more than she earned in a month. Then, with thunder crashing around us, with rain pouring, we gathered our things and plunged into the jungle.

CHAPTER SEVENTY-SEVEN

The Rain Forest

At daylight, drenched and miserable, we were on the trail again, struggling and slipping, heading upward into the rain, when we heard the helicopter.

We dove into the brush. It came closer, a menacing shadow of noise and metal, barely visible through the overhead foliage. Its roar shook the forest; a turbulent wind followed. Then it was gone, its sound melding into the jungle.

"Fucking Policarpo," Lannie muttered.

We brushed off, hiked up our packs, and were about to set off again when Policarpo and his mule came crashing up the trail, looking over his shoulder as if he'd seen the old forest devil.

"Brass buttons!" he shouted. "They got Saturnino and Machete Man."

He dashed right past us, slapping the mule with his hat, cursing in his Indian tongue.

"Wait," I yelled, and hurried to catch up. "The girl said they got you as well."

"Escaped. Ran away. Now I am here."

We loaded our backpacks on the mule and trekked on, but hadn't gone very far before the helicopter swept over us again, shaking the trees and setting off a spray of moisture.

It disappeared a moment, but just as suddenly came back, this time with guns blazing.

Bark splintered off the trees. Foliage and debris fell around us, bullets danced along the trail. From my hiding place, I caught a glimpse of a helmeted gunner. Lannie took a shot with his sniper rifle, and was maneuvering for another shot when it flew away.

Lannie stumbled up. His hat was gone, his hair and stubble matted with debris. "How the hell would they know where to shoot? They can't possibly see us."

I remembered the tracking device on Luís. Had they installed one on Policarpo? But there was no time to ask or search. No time to do anything except run, so we stumbled along riverbeds and ravines, cursing the steepness of the climb—up and still up until we found ourselves alongside the river Marisa had said to follow to Plan C. There, amid the boulders, we took a short break and were passing around cheese when the gunship swept over us again.

It flew low over the river, hovered a moment, and started back toward us.

Lannie worked the bolt on his sniper rifle. Bullets flew again, clipping limbs off trees, ricocheting off boulders, buzzing past us.

The mule took a direct hit and went down.

Policarpo retrieved his mandolin and took off.

Lannie and I grabbed our things off the mule and followed, zigzagging from tree to tree, diving into ravines, cursing, praying.

The shooting ended. The helicopter faded away, leaving behind it a blessed silence. When the last leaf had fallen, and the usual cries and croaks and chirps came back, and my heartbeat was almost back to normal, I struggled out of the ravine and looked around.

"Lannie, where are you?"

"Policarpo?"

The monkeys answered. The wind and the parrots answered. Lannie and Policarpo did not.

I ran back toward the river, retracing my steps. Surely they were okay. Lannie was like a rock—solid, dependable, always there.

"Answer me, Lannie. Can you hear me?"

"Over here."

He was leaning against a tree, his leg soaked with blood, trying to cut away the pants with his knife. He twitched. He groaned. His face had gone white.

"It's bad," he managed to say.

I took the knife and ripped open the cloth, but when I saw the blood and protruding bone, I wanted to cry. I staunched the bleeding as best I could, took a syringe from his first-aid kit, and gave him an injection of morphine.

"You'll be okay," I said, knowing he wouldn't.

The morphine took effect. He spoke, but his voice was barely a whisper. "Listen, old buddy, I need you to do me a favor. Call Easton and tell him what happened. Tell him about Cat Man."

"Tell him yourself, Lannie. I'm getting you out of here."

"No, Markus, please. My ass is rooted here. I'm finished."

"Where's Policarpo?"

"Halfway home by now. He went that way."

"We could surrender. They'll take care of you."

"Would you fucking listen to yourself? They'd just shoot us both." He took a series of deep breaths. "I want you to apologize to Sonia for me. Tell her I'm sorry it didn't work out."

By then I was in tears. I gave him water. He drank. He fumbled in his shirt and took out his wallet. "Look inside. There's a laminated business card for somebody named Marcie. See it? There's numbers on the back...code for my account in the

Bahamas. Lots of money. I want you to have it. Yesterday wasn't the first time I hit the jackpot."

"What about your family? Your ex-wife?"

"I don't have a family. My ex-wife ran off with a cowboy, a redneck from Texas."

I put a hand on his shoulder. "Listen, Lannie, I—"

He brought up his sniper rifle and poked me on the nose with the barrel. "Don't go pussy on me, Professor. Get away from here. Now. There's nothing more you can do."

He was right, of course. Already I could hear Sinchis calling out to one another, slashing at undergrowth with their machetes. But when I came to my feet and looked down at him, lying helpless in his own blood, I felt like a father about to abandon his child.

"One more thing, old buddy."

"What, Lannie?"

"I love you, man. Now go. Get your ass away from here. Live a long, happy life."

I stumbled away with his maps, pistol, binoculars, wallet, and cigarette lighter, wiping away tears, and was sloshing across a shallow stream when a single gunshot registered behind me.

The forest fell quiet. Even the monkeys ceased their chatter.

I was alone.

CHAPTER SEVENTY-EIGHT

The path led back to an animal trail alongside the river. I followed it upstream, in and out of ravines, sloshing through creeks, stumbling, running, looking over my shoulder, crying. I should have stayed with Lannie, should have died with him. I was a failure. All my noble efforts had come to grief. Even the birds seemed to be mocking me.

"Lannie, Lannie," they sang. "Failure, failure."

My head pounded. My lungs felt as if they would burst. I took a packet of coca tea from my pack, crammed it into my water bottle, and kept going. There were forks in the trail. I didn't know which to take. Lannie's map was no help either, so I took a break and thought of the Sinchis behind me and how young they were, and how their bodies were uniquely adapted to this kind of environment, and how mine wasn't. Time to lighten my load.

I flung my AK into the bushes, removed everything from my pack except bare necessities, and was rearranging the pack when I noticed the parrot.

The same damn parrot I'd first seen at the guerilla camp, all green and red and staring down from a tree limb, as fearless as a family pet. How could that be? That camp was miles away.

"Gringo," it squawked, and flapped to the trail on the right.

"Gringo," I squawked back, and followed, and somewhere in the recesses of my mind, where reality blends with madness, a spark ignited. This wasn't an ordinary parrot. It was a spy sent by the Sinchis, and it was communicating a message to Lieutenant Bravos at that very moment.

Squawk. He's following, Lieutenant. We've got him.

I trekked on.

By late afternoon, with the jungle stretching as far back as the eye could see, with angry clouds building up for a storm, with the parrot flapping along behind me, I came upon a magnificent canyon where the river went cascading over a cliff, disappearing into swirling mist. Everything around me was green, lush, and dripping. Songbirds and monkeys kept up their commotion, lost in a hundred shades of flowers, vines, and moss-covered trees.

Could this be it, Marisa's hideout of last resort? Plan C?

But where was the lookout tower? I saw only forest, mist, river, and that damned parrot.

I sat on a fallen tree and was consulting my map when an old woman appeared on the trail.

I jumped up. Was she real? Or another creation from the parrot world?

She came closer, a wrinkled old woman dressed in a long, shapeless dress that marked her as a Machiguenga. An amulet of bones swung from her neck. Her hair was long and scraggly, and her lips were moving as if singing.

"Hello," I said in Quechua.

She walked right past, lips still moving.

Was she blind? I followed her down a side path away from the canyon, hoping she'd lead me to her village. Machiguengas were friendly. They'd help.

She rounded a bend. I waited a moment and trotted to keep up.

But she was gone, as hidden as the monkeys and songbirds.

I stumbled on, straining my eyes in the growing darkness, looking for a village that didn't exist, followed by a parrot that might be a Sinchi spy. Why couldn't Machiguengas build their villages in the open? Why did they prefer the darkness of jungle?

Why didn't I shoot that squawking parrot?

The wind picked up, sending debris to the ground. Raindrops penetrated the overhead canopy, coming down in large, warm splats. Lightning flashed. Then a tree came down, with whip-lashing vines, cracking limbs, and a crash that shook the ground.

I retreated into a ravine, but the ravine flooded, and before long I was pulling myself up the embankment by roots and vines. How ironic that after all I'd been through, after all the bullets I'd dodged, I could drown in this stupid little stream.

The rain stopped as suddenly as it began, replaced by croaks, hoots, chirps, and the most hideous shrieks. The remaining light faded to dark. Not the dark of civilized places, but the blackness of the plagues of Egypt, blacker than black obsidian, blacker than my mood.

I fumbled in the pack for my flashlight and switched it on.

It didn't work.

I shook it. I cursed it. I banged it against my boots and finally got an orange glow that barely lit the palm of my hand. "Candles," said a voice in my head. Or maybe it was the parrot. I went back to my pack, found a couple of candles, stuck them in the ground, and to my amazement got them burning with Lannie's cigarette lighter.

In this little pool of light, I strung my nylon hammock between two trees.

Should I build a fire? No, that might attract the creatures I'd been warned about—man-eating peccaries and crocodilian-like caimans. Snakes large enough to swallow a cow.

Something moved.

I grabbed Lannie's pistol and peered into the shadows. Into the noise. A white figure emerged against the blackness. It took on the shape of a human. Now it seemed to be floating, growing more and more distinct, more sharply defined.

I tightened my finger on the trigger.

The old woman stepped into the light.

She was drenched, her hair a tangled mess. She was so tiny and shriveled that her dress dragged the ground. She spoke to me in Quechua. "They say that when a stranger lies down to sleep at night, he hears the footsteps of demons and witches."

"*Pin kanki?*" I asked. "Who are you?"

"I am the wind, *wiracocha*. I am the forest. I am the rain."

"Do you have a name, woman of the wind and rain?"

"I am called Sachamama—Mother of the Forest."

"Where is your village, Sachamama?"

"The forest is my village, *wiracocha*. The trees and the earth are my home."

She stepped closer. "You lost your friend today."

"How did you know?"

"The wind told me. Can you not hear it speak?"

I backed away. Obviously this was a troubled woman. She shuffled over and touched my forehead with her bony hand. It was cold. Her amulet dangled in my face. She closed her eyes and began mumbling in her ragged voice, filling my nostrils with a repulsive odor.

"You need not fret about the blue eyes, for I can see her."

"Where is she?"

"On the other side of the mountains, beyond the trees. In the wind."

Thunder shook the ground, adding stature to her words. A gust of wind stirred the soupy air, showering us with moisture. She spoke again.

"You have a visitor, *wiracocha*, behind you."

I spun around but saw only darkness.

"It is your dead friend. Do you not see his face, his clothes that are covered with blood?"

Goosebumps came over me. I wanted to run out of that cursed place as fast as my legs would carry me. "Do not be afraid, *wiracocha*. He will look after you."

"Who are you, old woman? How is it that you hear and see these things?"

"Ohhh, *wiracocha*, can you not see that I am part of the spirit world?"

She turned and melded into the night, leaving me shivering in my wet clothes, wondering if I'd seen her at all. Was all that coca tea affecting my brain?

I lathered myself with insect repellant, blew out the candles, crawled into the hammock with my Glock, and wrapped myself with the canvas tarp.

And it seemed as if I'd just fallen asleep when a rumble of thunder woke me.

Shafts of sunlight burned through the overhead canopy, mating with the mist. The birds and monkeys were at it again, and a low-lying fog hung over the ground, as depressing as my mood.

"Buenos dias, gringo."

I bolted up and looked into the rain-drenched face of Lieutenant Bravos.

CHAPTER SEVENTY-NINE

He looked as wretched as I felt, like he hadn't slept for days. The two Sinchis with him couldn't have been more than teenagers, but they had assault rifles and a look of determination. Bravos took my pistol and binoculars. Before I could ask how he found me, he dug into a side pocket of my pack and pulled out a homing device about the size of a silver dollar.

"Cat Man put it there. Too bad you shot him."

"I didn't shoot him."

"Your friend did. It's the same thing."

He dumped the contents of my pack on the ground. "Where's the money?"

"What money?"

He backhanded me so hard I fell against the hammock. "Tell me where you hid it, gringo."

I thought he'd search me, take my wallet and passport and the stolen twenty-thousand I'd stuffed into side pockets of my cargo pants. Beat the truth out of me. And he might have done all that except for the buzzing sound from the radio pack of one of the Sinchis.

"Helicopter," said the young man, and handed a microphone to Bravos.

"Where are you?" Bravos barked. "Over."

The radio crackled. Out of it came a tinny voice. "At the falls, I think. Over."

"What do mean—you think? Don't you know? Over."

"Negative, Lieutenant. Can't see anything in these clouds. We're blinded. Over."

"Can you see Sergeant Rojas and his men at the falls? Over."

"That's a negative, Lieutenant. Can't raise them on the radio either. Over."

"*Joda,*" Bravos said. "Return to base. Try again at ten hundred hours. At the falls. Copy?"

"Copy, Lieutenant. Returning to base. Rendezvous set for ten hundred hours."

Bravos handed back the mike, his face a picture of disgust. The other young Sinchi asked, "What do you think happened to them, Lieutenant?"

"How the hell should I know? Maybe their radio is bad. This Russian shit is worthless. Let's get to the falls." He consulted his watch and shoved me onto the trail, but we had taken no more than a few steps when from down the ravine came laughter, like a madman in a horror movie.

The Sinchis swung their assault rifles toward the sound. "What was that, Lieutenant?"

"Howler monkeys. They're all over the jungle. Now come on. Move it."

A rock flew into our midst, almost hitting Bravos.

All three Sinchis dropped to the ground, Bravos in a shooting stance, both hands on his pistol, swinging it side to side. His face had gone white.

"Who are you?" he yelled into the fog.

More rocks fell around us, followed by more laughter.

Bravos fired into the jungle. So did the other Sinchis, shooting into the trees, into the underbrush, adding smoke to the fog, stinking up the place with acrid smells.

When the shooting stopped, there was only the drip-drip of moisture.

"Let's move it," Bravos said.

He set a fast pace, pushing me ahead with his pistol, looking into trees, stopping now and then to listen, cursing the radioman for being too slow.

The Sinchi in the rear followed so close that he kept bumping into the lieutenant.

"Dammit, soldier. It's probably just a hunting party of Machiguengas."

"But don't they use poison darts?"

"Darts are no match for your AK."

There was movement off to our right, something crashing through the jungle. Ungas, I thought, coming to get me, to make me pay for stealing their money and burning their property.

A coconut flew into our midst, and by the time we came to another ravine, which had another creek running through it, I was as ready as the Sinchis to jump in and start swimming.

Bravos formed us up like a train, each holding on to the belt of the man in front, and we plunged in, sinking up to our chests, the radioman struggling to keep his footing, holding his radio over his head. The current was swift, the water cold and murky, with swirling leaves and debris, but we were finally on the opposite side, pulling ourselves out by tree roots.

The radioman crawled up the embankment, had a look, and waved us on.

Up we struggled, wet and muddy, cursing and grunting. We picked up the trail on the other side, followed it for maybe thirty yards, and came to a fork.

"*Mierda,*" Bravos said. "We'll never make it to Cuzco in time."

"What's in Cuzco?" I asked.

"Your *puta,* gringo." He shoved me aside and spoke to the radioman. "Is the radio working?"

"I think so."

"Get Sergeant Rojas."

The radioman shook off his pack, dropped to a knee, and put the phone to his ear.

"Sinchi Two, this is Sinchi One. Can you hear me? Over."

Out of it came a sound like running water, broken now and then by static, but there was no reply and no Sergeant Rojas. Bravos cursed again. The radioman kept trying. The other young Sinchi, his eyes as big as saucers, said, "What could have happened to them, Lieutenant?"

"Devil Man," I answered.

Bravos swirled on me. "Shut up, gringo."

"I saw him last night, running around on all fours, howling."

"I told you to shut up."

"Listen," said the Sinchi with the radio. "Something's coming."

All three dove for cover, leaving me alone at the fork. I stared into the fog, straining my eyes. A woman's voice came to my ears—the voice of the old woman.

The sound came closer. She materialized from the fog like a white ghost, hair plastered to her scalp, face smeared with mud, muttering to herself in her native tongue.

"It's just an old woman," I said to Bravos.

The woman walked right past me, trailing a scent of her foulness, heading toward the ravine.

The Sinchis came out of their cover. "Did you see that, Lieutenant? She was floating."

"No, you idiot. It's her long dress. It hides the movement of her legs."

The woman stopped and turned about. I could barely see her against the hazy backdrop, but when she spoke, the fog amplified her voice. "They say that when a traveler lies down to sleep at night, he hears the sounds of witches and demons."

Bravos puffed himself up. "What are you saying, old woman?"

She cupped a hand to her ear. "Listen, can you not hear it?"

"Hear what?"

"Devil Man. He is out there, waiting. Do you not hear his laughter?"

She turned her back and followed the trail into the ravine. Bravos grabbed the youngest Sinchi by the arm. "Bring her back. Maybe she saw Rojas."

"But Lieutenant, I—"

"I gave you an order, Flores. Go."

He trotted after her, calling out to her in the Quechua word for señora—"*Mamay, Mamay.*"

His head sank beneath the top of the ravine. His calls to the old woman melded into the jungle. Bravos cupped a hand to his mouth.

"Hurry up, Flores. Do you see her?"

No answer.

Bravos trotted to the ravine with his pistol and peered down into the fog. It ghosted up from the stream in patches, lighter here, thicker there.

"Flores, where are you? Answer me."

The monkeys and the thunder answered. Flores did not.

Bravos fired a shot into the air. Birds fluttered up, squawking their protests.

Another shower of rocks fell around us.

The radioman panicked and ran. I raced up the trail behind him, Bravos on my heels.

CHAPTER EIGHTY

We splashed through streams and crashed through brush, tripping, struggling, looking over our shoulders, limbs snapping back in faces.

"Almost there," Bravos said. "I can hear the falls."

The "falls" turned out to be another angry stream running through yet another gulley, another of those fog-enshrouded low places that only a snake would love.

The radioman plunged in and began crawling up the embankment on the far side.

Bravos pushed me into the water, holding the pistol to my back. But when we reached the other side, there was only the fog and the noise of the jungle.

The radioman had disappeared.

"Fuck," Bravos said. "Where is he?" He cocked the hammer on his pistol.

"Luna. Where are you? Answer me."

More rocks fell around us.

Bravos, looking like a wild man, prodded me up the embankment. At the top we lay flat on our stomachs and peered into the fog. Nothing but overhanging limbs, dangling vines, ferns, elephant ears—and that damned parrot, perched on the limb of a tree.

"Gringo," it squawked, and flapped ahead.

Bravos shoved me on, clutching my belt from behind, holding me like a human shield. In time we came to the same fallen tree that I remembered from the day before. From beyond it came the steady roar of the falls. "Thank God," Bravos said. "We're almost there."

I wound my way around the tree, stooping low to get beneath vines and other foliage.

And then I stopped cold.

There they were—a cluster of six dead Sinchis hanging upside down from a tree like Shining Path dogs, their throats slit, blood dripping, flies swarming.

"Dear God, no," Bravos moaned. "Not Sergeant Rojas."

He shifted his pistol from his right hand to his left and made the sign of the cross.

And that was when I rushed him.

He went down, his pistol clattering along the rocks. I dropped a knee in his stomach and got my hands around his throat. He kicked. He struggled. His face turned blue, his eyes bulged, and just when it seemed he was in the final moment of life, I let go.

I couldn't do it. It wasn't in me. I wasn't a killer.

"What is wrong?" said a familiar voice behind me. "Why don't you finish him?"

I spun around and stared into the ugly face of Tucno, all headband, scraggly hair, filthy clothes, AK and knife. He stepped closer and offered me his knife.

"Here, gringu, use this."

The brush parted behind him, and out came a party of half-naked Machiguengas with feathers and quills. With them were a few Shining Path regulars in their filthy clothes, all dripping wet.

Tucno, who couldn't have looked more sinister if he'd been carrying a pitchfork, delivered a savage kick to Bravos. Bravos groaned, rolled away, and tried to crawl into a patch of palmettos, but Tucno dragged him to his feet.

"Come on, Lieutenant, we're going to send your head to General Reál."

He shoved Bravos toward the falls and then swung his AK toward me.

"In fact, we might send two heads to General Reál."

The men behind me backed out of the line of fire.

Tucno prodded me with the muzzle of his AK. "What did you do with the money?"

"What money?"

"Don't play the fool with me. We saw the fire, the damage you did."

"Leave him alone," said a voice behind me.

Engineer straggled out of the jungle. The same Engineer who could have passed as Chairman Gonzalo. Behind him came the girl who'd incurred Tucno's wrath by lighting a cigarette back in the mountains, and even a few of my old comrades from Group Red.

They gathered around and slapped me on the back and embraced me and pumped my hand as if I were a celebrity. And just when I thought I was beyond shock, that I'd seen and heard everything there was to see and hear, there came a woman I thought I'd never see again.

Faviola, arisen from the grave.

CHAPTER EIGHTY-ONE

S he flung her arms around me. "Look at you, gringo. Look
at that white hair. Look at your bruises and scratches. What
have they done to you?"

I stared into her sunburned face and black Andean eyes,
taking in the frizzy hair, the red hibiscus in her cap, and the
grin that was as big as the jungle. Before I could ask how she
had survived, Engineer blew a whistle.

"Everyone to the falls. We've got an hour."

"An hour for what?" I asked Faviola.

"Sinchi helicopter. We're going to ambush it."

She fell in beside me for the march. She chattered endlessly, and by the time we reached the falls, I knew the guerillas
had a training camp nearby; that Bravos's soldiers had been
felled by poison darts; and that she, Faviola, had escaped death
at the Apurimac because she'd been in the ladies room when
the Sinchis came.

"There I was, combing my impossible hair, when I hear this
racket. I crawled out a back window and hid in the woods."

"But I saw your picture in the paper. They identified you as
among the dead."

"Do I look dead to you? That picture you saw was Tika. She
was dead already."

335

I hugged her again. She said someone should get word to Marisa that I was still alive. Then she glanced around and low-ered her voice. "I saw her a couple days ago."

"Where?"

"Here. Their helicopter landed at this very place. She told everyone who'd listen that you might be coming, that they'd better look out for you. She even told that old witch."

"What old witch?"

"Over there."

I followed her gaze to the old woman. She was sitting on a boulder, still babbling, eyes staring into nothingness. As we drew near, she came to her feet and grasped my sleeve. "They say that when a stranger lies down at night, he hears the sounds of demons and witches."

Faviola pulled me away. "She doesn't know what she's say-ing. The Machiguengas say she's been wandering the forest for years. She thinks she's a spirit."

"Is the parrot hers?"

"What parrot?"

I glanced around. The parrot was gone.

I was still looking for that stupid parrot when Engineer formed up his troops.

"It'll land here, on this flat space. Those of you with Sinchi uniforms will wave it in. The rest will hide over there, in the brush."

He put them through the drill—once, twice, three times—shouting and cursing, blowing his whistle, and the exercise didn't end until another party of Machiguengas emerged from the jungle with two prisoners. Luna and Flores.

Their eyes had the glazed look of drunken men. They were stumbling. Everyone gathered around them. Engineer con-sulted his watch. "Make it fast."

I looked at Faviola for an explanation.

"They're going to shoot them," she said.

"They're just kids. Why shoot them?"

"They shoot us; we shoot them. It's the way of the world."

I dashed over to Engineer. "Can I talk with them a minute?"

"We've already interrogated them."

"Did they tell you about their plans in Cuzco?"

"They're just common soldiers. What would they know?"

"Look, give me a minute, okay?"

Without waiting for his answer, I stepped over to the radio-man. "Listen, son, your lieutenant was going to harm an inno-cent woman tomorrow. You might be able to help her. Do you want to go to your maker and say you could have helped this woman, but didn't?"

"Fuck you, gringo."

They shot him and threw his body into the swirling mist. They did the same with the other young Sinchi. And then it was Bravos's turn.

"Wait," he said to me. "I need to confess. Will you hear my confession?"

"I'm not a priest, Lieutenant."

"Doesn't matter. I know I can trust you. I know you're a good man."

Engineer nodded approval. Bravos dropped to his knees in the impatiens beside me.

"Bless me, Father, for I have sinned."

With the Machiguengas watching from the side, and Engineer and Tucno giving me dirty looks, and the roar of the falls in my ears, he confessed that he'd been disobedient to his parents, that he'd deflowered a young girl named Viola, that he'd shamefully run away to join the army when she became pregnant. He said he'd done terrible things, like shooting innocent people and letting his men rape and plunder, and he ended by saying he'd collected money from the narcos for General Reál. He also told me the name of his priest in Cuzco, and asked if I'd notify him.

By then the sun had found a break in the clouds and Engineer was out of patience.

"You're out of time, Lieutenant."

"One more second. I'm almost finished." He waited for Engineer to step away and looked back at me. "General Reál knows who your woman is...the wife of the artist. He's going to arrest her tomorrow—at Inti Rayma, the Festival of the Sun. But that's not all." He lowered his voice. "He's also going to set off bombs, explosions. It'll kill innocent people."

"Why? For what purpose?"

"He's done it before. Blamed it on the terrorists. I can't go to my God with that on my soul."

"Enough," shouted Engineer. "Get on with it."

Bravos grabbed my arm. "Do you believe in heaven?"

"Yes, Lieutenant."

"I want to soar into heaven with the condors."

Before I could ask what he meant, he sprang to his feet, dashed to the canyon's edge, and plunged into the abyss. I rushed over for a look, and the last I saw of Lieutenant Bravos, he was spread-eagled like a sky jumper—like a condor—soaring into the mist below.

CHAPTER EIGHTY-TWO

Bravos soaring with the condors? The man who'd become the monster of my nightmares? Now gone? Before I could absorb the meaning, Faviola was at my side, asking what happened. Then it was Engineer and Tucno, cursing and threatening, demanding to know why I'd let him slip away, saying they wanted his head as a trophy.

"What did he tell you that was so important?" Engineer yelled above the roar.

He pulled me away from the falls so we could speak without shouting. I told him about the general's plans to disrupt the festival in Cuzco. He told me he didn't give a damn, and before long it seemed as if half the camp had gathered around to listen, even the Machiguengas with their feathers, quills, and long black hair.

"He going to blame you," I said. "All of you. Say you're the ones that set off the bombs."

"So what?" Engineer said. "They're always blaming us."

"They're also going to arrest the artist, Don Francisco."

"We're all dispensable," Tucno growled. "Especially you."

Tucno pulled out his knife, tested the sharpness, and turned to Engineer. "This gringo has been nothing but trouble. I say we send him into the mist as well."

"Are you crazy?" Faviola said. "Chairman Gonzalo will have your head."

Engineer pulled them away for a little Kangaroo Court in the jungle. Their voices rose and fell—Faviola arguing my case, Tucno glaring as if he wanted to slit my throat. I didn't know if it was going in my favor or not, and they were still going at it, arms waving, when a shout rang out.

"Helicopter! It's coming!"

There was a great trample of feet across the grounds, rebels running this way and that. The ones in Sinchi uniforms headed to the cliff's edge. Others scrambled into the bush. Faviola pulled me toward the trees, but Tucno, now wearing a Sinchi shirt and red beret, stopped me.

"No, gringu. You're the prisoner. That's what they're expecting to see."

He pushed me back toward the falls, nudging me ahead with the barrel of his AK. Engineer dashed back and forth, barking orders like the general he was.

"Those in the bush stay out of sight. If I see one head pop up, I'll shoot it off myself. Keep your eyes on me. Don't fire until I give the order. Is that understood?"

"Yes, Comrade Engineer."

The helicopter appeared in the canyon below us, following the bend of the river, its distinctive thump now audible over the roar of the falls. It came close and still closer—so close to the canyon wall, it was momentarily out of sight.

A guerrilla in a Sinchi shirt peered over the edge. "Here it comes. Get ready."

Tucno shoved me to a clear spot near the abyss's edge. Seven or eight others in Sinchi uniforms—supposedly Sergeant Rojas's men—stood behind me with their AKs.

The thump grew louder. Faviola's voice cut through the sound.

"Be careful, gringo. Hit the ground when the shooting starts."

Right—assuming Tucno didn't put a bullet into my back. I looked around for a boulder, for a low spot, for anything to use as cover, but saw only impatiens in bloom, a piece of flat earth between the canyon and the jungle, and Tucno with his AK.

The helicopter lifted over the edge and hovered like a prehistoric monster, its engine screaming, its turbulence throwing up sprays of moisture, blowing petals of impatiens into the air. God, how I hated that thing. It was more than the men inside, more than rivets and plastic and metal; it was an evil entity that didn't deserve to live.

It lifted higher, banking this way and that. From my position in front of Tucno, I could clearly see the helmeted gunner in the open port, swinging his machine gun side to side, looking us over. Probably the same gunner that killed Lannie. Bastard.

Behind the windshield sat the pilot in goggles, and beside him another man, surveying the area through binoculars. What if he grew suspicious?

What if the gunner opened fire?

What if Tucno shot me in the back?

The helicopter dropped lower. My hat blew off my head. The rebel pretending to be Bravos held on to his beret with one hand and motioned the pilot toward the flat area with the other.

Down it came, the gunner facing us, until at last it settled amid the impatiens.

The engine throttled down. The noise went from deafening shriek to almost bearable.

"Now!" shouted Engineer.

I dove for the ground.

A storm of bullets flew over me. Tracers slammed into the helicopter, chewing holes, ricocheting, throwing off sparks and pieces of debris. The windshield shattered, the tail rudder came off. And yet the pilot still managed to get his ship off the ground.

Only for a moment.

It pitched over and went into a crazy spiral, slamming into the ground near the edge of the cliff, spinning over the ground like a wobbly top.

A portion of the prop broke off and buzzed over my head. Then this entire piece of metal and men went over the edge, tumbling end over end into the mist, leaving behind a celebrating mob of terrorists and the smell of overheated oil, gun smoke, and scorched metal.

CHAPTER EIGHTY-THREE

The cheers and excitement and backslapping went on for a long time. Engineer made another victory speech, saying how proud he was of everyone, but reminding them of the struggles that lay ahead. The Machiguengas said their good-byes and faded into the jungle. Then the guerrillas gathered their gear, formed into a column, and began marching away.

Faviola came over as if to say good-bye, but Engineer waved her off and told her to keep going. Then he pointed an angry finger at me.

"Consider yourself lucky, gringo. Tucno wanted your scalp. He'd have it too if you didn't have friends in high places. I want you to forget what you saw here. Understand?"

"Yes, Comrade Engineer."

"And one more thing. We're going that way, south, but you're going that way, north." He pointed back down the trail I'd taken. "Now go, I never want to see your gringo face again."

"Can I at least have a gun?"

"Sorry, no gun. Maybe the Machiguengas will help."

He turned and marched off with the last of his column, leaving me on the trail without a weapon, food, or supplies. I slumped onto the boulder where the old woman had sat and watched the last of them disappear over a little rise.

Now what? To follow was suicidal. But so was turning back.

Dammit to hell. There had to be something I could do to help Marisa.

I stood and brushed myself off. No way in hell was I going back the way I came. Maybe I could find an Inca trail and follow it to Cuzco. Yes, why not?

I set off in the same direction as the rebels.

And met Faviola coming back the other way.

"Came back to say good-bye," she said, all grins.

"You'll get in trouble."

"I'm already in trouble. They're calling me a gringo-lover, and not in a good way." She led me to a crop of boulders that was surrounded by brush. There she looked around as if the trees had ears and lowered her voice. "I know how you can get to Cuzco. It's a big risk, but…"

"But what, Faviola?"

"We've got a helicopter. It's flying to Cuzco. Tonight."

She held up a hand. "Don't ask, just listen. It's huge, one of those Russian makes—three rows of seats. There's a storage area behind the back row. You can hide there."

She gave me details. We made our plans, then she set off and disappeared over the rise. A minute or so later, she reappeared and signaled me to follow. She hiked to the next bend and waved me on, and in this fashion I followed her all the way to the Inca lookout tower.

"This is as far as I go," she said. "The helicopter is that way."

She opened her pack and gave me a banana, a bar of soap, a square of cheese, and a little jar of liquid she called demon potion. "It's for the bugs. There's also a stream near the helicopter. You could use a bath. But be careful. There may be guards."

"Why are you doing this, Faviola?"

"Have you met Marisa's husband?"

"I've met him."

"Have you seen his paintings, the series called *Girls of Pachacuti*?"

"Don't tell me you were one of them?"

"I'm too old. But I've got a daughter—Celeste. She's fourteen, almost fifteen."

Hatred showed on her face. "If it was just the painting, it might have been okay, but he's a pervert, a *pedofilio*. I went straight to Marisa. She…"

"She what?"

"Helped me. Drove me to the place where he'd set her up. Confronted him with a pistol. She'd have shot him if I hadn't stopped her."

"Is Celeste okay?"

"She is now. Marisa helped me get back something that was precious to me. I'd like to do the same for her." Again, she kissed me good-bye and faded into the jungle.

CHAPTER EIGHTY-FOUR

I smelled it before I saw it, a mound of camouflage netting in a little clearing near the edge of the canyon, resting on its pad like a giant mosquito, stinking up the jungle with the odor of fuel and lubrication liquids. No guards that I could see. No trip wires either.

But what if someone was inside, sleeping or reading a book?

I crept closer, approaching as if it were a coiled snake, and crawled beneath the netting.

The markings identified it as a Petro-Peru helicopter, which it wasn't. No wonder they could fly around the country without getting shot down. Petro-Peru was the state-owned Peruvian Petroleum Corporation. They were so big and bloated that the bureaucrats who ran it probably had no idea the rebels had borrowed their good name.

Birds fluttered out of the netting. Monkeys screeched, but no movement came from the inside. No faces at the window either. Maybe they hadn't posted a guard. Why should they?

Only a lunatic would attempt what I had in mind.

The door was unlocked. I eased it open and clambered up, setting off a loud creak.

It was dark inside, and had the metallic and oily smell of an automobile repair shop. A tattered operations manual lay in the pilot's seat. So did a flashlight. I clicked it on and looked around at torn leather seats, wires and tubes dangling from the overhead, old newspapers and trash. Didn't they ever clean this piece of Russian crap? I couldn't picture Marisa sitting here, not the woman who surrounded herself with flowers and sweet-smelling things.

I kicked an Inca Kola bottle out of the way, strode to the back, and peered over the rear seats. Yes, just as Faviola had said—a wide cavity filled with boxes, blankets, cushions, and trash, spacious enough for a small horse. I shifted things around, made myself a bed, and climbed in.

Perfect. Better than first class. Now all I needed was a weapon.

I searched through bags and boxes. No weapons. I looked under the seats. Nothing. Then I dug through the hellhole on the side of the transmission well and found a flare gun with cartridges bigger than shotgun shells. Yes, it would have to do.

The flight to Cuzco was still hours away, so I plopped into a seat, picked up a newspaper someone had left, and noted another article about me—a contest sponsored by the editors for the best Shakespearean verse that summarized my circumstances.

The winning verse, Sonnet 116, came from a student at San Marcos.

> Love alters not with brief hours and weeks,
> But bears it out even to the edge of doom.

Exactly. Why else would I be in a Russian helicopter?

Voices and laughter came from the outside. Were they coming already?

Back to the rear I scrambled, back into my hole. Back into the edge of doom.

The door opened. A woman climbed in. Then a man. They were speaking Quechua, and from their conversation, I guessed they were part of the ground crew. But what if they were here to clean up? What if they noticed the missing flare gun?

Or the flashlight?

They had a boom box, and out of it came the familiar sounds of Radio Andino, direct from Cuzco. Things opened and closed. Metal clanged and clattered. They moved toward the back.

Then they were in the backseat, only inches away. Kissing and fondling.

"Don't you ever get enough?" said the woman.

"No, little flower. You are the light of my life. You make me crazy."

For God's sake. Not here. Go someplace else.

The seat shook. The helicopter creaked, the music played, and this couple whose faces I could only imagine began grunting and moaning and exchanging words that were meant only for each other. "There," she said. "Do it that way. Oh yes, oh yes. Dear God, yes."

In Quechua.

It went on and on—endlessly, until I smelled their love-making. I could even see the top of the woman's head in the opening between the seat and bulkhead. Up and down, back and forth, so close I could have reached out and pulled her hair.

"Oh yes…yes."

The shaking stopped.

"Why are you always so fast?" the woman complained.

"It's okay. I know how to take care of you. Just give me a minute."

A minute passed. Then about fifteen more before the shaking resumed. I wanted to scream, to pop out of my hiding place and give them a heart attack. Why did these things happen to me?

"Oh yes. Yes, yes, yes."

Again the shaking stopped. They lit up in spite of the *Se Prohibe Fumar* signs, filling the cabin with the smell of cigarettes. "Do you love me?" the woman purred.

"What do you think?"

"Say it. I want to hear you say it."

"I love you, little dumpling. I adore you. I worship you."

I wanted to puke.

"Too bad about the gringo," the man said. "I thought he was a pretty nice guy."

"What are they going to do with the gringo?"

"Didn't you hear? Tucno sent a squad after him. He'll never make it out alive."

They finally left. I went outside again, cleaned up in a little stream, waited until dark, and climbed back into my hiding place. Passengers and crew came around nine, during a driving rain, while I was lying in my hole with my stomach growling, dreaming about a burger and fries.

There was laughter, loud banter, a curse as someone stumbled in the darkness.

It was Tucno.

That son of a bitch. Maybe I could strangle him in the darkness.

Passengers plopped into the rear seat, knocking it against my shoulder. Bags dropped on top of me. Through the crack I saw a flashing red light.

The engine whirred, sputtered a couple of times, and roared to life. Rotors turned, rocking us gently from side to side. The motion intensified as the pilot warmed the engine. The craft vibrated and shook. The noise grew so loud, it hurt my ears.

Then we lifted into the clouds.

CHAPTER EIGHTY-FIVE

Cuzco

The helicopter lurched. It shook. It rocked me this way and that. Surely they'd discover me. Surely there'd be a confrontation that would get us all killed. Yet, aside from the noise and shaking, the darkness and the cold, I could just as well have been flying commercial. Hell, I could have climbed over the backseat and pranced around singing "God Bless America."

Or bashed in Tucno's head.

It was that dark and noisy.

It was going on midnight when we finally set down. By then I was so numb and cold and headachy and deprived of oxygen that all I wanted to do was sleep.

Cabin lights came on. The engine went from shriek to hum to silence.

Passengers debarked. Doors slammed, and then came the sound of a vehicle driving away.

I struggled free of my hole, hurried to the exit, and climbed out into a starry night. The air was bone-chilling cold. But why was it so dark? Cuzco was a large city. It should be glowing.

I pulled my blanket around me and headed toward the sight of moving cars, feeling my way like a blind man, cursing my clothes, which were still damp and smelly.

Dogs barked, a woman laughed, and then, as if I'd stepped on a trip wire, a light arced toward the heavens and burst into a dazzling display of colors.

I flattened myself on the tarmac, certain I'd been discovered.

More lights streaked up, turning darkness into daylight, followed by delayed pops and booms. All around were buildings, aircraft, and automobiles. I hadn't stepped on a trip wire. It was midnight in Cuzco, and the descendants of the sun-worshiping Incas were celebrating the arrival of the shortest day of the year.

I bounded up, strolled down to the main road, and hailed a taxi.

The driver told me the power was out. "Peru," he mumbled.

Traffic was heavy; the streets filled with revelers in colorful native dress. The driver said it would be difficult to find a hotel with a vacancy, so he dropped me near the famous wailing square of the Incas, where Inca Tupac Amaru had been drawn and quartered by the Spaniards.

The smell of outdoor cooking and eucalyptus smoke sharpened the emptiness of my stomach.

I pushed through the crowd and found myself in front of the Church of Santo Domingo, a colonial structure that had been built upon the ruins of the Coricancha, the heart of Inca worship, their Temple of the Sun. From the inside came a chorus of women's voices.

"Blessed art thou among women, and blessed is the fruit of thy womb..."

Too bad I wasn't Catholic, and wasn't so desperate to get to a phone. Otherwise, I'd have gone inside to say a prayer for Marisa and light a few candles for the dead.

Down the street came a candlelight procession of Runas, the men in red ponchos and knit caps, the women in swirling skirts and bowler hats, marching to the beat of drums. I fell in behind them, followed them around the block, and at

351

last stood before the graceful arches of the Hotel Cuzco where Marisa and I had once stayed. Back in my Peace Corps days.

The lobby was sinfully warm, lit by lamps and candles, with a clean, pleasant smell. No guerrillas, no Sinchis or parrots or screeching monkeys, only the concierge behind the counter in a little pool of lamplight, glaring at me as if I were a mystic from Katmandu.

"Señor?"

I took off my battered hat. "I need a room."

"Sorry, señor. It's the festival. Maybe tomorrow night."

I pulled out a hundred-dollar bill. "This is yours if you can find me a room."

He glanced around, took the money, and made a pretense of looking through the vacancies. "All we have is a luxury suite on the fifth floor. You'll have to pay in advance."

"Does it have a phone?"

"All our rooms have phones, but they don't work during power outages."

"What about water? I need to clean up and tend these insect bites."

"No water either. The pumps need electricity, but we keep a filled container in the bathroom for emergencies. I can get you an extra container if you need it."

I showed him my forged passport, signed in under the name of John Keats, handed him another hundred for the room, and followed a young man named Néstor to the second floor. He lit candles and lamps, illuminating the kind of luxury I hadn't seen for weeks.

"Does the hotel do laundry?" I asked him.

"Tomorrow."

"Tomorrow's too late. I need clean clothes first thing in the morning." I waved another hundred-dollar bill in his face. "This is yours if you if you can get it done tonight."

CHAPTER EIGHTY-SIX

Hotel Cuzco

C hurch bells woke me at sunrise, followed by loud cries and the beat of drums. I sprang out of the luxury of a queen-size bed and hurried to the window. Legions of barefooted Runas had come to life, greeting the first rays of sun with shouts and dancing.

I picked up the phone, got the downstairs operator, and within moments was speaking with Marisa's mom in Miami.

"Where are you?" she asked, her voice frantic. "Where's Marisa?"

I told her what happened and asked if she'd heard from Marisa. She hadn't, so I promised to find her and bring her home, and asked her to call Sonia and have her phone me at the hotel.

"But not from her house. Tell her to use a pay phone."

She promised. I hung up and bounced into the bathroom and took a gloriously hot shower. I also shaved a four-day growth of stubble, brushed, and flossed—thanks to the amenities provided by the hotel—and was doctoring cuts and bruises when Nestór arrived with breakfast and laundry, my clothes smelling like spring flowers.

I gave him the money I'd promised, led him to the window, and pointed out the Runas in their bright-red ponchos and knit caps.

"Can you get me an outfit like that?"

"Not a problem, caballero. We've got them in our tourist shop downstairs."

"A sweater too. Extra large. Also sunglasses, a large drawing pad, and a grease pencil."

I handed him two more hundred-dollar bills and told him to keep the change.

Sonia called while I was wolfing down breakfast. This was the moment I dreaded. I shoved away my plate and told her about Lannie.

She cried. I cried. I promised to give her details later and then told her what happened to Marisa, adding that the general knew her identity.

"I've got to find her, Sonia. She's in grave danger. Do you have any idea where she is?"

"All I know is what she told me a week or so ago, that her husband wants her beside him at the ceremony today. They're making him an honorary Inca for his support of their cause."

"Where and when?"

"Noon, at Fortress Sacsahuaman."

I asked if she could come to the hotel. She said she could. I told her I'd leave a package for her in the safety deposit box, and she could find the key at the top of the bathroom door-frame—in case I didn't return. "Tell the desk you're my wife. I'll tell them I'm expecting you."

My next call was to Holbrook Easton at the US Embassy in Lima. He bombarded me with questions in his refined voice, but I cut him off and told him about Lannie. I also told him about Cat Man and the Ungas and what we'd learned about the *narco-traficantes*, and about General Reál's plot to disrupt the festivities with a bomb.

"He's going to blame the terrorists."

"That's a serious allegation, Professor. What is your source?"

"Doesn't matter. Call Inspector Bocanegra. Call the Cuzco police. Call Radio Andino."

"I'll see what I can do, but listen. There's a missing Sinchi helicopter in the area where you were—also a squad of missing Sinchis. Do you know anything about it?"

I hung up on him and called Bravo's priest, and by the time we finished the conversation, the bells of the great cathedral told me it was already ten o'clock.

Dammit, where was Nestór? If he didn't show up within ten minutes, I'd have to head up to the fortress dressed as a gringo. I laid out my remaining possessions on the bed—Swiss Army knife, wallet and binoculars; the twenty thousand dollars we'd stolen from the Ungas; my passport, flare gun, and Marisa's rag witch.

Lannie's wallet went into the safety deposit box for Sonia. So did most of the twenty thousand. The rag witch was going with me.

Funny how it looked just like that old witch back in the jungle.

At last Nestór marched into the room with a bundle. I thanked him and began dressing as a Runa—knitted wool cap with earflaps, bright red poncho that reached my knees, sunglasses to hide my light-colored eyes. Who cared I wasn't wearing the traditional knee-length breeches and sandals, or that I stood a good eight inches taller than the average Runa?

The entire population of Cuzco would probably be drunk.

From the drawing pad I ripped off a sheet and wrote in all caps the word NORMAN.

I strapped Lannie's binoculars about my neck and stuffed the rag witch into my pocket.

Then I broke open the flare gun, slipped in a shell, and popped it shut.

Time to find Marisa.

CHAPTER EIGHTY-SEVEN

Fortress Sacsahuaman

The taxi swung around, made an illegal U-turn, and began a steep climb up Calle Saphi Plateros. Normally it would take about ten minutes to reach Sacsahuaman, but the streets were so filled with foot traffic that we crawled along in slow motion, stopping here, waiting for a noisy procession there, or taking a side street only to be waved off by cops.

The crowds swelled, the traffic grew heavier, and before long we were in a massive snarl, with blaring horns, red-faced drivers, and policemen trying to keep order. A drunk rolled across the hood and peered into the windshield. Children dressed as devils banged on the windows and shook their rattles. Then I heard my name on the car radio.

"*This just in: Professor Markus Thorsen, the man we've come to know as Romeo the Poet, is making serious allegations about General Clemente Reál...*"

I paid the fare, hopped out, and pushed along with the crowd, sticking to low spots to minimize my height. The road was steep. My lungs ached from the thin air. Here and there I ducked behind obstacles to avoid policemen, and I was sweating in spite of the mild temperature.

But at last I reached it, a sprawling monstrosity of cut boulders and triple walls, the scene of the final defeat of the Incas, now enveloped in a carnival atmosphere of noise and color.

Spectators in native dress lined the walls, legs dangling. Others sat on the cliffs or mingled on the parade field. And still they came, raising clouds of dust: women carrying infants in their shawls, old men on crutches, little children in colorful finery, demons and devils, and all manner of hideous-looking creatures with rattles and horns.

I threaded my way around tables where Runa women were selling roasted guinea pigs, climbed atop the outermost wall, and surveyed the parade ground with my binoculars, focusing on the VIP seating area. There sat generals in uniform, judges in dark robes, and politicians, mayors, clergy, diplomats, and other officials in civilian dress.

Marisa was not there. Neither was her husband.

Inca warriors were now performing a ritual dance, a swirl of shiny uniforms, shields, plumes, javelins, and other hand weapons. Female dancers came next—young, pretty, colorful. Then came the devil dancers, followed by flautists and a vocalist singing an Inca war tune.

> We'll drink chicha from your skull / Make a necklace from your teeth.
> A drum from your skin / And then we'll dance.

Conch shells blared, drums beat, and out from the great walls danced a line of girls strewing flowers from baskets. Behind them came a covered litter borne by twelve Inca warriors. In it sat the great Sapa Inca, as lordly as the surrounding snow-capped Andean peaks.

He was followed by the High Priest of the Sun in his golden robe, and then generals of the empire, princesses and princes, members of the court and the Chosen Women, and finally the soldiers, with javelins, shields, war clubs, and feathers.

The Inca stepped from his litter and ascended the same throne that had been carved for the real Sapa Inca hundreds of

357

years ago. Everyone stood. Cheers and applause rolled across the grounds. He turned to the VIP section and nodded. And that was when I saw Don Francisco de la Vega, honored guest, Marisa at his side, she in a fine white robe with purple embroidery, a golden medallion of the sun about her neck.

And she was biting her lower lip.

Run, I wanted to yell. *Get away*. But she couldn't even if she could hear me. Not with Tucno sitting behind her, all dressed up in jacket and tie.

One thing about Tucno: he got around.

Down to the next great zigzag wall I struggled. No one noticed. No one cared. I was just another Runa. I went over the inner wall as well, and at last was separated from Marisa by ropes, troops, and about half the length of a football field.

I waved. I took off my cap and shouted. I held up the sign on which I'd written NORMAN.

She didn't notice. Neither did anyone else, not in all the noise and commotion.

Now what? I thought about that indefinable little current that passed between us. Would it work here? I closed my eyes and summoned up all the will in my being.

Look at me, Marisa. I'm here, directly to your front.

I tried again and again, passionately, desperately, pausing to check her reaction through the binoculars. The drums and the music answered. Marisa did not.

Maybe if I sent her a poem. Not a Neruda poem, but a Mark poem—"Lily of Peru."

Again I closed my eyes and concentrated.

The noise of the festival faded. I heard songbirds and the wail of flutes. I smelled her perfume. I heard my own voice reciting words she loved to hear. And then, from somewhere within my soul, on the edge of perception, I felt her presence.

I raised the binoculars again. Yes, she had binoculars to her eyes, scanning the walls.

I held up the NORMAN sign, waving it back and forth.

She focused on me. Her expression changed from resignation to excitement.

I blew her a kiss and gestured toward the wall to her right. She shrugged as if she didn't understand. I wrote it on the back of my sign with the grease pencil—RUN!

She nodded and stood. Tucno pulled her back down.

Drums rolled. Conch shells blared.

And that was when the first bomb exploded, off to the left.

Gunfire erupted behind me.

"Run," I yelled at Marisa. "This way."

By then almost everyone in the VIP section was on their feet, looking around, some of them hurrying away. I ran toward them in a fury, waving my arms.

"Get away! Scatter!"

Marisa ran, stumbling over chairs and pushing past people who were too slow.

Her husband trotted behind her, cursing and yelling.

Tucno, faithful lapdog that he was, chased her down from behind.

He wrapped his arms around her, and they were struggling when the next bomb exploded.

In the VIP section.

A mushroom of fire and smoke lifted into the sky, sucking the air out of my lungs, blowing me off my feet and tumbling me over the field. Sparks, clothing, and other debris whizzed over my head. Chairs dropped around me. So did other things too terrible to mention.

CHAPTER EIGHTY-EIGHT

I struggled up, brushing dirt from my eyes. A cloud of suffocating smoke hung over the area. Ashes fell like raindrops. I stumbled toward the area where I'd last seen her.

"Marisa, where are you? Answer me?"

She was lying face-down beneath Tucno, trying to wriggle free. Tucno was dead, the back of his head crushed, his clothes smoldering. Don Francisco also lay nearby.

"Marisa," I cried. "It's me, Mark."

Her eyes opened. She squeezed my hand. "Mark, is it you?"

I choked up. "You're going to be okay. I'm going to get you out of this."

Her hand went limp. I begged her to hold on, but there was no response, no movement at all.

I rolled Tucno off her. Yes, she was breathing. No severe burns or broken bones that I could find, only singed hair, torn clothing, and a gash below the left temple. Tucno's body had saved her. But she still wasn't safe. General Reál knew who she was. She couldn't go to the hospital as Señora de la Vega. Hell no.

Her purse was strapped over her shoulder, with ID inside. I stuffed it under the body of a woman who lay a few feet away. No one noticed. There was too much noise and panic. I did the same with her golden sun disc. Then I found a poncho that was lying nearby and was working it over her head when she tried to sit up.

"No," I said. "Just relax."

She slumped back down and reached for my hand.

I brushed soot off her face. "Listen, sweetheart, when the ambulance comes, I want you to tell them your name is Lori Easton. Wife of Holbrook Easton. Got it?"

"Lori Easton," she mumbled. "What happened to Tucno?"

"He won't be bothering you again. Neither will your ex."

"Am I going to die?"

"No, sweetheart. You'll be fine."

I made her say Lori Easton again and was telling her how much I loved her when a woman in scrubs examined her and waved over stretcher-bearers. Someone handed me an identification tag and asked me to write her name. I wrote Lori Easton and the number for Holbrook Easton.

They shoved her into an ambulance with at least a half-dozen other bloodied survivors. A medic tied the tag to her wrist. I tried to crawl in beside her.

"No," the medic said. "There's no room."

"But I'm her husband."

"You can visit her at the hospital. We don't know which yet."

The door slammed. The ambulance pulled away, lights flashing, siren wailing, leaving me in tears. *Please, dear God, let her be okay.*

More ambulances rolled onto the field. A news helicopter buzzed low over the fortress. I took another look at Tucno and her husband to be sure they were dead, and was thinking to get down to Cuzco when the PA system crackled to life. Over it came the raspy voice of General Reál.

"*Atención. Atención,* we have the situation under control. Please remain calm."

There he stood, the bastard, his hair and uniform covered with dust, barking out orders to five or six Sinchis, sending them left and right, trying to bring order to the chaos he'd created.

He ascended the throne like an Inca lord. A small army of reporters with cameras and microphone followed, all of them asking what he knew about the perpetrators.

"The terrorists," he snorted. "They did this. But they'll be brought to justice."

The noise and the chaos made it almost impossible to hear, but the general didn't care. The cameras were rolling. His face would be on the news—and on the front page of every newspaper in Peru: GENERAL REÁL RISKS HIS LIFE AT SACSAHUAMAN.

Damned right he was going to risk his life! Lose it too if I had my way.

I sprang onto the throne and yanked off my little Inca cap.

"You," he said, and reached for the pistol in his holster.

I flew into him with such fury that it took us both over the side.

The pistol went flying. Journalists and reporters jumped aside.

He looked left and right for his Sinchis, panic in his face.

But there were no soldiers in sight, only the press corps, and they didn't like the son of a bitch either. They weren't going to interfere. They knew a good story when they saw it.

I took another step toward him, thinking he'd put up a fight for the cameras. Or point a finger and start making accusations. Instead, he turned and ran.

CHAPTER EIGHTY-NINE

At 11,200 feet, Fortress Sacsahuaman is not the place for a gringo to go jogging, and certainly not the place to get into a footrace with a native Peruvian. General Reál had the blood of the Andes in him. I didn't. His body was uniquely adapted to the thin air of such places. Mine wasn't.

But on I went, driven by rage and hatred and the certainty that if I didn't stop him, he'd get away with his atrocities and find Marisa in the hospital, and we'd both end up at Dracula's House, and he'd probably be elevated to a national hero.

He skirted a rocky knoll known as the Rodadero—the children's rock slide—and crossed the road above, taking a steep trail upwards. I followed. But at 11,600 feet, near the site of a modern lime crusher, I slowed to a walk.

My lungs burned. My injured leg hurt. Everything hurt, and I'd been running for only a few hundred yards. I was defeated. Time for Plan B. Or was it Plan C?

Get down to the hospital, find Marisa, and get her into hiding. Again.

But the elevation was getting to the general too. There he stood, the son of a bitch, no more than fifty or sixty yards ahead, bent double near an old Inca bath, hands on knees, sucking in the thin air. He'd probably been debauching all over Peru while I was hiking up mountains. Maybe he'd had a few pisco sours before the ceremony and whores all night long.

I pushed on, up and still up.

At 12,200 feet, about a kilometer north of Sacsahuaman, the general looked back. By then I'd closed the distance. The better news was that it was all downhill from here, down toward the Saphi River valley, where a refreshing ribbon of water cut through groves of eucalyptus trees.

I said a silent prayer for Marisa and kept going. With any luck at all, I'd catch the general before we reached the Chacán, a great natural barrier straddling the Rio Tica Tica. Then I was going to beat his face to a pulp, strangle him with my bare hands.

Twenty paces and closing. Now I could hear his grunts, the crunch of his feet.

Fifteen paces.

Ten.

He reached the bridge, stopped, and spun around. In his hand was a pistol, one of those small-caliber, one-shot affairs that a gambler might hide up his sleeve.

I saw the flash, felt the jolt of impact, felt my right side go numb, and I crashed into the general like a sack of potatoes, knocking us both to the ground.

I tried to struggle up, but the strength had gone out of my legs and arms. I fumbled beneath my poncho for the flare gun and got my hands around the familiar grip. But I couldn't get it out of my belt. My thumb was too slippery, too bloody, too numb.

I tried the left hand. It didn't work either.

The general made it to his feet and stood over me, his breath coming in ragged gasps.

He delivered a vicious kick to my side. "Was it worth it, gringo? You could have walked away…gone back to your academic world. But, no, that wasn't good enough. You killed my lieutenant…and Cat Man, and Gordo…and all those other good men."

He kicked me again. "Now look at you…your best friend dead. Your little slut dead. And you about to join them."

He ejected his spent cartridge and reached into his pocket for another.

I pushed backwards on the graveled trail, back and still back until my head and shoulders rested against the remains of an Inca aqueduct. From it came a bubbling sound, as if it were still carrying water down to Cuzco, but when I heard the wheeze, the gurgles, and saw the blood on my hand, I realized the bubbling came from my chest.

A hazy crimson mist settled over me. The general's words melded into the thump of the helicopter. He said something about the bomb blast, and the drug-running operation that he controlled, and I'm pretty sure he admitted his main reason for wanting Chairman Gonzalo was to eliminate the competition.

The mist grew heavier. The buzz I'd thought was the helicopter was in my own head.

So this is what dying is like, I thought. Close your eyes, give up, and go to sleep. No fear, no regrets, only a dark, peaceful haze. Not even my life flashing before my eyes.

That was when the parrot appeared. It squawked a few times, ran along the railing of the bridge, and turned into Lannie Torres.

He knelt beside me. "The hell's wrong with you, Mark?"

He popped me on the head. "Don't go pussy on me now. You can do it."

Behind him stood a little gathering of the dead—Luís, Gordo, Tucno, Don Francisco, Cat Man, Bravos, the Sinchi photographer, Puppy Sad Eyes, and even those damned mules, as if they'd stopped by to welcome me into their world.

"Come on," Lannie said. "It's not your time yet. Get out that flare."

Again I reached beneath the poncho, struggling with the flare gun, trying to work it loose.

It came out.

"Cock the hammer," said Lannie. "Use both hands. You can do it."

The general didn't notice my efforts. Or if he did, he must have thought I was holding my hands over the wound. He took his time reloading his little pistol and snapping it shut.

He stepped closer, still gasping for breath, his boots crunching on the loose gravel.

Now he was standing over me.

He thumbed back the hammer and lifted the pistol toward my head.

"The hell?" Lannie shouted in my ear. "You gonna let him shoot you?"

I swept aside the poncho and pulled the trigger.

The blast levitated the general and blew him right off the bridge.

The people and animals on the bridge faded away, taking the general with them, and suddenly it all made sense. They'd come for the general, not me.

Lannie patted my shoulder. "Good job, old buddy." Then, like the head of Inca Tupac Amaru, he turned into a condor, flapped along the bridge, and soared into the mist.

CHAPTER NINETY

Cuzco Memorial Hospital

They called her Nurse Zara, and she had the voice of an angel. How I knew her name I don't know, but I recognized her the instant I woke up and found her running a ruler along the bottom of my feet. I jerked back and tried to sit up, but the pain was too great. I tried to talk, to ask about Marisa, but the tubes got in the way, words wouldn't come out, and I fell back into the pillow.

"It's all right," she said in that angelic voice. "Just lie still."

She told me that I was in Cuzco Memorial and that I'd been there for two days.

"Do you know your name?"

I did, but wasn't about to tell her, not until I learned what she knew.

"No point keeping it a secret," she said. "We know who you are."

She went to the door and called out to someone in the hallway. This brought in a dark-haired little man in a white smock. He bent over me with his stethoscope and did the usual thing doctors do, and then told me the bullet had glanced off a rib, collapsed a lung, and lodged against muscle tissue near my spine. "With therapy you should fully recover."

Fully recover? What was he talking about? My life expectancy was no better than a rabid dog's. I was surprised they hadn't already given me a lethal injection.

"Don't get any ideas about escaping," he said. "There's a Peep guard outside."

Nurse Zara pulled up a chair as soon as he left, and for the first time I noticed her almond-shaped black eyes and how young and pretty she was. She handed me my little rag witch.

"Here, thought you might want this back. Peep took everything else."

I choked up at the sight of my little friend. Was she the reason I hadn't bled to death?

Zara looked as if she too was about to burst into tears. "You've been asking about Marisa," she said in that soft voice. "I'm sorry to have to tell you she didn't make it."

My stomach twisted. She was wrong. Marisa was alive when I'd last seen her. But I wasn't about to mention the name Lori Easton. For all I knew, Nurse Zara could be Peep Agent Zara.

"How do you know this?" I asked.

"It was in the papers. What a shock to hear she was married to that famous artist."

"Where did they find her body?"

"I don't know. Maybe I can get you a paper."

No sooner had she left than the door opened and in marched Inspector Bocanegra and his cigar, Chino at his side. "You're one lucky *hijo de puta*," he growled. "If it hadn't been for that false passport, you'd be in a prison ward. Instead, you're here, the hospital's VIP room."

He took off his jacket as if he were a guest and pulled up a chair. Chino yanked my right arm so hard that I felt my wound tear. "Does that hurt?" he asked in singsong Spanish.

They cranked up my bed, putting more stress on the injury. Bocanegra rattled off the charges against me, counting with his fingers—the manslaughter of a Peep detective, the sniper killing of El Gato, the murder of Lieutenant Bravos and an entire squad of Sinchis, the destruction of an army helicopter and death of its crew, the assassination of a general of the army.

He took a puff and blew it into my face. "So what I'm saying, gringo, is you're facing life sentence in Lurigancho—assuming someone doesn't slit your throat first."

He leaned closer. "But don't despair. The president doesn't care about you. The person he wants is Chairman Gonzalo. You help us find him and maybe you'll get only ten years."

He was still glaring at me, waiting for an answer, when Nurse Zara came back in, pushing a cart. "What is going on? This is a no-smoking room."

Bocanegra stood and pulled on his jacket. At the door he said, "I'll be back."

Zara slammed the door behind them.

"Bastards. They ought to give you a medal for killing that general." She changed the dressing that was now bloody, served me a bowl of vegetable soup, and gave me an injection for pain. Then she took a newspaper from the bottom rung of the cart.

"Better read fast. You've got about ten minutes before the drug kicks in."

Marisa's photograph jumped out at me. So did the photo of her famous husband. And the Shakespearean headline: DONE TO DEATH BY SCOUNDRELS FOUL.

They'd found both bodies at the fortress, side by side. My switch had worked. But what about the Marisa I'd put in the ambulance as Lori Easton?

I ripped through the pages. Here were photographs of the carnage and overhead photos of me chasing the general, and the shootout at the bridge, and a headline that read: GENERAL REÁL DENIED MILITARY FUNERAL.

At last I found it, buried on a back page under a long list of injured and dead.

Señora Lori Easton, wife of an official at the US Embassy in Lima, expired.

CHAPTER NINETY-ONE

Holbrook Easton came the next morning, while I was wallowing in misery. I knew it was him when I heard his refined voice in the hallway, talking to the guard. Though I'd never seen him, I had a mental picture of him as a tall, dignified-looking man in a three-piece suit with graying hair and a briefcase. He turned out to be all those things.

And he was also the blackest black man I'd ever seen.

He shook my hand and told me how sorry he was about Marisa, and how sorry he was to trouble me at this time of my grief, but there were serious issues that had to be settled, before things took a turn for the worse.

"How could things possibly be worse?" I asked him.

"Rumor has it there's a contract out on you."

I shrugged. He went on. "You've made enemies with just about every power group in the country—Peep, the Shining Path, the army, right-wing death squads, even the Ungas. We'd like to move you to one of our safe houses until the trial, but they're not cooperating. They've posted only one guard, and a Peep agent at that."

He took a tape recorder from his briefcase and set it on the nightstand. "We need to get a statement while you're still available to us. Do you mind if I record our conversation?"

"Did you find Lannie's body?"

"Not a trace. I'm told they searched the entire area."

A long silence passed. I thought of the animals and birds that had probably moved in on Lannie before his blood was cold. Easton cranked up my bed, slowly, and reached over to switch on the recorder.

"Wait," I said. "Tell me what happened to Lori Easton?"

"Who is Lori Easton?"

"The papers say she was your wife."

"My wife's name is Trish. I don't know anyone named Lori."

"How could you not have heard? She was identified as the wife of an official at the US Embassy in Lima. Her name is Easton. Your name is Easton. Surely they contacted you."

He swallowed hard and looked away, avoiding my eyes.

"I'll look into it. Right now we need to get a statement." He turned on the recorder, identified himself, the location and date, and asked me to state my full name and birth date.

"Shouldn't I have the benefit of counsel?"

"I'm your counsel, Professor. Anything you say will be just between us."

I answered all his questions about Gordo and the little no-name battle in the mountains and El Gato and the sniper shootings and the Unga village, and how we'd been attacked by the helicopter, and how I'd been captured by Lieutenant Bravos. But I refused to tell him where I'd been hiding and who helped me other than Lannie. No way was I going to implicate Sonia, Faviola, or Condor. I didn't even tell him about Engineer.

"Let me see if I have this straight," Easton said. "You were captured by the Sinchis. You heard them discussing General Reál's plot. You wanted to save Marisa, so you escaped by plunging into a swollen river during a rainstorm. How did you get back to Cuzco?"

"Caught a train."

He rolled his eyes and switched off the recorder. "There was only one way to get back to Cuzco, Professor, and that was with the help of insurgents. Why are you protecting them?"

By then my head was pounding, my wound hurting, my soul bleeding. Easton took a deep breath. "Look, Professor, either you cooperate fully and truthfully, or you'll probably spend the rest of your life in Lurigancho."

He paused as if to let the gravity sink in and then lifted a finger. "But there's another option."

"What option?"

"I've been in touch with the powers that be, including Commissioner Amado and the president's office. As far as they're concerned, you're small potatoes. The man they're after is Chairman Gonzalo. Their offer is this: help them capture him and walk free."

I sank back into my pillow. "Bocanegra says I'd still get ten years."

"Bocanegra doesn't make that decision. Besides, he's still sore he couldn't catch you."

"It's a moot issue anyway. I have no idea where Gonzalo is hiding."

"But surely you heard something. A city? A neighborhood?"

"They didn't confide in me."

Easton sighed, stood, and began gathering his things. "I wish there were other options, but that's the only one we have." He thanked me and went out the door.

CHAPTER NINETY-TWO

My mood blackened. I sank into one of those morbid states that suicide victims go through before plunging off a bridge. Daylight faded into darkness. I grew weak. Zara tried to lift my spirits by telling me the Amado Commission was investigating General Reál, and that the death toll would have been higher except for my warning, and that people were saying I wasn't a terrorist after all, just a love-sick professor, and there was talk of a Mark and Marisa movie.

"It'd be a sad movie," I said. "Movie-goers want a happy ending."

"No, that's not true. Lots of movies and books have tragic endings." She ticked off a list—*A Farewell to Arms, Madame Bovary, Love Story, Romeo and Juliet.* "Besides, for all you know, Marisa's not even dead. Ever thought of that?"

"What are you talking about?"

"You know how it is in this country. People die who don't really die—people in debt or in trouble with the law, or trying to get out of a bad marriage. Last week I read about this man, supposedly dead, whose wife found him shacked up with a teenager. Now he really is dead."

She was still rattling about fake deaths when I heard voices outside the room, a woman talking with the guard. A familiar voice. Sonia? Could it be?

I sat up. Yes, I could see her at an angle, dressed like a doctor. She locked eyes with me, nodded as if to say all was well, and hurried away, her footfalls slapping on the floor.

"Do you know that doctor?" I asked Zara.

"Never seen her before. She must be new."

She stepped outside and came back a minute or so later waving an envelope.

"For you," she said. "It was in my mailbox. Maybe it's from that new doctor."

My heart jumped. I ripped open the envelope and saw three words:

Chaupi tuta hamusac. Midnight I will come.

What the hell was this? Sonia wouldn't have written in Quechua. Besides, the penmanship was sloppy, crude, and had a hard edge to it, like a threat.

"We should alert the guard," Zara said.

"No, let's wait and see."

The rest of the day passed in slow motion. The note hung over me like a Shining Path dog. Daylight turned to dark. Moonlight shone through slats in the windows.

Zara, who wasn't on duty that night, showed up around eleven anyway, and pulled from her pocket a butcher knife and a canister of Mace.

"Are you crazy? You could get in trouble."

"It's okay. Jorge's on duty. Haven't you seen the way he looks at me?"

She sat down and waited, knife and Mace within reach. At the stroke of midnight, while church bells were tolling all over Cuzco, there came the sound of wheels rolling down the hall, loud, like a wagon bearing the Grim Reaper.

Zara's eyes widened. I stiffened. Could this be it? Ungas coming to get me. Or right-wing assassins. Zara switched off the lights and peeked out.

"It's a gurney," she whispered. "An old man being pushed by an orderly."

The man coughed. It was a nasty, hacking cough.

"I know him," Zara hissed. "He's from the *maricón* ward. He's got that disease."

The gurney stopped.

"What do you want?" The guard asked.

"He wants to visit the gringo."

"Forget it. No one goes in there without authorization. Now go, get away."

The man on the gurney spoke. It was barely a whisper.

"Tell the gringo this. Except for power, everything is an illusion."

Condor? Was it him? He said it a second time, and a third, loud, his words reverberating around the room. "EXCEPT FOR POWER, EVERYTHING IS AN ILLUSION."

The orderly wheeled him away. Zara looked at me. "What does that mean?"

I knew exactly what it meant: *Marisa was alive.*

She came to me in my sleep and crawled in bed beside me. I felt her heartbeat, her warmth, her breath against my neck. I even smelled her perfume. "How did you do it?" I asked her.

"It's a hospital. Hospitals have bodies."

I woke up. Was it possible? Had Marisa somehow managed to put a body in her hospital room? In her bed, possibly with Condor's help—or Sonia's?

It was almost nine when Zara woke me out of another dream.

"Guess what," she said. "They're bringing flowers and get-well cards with breakfast."

In rolled a food cart. Then another on which rested flowers and cards. There were well-wishes from Sonia and Faviola, and my beautiful daughter, Cristina, and my colleagues at South

Florida, and my ex-wife, Denise, and offers of marriage from women I'd never heard of.

Zara read each card aloud and held up the corresponding flowers—snapdragons, roses, daisy pompons, larkspurs, Peruvian lilies.

Lilies? I took the card and breathed in the lingering scent of Lily of Peru. My heart raced. I ripped it open and read at a glance the words it contained:

> Go away with me and be my love / and father our children too.
> And I will bring you blue-bells / and lilies from Peru.

It wasn't signed; it didn't have to be.

"You're crying?" Zara said.

I could no longer hide my secret. I had to trust someone. "Have you ever wanted to get out of here and go to the States?" I asked Zara. "Maybe Miami?"

"Are you offering to marry me?"

I motioned her into the chair. It was time to make the sell. To use that twenty thousand Sonia was holding. I kept my voice low.

"Suppose I offered you five thousand dollars now and another fifteen thousand when we get to Miami? Suppose I could get you into a university, or a job at a hospital, and find you a place to live? If I could do all that, would you help me bust out of here?"

Her face lit up. "What is it you want me to do?"

CHAPTER NINETY-THREE
The Great Escape

It took two days to work out the details. During this time I also wrote verses of my adventures in the jungle and had Zara mail them to the newspapers. But still I worried.

Suppose Bocanegra transferred me to Lima before we could pull it off?

All my other plans had come to grief. Why should this one be different?

On the third evening, when all was in readiness, I lay in bed waiting for midnight, breathing in the unpleasant smell of hair coloring that had turned my hair black. Zara was five thousand dollars richer, thanks to Sonia. I was a bit fitter, thanks to exercising and gorging myself on hospital food. I was also dressed in doctor's scrubs and smock, stethoscope around my neck, clipboard in hand, the little witch in my pocket.

At precisely midnight Zara plunged a syringe into the back of the Peep guard.

"What the hell was that?" he said, and slumped in his chair.

Zara peeked into the room. "Wait until you hear the elevator."

I eased out of bed and remade it to look like I was still in it. The guard sat at his desk behind his sunglasses, breathing deeply in his drug-induced sleep, feet propped up, newspaper open on his lap. Poor bastard, he was going to catch hell from Bocanegra.

It was so quiet, I could hear the buzz of the fluorescents.

The elevator jarred to a stop. I eased into the hallway, patted the guard on the head, and limped toward the elevator where Zara was waiting.

She punched a button. The door closed, slowly. Down we went, traveling at the speed of a snail. Suppose someone else got on? Suppose Zara was working for Peep, or the Ungas, or the Shining Path? Give her an AK-47, get her dressed up in dirty fatigues and a beret, and she'd look just like one of those Pachacuti-chanting girls in the mountains.

The elevator stopped on the bottom floor. The door opened, and there stood Sonia in a doctor's outfit, all wide-eyed, smoking a cigarette, and looking as if she'd rather be anywhere but here. A video camera was strapped around her neck.

"Plans have changed," she said. "No time to explain. Just do what we tell you."

Zara opened the exit door and struck off into the cool night air, fading into the blackness. Sonia pointed out an older car that was parked nearby, dimly illuminated in the streetlights.

A man stood next to it—a man with an assault rifle. He trotted toward us.

Jorge, one of the Peep guards.

"Don't panic," Sonia said. "He's part of the plan."

Jorge took up a position with his AK next to me. Sonia adjusted her camera and again pointed to the car. "Walk toward it like you're looking for a car to steal. Okay? Open the door and look back so I can get a good shot with the camera. Try to look scared."

Scared? How could I not look scared?

I lumbered across the lot, glancing from side to side like the fugitive I was, trying to beat down the impulse to bolt.

Behind me, Jorge chambered a round in his rifle.

The car Sonia had pointed out was battered and old, probably stolen. It also reeked of gasoline, as if Jorge had given it a good drenching. A man sat in the driver's seat, slumped against the steering wheel. He didn't move.

I opened the door, half expecting the car to explode.

Shit. The man sitting there was dead, but even in the poor light I recognized him.

Apu Condor.

Somewhere a car roared to life. And there it was, coming straight at me—a black Mercedes, the kind favored by Peep.

It drove right past me and screeched to a halt about fifty feet away.

The back door flew open. Out of it came Nurse Zara.

"Over here, gringo. Come on. Run!"

Behind me, Jorge was yelling like a madman. "Stop, gringo. Stop, or I'll shoot."

I ran. Jorge opened fire. I stupidly dove to the ground, thinking he was shooting at me, but when I glanced back, he was firing into the car that held Condor's body.

Glass shattered. Tires popped. Things flew into the air. Then it ignited in a blazing whoosh, lighting up the parking lot, the rear of the hospital, and the trees alongside Rio Saphi.

Zara yanked me to my feet and helped me into the Mercedes. She was laughing.

"Why did you go down on the asphalt? You could have hurt yourself."

"I tripped."

Sonia piled into the backseat next to me. "What a way to go. Condor would love this."

Doors slammed. There was laughter, and we roared into the night, tires screeching, Zara whooping as if we'd just pulled off the robbery of the century. This wasn't at all the escape I'd planned, and it got even more confusing when we stopped at a traffic light, and I saw the driver.

Holbrook Easton.

And in the passenger seat beside him sat Faviola.

"Will someone please tell me what's going on?"

Easton laughed. "Looks to me like you just died back there, Professor, burned to a crisp. Sonia even got it on film. What a story it'll make for the papers."

CHAPTER NINETY-FOUR
Lima

Not until we reached the airport and climbed out near a waiting Lear jet did I notice that Faviola, who before had always worn fatigues, beret, and boots, was now dressed in dark jacket, skirt, and heels, looking like a professional business-woman. No AK either.

"Don't ask," she said, and climbed aboard the Lear.

I didn't. I'd already asked about Marisa three or four times and couldn't get an answer.

We landed in Lima at dawn. An embassy Cadillac drove us through the coastal fog to a walled compound that I assumed was a safe house. An armed guard swung open the gates.

"Better get cleaned up," Easton said. "You've got an impor-tant meeting."

No point asking for details, so I followed him into a bedroom and for the third time, found my suitcase and the clothes I'd abandoned in Lima, all washed and pressed, the shoes shined, underwear folded. I almost cried when I saw my leather jacket.

I picked up the jacket and breathed in its richness, and for a moment I was back in my hotel room on that first day, wondering what to wear for my meeting with Marisa. I chose leather, just as I had then, laid out the matching pullover, and headed for the shower.

An hour or so later, with my clothes hanging loosely on my skinny frame, we were back in the Cadillac, Holbrook Easton at the wheel, Nurse Zara in front, Sonia in back with me, looking like Marisa in black dress, heels, dangling pearl earrings, and sunglasses in spite of the fog.

"What happened to Faviola?" I asked.

"Who is Faviola?" Easton answered.

He swung the Cadillac off the main street and drove to the same place where I'd hidden out with Sonia some seven weeks earlier—Chateau Beige with its bougainvillea trellis, armed guard, and the apartment that contained de la Vega's paintings of the *Girls of Pachacuti.*

Had he known about this place before, even when I was here with Sonia?

The guard waved us through the gate as if we were residents. Zara hopped out and ran inside. Sonia leaned over and kissed me on the cheek.

"Wait here. Be right back."

Easton twisted around in his seat. "Just so you know, we were planning to bust you out all along. Your plan dovetailed nicely with ours. But it was really Condor's plan."

"Condor was working with you?"

"Condor worked only for Condor. Remember what he said about illusions?"

I fell back into my seat, trying to make sense of it. But I was so weary, so confused that I didn't notice Sonia until she opened the door and slid into the seat beside me.

Except it wasn't Sonia.

"Behold," Easton said, "I give you Lori Easton."

The world stood still, and I was vaguely aware that we were on the road again, driving past the Gran Hotel Bolívar where I'd waited for Marisa that first day, and around Plaza San Martín with its demonstrators, and down Jirón de la Unión, past its shops that advertised Inca gold.

The guards at the presidential palace waved us through the gate as if they'd been expecting us, and we ended up in the same parking space where Lannie and I had parked.

"Wait here," Easton said to Marisa. "This shouldn't take long."

Easton held the door for me, and as I stepped out into the same parking lot where mortars had dropped and a car had been crushed by a tank, I imagined I could hear Lannie's voice.

"Come on, old buddy. This way."

The tears welled up again. Damn, how I missed him.

A side door to the palace opened, and there stood Inspector Bocanegra, smoking a cigar.

With him was Commissioner Amado.

Holbrook Easton took a thin envelope from his inside pocket and handed it to me.

"Here, as soon as we're inside, give this to them."

"What is it?"

"An address, Condor's wedding gift to you and Marisa."

The transaction took less than a minute. Papers were signed by all parties, in triplicate. No words were spoken. No hand-shakes either.

Back in the parking lot, just before we reached the Cadillac, Easton said, "There's one more little detail I didn't mention."

"What detail?"

"Markus Thorsen is permanently dead. So is Marisa. There's no other way."

I opened the door and crawled in beside Marisa.

She was the best-looking dead woman I'd ever seen.

Epilogue

Sonia's video of my "death" made the evening news and the extra edition of newspapers all over Peru. Headlines read: ROMEO AND JULIET REUNITED IN DEATH.

Nurse Zara took an early flight to Miami. I never saw her again.

My adventures became the subject of talk shows, university seminars, and endless debate. It seemed that everyone who'd met me, including taxi drivers, hotel employees, soldiers, prisoners, and even Policarpo came forth with their own version of events, embellished, of course.

Inspector Bocanegra claimed that I was never out of his sight, and that I'd done exactly what he'd set me up to do—lead him to the hideout of Chairman Gonzalo.

The embassy held a memorial service for Lannie Torres.

My colleagues at South Florida held a memorial service for me.

Chairman Gonzalo was captured on a dreary Saturday morning by counter-terrorist agents disguised as ice-cream vendors, lovers in parked cars, and street sweepers. He'd been shacked up with a ballet dancer in a quiet Lima neighborhood. No one was killed in the raid.

The US ambassador to Peru left the country the next day. The embassy claimed his departure at that time was purely coincidental. Cynics believed otherwise.

The Amado Commission concluded that General Reál had indeed been involved in drug trafficking. The same report noted that although I'd acted irrationally, my link to the terrorists was purely circumstantial, motivated by an illicit love affair. They ended their report with a verse from *Hamlet* that pretty much summed up my adventures.

> When sorrows come, they come not single spies
> But in battalions.

Holbrook Easton was reassigned to Nicaragua, another hot spot, and fell into a similar mess created by a young American archaeologist. But not before helping me get a new identity. He also helped me liquidate all my old assets and transfer them into a new account.

Not that we became paupers. There were all those de la Vega paintings Marisa shipped back to Miami, and the dirty money in her late husband's account, and the money she and Sonia inherited from Condor, and the money in Lannie's secret account...

A group calling itself the Underground Press of Lima published my poetry and love letters in a little book called *Lirio del Peru*—Lily of Peru. It was all there, everything from the erotic and romantic to the corny and maudlin. The verses I'd written so stiffly in English came alive in the Spanish translation, with rhythmic flows and subtle symbolism that had always evaded me. It became a best seller in Peru. The only complaint was from a mother who claimed her daughter became pregnant after reading it.

At last I was a published poet.

But a dead poet.

Twenty-two years have passed since that horrible experience, and not one day has gone by that I haven't thought about all the good men and bad who might still be alive if I'd just stayed home. Call it survivor's guilt. Call it nonsense. It still haunts me.

Marisa refuses to hang any of Francisco de la Vega's paintings in our home. We recently donated one of his *Girls of Pachacuti* to a museum. It was appraised at more than eight hundred thousand dollars. Next time we'll sell.

Sonia returned to the States with a false passport and new name and married a dentist.

Cristina married a rock musician. She delivered our first grandchild a few months ago.

The child we conceived in Peru is now studying for his masters. We named him Lannie.

Faviola is a schoolteacher in Florida. She finished her memoir, but hasn't published it for fear of reprisal. She may publish it as fiction. In ten years or twenty years.

As for the money we took from the Ungas, I'm guessing it's still buried at the Inca ruins, beneath the thirteenth stone on the walkway toward the river. A hundred years from now some archaeologist will probably dig it up and wonder how it got there.

Or maybe not.

I have this recurring dream that Lannie survived and was nursed back to health by the Machiguengas. It's not that farfetched. I came back from the dead. Do did Faviola and Marisa. Maybe he went back for the money and is now living in luxury in Brazil. Maybe the phone will ring one of these evenings while Marisa and I are sitting by the pool sipping pisco sours, and I'll hear that Tex-Mex voice again:

"Hey, old buddy, the hell's going on?"

Reality Vs. Fiction

The backdrop for *LILY OF PERU* is authentic. The story is fiction. It was inspired by an article in an underground newsletter that claimed Chairman Gonzalo was betrayed by a gringo professor with links to the Shining Path "by virtue of his illicit affair with a woman in the movement."

Dracula's House and the garbage dump called El Infiernillo have been documented by numerous independent sources, including America's Watch and Amnesty International. Ditto for the assassinations, hanging dogs, disappearances, summary executions, illegal arrests, kidnappings, rapes, murders, battles, and bombings.

San Juan de Lurigancho prison exists as described. It was there, during my research for this book, that I met inmates on whom the characters of Tucno and Luís were based.

Apu Condor was the *nom de guerre* of a Shining Path guerrilla I interviewed in a Lima café. From him I first heard the phrase, "Except for power, everything is an illusion."

The Amado Commission was inspired by the Inter-American Commission on Human Rights.

A number of Europeans and Americans were drawn to the conflict. Some threw in with the insurgents. Some were killed. Others were innocent. The most intriguing case is that of a young writer from New York named Lori Berenson. She was arrested on a Lima bus, tried by a military tribunal of hooded judges, and—although she claimed to be innocent—served nineteen years in a Peruvian prison for "high treason and crimes against the state."

Ms. Berenson was released in 2014.

The Ungas do not exist, though such people and such villages do exist.

The Machiguengas live peacefully in the eastern jungles of Peru.

The Festival of Inti Raymi was not disrupted by a bomb blast, although a bomb did destroy several cars of the Cuzco-Machu Picchu train at that time, killing a number of tourists.

The mortar attack on the presidential palace occurred more or less as described.

The Shining Path and its sister organization, the Movimiento Revolucionario Tupac Amaru, is still operating, but in a much diminished capacity. The latter group's most spectacular success—a raid on the Japanese embassy—was fictionalized in the book *Bel Canto* by Ann Patchett.

Abimael Guzmán, a.k.a. Chairman Gonzalo, was in fact a philosophy professor at a university in Ayacucho. He is currently serving a life sentence in a high-security prison at a naval base in Callao, near Lima. A fictionalized account of his capture was the subject of the movie, *The Dancer Upstairs*. It was based on a work by Nicholas Shakespeare.

Another excellent novel of this troubled period is *Chasing the Sun* by Natalia Sylvester.

President Fujimori was stripped of his office as "morally unfit" to rule in November 2000. He was charged for his role in summary executions, torture, illegal arrests, and a 1991 massacre of civilians. He subsequently fled to Japan, the country of his birth, but was arrested in Chile and extradited to Peru. He was tried, convicted, and sentenced to twenty-five years in prison.

Peace has returned to Peru. It is now as colorful and beautiful as always.

Acknowledgments

*L*ILY OF PERU would not have been possible without the support, encouragement and critical eye of many friends, university associates, embassy personnel in Peru, DEA and Treasury agents, spooks, fellow writers, family members, returned Peace Corps Volunteers, former students, and even a few insurgents and prison inmates. Most of my Peruvian connections have requested anonymity. Any other omissions result from a lapse of the mind rather than the heart.

In Cajun country, I am deeply indebted to Lucinda Sibille, who was present at the creation. My thanks also to John and Patsy Fontenot, Gary and Leslie Kinsland, Nancy Rumore, Karen Burlet, Talis Byers, Doug Womack, Lisa Shirley, Bea Angelle, and Dr. Richard Saloom. Also to my good friends in the Writers' Guild of Acadiana—Ro Foley, Jessy Ferguson, Christine Word, Renee Goudeau, and Barbara Veillon.

Dr. Michael Maher, Head of Communications at the University of Louisiana/Lafayette, read and edited the first draft and taught me a thing or two about creative writing. Thanks also to Cynthia Thomas for her newspaper clippings and many helpful suggestions.

Among my Chile IV Peace Corps friends who listened, read my chapters, or otherwise shared their thoughts are George Pope, Bill Callahan, Mary Ellen Wynhausen, Karen Mitchell, and Myrna Gary. Thanks also to RPCVs Barbara Letvin, Valerie Perez, and Marian Haley Beil of Peace Corps Worldwide.

In Florida I am no less grateful to the Tarpon Springs Library Writers' Group and fellow travelers—Bob Dockery, Georgia Post, Mary Dresser, Rebecca Roberts, Claudia Sodaro, Sonia Linke, Stephanie Geddes, Lloyd Wilson, Ann O'Farrell, Margaret Saxon, Abe Spevak, Denis Gaston, Jerry Grant, Susan Ingold, Mickey Davis, Barbara Harrington, Carol Gilardi, Gwen Hamlin, Sarah Pletts, John DiSanza, Meg Skinitis, Brian Roth, Heather McCauley, Jerome Kynion, Louise Collins, Joseph Mendonca, Dexter Jerome, and Lourdes Brindis.

Ditto for my writer friends in the Fiction Writers' Group of Tarpon Springs. Thank you, Gino Bardi, Dianna Thiel, Mark Turley, Laura Kennedy Bell, Liz Drayer, Ken Dye, Lee Blimes, Sali Dalton, Jean Gogolin, Roger Hoffine, Beth Hovind, Rich Ippolito, Dorte Zuckerman, Donna Lengel, Shannon O'Leary-Beck, Eleni Papanou, Tommy Dominos, and Jim Valco.

The TS Library director, Cari Rupkalvis, deserves credit for putting up with us over the years.

Thanks also to my dear friends with a St. Petersburg College connection—Barbara Glowaski, Susan and Terry Parchetta, and Dr. Vilma and Joe Zalupski.

And my good friends at Calhoun High—Ken Rayborn, Freda Herrington Wilson, Rebecca Bush Hopkins, Jeanine Jacks Stone, Don and Elaine Herrington, and Nell Sims Harrod.

A *big* special thanks to Pamela Lopez, who put a gallon of red ink on the pages, and Elizabeth Indianos, artiste extraordinaire, who beat the drums for me and created the cover art.

Finally, I could not have done any of this without the love and encouragement of the real Lily of my life, my beautiful bride, Maria.

DR. DAVID C. EDMONDS was raised in Mississippi and Louisiana and is a former marine, Peace Corps volunteer, Senior Fulbright Professor of Economics, and academic dean. He has spent considerable time in Latin America as both a US government official and a scholar. He and his wife now live in Florida.

OTHER BOOKS BY DAVID C. EDMONDS

Yankee Autumn in Acadiana
The Vigilante Committees of the Attakapas
The Guns of Port Hudson: the River Campaign
The Guns of Port Hudson: the Investment, Siege and Reduction
The Conduct of Federal Troops in Louisiana

TO BE PUBLISHED IN 2015

The Girl in the Glyphs, with Maria Nieves Edmonds

Did a holy woman visit the Americas in antiquity with a list of commandments for the natives? Jennifer Bowman-Cruz, a Smithsonian specialist in ancient writing, thinks so and she's determined to prove it. The answer lies in a cave on an uninhabited island on Lake Nicaragua. If she can find the cave, she'll make a name for herself in archaeology. But first she has to deal with a cheating husband, romance with a young man at the US Embassy, an old Indian couple who may or may not be ghosts, a local journalist who dogs her every step, and a nasty band of tomb looters. The looters are also searching for the cave, not for ancient writing but for millions in pirate gold. They've already murdered one of Jennifer's associates—and now they're closing in on her.